SHADOWS OF WINTER

THE CURSE AND THE CROWN

LINDSAY BUROKER

FOREWORD

Greetings, good reader! Thank you for picking up *Shadows of Winter*. With this story, I'm delighted to return to high-fantasy romance after a break of a couple of years. I hope you'll enjoy the new adventure.

Before you get started, please let me thank my steadfast beta readers, Sarah Engelke and Cindy Wilkinson, and also my editor, Shelley Holloway. Thank you as well to Deranged Doctor Design for the cover art. Now, let's jump in!

1

———————

*BENEATH THE MOUNTAINS OF EVARDOR, WINTER'S SHADOWS FOREVER
linger.*
   ~ "Spring Cowers" by Erazidar the Poet

"It's magnificent." Kaylina clasped her hands and gazed
enraptured at the dilapidated stone inn.

The walls were cracked and crumbling, seagull droppings
spattered the rusty gate, and cracks wide enough to swallow stray
cats plagued what she could see of the courtyard, but the location
was perfect. Only ten blocks from King's Cliff, with the Stillguard
River flowing behind it, the fortified structure would draw all
kinds of foot traffic. She wagered there was a view of the harbor
from the—

"It's a *castle*," her younger brother, Frayvar, said. "We're not
fortifying ourselves to withstand sieges and invading armies. We're
starting a meadery."

"Don't forget the eating house. I saw how many cookbooks you
brought." Kaylina waved to the trunks they'd rolled up from the

harbor on a rickety cart. As it had clattered over the cobblestones, getting stuck in ruts, horse droppings, and mounds of semi-cleared snow, she'd briefly lamented the number of romance and adventure novels she'd brought along, but a girl couldn't be bereft on a long trip. "Our diners will feel safe and protected while they enjoy our offerings. This is the rugged north. People here probably *insist* on a secure place to eat."

"Are you suggesting our diners will require an eating house containing both murder holes and machicolations?"

"*Of course.*"

Machio-what?

Frayvar sighed. "There's no way we can afford the rent on a place this big."

"You might be surprised." The graying land agent they'd found in the market square smiled warmly as pedestrians and horse-drawn carriages and wagons passed on the boulevard behind them, the people casting curious—or were those *wary*—looks in their direction. "It's been centuries since the Stillguard Inn went out of business, and the castle has been vacant for most of that time."

Frayvar nudged a section of the courtyard wall with his boot, and the crumbling mortar gave way, a stone falling. "Kay, all we need is a dining room, a kitchen, a lavatory, and a well out back. Not this... monstrosity."

A red-breasted bird chirped from a great oak rising at the corner of the property, the dark skeletal branches in contrast to the icy snow-smothered mountains towering beyond the city. It flew down and landed on Kaylina's shoulder.

She pointed to it. "This is a good omen, right?"

"Animals befriend you everywhere," Frayvar said. "If anything, it's probably trying to warn you that this is a bad idea."

The bird's head rotated toward Kaylina, toward the castle, and toward her again. It emitted a concerned cheep.

Was Frayvar right?

No, Kaylina refused to believe that. The bird flew off when she lifted her arms and faced the castle, her dream so intense that she had no trouble envisioning it. Their meadery would be an extension of the family business that thrived far to the south, a chance to bring their food and drink to Port Jirador, the capital of the Zaldor Kingdom. It would be visited by lords and ladies and maybe the queen herself. People rich and poor would flock to taste mead crafted from Grandpa's exquisite honey using Grandma's recipes. Kaylina would bring pride to the family name of Korbian, and everyone would realize she wasn't a screwup. She had what it took to build a successful business of her own, to find the contentment that had eluded her at home where others were always telling her what to do.

"Imagine it, Frayvar," she breathed when she realized she was babbling the details of her vision aloud. "Can you see it?"

"No. I don't hallucinate the way you do."

Kaylina lowered her arms, frustrated, not for the first time, that Grandma had sent him to tag along and keep an eye on her.

"I don't hallucinate," she snapped. "I have dreams of what can be, what *will* be."

"Dreams that you see when your eyes are open." Frayvar turned to the land agent. "What is the cost of leasing this... establishment, and will repairs be included?"

"Certainly, certainly. With an acceptably lengthy lease agreement of course. No fewer than ten years."

Kaylina gaped. Ten *years*? Was that normal? That was almost half her life.

"Commercial lease agreements in the kingdom are typically three to five years," Frayvar said with certainty.

Given how much nonfiction he read, Kaylina suspected he knew that for a fact.

"Yes, but this is prime territory alongside the river and near the royal castle and the harbor. It also has a view of the mountains. *Very* desirable. Just yesterday, I had someone interested in leasing it, but he would only commit to five years. I was forced to pass. The landowner wants a longer contract."

"How much is the rent?" Kaylina asked.

"All this can be yours for two thousand liviti a month." The land agent winked at her, ignoring her brother.

"How much was it *before* my sister said it's magnificent?" Frayvar asked.

Kaylina grimaced. He was right. She shouldn't have been so transparent when they had to negotiate.

"It's perfect for your needs. Very spacious." The agent smiled, not answering Frayvar's question. "Assuming you do indeed have funds? You're young for this endeavor, aren't you?"

He eyed Kaylina, her raven hair swept back in a ponytail, and considered her trousers, tunic, parka, and low boots. The clothes were practical for travel, if not the most feminine garments she might have chosen. At least she'd cleaned off the grime of the sea voyage in a washbasin that morning. She'd anticipated having to prove that she was serious, capable, and not without coin.

Her brother... She hadn't been able to talk him out of wearing his rumpled hemp shirt with missing buttons and a fluffy prancing taybarri embroidered on the front. The noble creatures, ridden into battle by the elite royal rangers, were *fierce*, not fluffy. Admittedly, taybarri were rare in the south, and she'd only seen them from a distance, but the history books promised ferocity.

"I'm twenty-one," Kaylina said, "and my brother is a very old and crotchety seventeen." Despite the furry blue creatures prancing across his chest.

"Young for starting a business," the agent said.

"Rangers are recruited to risk their lives and protect the kingdom as early as sixteen," she pointed out.

"Rangers are *chosen*, not recruited." The agent glanced up and down the street, then asked again, "Do you have funds?"

"Yes," Frayvar said.

He was the one who'd brought a purse. Kaylina, who'd left in more of a hurry—or, as Mom would call it, a *huff*—than she wanted to admit, had planned to work for someone else to save up funds for the first few months. As much as she hated having her younger brother watch over her, his coin would be helpful.

"We also have Grandpa's special yeast and honeycomb." Kaylina patted one of the trunks.

A squawk came from a tower, and three pigeons flew out, complaining about something. Unlike the other, these birds weren't inclined to visit her shoulder. One pooped on the walkway three feet from them before flapping away.

"You'll want to clean that up before the queen arrives," Frayvar told her.

"As my assistant, you can handle that."

"Hilarious. Grandma sent me along to keep the books, prevent you from being swindled, and ensure her recipes are accurately represented."

"Also so you wouldn't be beaten up again by the Bustinor brothers." Kaylina waved at his shirt, though it was more his spindly arms, gangly height, and tendency to wheeze and pass out that made him a target for bullies.

Frayvar lifted a finger, as if he might protest, but he only sighed and added, "Or the Bustinor *sisters*."

"Craters of the moon, they're worse than the brothers."

"Tell me about it."

After another glance down the street, the agent gestured at the castle. "Why don't you look around the property while you think about it? I'll wait here and find my paperwork in case you decide you're interested." He patted a brown satchel.

It wouldn't hurt to check the place out.

Smiling as her vision wafted through her mind again, Kaylina leaped the cracks of the courtyard and jogged to the double doors leading into the keep. The stout wood creaked as she pushed one side open. She almost ran through a grand vestibule and into a great hall with wrought-iron chandeliers hanging from high ceiling beams. This would be a wonderful place to seat diners.

Dust tickled her nose as she stumbled into cobwebs hanging from those beams, but she didn't care. Already, she could see the hall cleaned up and full of tables, every patron sipping her mead and proclaiming its brilliance.

An archway led to a smaller room with cabinets and counters. They could put the mead-making equipment there, and she could give talks about the process. Demonstrations. And was that a kitchen beyond? A *huge* kitchen.

"Look, Fray." Kaylina spun a pirouette before pointing. "There's room for all your pots and pans, and I bet there's a huge pantry. Once we're successful, you can buy every spice in the world. And you can spend your days gleefully organizing and reorganizing the jars, an activity I'm positive you love as much as cooking."

"I don't *love* cooking." Sneezes came from behind her, announcing her brother following, though his watering eyes might be keeping him from seeing her vision. "I got into it because I'm allergic to everything, and I have trust issues about taking food from strangers."

"And family."

"Family who aren't meticulous in the kitchen, yes. Silana has tried to poison me *three* times."

"She gave you nutmeg."

"*Poison.*" He sneezed again.

His dourness couldn't make Kaylina's vision falter or still the energy humming through her. She couldn't wait to sign that lease and take ownership of this place, to clean it up and—

The heavy front door slammed shut, the thud echoing from the stone walls.

Had that been... the wind?

As if in response to her thought, a creepy draft whispered across the back of Kaylina's neck, sending a chill to her core. With her instincts warning her of danger, she ran to the front door and tried to open it. It didn't budge.

"That guy locked us in?" Kaylina darted to a window as tall as she, heavy shutters covering it. She grunted as she tried to open one. "Do you still have your purse?"

Coins jangled.

"Yes, but we left our trunks out there." Frayvar's voice lowered. "I'll bet he set us up to be robbed. I *knew* he wasn't legitimate."

"If you knew that, why didn't you say something back at the *market*?" Again, Kaylina pushed at the shutter, but it didn't move.

"I didn't know until he quoted the rate. I'm not that good at reading people. You know that. *You're* supposed to have a woman's intuition."

"You're thinking of Silana. I have..." What? If Kaylina knew, maybe she wouldn't have felt compelled to make this journey to prove herself.

"Schemes."

"*Dreams.*"

A clank came from the back of the castle. The kitchen? It sounded like someone had kicked a pot. Someone sneaking through the shadows to waylay them?

"I hope they can defend us from thieves and cutthroats." Frayvar turned toward the kitchen.

Kaylina reached for her belt, for the only weapon besides her utility knife that she carried. But the sling was for hunting grouse, not braining thieves. If it hadn't been a gift from Grandpa, she might not have brought it, but she'd wanted it in case she didn't get to go home again for a long time.

Behind them, the shutters flew open. Light shone in around the blue-furred head of a towering taybarri, its soft floppy ears contrasting with the fangs revealed when its jaws parted. Its breath steamed into the room, fogging the cold air.

Kaylina stumbled back, screaming before she caught herself.

The creature's large nostrils twitched. Because it was sniffing her? Because she smelled like dinner? What did taybarri like to eat?

Appearing far different from the image on her brother's shirt, the long-bodied, four-legged beings were supposed to be at home on the Plains of Tiardia, where their height, greater than that of a horse, allowed them to see over the tall blue grasses and stalk prey as they swished their thick, long tails behind them. The stories said those tails were as much weapons as their claws, fangs, and flash magic. Their floppy ears made them look cute when they were at rest, but when the taybarri sprang into battle, even the fearsome Kar'ruk warriors scattered.

This one leaned closer, its jaws parting farther. The fangs drew Kaylina's gaze, almost mesmerizing her. The taybarri's nostrils twitched again, but it didn't look at her face or what might be her delicious torso. Instead, it peered over her shoulder to her pack.

Kaylina pulled it off and set it on the floor, thinking the taybarri might want the handful of snacks she'd taken from the galley before they disembarked. Or maybe the creature smelled her grandfather's honey. Not fully trusting that the trunks wouldn't be lost, she had stashed some in her pack. But would something with that many fangs eat sweets? Those teeth and that powerful jaw had to be for tearing meat from bones.

As its head dipped toward the pack, Kaylina noticed the rider for the first time.

When she met the icy blue eyes of the pale-skinned man, she didn't grow any more certain of her fate. He wasn't much older than she and might have been handsome once, with a square jaw, straight nose, and cleft chin, but one of three parallel scars pulled down his left eye at the corner. Marks made by claws? His short red-brown hair was trimmed so close that it revealed more scars on his scalp. They also looked like they'd been left by an animal rather than a blade.

Dressed in the black leather armor of a ranger, he had to be one of the fabled protectors of the kingdom, and she shouldn't have needed to fear him. His face was cold and distant but not cruel, and he sat calmly on his mount, barely stirring. Even so, her instincts warned her of something dangerous about him, not only dangerous to enemies of the kingdom but to *her*.

"I am Lord Vlerion," he stated with little inflection. It reminded her of her brother's tone, especially when Frayvar was tired and not putting effort into being expressive, but the coldness in the ranger's eyes made his voice more menacing. Or maybe it was the fact that his hand rested on the hilt of a sword. "You will come out of the castle."

His taybarri shifted slightly, enough for her to see another standing in the courtyard, a strikingly handsome man mounted atop it. He also gripped the hilt of a sword, promising he was a threat as well. Despite his good looks, he regarded her with the same coolness as the other man—Vlerion.

His taybarri's jaws parted, and it looked at her like she was dinner. There was no curious sniffing. A wide pink tongue slid between its pointed teeth to wipe saliva from its jowls.

"Actually, we're in the middle of a tour." Kaylina was proud that her voice didn't squeak. "Maybe you could speak with..." She glanced at her brother. "What was his name?"

"Naybor," Frayvar whispered.

"Naybor," she repeated with a smile for Vlerion.

He didn't smile back. Something told her the guy never smiled.

The handsome ranger looked around, elegant blond eyebrows rising. "There's nobody else here."

"You will come out." Vlerion held Kaylina's gaze. "Trespassing on private property in Port Jirador is illegal." His eyes closed to slits. "Trespassing with the intent to foment an insurrection is treason, punishable by death."

Kaylina stared at him. Insurrection? *What* insurrection?

"We just *got* here," she blurted.

Maybe that wasn't a defense. Maybe if she had a minute, she could come up with something more articulate, but he didn't give her a minute.

"Only the so-called *virtuous* cohort and their spies lurk around the cursed castle." Vlerion drew a long sword, nicks along the blade promising it had seen frequent use. "And only the Virts have the motivation to murder unarmed aristocrats."

"I—"

Murder? What was he talking about?

"If you are not guilty, you will come out and explain yourselves," Vlerion said. "If you run, your guilt will be assumed."

And I'll kill you, his cold eyes said.

Would he enjoy it? Or remain as dispassionate throughout as he was sitting on his mount?

"The front door is locked," Kaylina remembered. "Naybor trapped us inside."

"During your tour." His flat tone made it a statement, not a question.

"Before it started."

"It was a self-guided tour," Frayvar said. "Naybor—he called himself a local land agent—told us to check out the place. We're prospective tenants."

Vlerion's expression never changed, but his earlier words, *cursed castle,* made Kaylina think the idea of anyone renting this place was ludicrous. Maybe that was something the locals all knew.

"Jankarr." Vlerion looked to the other ranger.

He appeared to be older, but he bobbed his head and hopped down as if he'd been given an order by a superior. He trotted to the great oaken double doors and swung one open easily, as if its hinges had been oiled recently.

What in all the altered orchards? It had been locked a minute ago. Kaylina wasn't crazy. She'd *checked*.

"Come outside, Virts," Jankarr called, "if you want a chance to defend yourselves."

"Defend ourselves?" Frayvar whispered, walking hesitantly toward the door. "Does he mean with weapons or words?"

Though she didn't want to go out, Kaylina had to watch out for her little brother, so she hurried to step in front of him. "You know a lot more about words than weapons, so you'd better hope for that."

"I know more about *numbers* than either."

"You want me to ask him to set up some math problems?" Kaylina crept warily toward the door, eyeing Jankarr, who held it open, as if he were a polite gentleman instead of a fearsome ranger who was also fondling his sword hilt.

"Would you?" Frayvar asked.

"*Math* isn't going to prove our innocence. You—"

As Kaylina stepped out, a shadow moved to the side. Before she could so much as twitch, a sword swept in, the cool kiss of sharp steel touching her throat.

Fear slammed into her like a stake to the heart. She stared into Vlerion's cold eyes, certain he had no idea who she was but equally certain he was going to kill her.

2

PANIC STEALS OPPORTUNITY.
  ~ Lord General Avingatar

Vlerion didn't kill Kaylina. With his blade resting against her throat, he said, "Walk," and jerked his chin toward a tower at the corner of the castle.

"When do we get to defend ourselves?" Kaylina held her hands out, not wanting to make trouble, but also not wanting to be run through for something she hadn't done. She glanced around as much as she dared with the blade touching her throat.

Jankarr was right. Their *land agent* was nowhere to be seen.

"Walk," Vlerion repeated softly, shifting to stand beside Kaylina and grip her arm while keeping his sword against her throat.

"Since you're being so polite about it, I'd love to go anywhere with you. I can tell you're a fantastic date."

Something flashed in those cold blue eyes. Irritation? Maybe she was supposed to call him *Lord* Vlerion when she spoke and genuflect a few times at the end of each sentence.

"You want me to bring the kid?" Jankarr asked.

"He didn't murder anyone," Vlerion said.

Though Kaylina was glad they were dismissing Frayvar as a non-threat, she couldn't help but blurt, "And you think *I* did? Is it the deadly sling I carry? Or the great brawn of my arms?" The blade at her throat continued to unnerve her, but Kaylina lifted her arms to show them off, though the parka sleeves hid their slenderness. "I got my muscles cleaning my grandma's big glass carboys, in case you're wondering."

Vlerion guided her around the corner of the tower without responding, though he glanced at her sling and the pouch of rounds that hung next to them. He *couldn't* think she'd murdered someone with one of the lead balls.

"That wasn't as much of an answer as you might think," Jankarr called after them.

Vlerion didn't respond to that either, only walking Kaylina through the uneven courtyard that surrounded the keep, half-crumbled stones littering it. An eerie moan came from somewhere above, and a stone fell from the wall not ten feet in front of them. It hit the ground and broke into a dozen pieces.

Maybe the castle *was* cursed.

Vlerion lowered his sword, but the grip on Kaylina's arm remained, and he walked close, eyeing the wall ahead warily. She could almost feel the heat of his body in contrast to the frosty air. His muscles bulged against the seams of the black shirt under his armor, and she decided not to challenge him to an arm-wrestling match.

"I was more interested in a tour of the *inside* of the castle. Did I tell you we're going to start a meadery? Though I'm gathering this place might not be as for rent as Naybor said." Kaylina walked obediently as Vlerion guided her around another tower at the back corner, but she decided to elaborate while she had a chance. "We're new to the city. We were cooped up on a ship for *weeks* to get here and just arrived a few hours ago. It was called the *Windborn Taybarri*. Maybe you'd like to check with the crew. I'm sure someone can show you that our names were on the manifest, so we couldn't possibly be the spies or, uhm, murderers you're looking for."

Vlerion stopped at a back gatehouse that led out to a wide trail along the river, more skeletal trees stretching branches over water framed by several feet of ice along the banks. Thanks to a raised portcullis casting shadows, they didn't see the body lying in the gatehouse until they stopped in front of it.

Kaylina had never seen the pale-skinned, white-haired gentleman sprawled on his back on the ground, his eyes frozen open in death, but she gaped, stunned. Had this *just* happened? She remembered the rattle she'd heard in the kitchen, but, with blood matting the side of his head, he looked to have been hit by a club or mace.

Vlerion glanced at her sling again.

She shook her head. A small lead round wouldn't have done that much damage. Vlerion couldn't *possibly* think she'd done this.

Except... from his point of view, Kaylina and Frayvar were the only ones around. Unlike in the street out front, there was no foot traffic back here, nobody ambling along the river trail. Was that chance? Or did people avoid walking close to the city's cursed castle?

Aware of Vlerion watching her—judging her guilt or innocence by her reaction?—Kaylina shook her head again. "I'm sorry if he meant something to you, but I didn't have anything to do with this."

"The death of any kingdom subject means something to me." Again, his words were without inflection, making it hard to tell if they were true, if he did care.

"I'm a kingdom subject," she said.

"Are you?" Vlerion's gaze flicked downward dismissively, not lingering on her curves, her brown skin, or her dark hair. He had to have taken in everything about her when his taybarri had been sniffing her through the window.

"I don't know if you read history books, but the kingdom annexed the southern region, including my island chain of Vamorka, more than a hundred years ago. We're *all* subjects now. Not only those of you who live up in the gold-mining, whale-hunting, frigid-most-of-the-year north."

"I have read *many* history books." His tone remained flat, and he didn't add *way more than you* in a snotty voice, but she heard it anyway.

"I'm a loyal subject, the same as you. I came to spread my family's business to the capital and make a name for myself."

His gaze dropped to the dead man.

Kaylina grimaced, not knowing if Naybor had set her up, or if she'd stumbled into a crime scene due to her own bad luck. The latter wouldn't surprise her much.

"I'm not a spy," she added. "And I'm absolutely not a murderer."

"Even those who don't deliver the killing blow can watch the river for the approach of witnesses," Vlerion said softly.

"Listen, my name is Kaylina Korbian, and I told you the truth. My family is loyal to the king."

Technically, her family was loyal to their kin, their customers, three out of the twelve moon gods, and their roots in the island community. But they paid their taxes and never made trouble for the lord who ruled in the king's name over their southern province.

"We'll see." After a grave nod for the fallen man, Vlerion turned Kaylina back toward the front of the castle. "Because you were, at the least, present when a noble was murdered, I'm taking you to jail. You may speak to the adjudicator about your ship and journey, and *he* can determine if you are a spy or not." Vlerion paused before rounding the tower at the front corner, and his fingers tightened on her arm. "If you assisted in the murder of one of the king's chosen tax collectors, I will slay you myself."

"Oh, goodie. I was afraid an underling with a shaky hand would do it."

Something dark and dangerous sparked in his eyes, fire scorching away the ice. Kaylina stumbled, fear making her wish she could retract her words.

The fiery spark disappeared, and Vlerion's cold facade returned.

Had she imagined the change? No. A shiver went through her, and she told herself to refrain from ticking him off. He had a temper. Who knew what he did when he exploded?

Kaylina hoped the adjudicator he'd mentioned cared enough about justice and the rights of kingdom subjects to research her story. She had told the truth, that her name was on the ship's manifest. Thanks to the funds her brother had brought, they'd both bought passage legally. When she'd left on her own with scarcely any coin and only the honeycomb and yeast, she'd planned to stow away or trade and barter her way here. Now, she was relieved that hadn't been necessary.

Vlerion guided her to the front doors to rejoin his comrade. Jankarr had his sword pointed vaguely in Frayvar's direction but didn't appear worried about him. He smirked as he glanced at the taybarri shirt.

"What do you think, my lord?" Jankarr tilted his head toward the doors—no, he was indicating the body out back.

Vlerion looked at Frayvar before giving Kaylina a long moment of consideration.

Though she bristled under the cool study, she kept her mouth shut, reminding herself she also wanted to be dismissed as a non-threat. And she *wasn't* a threat. Just because she came from the most recently annexed part of the kingdom didn't mean she cavorted with spies and murderers.

"I deem it unlikely they had anything to do with Lord Darringtar's death," Vlerion finally said. "I suspect they are the ignorant tourists that they claim to be."

Kaylina bristled even more—they weren't *ignorant* because they'd arrived that morning and hadn't been filled in on local threats—but Frayvar spoke before she could say anything unwise.

"*Yes.*"

Jankarr snorted. "Let them go?"

"No," Vlerion said without hesitation. "We've been duped before by spies who appeared innocent. We'll take them to the adjudicator for questioning." He watched for Kaylina's reaction when he added, "Under the influence of kafdari root."

While she scraped through her mind in an attempt to remember why that was familiar, Frayvar reacted. His eyes bulged with terror.

Confusion swept through Kaylina. She'd only seen him react that viscerally to the promise of some tincture or potion if—

Frayvar sprinted away, charging for the corner of the tower.

"Shit," Jankarr said, starting after him.

"Stay with her." Vlerion's cool voice didn't change, but when he glanced at Kaylina, his eyes burned with the certainty that he'd unearthed a traitor—a *spy*.

"No," she blurted as he raced after Frayvar.

Vlerion drew his sword as he ran. By the moons, would he *kill* Frayvar?

Jankarr reached for Kaylina, but she dodged and sprinted after Vlerion, yanking out her sling. Terrified for her brother, she didn't consider the ramifications of using a weapon on a ranger.

With longer and stronger legs, Vlerion was seconds from

catching up to Frayvar. Kaylina hurled one of her lead rounds, adjusting her target at the last instant from his back to his head. That leather armor would keep the round from doing any damage, and she *had* to stop him. She couldn't let him hurt her brother.

An arm wrapped around her from behind, yanking her off her feet. Not before she glimpsed her round slam into the back of Vlerion's head. *Hard.*

Though the blow had to have hurt, he didn't slow down. He glanced back with ice in his eyes, ice and *calculation* as he doubtless reconsidered if she was capable of murdering someone.

"Leave him alone!" Kaylina yelled as she lost sight of Frayvar. "He didn't do anything."

Jankarr flipped her around to face him, then slung her over his shoulder. He ripped her sling from her hand.

A cry of pain came from Frayvar. Vlerion had caught him. Caught him or *worse?*

Jerking and twisting, Kaylina tried to escape, but the ranger had her pinned. Her knee thudded against his chest, but the leather armor might as well have been steel for all the good her blows did.

Her captor headed back to the front of the castle, toting her like a sack of potatoes.

"Jankarr, when I said *watch her,* I assumed that would also imply you should keep her from attacking me," Vlerion said calmly from a few steps behind.

Kaylina twisted enough to see under her captor's armpit. Vlerion gripped his sword in one hand and used the other to grasp Frayvar's arm and force him to walk with him, the same as he'd done with her moments before. There wasn't any blood on that blade, but it was hard to tell from Frayvar's red face if he'd been hurt. His eyes remained wide, panic making the whites visible around his pupils.

"I wanted to see if she could use that sling." Jankarr sounded amused.

"Effectively." Vlerion grimaced when he touched the back of his head. When he considered Kaylina again, that cold calculation remained in his eyes.

Her heart pounded in her eardrums as she realized he'd reclassified her from not-a-threat to dangerous. And capable of being a spy, if not a murderer.

How had things gone so wrong so quickly?

3

GIVE THE TRAITOR ENOUGH FREEDOM TO CONDEMN HIMSELF.
   ~ King Gavatorin the Elder

The cold of the stone bench seeped through Kaylina's parka and trousers, numbing her body, as heartless as the glacier-filled mountains looming behind the city. Common sense told her to stand up, move around, and figure out how to get out of the cell. Instead, her treacherous mind fixated on the confrontation with the rangers, on what she *should* have said to Vlerion, on how she shouldn't have lost her temper, on how, on how, on how—

"It's not my fault," Frayvar said for the fifth time. "Kafdari root is from the altered myristica fragrans tree."

"I know," Kaylina murmured.

She *hadn't* known when the rangers had spoken of it, but Frayvar had been apologizing and explaining ever since they'd been locked in the cell.

"It's magical," he said, "like all altered plants are, but that's not the problem. It's from the same tree as nutmeg and mace. That means I'm almost certainly allergic to it. If they make me ingest it, I could die."

"I know."

"They execute spies and traitors." Frayvar paced as he spoke. Five steps to one wall. A thump as he pushed off it with his hands. Five steps to the other. Thump.

Kaylina did her best not to find the thumps irritating. Better to be with her brother than alone. "I know that too."

"We have to figure a way out of here."

"Yeah." She stared up at the dark ceiling. A single north-facing window high on the stone wall let in little light.

"Unless we get an adjudicator who's *much* more reasonable than the rangers, we could be put to death by sunset."

"Yeah."

"You know I normally find solace in obeying laws and rules, since they're barometers for what's socially appropriate behavior, but in this case, I think we have to break out of jail, escape back to the south, and hope the rangers have more pressing concerns than coming after us."

Back to the south... as failures.

Kaylina grimaced at the cobwebs in the corner of the shadowy ceiling. She'd come to prove herself. How, after less than a day here, could she already be defeated?

No, she wasn't defeated. She couldn't give up yet. She had to do something. But what? Her earlier energy had faded, and intense fatigue bound her to the bench as surely as chains.

"*Kaylina.*" Frayvar halted, spun toward her, and planted his fists on his hips. "This isn't a logical time for one of your funks."

"Is there ever a logical time for a funk?" she murmured.

"When we're not about to be *executed.*" His voice squeaked like it had when he'd been thirteen.

When she met his imploring eyes, he didn't look much older than that now. He was still gangly and frail, a target for bullies. For an asshole *lord* who thought nothing of slamming him to the ground with his overly muscled weight.

Protective anger simmered, helping to push back the malaise. Kaylina sat up, swinging her legs to the floor. "Do you have any ideas for escaping?"

"*You're* the schemer."

"Yeah, but you're—"

A scream interrupted her, sending a chill down her spine. It came from one of the other cells they'd passed on the way in. A prisoner being questioned? Being *tortured?*

The scream faded and didn't repeat. Kaylina found that more ominous than promising.

"You're the one who's read every encyclopedia and textbook in the town library," she said quietly. "Didn't any of them discuss jailbreaks?"

"In nonfiction, that comes up less often than you'd think." Frayvar eyed the iron bars of the window. "Metal contracts when it's cold and expands with heat, which can break or at least loosen bonds. Unfortunately, the inconsiderate guards didn't give us a torch."

"These northerners are a rude lot."

"Extremely."

Kaylina rose and tried to get her sluggish brain thinking. It was hard. For the whole journey, she'd been on a cloud, planning what she would do when they arrived, lying awake nights, her brain too busy for sleep. But that alertness had been knocked out of her, as if *she'd* been the one to take a lead ball to the head.

"You can do this," she whispered to herself.

Kaylina didn't think she was a schemer—maybe a *dreamer*— but she would do what she could. She walked to the door and knocked, the cold oak so dense it hurt her knuckles.

What she would say if someone answered, she didn't know, but she had to barter and negotiate if at all possible. She couldn't let Frayvar be killed because of her dream.

Nobody answered. She pressed her ear to the door. Was anyone on guard in the corridor?

"I'm sorry Grandma sent you after me," she told Frayvar in case there wasn't a chance later. In case she *couldn't* negotiate his freedom. "When I left—" *fled*, the insidious part of her mind inserted, "—I didn't think anyone would come after me. After what I said to her... Well, you were there." Kaylina rubbed her face, regret lurking. Always lurking.

Frayvar looked toward the window. "Grandma didn't send me."

"Was it Mom?"

"No. Nobody."

"What do you mean? You told me the family sent you."

"I *lied*, Kaylina. I can't believe you didn't see through it. I'm a horrible liar."

"Well, I'm used to you not looking me in the eyes, so I didn't think anything of it."

He snorted. "I thought you would need someone to keep the books, to be the practical one, and to help make your business successful. I also worried you were in over your head. The north is harder than the south." He glanced at the bars in the window and the thick stone walls. The jail in their town back home was made from bamboo, the roof from reeds. "Besides, I owe you. You've... you've always watched out for me. It's not like the rest of the family doesn't, but Grandma is the only one who *gets* me. Her and you."

"I don't get you either, but you're my brother."

"I guess that's sufficient. I appreciate you trying to keep that hulking troglodyte from pummeling me."

"Any time. If the family didn't send you, where'd you get the seed money?"

"It's my savings."

"Twelve gods, Fray." Kaylina slumped against the door. Now,

she *really* had to get her brother out of there. "Did you tell Mom you were coming? Grandma? Anyone?"

"I left a note."

Yeah, that was his style. No direct confrontation.

Kaylina couldn't blame him. Confrontations tended to escalate, even with those you loved. Or *especially* with those you loved.

"Did you leave a *note*? Or was it an essay detailing the reasons for your departure over multiple pages?" She tried to smile for him, certain she already knew the answer.

Frayvar hesitated. "There *were* multiple pages. There was also a business plan. And a pro forma."

"I don't know what that is."

"A financial statement calculating potential earnings based on projections and presumptions."

"So, it was the typical runaway letter." Her second smile was more genuine, though the weight of responsibility threatened to send her back to the bench. More than ever, she felt it was her duty to keep him safe.

Rising on tiptoes, she checked the bars in the window, attempting to twist them. Their coldness bit into her palms. She supposed blowing hot air on them wouldn't be enough for Frayvar's expansion of metal.

"May I ask you something?" he asked with more diffidence than usual.

"Yup."

"Is this adventure truly about proving yourself... or is it about Domas?"

"It has nothing to do with him."

Liar, her mind accused, a memory rearing up like an angry horse. Domas backing away from their bed with a blanket around his waist and scowling. "*What is* wrong *with you? You look so normal.*"

He'd said that more than once when they'd been together. *You look so normal.*

Strangely damning words. Like if she'd been born clubfooted with four eyes, her mood swings, her *funks*, as Frayvar called them, might have been more acceptable.

Kaylina shook her head, reluctant, as always, to open up to anyone, even family members. But Frayvar had come clean to her. Didn't she owe it to him to tell the truth? Especially now?

"Silana said it was," he added.

Silana. Their always-smiling older sister who had a husband, two daughters, and happiness and contentment others could only aspire to.

"She wasn't there," was all Kaylina said.

"Domas broke up with you, though, right?"

"It was mutual."

"A simultaneous and equally desired agreement to part ways?" Frayvar sounded skeptical for someone with zero experience with relationships. Maybe logic prompted the question rather than intuition.

"Something like that. Breaking up might have been what prompted the timing of me leaving, but it wasn't everything. For years, I've had this dream."

"So, it was the catalyst," Frayvar said.

"Sure."

Leave it to him to use a vocabulary word to describe her emotional outbursts.

Some intuition took Kaylina to the door again, and she pressed her ear against it. Footsteps sounded in the corridor.

"Someone's coming," she whispered.

"We'll tell them the truth once more. Calmly, so they'll take us seriously."

"It's hard to get people to take you seriously when there's nobody behind you."

His lips flattened, but he didn't deny that. After all his encounters with bullies in school, he had to know that better than she.

"If we have to, we'll request that the adjudicator send a letter home to verify we are who we say we are," Kaylina said. "I hate the thought of needing help, but Grandma will vouch for us."

"It'll take three weeks for round-trip communication."

"Three weeks when they'll have to keep us alive. Time for us to come up with something."

"All right." His bleak expression didn't suggest agreement, but he probably had nothing better.

The lock turned, and Kaylina stepped back.

When the door opened, Lord Vlerion's broad shoulders filled the frame. Damn it, where was that adjudicator? Someone impartial and fair who would hear them?

Vlerion carried his sword in hand, like an executioner's axe ready to swing.

When his cold gaze met hers, Kaylina stepped back before she caught herself. Irritation swept through her, more at her automatic response than at anything he'd done. But her brother would point out it was *logical* to get out of the way of someone with a huge sword.

His face impassive, Vlerion walked into the cell, making room for an older man in ranger blacks to step in after him. A few grays dotted the new man's brown hair, but he looked lean and fit under his armor.

When Vlerion turned, light from the corridor allowed her to see the red lump on the back of his head. Kaylina couldn't regret hitting him, not when he'd been going after Frayvar with a sword, but there might be repercussions.

With a sword and dagger belted at his waist and more visible scars than Vlerion had, the second ranger looked as fair and impartial as a badger defending a cub. He surveyed them as

Vlerion rested the tip of his long blade on the stone floor and waited.

"This is the girl who hit you on the head?" Was that amusement in the new ranger's eyes?

"She is." Vlerion touched something tucked into his belt opposite a dagger. Her sling.

Kaylina's fingers twitched involuntarily toward it. Not because she longed to brain him—*much*—but because she couldn't lose Grandpa's gift.

"She wants to do it again." Yes, that *was* amusement in the other man's eyes.

Kaylina lowered her hand.

"Many do," was all Vlerion said.

The older ranger considered Kaylina and Frayvar. "They're young for spies and murderers."

Vlerion eyed Kaylina. "She's close to my age."

"*You're* young too." Humor glinted in the ranger's brown eyes again.

Dare they hope he would be more reasonable than the uptight lord?

"Captain." The first hint of emotion entered Vlerion's voice—mild indignation. "For six years, I've patrolled the Evardor Mountains and climbed the Twin Sisters to fight the Scourge beasts and Kar'ruk spies. I've seen as many battles as your gray-haired veterans."

"As *some* of my gray-haired veterans, perhaps." The ranger—the *captain* of the rangers?—touched a scar along his jaw.

"The Virts have used children as spies before," Vlerion said.

Kaylina wanted to bristle at being lumped in with *children*—she was twenty-one, damn it—but she managed to keep her mouth shut.

"They have, but we aren't at war with the entire proletariat, and we can't assume everyone who isn't a noble is an enemy."

The captain's jaw tightened in a clench. "They're our own people."

"Even those who don't raise weapons against the nobility would cheer to see us burn." Vlerion's tone was back to emotionless, but his face conveyed an aloof haughtiness.

"Don't let your heritage define you, Vlerion."

"It would be... quite impossible for it not to." Their gazes met with the understanding of some shared knowledge. Or... a shared secret?

Whatever it was, Kaylina doubted it had anything to do with her. Deciding she didn't care about their secrets, she raised a finger. "May we explain what led us to that castle? And *who*?"

"The land agent who mysteriously disappeared?" Vlerion asked coolly.

"Naybor was his name. And when armed rangers on giant hairy beasts show up, people disappearing can't be that mysterious."

That spark of irritation—of *danger*—flared in his eyes again.

Kaylina reminded herself not to intentionally goad him. He clearly didn't like her, probably because she was a commoner. That was fine. She didn't like him either. Asshole.

"I'm Captain Targon. Tell *me* what led you to the cursed castle."

"Have you the authority to weigh guilt and innocence and release the wrongfully accused from incarceration?" Frayvar asked.

Targon, whom Kaylina had dubbed the more likely of the two to listen, narrowed his eyes. Perceiving the question as disrespect? Maybe *his* heritage defined him too. Or he at least believed people should bow down to his rank.

"I command the rangers and report to the king," Targon said. "I carry *his* authority when it comes to defending Zaldor against threats, foreign and domestic."

Kaylina held her hand up to keep her brother from speaking again and launched into a more complete version of what had happened since they'd landed. She was almost surprised when Targon listened. Vlerion also listened, but his eyes said he'd already condemned them as spies.

When she finished, she lifted her hands. "I'm willing to eat that root and answer questions under its influence. It's a truth drug, right? If it can clear my name, I'm *especially* willing to eat it, but you can't give it to my brother, okay? He's allergic to stuff from the tree it comes from." Kaylina looked at Vlerion. "*That's* why he ran. Not because he was guilty of anything. He was scared for his life."

Vlerion's expression didn't change, and she couldn't tell if he believed her. She looked back to Targon, deeming him the more sympathetic.

"I volunteer to take that root and be questioned," she repeated, "if you don't give it to my brother."

"You will take the root and be questioned whether you volunteer or not," Vlerion said.

Targon glanced at him but didn't naysay the statement.

"I thought it might be helpful if you had my cooperation instead of me biting you when you try to shove something in my mouth." Kaylina bared her teeth at Vlerion.

"She *definitely* wants to hit you again," Targon told him.

"Yes," Vlerion agreed with an indifferent shrug.

Targon focused on Kaylina. "You two do look like siblings, even if you're a lot more appealing than he is."

Frayvar lifted a finger, as if he might object, but he lowered it and said nothing. Good. Kaylina didn't want him drawing attention to himself. She didn't want to be called *appealing* by a scarred-up forty-year-old guy, but he hadn't ogled her chest or her ass, so she could deal with it.

"For now," Targon continued, "unless your answers lead us to believe there's more that we must unearth, I'm willing to question you in lieu of your brother."

"Good," she said. "I'm ready."

Targon held up a hand. "Have you been given kafdari root before?"

"No." Only after she spoke did Kaylina realize the question might have been a test. If she had said yes, would Targon have believed she'd been in trouble with the law before?

"Then you're not aware of its side effects and how you might react under the influence."

"It just makes you tell the truth, doesn't it?" Kaylina looked at her brother.

"Assuming you're not allergic to it," Frayvar said, "it lowers your inhibitions, like alcohol. But it's even more potent. It makes you eager to share information, but it also removes any reluctance to hide or sublimate your emotions. Depending on the person, its use can result in weeping or rage or both."

Great. Kaylina couldn't wait to bare her soul and *weep* in front of the stone-faced Vlerion and his boss.

Or *was* the ranger captain his boss? He ought to be, but they stood shoulder to shoulder, and they'd bantered like equals.

"The kid knows a lot about it for someone who isn't a spy," Vlerion noted.

"He knows a lot about everything." Kaylina balled her fingers into a fist, frustration with the situation still simmering. "He reads books."

She kept herself from implying that Vlerion didn't—or couldn't—barely.

"On roots?" Targon asked mildly.

That humor remained on his face, but his eyes were intent, and she knew he was testing them, waiting to see if they would inadvertently condemn themselves. What was going on in the capital that the rangers were so on edge? That they jumped straight to believing that people *accidentally* trespassing were spies?

The memory of the dead lord floated into her mind, answering her own question. She wished she'd spent more time reading the kingdom newspapers of late. Whatever was going on up here was probably being published in all the major cities, but she'd been too immersed in her own world to pay attention.

"He's a chef at the Spitting Gull, our family's meadery and eating house," Kaylina said to answer Targon's question. "If something is edible, magical or mundane, he's read about it."

Frayvar nodded.

"We'll see." Targon raised his eyebrows. "Do you still consent to taking the kafdari root and being questioned?"

Vlerion had implied that she would be questioned whether there was consent or not, but maybe those words had been meant to scare her into compliance. Maybe they had some laws about questioning their own people and needed her permission.

Another scream echoed through the stone walls, one of pain. Neither ranger blanched or reacted in any way. Targon continued to watch her intently.

"Did that guy *not* consent?" Kaylina didn't manage to keep the squeak of alarm out of her voice.

"He did not. Evdar Wedgewick..." Targon paused, watching her eyes. To see if she recognized the name? She didn't. "...is a known terrorist leader who's been behind explosions around the city that have caused the deaths of innocents, working class *and* aristocrats. He is being questioned by force since he eluded the effects of the kafdari root and didn't tell us the locations of the Virt bases."

It was possible to elude the truth drug? Did that mean that her words wouldn't automatically clear her?

Kaylina hoped that wouldn't be the case. She had nothing to hide and wouldn't fight the questioning. But would they believe her? What if the root addled her so much that she couldn't think straight, and she somehow said something that would condemn them?

She looked at Frayvar, but he didn't nod or encourage her in any way. His solemn eyes seemed to say it was up to her.

Since he couldn't be questioned with the root, she had to do this.

"I consent, and I'm ready." Kaylina wanted to get away from the sound of a man being tortured and back to fulfilling her dream as soon as possible.

Targon nodded and withdrew something from a pouch on his belt. The cream-colored ball looked like wadded-up chicle. Kaylina assumed powdered kafdari root was mixed into it.

As Targon approached, Vlerion did too, moving to stand behind her.

Kaylina tensed, alarmed by the big men hemming her in.

"Vlerion will hold you in case you grow violent under the influence of the root. It's for your own good as well as to prevent him from suffering grievous injury at your hands again." Targon grinned at Vlerion.

He sighed. "Do you have to take so much delight in my bruise?"

Bruise. He probably had a concussion. Kaylina hoped he did.

"Yes." Targon's grin widened. "Hardly anyone *ever* touches you in a fight."

"If that were true, I'd have a prettier face."

"Weren't those scars from a tangle with your father when you were young? When he was..." Targon glanced at Kaylina and finished with a vague wave.

"Yes."

"I haven't seen anyone hit you since your first days of training. You'll pardon me if I wish I'd seen her crack you in the head."

"Jankarr allowed it because he wanted to see how good her *aim* is. I would appreciate it if you put him on potato-peeling duty for a few days."

Listening to them banter almost made Kaylina forget about the screams and think she and Frayvar might be okay, that these men were reasonable enough to believe the truth and let them walk. But when Vlerion stepped closer, his torso brushing her back, and gripped her upper arms, her anxiety returned. The tall men shared looks over her head, the humor in Targon's eyes shifting to grimness as he raised the cream-colored ball.

Something told Kaylina this wouldn't go well.

4

In shame lies the fear of being driven into isolation.
    ~ *Ganizbar, the poet*

The gummy ball was too large to swallow, so Kaylina made herself chew it. A sweet maple flavor and rubbery texture didn't fully hide the gritty, bitter powder mixed in. The kafdari root.

Aware of Targon's gaze upon her, and Vlerion's grip around her upper arms, she resisted the urge to spit it out and swallowed.

Nothing happened, but that wasn't surprising. It would take time to digest the root. But how much time? Would she have to stand between the two men like this for a half hour before anything happened?

Vlerion's grip wasn't painful—especially considering he had to be irked that she'd hit him in the head—but it wasn't so delightful that she wanted to linger like that.

Her tongue tingled, as if the powder seeped through it and directly into her bloodstream. Was that possible?

Another scream sounded elsewhere in the jail, and it sent a shiver of dread through her. What if the root didn't work on her? Would the rangers use more physical means to question her?

"I hope Bartron gets the bases out of him," Targon said quietly, meeting Vlerion's gaze over Kaylina's head.

They were both tall enough to see over her. The warmth of Vlerion's breaths stirred her hair.

"I'm tired of fighting our own people," Targon added. "I never thought I'd long for the frigid mountains and being attacked by Scourge beasts and packs of yekizar, but..."

"I also prefer the wilds and clearcut foes," Vlerion replied, "not the hordes of people in the city, people whose sharp, disrespectful tongues test your equanimity more than fangs or even the blades of the Kar'ruk."

Certain he looked at *her* when he said that, Kaylina blurted, "Screw you, pirate."

Targon arched his eyebrows as Vlerion's grip tightened on her arms. "Is it kicking in already, or was she that mouthy before you dragged her in?"

"She does not treat rangers with appropriate respect," Vlerion said.

"If she's from the south and doesn't face anything more dangerous than pirates regularly, she might not have the appreciation for rangers that those whose lives depend on us do. The laws about disrespecting nobles are enforced throughout the kingdom though."

Five lashes for cursing at an aristocrat, ten for obstructing his path, and twenty for raising a hand toward one, unless within the boundaries of a mutually agreed upon duel. Kaylina knew the rules, but so few lords came to their islands that she'd rarely had to think about them. It hadn't occurred to her that there were places in the kingdom where laws like that were enforced.

"Do you want her flogged after this?" Targon added.

Frayvar stirred, indignation in his eyes, though he was doing as Kaylina had asked and staying out of this. She raised a hand toward him, inasmuch as she could with her arms trapped.

"No," Vlerion said. "It would not be fair to punish her for words uttered under the influence of a drug."

Targon nodded, as if that was the answer he'd hoped for.

Kaylina should have been relieved, but tension had crept into her, bunching her shoulders and tightening every muscle in her body. It frustrated her that these people had the right to flog her. And more. She shouldn't be here in this jail. This was all a mistake.

With a surge of anger, she twisted, trying to break Vlerion's grip on her. His muscles flexed against his sleeves, but his hands didn't budge. He easily shifted her back to face Targon.

"Your name?" the captain asked.

She'd already given it but blurted, "Kaylina Korbian," as if she couldn't wait to share. Then she found herself volunteering more. "My brother is Frayvar. My *little* brother. I thought Grandma sent him after me because she didn't think I could do this on my own, but he ran away because he thought I needed help. I can't let him be hurt or get in trouble because of my plan." Again, she struggled, wanting to escape the big man holding her, frantic to have her freedom. Her blood scoured her veins as it flowed through them, hot and tingly. Something was affecting her so strangely.

She'd eaten a weird ball, hadn't she? Memories from moments before flitted away, difficult to grasp, with the past coming to the forefront of her mind.

"What is your plan?" The man in front of her didn't stir as she thrashed against the guy holding her from behind.

She spat at him. He tilted his head in time so that it sailed past.

"State your plan, Kaylina Korbian," he said.

"To open a meadery using my family's recipes and our honey —the bees on the islands forage on altered plants, you know, so it's really good. One day, I'm going to be as successful as Grandma. And Grandpa too. He helps at the Spitting Gull, so he's just as responsible for its success. Of course, he's usually out with the bees or hunting or fishing to bring in fresh fare for the eating house. Frayvar helps Silana cook, and her kids are serving now too. Our cousins do the repairs for the place and keep out the riffraff. The whole family works at the Gull, and I'm proud of what they've made, but I blend in, disappear. I'm nobody there. And some days, it's so hard to get out of bed and do the chores, to have people tell me what to do. I get cranky." Her voice fell to a whisper as she continued, forgetting that men were watching her, forgetting where she was. Why was it so hot? And why wouldn't the guy behind her let her go? "I don't mean to be like that—I *hate* that I can't control my temper and snap at people. Why can't I be, I don't know, *happy*? The way Silana is. Nothing ever fazes her. She's so comfortable in her life and in the family and on the island, but I ... I need something more and to be away from everyone, because I lose it sometimes. I feel trapped, say things I regret. It hurts them, and I hate myself later."

Kaylina twisted again, needing freedom, needing the cool air from the window to push away the heat flushing her face, her entire body. A bead of sweat ran down her spine.

"Let me go." Kaylina grunted under the restraint, more tension tightening her muscles. She shifted her weight and kicked out, wanting the man questioning her to stop. But she couldn't reach him. "I need to go. I need to prove to them that I'm not a screw up, but I need my own place to do it. A meadery of my own. Or an *inn*. That castle place is perfect. We're going to rent it. With some work, it'll be amazing. I could share our family's mead with everyone in the capital, our award-winning recipes. I could help my family without, without... I need freedom and a chance," she finished with a whisper.

"Are you a spy?" the man in front of her asked.

"A spy?" Kaylina peered at him with confusion, trying to dredge an appropriate answer from her memory. She couldn't remember why, but she had to say the right things, tell these people what they wanted to hear, even though they were imprisoning her. That grip. Why wouldn't it let her go?

She thrashed again, some weird power giving her more strength than usual. For an instant, she escaped one of the hands grasping her, and she tasted her freedom. But an entire muscled arm wrapped around her torso, pulling her back, and she found herself pinned to a big man's chest. She tried to jerk her head back, to thump him in the nose, but he was too tall. All she hit was armor. Leather armor. Black like a ranger. Wait, *was* he a ranger?

"Are you a spy?" the question repeated.

"No. I caught Mavari Bustinor spying on the Gull once. She was trying to steal Grandma's recipes. Those sisters are *always* trying to get our secrets. Their parents run the Cock's Crow, and they think they can get our customers, but their food isn't anywhere close to as good as ours. And they serve that awful grog instead of mead. Even if they *had* our recipes, they couldn't make them like Fray and Silana do."

The man's eyes lifted. "You still think she's a spy?" he asked dryly.

"Ask her about Darringtar."

"Do you know what happened to Lord Darringtar?" the man in front asked.

"I don't know who that is." Kaylina ducked, trying to pull away from the arm restraining her. This was worse than before. So hard and hot. Sweat bathed her face.

She squirmed, stomping a foot down on her captor's, but it

mustn't have hurt him. His arm didn't budge. A statue couldn't have been more impervious.

"Have you ever killed anyone?"

"No, of course not."

"Have you ever struck a noble?"

"No, nobles hardly ever visit the Vamorka Islands. Oh, wait!" A satisfying memory surged to the forefront of her mind, clearer than the rest. "I hit a ranger with a round from Grandpa's sling." She grinned fiercely before remembering something. "You're not supposed to attack law enforcers, and *definitely* not rangers, but he was such an ass. He was going to kill Fray. I had to. He's my brother. Even if they sometimes piss you off, family is still family. You have to protect family."

The man in front of her looked up again.

"I chased the kid because he fled," her captor said calmly, as if she weren't squirming and trying to twist away from him. "I wasn't going to kill him."

"Chased him with your sword raised," Kaylina spat over her shoulder. Then added, "Asshole," again.

"She really likes you," the other man said.

"As we've established. The squagar juice?"

"Yes. This has been a waste of time."

"I apologize," her captor said, the words clipped. He didn't sound like someone who said those words often. "I'll find Darringtar's murderer before my squad goes back to the mountains."

The man stepped into the hall outside, disappearing from view, and Kaylina renewed her effort to free herself. By now, she was panting as well as being hot and thirsty.

"It's over," her captor said quietly in her ear. "Drink the juice Targon brings. It's not exactly an antidote, but it'll clear your head faster."

That seemed reasonable, but she couldn't control her body,

couldn't stop fighting the grip restraining her. But her captor was strong, so muscular.

What would it be like to sleep with someone like that? All hard ridges and power.

Domas had been all right, but he wasn't a warrior. He was a fisherman. Handsome, maybe, but not that nice. Why had she had sex with him? Because she'd thought it would make her happy to be in a relationship? The way her sister was?

The man returned with a flask, pausing to watch her writhing before raising his eyebrows. "I'd ask if you were enjoying that, Vlerion, but I suppose you keep yourself too strapped down to experience lust."

Enjoying... her squirming? Like her captor might be thinking about sex too?

"Give her the juice. It was a mistake to bring them here."

No, he wasn't interested in sex. And she wasn't either. Not with *him*. Why had her mind brought up those thoughts?

"I don't blame you for thinking they had something to do with Darringtar's death." The man barked a laugh as he approached with the flask. "But I can't believe they want to rent the cursed castle. What fools. They *must* have just arrived on that ship."

Indignation flared in Kaylina. When the man came close enough, she tried to kick him.

Unfortunately, he saw it coming and dodged. Too bad. He would look good with his testicles lodged up his ass.

"She doesn't like you either," her captor said dryly.

"It's the kafdari root. She'll find me a delight once she recovers." The man considered approaching her, but Kaylina bared her teeth, prepared to kick him again. "You give it to her." He angled in from behind her captor, a direction she couldn't kick, and offered the flask to him.

Vlerion, she remembered, her mind growing less scattered.

"Coward," Vlerion said.

"I've faced Kar'ruk armies and have been battling Scourge monsters since before you were born." That didn't keep the man—Targon—from foisting the flask on Vlerion.

He managed to grab it, thumb the cap off, and keep Kaylina restrained at the same time.

"Take this," Vlerion told her, not rescinding the coward comment for his comrade. "Once you calm down, I'll release you."

Kaylina wanted that, but she eyed the lip of the flask warily, afraid of what she would remember when her mind returned fully to her. Already, she sensed that she'd bared her soul to complete strangers, saying things she didn't even talk about with her family. Not only strangers but pompous rangers who'd believed her guilty of a crime she'd had nothing to do with.

"Take it." Vlerion brought the flask to her lips.

"Do it, Kay," a new voice urged. Frayvar.

She'd forgotten he was there. He'd witnessed everything too.

She groaned, her head falling back against a hard shoulder as shame crept into her.

With her head back, she could see Vlerion's scarred jaw, as well as the rest of his haughty face. His blue eyes were as cool and impassive as ever. Maybe he didn't care that she'd spilled the contents of her soul. Maybe he hadn't been listening.

With one arm still wrapped around her, pinning her against him, Vlerion tilted the flask. A tart berry juice she hadn't had before trickled down her throat, and she had to swallow.

The fight bled out of her, the heat and energy that had filled her fading. She didn't object to the juice. Despite its tartness, it was cool and appealing on her tongue.

Kaylina closed her eyes and slumped, briefly forgetting whose arms were around her and that she didn't like the owner of them. As she again noticed the chill of the cell, his warmth grew appealing. A weird urge to snuggle back into him swept over her.

Her earlier feeling of being trapped disappeared, and she

admitted it was nice being held by a man, a tall strong man who smelled of leather and lye soap and faintly of the crisp, snowy mountains. Maybe he wouldn't ask her why she couldn't be more like her sister. Maybe he wouldn't call her sexy but frustrating. Maybe he wouldn't say, *You look so normal.*

"Do you want more juice?" Vlerion's grip loosened, but he watched her closely and didn't yet release her.

Kaylina opened her eyes. Was she better? She didn't know.

She felt woozy and like her mind wasn't entirely hers. The thought of more juice appealed, and she nodded and licked her lips.

Vlerion's gaze shifted to watch her mouth as he tipped the flask back. Had his eyes not continued to be impassive, she might have thought him a little interested in her.

A great *boom* erupted outside, close enough that it rattled the iron bars in the window and shook the floor.

Vlerion sprang away so fast that Kaylina almost fell. He dropped the flask and, not glancing back, grabbed his sword and ran out of the cell. Targon had already disappeared into the corridor and was shouting orders at someone.

Kaylina had barely recovered her balance when the door slammed shut. A scream sounded, a woman this time, and it came from outside the jail. Bangs and thumps followed.

"Terrorists!" someone cried.

"Are you okay?" Frayvar, who rarely touched and never hugged, gripped Kaylina's wrist.

"No." Memories of all she'd uttered flooded her with embarrassment. Embarrassment and *anger.* She resented the rangers for making her drop her defenses and share everything. She hadn't meant to consent to *that.* When she noticed her brother's worried face, she made herself change her answer. "Yes."

She grabbed the flask off the floor. Some of the juice had dribbled out, but she swallowed the rest.

Outside, clangs rang out. A sword fight?

"This would be a good time to leave." Frayvar pointed to the door. "They didn't pardon us, but we were never formally charged of a crime either."

Nodding, Kaylina dropped the empty flask and headed toward the door, wobbly but determined. She tried the latch, then groaned. She didn't know if the rangers had done it or some guard had hurried down the corridor to check all the doors, but it was locked, and there was no other way out.

5

ONLY A BEAST MAY WIN A BATTLE AGAINST A BEAST.
  ~ Kar'ruk proverb

"They locked us in?" Frayvar asked as more shouts came from outside, punctuated by the clangs of swords. "It sounded like they were on the verge of letting us go. That's the only reason I didn't leap in and save you when that brute had you pinned."

"*That's* the reason?" Kaylina walked toward the window, struggling to push aside the lingering effects of the root. "Not that he's twice your weight, has muscles harder than steel pillars, and wears armor instead of a rumpled taybarri shirt?"

"My *shirt* doesn't affect my fighting prowess."

Kaylina wasn't tall enough to see out the window. She gripped the bars with thoughts of pulling herself up, but the wall offered no footholds. Even when she felt perky, she didn't have the strength to hold her body weight up for long.

"His muscles might have been a consideration," Frayvar added. "And his sword."

"*All* of him." Even if she hadn't been in control of her tongue, and her thoughts had been addled, she had no trouble remembering that Vlerion hadn't budged during all her struggles.

"Yeah."

A boom less substantial than the last thundered. It sounded like Grandpa's blunderbuss and brought memories of pirate raids and defending the Gull from the wooden decks surrounding the elevated eating house. Vlerion wasn't the first man that Kaylina had cracked in the head with a sling round.

"Can you boost me up?" She would have asked her taller brother to look out the window, but curiosity made her want to see for herself what was going on.

"*My* muscles aren't harder than steel pillars," Frayvar grumbled, but he did come to assist her.

"Oh, I know. I've helped you carry the stock pot to keep you from dumping boiling water on your sandals *often*."

"When it's full, that pot is heavy for *everyone*." Frayvar lifted his hands in the air as he considered where to grab her, then tried her waist, as if he might heft her like a vase.

Feet not raising an inch, Kaylina rolled her eyes. "This from the mind of a mathematical genius. Squat down so I can stand on your back."

Grumbling again, he did, making a stool. The grumbles turned into grunts as she stepped up. Even through her boots, she could feel the frailness of his build and vowed not to stay up for long.

She gripped the bars, shifting her weight off Frayvar as much as she could as she peered out. Finally, she could see.

Twilight had fallen, but streetlamps burned along the road, a canal that passed the jail, and a bridge that was... half missing. Rubble littered the cobblestones on one side, and men fought on the half of it that was still intact. That could *not* be a stable perch.

Kaylina shook her head grimly. The rangers had marched her and Frayvar over that bridge on the way to the jail. What if the explosion—had it been a keg of black powder?—had gone off when they'd been on it?

Two of the fighting figures wore black—Targon and Vlerion. They crouched back to back at the base of the bridge, not ten yards away from the jail. Men and a few women in a hodgepodge of chain mail, leather armor, and rusty plate—the pieces were mixed as if they'd been selected at random—attacked the rangers with swords and cudgels.

Three archers and a woman who was reloading a single-round blunderbuss stood farther down the canal, using a lamppost and a tree for cover while leaning out to fire at the rangers.

A war horn rang out somewhere in the city. A warning to desist. The attackers did not.

"For the righteous and virtuous!" someone bellowed. "For the commoners!"

Another archer stood at the corner of the jail building. He fired not at the rangers but at the other bowmen. An ally for Vlerion and Targon. But someone in black clothing with a knife crawled out of the canal—was there a boat down there?—and crept through the shadows toward the archer.

Kaylina bit her lip, not certain if she should call a warning or not. On the one hand, rangers were law enforcers in the kingdom, as well as defenders of its borders, and she should have felt loyal to them. On the other, Targon and Vlerion hadn't given her any reason to love them, and if this was a class battle, she didn't want to side with the aristocrats. There wasn't a drop of noble blood in her veins. Besides, the aristocrats had advantages enough.

But they *were* outnumbered in this battle...

More men with knives climbed out of the canal. They glanced at the fight at the base of the bridge, then headed for the jail instead.

Given the number of enemies, the rangers should have gone down quickly, but they had the better training. *Far* better training.

Kaylina stared as Vlerion somehow sensed an arrow zipping toward his head and deflected it with his sword at the same time as he used a dagger to parry an attacker's cudgel. Not glancing at the archer, he kicked the closer foe back and spun to his side to protect Targon from another swordsman.

His movements were so fast that they blurred, making them hard to follow. Targon was competent as well, extremely competent, but he didn't have the same preternatural speed as Vlerion. Far greater speed and grace than Kaylina would have expected from a big man. Something about the way Vlerion moved his feet and whipped his limbs about, blocking every attack and deploying several of his own, made her think of panthers chasing prey in the reeds along the marshy shoreline back home. He didn't seem quite... human.

She snorted at herself. What else could he be? Half Kar'ruk? He didn't have horns and fangs.

Further, Vlerion's face wasn't savage as he fought. No, it was the opposite. Enough light came from a lamp burning at the base of the bridge for her to see his expression. He looked like he was concentrating, his focus absolute. No battle lust burned in his eyes, nor did he show any sign of fear or anger or aggression of any kind. His lack of reaction in the face of his enraged foes was strange. The words *not quite human* came to mind again.

In contrast, Targon grunted, cursed, and let out a triumphant, "Got you!" as he took down an opponent in front of him.

The rangers were frustrating their attackers, who snarled, spat, and maligned aristocrats as they swung their weapons. As their numbers diminished, their blows grew more desperate. Kaylina couldn't believe they were still attacking. They had to realize that, even with archers trying to pepper the rangers, they weren't going to win. One man kept glancing toward the jail, as if expecting something to happen there.

Those glances cost him his life. Vlerion swung his sword horizontally and took off his head.

Kaylina swore as it thudded to the ground and rolled into the canal. Again, she reminded herself not to insult Vlerion.

A barge floated down the river toward the destroyed bridge, and she imagined the crew being confused—and horrified—as a head bumped against their hull.

Several of them were out on deck, watching the battle. No, they were fiddling with a large rectangular object on the deck, something taller than they. Was that a cage? Yes, a black animal moved inside. Something bigger than the panther she'd been imagining. A cragwalker? A bearslayer? A trained yekizar? Some deadly animal she'd only read about in books, that was certain.

Frayvar groaned and shifted. "How much longer do you need a front-row seat to whatever is happening out there?"

"Another minute. I think that barge is part of it." Biceps and forearms quivering, Kaylina pulled herself higher, pressing her face to the bars for a better view.

A clang sounded as the cage door opened, slamming to the deck. With a lion-like roar, the muscled black creature ran out and sprang for the street—for the battle. A yekizar.

On powerful limbs, it bounded toward the fray, its golden eyes catching the lamplight. They were focused not randomly on the crowd but on the rangers.

A chill swept through Kaylina. Her books had never spoken of that kind of intelligence in the beasts of the north, that they could recognize and choose their prey.

Different roars sounded in the distance, from the same direction that horn had been blown. Those she'd heard before. Taybarri.

More rangers had to be coming to help, but would they be in time? The yekizar might be too much even for Vlerion.

He glanced toward it as he knocked two attackers away, one

gripping his bleeding side as he stumbled and fell into the canal. That made room for Vlerion to spring out of the knot of men, landing in a crouch facing the approaching beast. Again, his face was impassive. Eerily calm.

Mesmerized by the battle, by *him*, Kaylina almost missed movement to her left. Someone darted across the cobblestone street between the jail and the canal. Another shadowy figure. No, two of them. They carried small boxes instead of knives. The archer who'd been helping the rangers had disappeared. Or had he been killed?

One of the men stopped under the window of a cell near hers, placing a box against the wall. No, those weren't boxes. They were kegs.

He ran to her cell and left another box. With the help of his allies, four more kegs were placed.

The screech of the yekizar rang out as it reached Vlerion. He dodged lightning-fast swipes from forelimbs ending in claws like daggers, then angled in from the side to slash his sword toward the beast.

Though Kaylina wanted to see the rest of his battle, the flame of a match flared, a man lighting a fuse on one of the kegs. He moved quickly to the others, including the one placed beneath her window.

"Back, back." Kaylina jumped down and grabbed her brother, pulling him to his feet.

"What?"

With no time to explain, she yanked him to the far side of the cell. "Cover your head."

A great explosion almost drowned out her last word.

Even closer than the thunderous boom that had started everything, it not only made the floor quake, but the cell wall blew inward. Stones tumbled from the ceiling and Kaylina cursed her decision to leave home as she wrapped her arms protectively over her head and knelt against the bench, wishing there were cover in the empty cell.

More explosions followed the first. Those guys were blowing open every cell in the jail. As more stone tumbled down, the entire ceiling threatening to cave in, Kaylina worried she and Frayvar would be buried.

She glanced toward the exterior wall, wondering if they could get out that way now, but thick smoke hid everything.

More clangs, another roar from the beast, and the firing of a blunderbuss promised the battle hadn't ended, but she couldn't see it. A shadow stirred in the smoke, and a cloaked woman peered into their cell.

"Hurry, hurry," she whispered. "Everyone out."

Frayvar looked at her and didn't budge. "We're not with you, thanks."

Someone else appeared beside the woman, a man with blood dripping from his fingers, bruises mottling his face, and an arm gripped to his ribs. Those wounds hadn't come from a sword fight —and the bruises were at least a day old. He had to be the prisoner who'd been tortured. Evdar Wedgewick.

"We saved you," he rasped. "You owe us."

The woman waved the words away. "You don't owe us, but we'll accept fresh blood for the cause if you're game. Don't stay and let the rangers round you up."

A pained screech, the sound of a dying animal, filled the night. Had Vlerion gotten the best of the yekizar?

"You can come with us," the woman added in a whisper. "We'll hide you!"

She waved again before she and the man ran to the next cell.

The rubble stopped falling from the ceiling. Great cracks ran along it, and the night sky was visible through holes, but it hadn't fallen completely. Not yet, anyway. Kaylina pushed herself to her feet, gripping Frayvar to help him up.

"Maybe we should go with them," she whispered, not daring to speak loudly since the battle was dying down. Their opportunity to escape would be brief. But should they use it? A hint of a plan formed in her mind. "We could find out where their bases are and..."

And what? Report back to the rangers? Become spies for *them*? She didn't even like them. But... if she and Frayvar helped the rangers, that could clear them of all suspicion of being tied in with the murder. Had her babbling under the root's influence done that? She didn't know. Mostly, she remembered ranting about her family life.

Frayvar grabbed her arm, making her realize she'd taken two steps toward the hole in the wall.

"They were about to let us go," he said. "We don't need to run. We absolutely do not need to join a rebellion or whatever is going on up here. We don't know anything about it. And do you want that big brute chasing after us for *real*?"

He flung a finger toward the bridge, and she had no doubt which *brute* he meant. Frayvar might not have seen the battle, but he'd been flattened by Vlerion. He understood the ranger's capabilities perfectly well.

"No." Kaylina couldn't see Vlerion and Targon, but the smoke was thinning, the sounds of chaos lessening. Nearby, snorts, chuffs, and whuffs meant the taybarri, and however many rangers were riding them, had arrived. "But if we have the opportunity to leave and don't take it, we might regret it later."

She glanced toward the door—the *locked* door.

"You gave them our names and the name of the eating house, Kay. If we disappear, the rangers could have the Kingdom Guard sent to Grandma and Grandpa's door to question *them*."

Kaylina didn't want to imagine the authorities doing anything vile to elderly law-abiding subjects, but Frayvar was right. If they fled, it would be suspicious, and they might no longer be deemed law-abiding subjects themselves.

"They'll let us go," Frayvar repeated. "We've done nothing wrong."

"Except for being ignorant tourists?" She bristled as she quoted Vlerion.

"That's not a crime. Besides, if we run, you won't get your sling back."

Shit. That was a good point.

"Fine." Kaylina pushed rocks and dust off the bench and sat with her arms folded across her chest to wait.

Frayvar arched his eyebrows. "Are you sulking or scheming? I can't always tell."

"I'm debating what to do next to make sure I get my sling *and* our honey back." She well remembered that her pack and their trunks had been left in the castle courtyard and hoped nobody had stolen them.

"So, scheming." Frayvar sat beside her. "Good."

6

ADAPTABILITY IS THE GREATEST QUALITY ON THE BATTLEFIELD.
  ~ Ranger Captain Targon

Fifteen or twenty minutes passed before anyone came to check on
the jail cells. The smoke had cleared, and a horse-drawn wagon
had arrived, stopping beside the unmoving body of the beast that
had attacked Vlerion. Attacked him and lost.

Kaylina hadn't seen the barge after its crew released the
yekizar, but she guessed it had continued down the canal and out
to the harbor.

Two men in gray-and-black Kingdom Guard uniforms ignored
the fallen beast and lifted human bodies into the back of the
wagon. They used more care than one might expect, given that the
dead had been facilitating a jailbreak.

Kaylina's stomach turned when the guards lifted the headless
body. She looked away, reminded of how Vlerion had decapitated
the man with no change of expression, no anger, no satisfaction,
no glee.

How many had he killed in his life to be completely unaffected like that? The songs and stories about the rangers always told of their heroics in defending the borders, in riding through the wilderness and protecting villages and watchtowers from the human-loathing Kar'ruk and the great mountain beasts that hungered for the flesh of men. She couldn't remember tales that spoke of rangers putting down rebellions and killing human beings, but she supposed their duties implied they would do that when the Guard wasn't sufficient to handle uprisings.

"I believe our opportunity to escape has ended," Frayvar murmured as a taybarri ambled into view on stout blue-furred legs and stopped, blocking the view of the canal. Nobody sat astride its back, but its ranger rider had to be nearby.

"Don't tell me you're changing your mind about that after you wouldn't let me walk out."

"You wanted to join rebels and find their *bases*." He gave her an aggrieved look as he wiped his palms on his trousers.

Nervous, was he? That they'd made the wrong decision?

So was she.

"I would have objected less to sneaking away and creeping back to the castle to gather our belongings, board a ship, and go home."

"We're not going home." No way would Kaylina let one little mishap destroy her dream.

Frayvar winced, a reminder that he'd only come because he'd thought she needed help starting the business. On their first day, he'd gotten far more adventure than he'd wanted, she had no doubt.

"*I'm* not going home," she amended.

As much as the money he'd brought would be helpful, she didn't want him to stay if he didn't want to. Being alone here would be scary, but she wouldn't have to worry about him as much if he went home.

Frayvar opened his mouth, but before he could speak, two men walked into view, stopping between the taybarri and the hole in the cell. Vlerion and Targon gazed in at Kaylina and Frayvar.

Dried blood smeared the side of Targon's head, and a cut had opened his leather armor, revealing a long gash along his ribs. Vlerion, other than someone else's blood spattered on the back of his hand and soot smearing one cheek, looked little different from when the rangers had questioned Kaylina.

Targon's words to Vlerion came to mind: *Hardly anyone ever touches you in a fight.*

"Huh," Targon said when he picked Kaylina and Frayvar out of the shadows.

When Vlerion met Kaylina's gaze, he arched his eyebrows. An expression of surprise? Or was he thinking what idiots they'd been not to leave?

Kaylina cleared her throat. "We had some time to think while you were fighting, and I was wondering..." She pointed in the direction of the former Stillguard Inn, though the crumbling castle was blocks away, and intervening trees and buildings hid it from view. "If that place is cursed, the owner might be willing to lease it at a discount. Do you know if he or she would be available for a business meeting?"

Beside her, Frayvar's mouth gaped open in surprise but only for a moment before he nodded.

The rangers stared at Kaylina for a much longer moment before Targon threw his head back and laughed. It was a short laugh that turned into a wince as he gripped his ribs.

"I admire your audacity, girl," he said.

"Nobody *leases* the cursed castle," Vlerion said without any sign of appreciation for audacity. His eyes were as cold as ever.

"Because the current owners are unwilling to rent it out?" Kaylina asked. "Or because its reputation keeps potential business owners from wanting to invest in it?"

"There's ancient magic woven into it that makes it dangerous," Vlerion said. "The catacombs underneath are traversed by criminals, it's notorious throughout the city, and Lord Darringtar was just murdered on the grounds."

"So... more of a reputation problem?"

Vlerion looked at Targon. Waiting for his boss to quash the ludicrous idea?

Targon smiled and stroked his chin, his eyes speculative. Kaylina didn't know if she should like that look or not.

"The Saybrooks are the owners of the castle, aren't they?" Targon asked Vlerion. "Of everything between the park and the river on that block, if I recall correctly."

"Yes."

"Didn't you used to play with the Saybrook girls when you were a boy?"

Vlerion lifted his chin. "I watched over them while their grandfather attended business meetings."

"You made a tree fort and pretended to be rangers and robbers with them. Wasn't there a dog too? That you dressed up like a taybarri?"

"*They* dressed up the dog, and how do you know what I was doing when I was nine?"

Targon grinned. "As you well know, the rangers have always kept an eye on your family. You've been of particular interest since you declared your intent to be something besides a farmer or goatherd wandering your ancestral lands." Their gazes locked, something passing between them again. A secret unspoken. "I believe you were six when that happened."

"One wouldn't think grown men would put much stock in the blatherings of children."

"Not *all* children." Targon looked at Kaylina and Frayvar, then tilted his head toward the street.

The rangers withdrew to speak in private.

Frayvar scratched his cheek. "Are they going to help us? I didn't expect that. I was second-guessing that they would even release us."

"After you insisted we stay—I noticed." Kaylina shifted on the bench, tempted to creep over to the wall to eavesdrop. The taybarri had moved, and the rangers hadn't gone far. "If they're going to help us, it's because that captain thinks he can get something out of it."

She struggled to imagine *what*. That comment about criminals using catacombs under the castle made her wonder if she and Frayvar might end up being spies for the rangers whether they wanted to or not. Or, if not spies, at least asked to keep their eyes open and report if they saw anything.

"Vlerion hasn't given his surname to us, has he?" Kaylina asked. "He's not one of the king's heirs, right? Why would the rangers have been watching him?"

Though she paid little attention to the politics of the kingdom, she knew the prince and heir was Enrikon, a man of thirty, and he had two younger sisters. If there were illegitimate sons, she hadn't heard about it, but she didn't know why else a young noble would be considered important enough to keep an eye on, other than that the aristocrats had a checkered history of raising armies and trying to overthrow monarchs. Maybe the noble families were watched for signs of that.

"He didn't mention it as he was mashing me to the ground, no. Strangely, I forgot to ask." After a pause, Frayvar added, "I have read about the Saybrooks in history books. They were one of the founding families of the kingdom and have a lot of land, both agricultural all up and down the coastal valleys, and industrial and commercial in Port Jirador and other major cities."

"So... they're incredibly rich?"

"Undoubtedly."

Kaylina bit her lip, doubting people that wealthy cared that their cursed castle wasn't bringing in any rent. She might *need* the rangers' help to convince the Saybrooks to lease it to her.

As if he knew what she was thinking, Frayvar said, "There are other places we can find to rent, places that aren't cursed. If that ranger thinks there's magic there, then there probably is. The Kar'ruk might have lived here once, but this whole land once belonged to the ancient Daygarii druids. They're the people who enchanted plants and animals before abandoning this realm and returning to the Vale of Origins."

"Other places would be more expensive though. And less... *epic*." Kaylina spread her arms, still able to envision how grand having a castle for their meadery and eating house would be. "People might come just because we're in such a unique building."

"People might *avoid* us because of the building. It could go either way."

"Hm." Kaylina stood.

Targon and Vlerion were still speaking, Targon doing most of the talking while Vlerion stood flint-faced, his arms crossed over his chest. From her position, it looked like Targon was the subordinate instead of the superior.

"Where are you going?" Frayvar whispered.

"Nowhere." They weren't looking at her, so she stepped out of their view to approach the wall. Using it for cover she turned her head toward the hole, hoping to catch a few words.

"...finished here, I could return to the mountains," Vlerion said.

"We need you here."

"Killing humans."

"Humans plotting to assassinate the king and overthrow the government? Yes, that's a priority right now."

"If King Gavatorin passed a few laws to give the Virts the work conditions they want, maybe there wouldn't *be* a rebellion brewing. His father would have at least negotiated with them."

Kaylina raised her eyebrows. She wouldn't have thought Vlerion would be the more reasonable of the two, or at least more openminded. Maybe she shouldn't have called him an asshole.

"Ssh, Vlerion. Watch your tongue. I can't protect you if the king's agents hear seditious words from your mouth."

Vlerion grunted. "When did it become sedition to speak about politics and economics? I'm not joining the commoners, simply saying that some concessions might appease them. They're simple people. They don't want much."

She rolled her eyes at the superciliousness. Asshole had been the right word.

"Your family lost its right to have control over such matters when your great-great-grandfather abdicated," Targon said.

"I'm aware. I..."

Frowning, Kaylina leaned her ear closer to the hole. Had they turned their backs?

A shadow loomed in the opening, and she stumbled backward. Vlerion grabbed her and pulled her outside while skewering the captain with his icy eyes.

"This one is trouble," Vlerion said. "You'd better forget any plan you have that involves relying on them."

"We're not relying on them." Targon waved an arm, as if indifferent to Kaylina's spying.

But Vlerion's grip bit in, and he eyed her sidelong.

"We're just using something that happens to have been made available to us. We need extra eyes around the city, eyes that aren't known to Wedgewick, Cougar, and their legions."

"When did you change from ranger captain to spymaster?"

"In times like these, our duties require us to wear many mantles." Targon's tone grew firmer when he said, "Go see Lord Saybrook, Vlerion. Or one of the girls. Don't they run half the businesses for him now?"

"Ghara does, yes."

"Is she the pretty one or the prettier one?"

"Does the king pay you to categorize noblewomen like that? Ghara is the one who apprenticed to a bookkeeper and can out-calculate an abacus."

Frayvar had crept closer when Kaylina had been caught, and his ears perked with interest.

"So the less pretty one," Targon said dryly.

Vlerion sighed.

"The king pays me to run the rangers, oversee recruit training, and protect the nation. He's indifferent to how I describe women."

"He's indifferent to a lot these days," Vlerion said.

"Your tongue is flapping too much tonight."

"It never occurred to you that there's a *reason* the crown has preferred I be in the hinterlands?"

"Oh, I'm aware. As the captain, I do have *some* say in the scheduling, you know." There was that dryness again.

"Some but not all, right?"

Targon was slow to answer. "I'd deny knowing what you're talking about, but you're a hard man to fool, despite your long absences from the city. Go see the bookkeeper girl. Wink at her, and get her to draw up a lease for those two."

"And the curse?"

"Maybe the ghosts of the druids like mead." Targon looked at Kaylina for the first time in several minutes—he hadn't reacted in the least when Vlerion had pulled her out. "You can wander by now and then to make sure they're not dead."

If Vlerion was seething inside, it didn't show on his face, but the tense set of his jaw and his tight grip promised he wanted nothing to do with Kaylina and Frayvar. She didn't want anything to do with *him* either.

"Do you two have a place to stay tonight?" Targon asked, waving for Vlerion to release Kaylina.

He did so, but he didn't step away, instead looming over her.

She resisted the urge to move, though she would have preferred not to stay within grab range.

Frayvar shook his head. "We ran into the land agent almost as soon as we got off the ship."

"We didn't get to see much of the city," Kaylina added. "Other than the now well-ventilated jail."

"Unfortunately," Targon murmured, glancing at the wagon as it rolled away, the bodies being taken who knew where. "The ranger barracks—"

"Are for rangers," Vlerion interrupted.

Targon pointed at Kaylina and Frayvar and opened his mouth.

"*They* can spend the night in the castle they want to lease." Vlerion gave Kaylina a challenging look.

Heat flushed her cheeks. What? Did he think they couldn't handle spending the night on a cold stone floor?

"That's fine," she said. "Saves us having to pay for a room at an inn."

"They haven't leased it yet," Targon pointed out.

"By morning, they might not want to." Vlerion continued to hold Kaylina's gaze.

"Would you mind not meddling with my plan?" Targon asked. "Just drop them off somewhere, and visit the Saybrooks in the morning."

"Of course, my captain." Vlerion bowed to him.

"You're an abysmal subordinate. The king isn't the *only* reason you keep getting banished to the mountains."

It might have been a joke, but Vlerion's blue eyes grew hooded, his face grim. "I'm aware."

7

TO BE TESTED AND FAIL IS DISAPPOINTING BUT NOT SO DISAPPOINTING AS to never be tested at all.
~ *Elder Taybarri Ravarn*

Riding a taybarri and stroking her fingers through its thick, lush fur was *amazing*. Too bad Kaylina had to share the mount with Frayvar and Vlerion. The stuffy ranger lord hadn't spoken a word since giving her the challenging you're-going-to-be-scared-spit-less-tonight-in-that-castle stare.

At least she'd talked Frayvar into being the one to ride directly behind Vlerion, with her behind them. That way, she wouldn't have to wrap her arms around the ranger if the taybarri broke into a gallop. There'd been far too much touching that day for her tastes.

Full night darkened the city as the furry creature ambled down the street paralleling the river and leading to the castle. Its back could have carried even more than three people. Their powerful muscles and inherent magic made the taybarri strong enough for loads that would have dropped horses. Not that anyone had ever hooked one of their kind up to a plow. From what she'd read, they were far too intelligent—and powerful—to allow themselves to be used in any way except as they wished.

The handful of people running late errands or returning from drinking bowed as Vlerion passed on his mount, only glancing at the riders behind him. Per Targon's order, Kaylina and Frayvar wore borrowed cloaks with the hoods pulled up to hide their faces.

The ranger captain hadn't said he didn't want anyone to associate Vlerion with them, but Kaylina assumed that was the reason. They couldn't be spies for the nobles if the Virts knew they had a relationship.

Not that Kaylina *wanted* to have a relationship with the nobles. If she'd known where to find the Saybrooks, she might have tried to negotiate a lease herself. Reluctantly, she admitted that Vlerion, who'd built play forts with the girls, might get them a better deal.

When the castle came into view, a black monolith against the night, the skeletal trees rattling in a breeze, there was nothing inviting about it.

Kaylina wouldn't be deterred. She leaned around her brother to tell Vlerion, "We have five hundred a month to spend on the lease."

"That's enough to rent a stable for one horse," Vlerion said without looking back.

"If the castle is so cursed you don't think we'll survive a night there, that should be about right, wouldn't you think?"

"I didn't say you wouldn't survive."

"You only think we'll be so scared that we'll wet ourselves and run screaming to the docks to buy passage on the first ship heading home?"

"That would be the *smart* thing for you to do. The north isn't a place for southern innkeepers."

The taybarri whuffed and shook himself, making Kaylina lunge to grip its fur, lest she fall off. Frayvar flailed and grabbed Vlerion.

"Crenoch is disturbed when people who ride him speak of wetting themselves," Vlerion said blandly.

Frayvar recovered and stroked a curious hand through the taybarri's fur, much as Kaylina had. "Can he understand us?"

"To some extent. The elder taybarri most assuredly can, and they watch out for their young."

Kaylina had heard stories that taybarri gained great intelligence if they survived their long childhoods. The elders had been the ones who had, centuries earlier, allied with humans, letting rangers ride their young into battle to improve the odds that the desirable lands west of the mountains remained safe for both their peoples. It was hard to imagine the two-thousand-pound creature they rode being a baby.

"How old is Crenoch?" she asked.

"Five years. He's smart and knows a lot of commands—when he chooses to obey them. He loves riding into battle and chomping down enemies." Vlerion's voice lowered, and she almost missed the rest. "He's less pleased to run down humans in the streets of the city."

Crenoch was or *Vlerion* was?

Kaylina wondered if the rangers had caught the prisoners who'd broken out of jail and almost asked, but did she want to know? The memory of the man's head being lopped off swept through her, and she shivered. Had she and Frayvar run, would Vlerion and his mount have chased them down and given them the same treatment?

If she and Frayvar died in the north, who would send word

back home? Even if he'd left a note—an *essay*—their family had to be worried about them. Guilt crept into Kaylina. Even if her kin were stifling and sometimes judgmental, they cared. It was *why* they were stifling and judgmental.

Crenoch stopped at the open courtyard gate of the castle, no lights burning in the nearby streetlamps, as if the city worker who lit them didn't want to give people reason to come this way.

Kaylina would have to provide her *own* lights if she wanted evening visitors to the meadery. Unfortunately, they were a long way from being ready for visitors of any kind. If they were able to sign a lease, that would only be Step One.

As she gazed through the gate at the crumbling castle, the stones silver under the glow of a half moon, the enormity of the task ahead came to her. The repairs and cleaning they would have to do. All the supplies they would have to buy before she could ferment her first batch of mead and Frayvar could cook his first meal. Was there even any firewood for the hearths? Probably not. They might freeze on their first night here.

The fatigue that had been catching up to her before her questioning and the jailbreak threatened to overwhelm her. At least it was nighttime. They could sleep, and tomorrow... She would figure out tomorrow when it came.

Vlerion slid off, producing something from his pocket. The big taybarri head swung over, sniffing at his hand.

"Sugar cube?" Kaylina guessed. "Or dried apple?"

That was what Grandpa's mare liked.

"He's not a horse," Vlerion said. "It's dried meat pulverized and packed into a cube."

"Tasty." Frayvar slid off the taybarri a lot less gracefully, his heel skidding on a patch of ice.

Vlerion caught him, keeping him from falling. "Crenoch likes it."

Careful not to land in the same icy patch, since she didn't want Vlerion grabbing *her* again, Kaylina dropped down.

He stepped closer and reached for something on his belt. A weapon?

Fear surged into her as she remembered his deadly fighting prowess, and she stepped back. She bumped into the taybarri, the creature as immovable as a wall, and felt trapped.

"What are you doing, pirate?" Kaylina blurted, trying to sound tough, but her voice squeaked on the last word.

Vlerion snorted. "Your mouth might get you killed before you make your first batch of wine."

"Mead."

"Watch who you call pirate—or anything else derogatory. The nobles can be prickly, especially now."

The law about flogging came to mind, one she'd never worried about back home. "We don't have a lot of nobles in the south."

"The south doesn't have much agriculture and mining or many factories. The kingdom mostly annexed it so it couldn't be used as a staging ground by enemies or to house pirate strongholds."

"Meaning the south doesn't *need* nobles?"

"Meaning you aren't a priority."

Did he mean that *you* to be personal?

Vlerion held up what he'd been reaching for, offering it to her. Her grandpa's sling and pouch of lead rounds.

"Uhm, what is that?" Frayvar's voice came out even squeakier than hers had a moment earlier. He was pointing toward one of the two front towers at the corners of the castle.

Kaylina stepped away from the taybarri to follow his gaze. An unshuttered window emitted a steady red glow.

"I... don't know." Kaylina had seen animals and insects in nature give off photoluminescent greens and blues, and she'd seen altered plants and trees in the wild that glowed at night but not red.

"Lord Vlerion?" Frayvar's tone was a lot more diffident than hers.

"As I've been telling you, the castle is cursed." Vlerion sounded indifferent and unfazed by the glow, but he turned to watch Kaylina. "Maybe you can figure it out while you're spending the night."

Did he sound amused? What a bastard.

A breeze swept through, a few snowflakes floating down, and an eerie moan came from the castle. The wind blowing across an opening or maybe those crenelations, Kaylina told herself.

"We will," she said firmly. "A little magic might be a boon. It will add to the appeal of our establishment and help draw curious customers."

"Nobody's going to spend the night there."

"We weren't planning to start an inn."

Of course, if the meadery and eating house did well, they could expand.

"Only foolish tourists would come this close to the castle."

"And the rangers sent to guide them?"

"Per my captain's orders. Rangers go where they must."

A screech came from the tower window, and Kaylina and Frayvar jumped. Two huge bats flew out and sailed toward them, screeching again.

Kaylina stepped back, bumping into Vlerion this time, and irritation at herself flared. She fumbled for a sling round, not wanting to appear cowardly in front of him. But would the bats *attack*?

No, they flew low over their heads, but Crenoch let out a warning roar, and they flapped their dark wings to angle over the river and disappear into the night.

"Northern fang bats," Vlerion said calmly. "They drink the blood of their prey."

He hadn't taken a step back or reached for his weapon.

"Are they edible?" Kaylina didn't want him to think their presence concerned her. "We could put them on the menu."

Frayvar blanched and rested a hand on his stomach. Maybe it took more than a special spice rub to make bats appetizing.

"I'll head out tonight so I can reach Saybrook Manor by morning," Vlerion said, not deigning to respond to her question. "Should you find your accommodations unpalatable, Headwaters Inn is two blocks to the east."

Surprisingly, he rested a hand on Kaylina's shoulder. Earlier, she hadn't wanted him to touch her, but it was reassuring now, having him and his weapons at her side. She couldn't bring herself to step away, even though his tone was smug, promising he expected to find them in that inn when he returned.

"That won't be necessary," Kaylina said, "but we'll keep your recommendation in mind."

"How much is a room there?" Frayvar asked wistfully, his eyes locked again on the glowing window. The bats' departure hadn't changed anything about it.

"Rangers don't get charged, so I don't know, but it's not a ritzy area."

Of course they didn't get charged. The working-class owner probably had to suck up the expense of hosting them himself. No wonder people were rebelling here.

Hand still on Kaylina's shoulder, Vlerion stepped closer to her, leaning his face toward hers.

In the still quiet of the night, she felt her heart speed up, even more than it had when the bats had flown out. He was more of a threat than they.

"I doubt he wants me to share this warning," Vlerion said softly, the words only for her as his warm breath whispered against her ear, "but if you decide to leave the city, you'll find no shipmasters in the harbor who will give you passage. Captain Targon is making sure of that."

That did nothing to calm her racing heart.

"Why? Is that *legal*?"

"Targon can do whatever he wishes for the safety of the kingdom."

"We're not a threat."

Vlerion snorted softly. Derisively? "No, but he wants to use you."

Her earlier premonition returned, that Targon thought their future meadery and eating house might become a gathering place and that Kaylina could share information they overheard with the rangers. Or did the captain want her to do even more than that? To actively seek out information? To become the spy Vlerion had originally accused her of being? But for the other side?

"Why us? There have to be dozens of inns and eating houses in town."

"There are, but they are long-established with the allegiances of the owners known. Certain groups eat in certain places." That had to be his way of saying the nobles wouldn't dine with commoners. "Should you succeed in opening something new, boundaries won't yet be established. Nobody here knows you. You might be recruited by the Virts." Vlerion sounded indifferent to the idea. Because it wasn't his plan but his captain's?

"Or by the nobles? As you're attempting to do right now?" Kaylina asked.

The hand on her shoulder that had briefly been reassuring now felt like a shackle, binding her to him—to them. The rangers. The nobility. She'd dreamed of serving her drinks to the king and queen, but she'd never thought a mead maker would have to choose sides.

"I am merely giving you a warning." Vlerion squeezed her

shoulder before releasing it and stepping back. After glancing toward the window, he added, "Enjoy your night."

He leaped onto Crenoch, the taybarri swishing his wide tail, and rode in the direction of the mountains, their snowy peaks stark and visible even by night.

"What did he say?" Frayvar asked.

"We can't go home."

8

THE GREATEST DANGER STALKS AT NIGHT.
~ *Elder Taybarri Seerathi*

The air seemed to grow colder after Vlerion left, and it chilled Kaylina to her southern bones.

She eyed the red glow, the window thirty or forty feet off the ground. It was the only one in the tower.

The castle itself looked to have only two main levels, the lower with the vestibule, great hall, dining hall, library, and kitchen, and the upper, which likely held inn rooms. But the four towers, one at each corner, rose higher than the keep. They were wide enough to have rooms stacked atop each other, but they might also contain nothing more than a winding staircase leading up to a lone room —or guard chamber—at the top.

The single narrow window had been designed for archers to shoot through. When the castle had been built, Port Jirador might have been nothing more than a town dotted with logging and hunting shanties. Kaylina wasn't the best history student but knew the kingdom's original capital was farther south. The throne had transferred to the north only after the discovery of rich gold veins in the mountains. At that point, thousands of people had flowed into the area to prospect.

"Let's see if our stuff is still inside." Kaylina patted her brother on the shoulder.

Frayvar tore his gaze from the unwavering red glow. It might have been there during the day, but they hadn't noticed it when the sun had been out.

"Do you think we should, ah, check that?" He pointed.

"To what end? Do you want to say *hi* to whatever magical doodad is making it?"

"Magical *doodads* don't exist."

"Don't witches and alchemists make idols or artifacts or something?" Kaylina had heard of such things, though magic of any kind was scarce on the islands, unless one counted the watcher whales that used their power to protect their pods—and their hunting coves.

"The only way humans can create items with magic is to sprinkle berry powder or otherwise incorporate altered plant material into them. As far as we know, that's what Kar'ruk shamans do too when they craft their magical weapons. *What* plants they use, we don't know. Humans would pay dearly for that information." Frayvar shrugged. "Unless you count the taybarri, the druids were the only intelligent beings born with the ability to wield magic, and they're believed gone from this world."

"I would count the taybarri." Kaylina hadn't seen them employ magic, but she'd heard of their flash power.

After finding their trunks where they'd left them in the courtyard and reassuring herself that nobody had disturbed them, she dragged them to the front door with determination. Not only would she spend the night in the cursed castle, but she would sleep like a crocodile sunning itself on the beach, then greet Vlerion rested and relaxed when he returned.

Another breeze blew down from the mountains, creating an eerie sound as it whispered through the crenellations along the outer wall.

Well, she would at least *greet* him. She might not be rested or relaxed, but she damn well wouldn't be at that inn. The pompous bastard would probably check there first when he returned, certain they wouldn't have stuck it out here.

The door opened when Kaylina pushed, and she spotted her pack on the floor where she'd left it. That was one small relief. If the city's populace feared this place, maybe one could leave gold bullion scattered on the floor and nobody would touch it. Naybor, she remembered, hadn't come inside with them.

But what of the criminals Targon had mentioned? Taking advantage of the castle's reputation to make it a meeting spot? That might be another reason the ranger captain wanted Kaylina and Frayvar to open their meadery here. Their presence could make such meetings more difficult. Assuming the criminals didn't kill them in their sleep for inconveniencing them. After all, *someone* had killed that lord.

A scraping sound made Kaylina jump.

Frayvar dragged in a heavy piece of rubble to prop open the door.

"Good idea." She remembered it locking earlier.

That might have been Naybor's doing. It might not have been. *Something* was making that tower window glow. There could be actual magic—a genuine curse—incorporated into the castle.

Between their long, harsh winters and the dangerous beasts that wandered down from those mountains, the northerners were tough people. She doubted stories would scare them if there wasn't any truth to them.

"I didn't see torches when we were in here earlier," Frayvar said. "Do you have candles or a lantern?"

"I have *both*. And matches." Kaylina rummaged in her pack for the bundle of wooden matches the alchemist in their town made with altered cinderrock plants. "I travel prepared."

"You just wanted to make sure you could read your novels."

"That is what I'm prepared to do."

Kaylina struck one of the bulbous matches and lit her small lantern, wishing the tiny flame provided warmth as well as light. Weariness and the pervasive chill made her long for her cozy bed back home. The thought crept into her that she had possibly acted rashly and that leaving had been a mistake.

She quashed it. "We need to make a fire so we don't freeze, but I'm going to look around first."

"Me too." Frayvar stuck close as they passed through the great hall and library, the latter filled with tables and booths instead of books, and headed toward the kitchen. It would have a large hearth and doors that closed to keep in warmth, so it would be a logical place to bed down for the night.

Remembering the noise she'd heard back there earlier, Kaylina hesitated to enter. But she had to be brave. She wouldn't let the smug and haughty Vlerion be right.

Frayvar must have been eager to see the room that would be most important to him, because he eased past her to lead the way.

A cast-iron pan lay on the floor. When Kaylina picked it up, it had the heft of a weapon, not an omelet maker. She had to set the lantern down and use both hands to turn it over. That lord had been killed by a blunt object, but she didn't see any hair or blood on the pan.

"Doesn't mean that much," she murmured, setting it down on a chipped travertine countertop. The clank echoed in the cavernous space, and something small skittered across a huge wrought-iron pot rack attached to a thick ceiling beam. "Mouse," she murmured, hoping that was all it was. She hung the pan from the holder, where other large pots dangled.

A moan came from the floor above. A *human* moan?

No, it had to be the wind. Maybe.

Kaylina grimaced. As brave as she wanted to be, this place was creepy.

"Did that moan come from the same tower as the red light?" Frayvar asked.

"I don't know. It's probably the wind blowing over the roof again."

He looked skeptically at her. "I'll make a fire if you want to explore."

He waved to a box by the hearth, logs filling it, the quartered wood so dry and dusty it might have been there for decades. Or centuries? From halfway across the kitchen, Kaylina could see thick cobwebs between the logs, one with a large spider hunkered in it.

"Sure. I'm not afraid to look around by myself." Kaylina said that more to convince herself it was the truth than out of a desire to display bravado for her brother.

"I would be," he muttered.

Before leaving, she lit a few stout candles so he would have light. The tops were as dusty as everything else, and it took several tries to get the wicks to burn.

She sniffed at an odd milky scent that wafted from them. "These aren't beeswax."

"A lot of things up here are made from whale oil. Those are probably spermaceti candles. That's a waxy substance you can scrape out of the head cavities of sperm whales."

"How come you know things like that but not how to escape from jail cells?"

"My education isn't as complete as I'd believed."

"Clearly."

Between the kitchen and the original dining hall, Kaylina found wooden stairs leading upward. There were no windows to let in moonlight, only the gray rectangular stones that made up the walls, the chill of winter radiating off them.

She held the lantern ahead of her as she climbed, each step making the ancient oak treads creak. A *ping, ping, ping* came from somewhere above. She couldn't blame the wind for that.

Before reaching the top, Kaylina tucked a lead round into her sling and carried it in her free hand. To deal with criminals who might be hiding out, she told herself, not a curse.

Two hallways, one wide and one narrow, met at a landing at the top of the stairs. Both were lined with doors, most closed. Windows at the ends of the hallways made the darkness less absolute, but the panes were filmed or broken. A cold breeze drifted through, tempting her to dismiss the moans she'd heard as being caused by the broken window. But the movement of air didn't make any sounds while she stood there. It merely brushed her cheeks with its chill.

Kaylina chose the wide hallway, but she didn't see stairs in any direction. Was there no way to access the towers from this level?

After a few steps, light came from an open doorway, and a man in black stumbled backward into the hallway.

Startled, Kaylina jerked her sling up, almost losing the round with the erratic motion. The man's back struck the wall opposite the doorway as he gripped something at his throat. A snake? A vine? Whatever it was had wrapped around his neck. The rest of it trailed down his body and back through the doorway of the room he'd exited.

He thrashed as he tried to tear it away. Strangely, he didn't make a sound.

When he twisted partially toward Kaylina, she got a look at his black armor and a silver tree crest on the chest. Was he a ranger?

Vlerion's armor hadn't held a tree, but it had otherwise been similar.

A gold medallion on a chain bounced as the man jerked about, trying to free himself.

His face was red. Whatever had him was cutting off his air.

Fear froze Kaylina's feet to the floorboards. Was she supposed to help? *Could* she? She couldn't target the snake without risking hitting the man.

He dropped to one knee, his face darkening from red to purple. Even though his head turned toward her, he didn't seem to see her. He didn't cry out for help.

Kaylina drew her knife and crept forward, afraid of him, of the snake, and also of doing nothing at all. She didn't want to watch a man die. If he was a colleague of Vlerion's, he might throw her back in jail for not helping.

Knife extended, she eased closer, hoping she could cut the thing away. Before she reached the man, he disappeared. Everything did, and the hall dimmed, the light disappearing.

She stared at the empty space he'd occupied. Had that been her imagination? A hallucination?

Maybe there was something in the air that caused an altered state of mind. She'd heard of fungi spores that could do that.

Not certain of anything, Kaylina peered around the jamb of the open door. Shadowy bedroom furniture loomed inside, and something pale lay on the stone floor in front of the hearth. Was that... a skeleton?

She stuck her arm inside and lifted her lantern. Yes, it was.

Whatever clothing the owner had once worn had disintegrated with time—or been eaten by rats—but a gold chain remained, the medallion dipped between two ribs.

"Another hallucination," she tried to tell herself, but the need to know prompted her to take a couple of steps into the room.

With the toe of her boot, she nudged the foot of the skeleton. It moved. It was real.

She sprang back through the doorway, as if the skeleton might rise up and lunge at her. It didn't. That didn't keep her heart from pounding against her ribs.

Kaylina didn't know what magic could have showed her how a man had died, but she had little doubt she had witnessed that, and that these were the ranger's remains.

With no interest in exploring that room further, she shut the door. The hinges creaked, and it wouldn't close all the way.

"We'll rent that room for a discount," she muttered.

A creak from the stairs made her spin, but the thud-thuds of fast footsteps promised it was her brother, not a hallucination. His eyes were round when he reached the landing and spotted her.

"Is someone after you?" She drew her sling again.

"Uh." He glanced over his shoulder as he moved away from the stairs, putting his back to one of the walls. "Not *someone,* no. I... thought you might be lonely up here. That's all."

"Uh-huh. Did the spider bite you?"

"There was a spider?"

"In the wood box."

"No. I heard something and thought I saw something." He shrugged. "It was probably nothing."

"It wasn't a vision of somebody being killed, was it?"

"No." Frayvar squinted at her. "Why do you ask?"

"No reason." After glancing at the not-entirely-closed door, Kaylina continued down the hall. "But these rooms will need to be cleaned out before we rent them."

"This whole place needs to be cleaned."

Not of bones, she thought but didn't say.

As they passed more closed doors, Kaylina left them alone, not wanting to see if more skeletons lurked in the rooms. Maybe by day she would investigate more thoroughly.

There was a final door at the end of the hallway by the window, a tower carved into the wood. Maybe they'd found the entrance to the stairs leading up to the red glow.

When she glanced out the dark window, Kaylina didn't expect to see anything but the rubble-strewn courtyard. Instead, an ancient forest rose from loamy earth, the trees so tall and thick that the area couldn't ever have been logged.

"That... is *not* out there." She'd chased Vlerion around that side of the castle when he'd gone after her brother.

"Nope," Frayvar said.

"You can see it?" That surprised her. She'd thought the hallucination had been hers alone.

"A forest with a hunter? Yes."

Kaylina started to say that she didn't see a hunter, but movement behind a tree drew her eye. A gaunt man in surprisingly lush silks and a cloak trimmed with ermine fur crept through the forest with a bow in hand, a quiver of arrows on his back. He knelt to check for sign in the pine needles at his feet. A thick vine snaked down from a branch above.

"Look out," Kaylina blurted, as if she could warn him.

As with the ranger, he didn't glance toward her or seem aware of her. When he started to rise, the vine struck like a cobra and wrapped around his neck. He dropped his bow and tried to lunge away as he grasped it, but it wouldn't release him. When his fingers dug into it, the vine tightened with the strength of steel.

Kaylina turned away from the window, not wanting to witness another death.

Grim-faced, her brother watched another minute. "This place is eerie."

"Yeah."

"A bunch of clanks came from underneath the kitchen, and then I saw something similar happen." Frayvar waved toward the window.

"A man getting killed by a vine?"

"It was a woman. She was serving rangers—I think they were rangers, but the uniforms were different from now—and a wind blew open shutters and blasted her into the hearth, forcing her to stay there until she burned alive."

"Gods of the moons, that's even worse than the vines." Before she could catch herself, Kaylina glanced out the window.

The man lay dead, strangled by the vine. It had gone slack and now hung limply from the branch, as if it had never stirred.

"There were bones in the back of the hearth," Frayvar whispered. "*Her* bones. I mean, I don't know that, but..."

"I think these things really happened."

He nodded. "Yeah."

"Is the castle showing us these visions of the past to threaten us? To let us know vines will come attack *us* if we stay?"

Frayvar spread his arms. "Tomorrow, I can find the city library and see if there's information on this place."

"If we survive that long," she muttered.

He frowned.

"I'm joking." She hoped. "We're not rangers, so maybe the castle won't find us offensive."

If criminals used this place to hide out, the curse couldn't kill everyone. Of course, she didn't know if they hid inside the castle or only lurked in the catacombs underneath it.

"The woman wasn't a ranger. *He* doesn't look like a ranger." Frayvar pointed at the dead man in his ermine cloak. "Didn't," he corrected.

"But you said she was feeding them? Maybe these were allies of theirs." Kaylina tried the door, wondering if they would find answers in the room with the red glow.

It opened, and a narrow windowless hallway led toward the tower, but the shadows were too deep for them to see to the end. Lantern aloft, Kaylina led the way. Even though she wasn't broad of shoulder, the tightness made her brush against an empty wall sconce. Soot remained on the stones above it, but she doubted a torch had burned there for a long time.

At the end, the hallway opened into a circular room. The tower.

Expecting stairs, Kaylina looked around, but there weren't any, save for a few iron brackets on the wall that might once have supported them. Overhead, clumsily nailed boards covered what may have been open air at one time. Or a partial platform that archers would have stood on to fire out the window. Either way, there was no way up there now.

"Guess the owners of the castle want to keep people out of the towers," Frayvar said.

"Do they want to keep people out? Or something else *in*?"

Another eerie moan swept through the castle.

"That inn Lord Vlerion mentioned sounded kind of nice," Frayvar offered.

Kaylina scowled at him. "We're not leaving with our tails between our legs like cowards."

"What if we strode out with our chins held high? Like heroes?"

"We'll start a fire and sleep in the kitchen. There's some furniture left around. We can drag it in front of the doors so nothing can get in and bother us."

Frayvar bit his lip. "I'm not an expert on curses, but I kind of doubt a chair propped under a doorknob is going to keep us safe."

"Do you have a better idea?"

He opened his mouth.

"*Not* the inn," she said before he could speak.

He hesitated. "Then, no."

"It'll be all right. In the morning, we'll see if we can find a ladder to take these boards down."

"That might not be a good idea."

"Weren't you the one who thought we should figure out the red light?"

"I've changed my mind."

"It'll be fine, Fray." Kaylina led him back toward the main hallway. "We're not rangers, and we're not *allies* of rangers. Whatever happened here in the past, the castle shouldn't have anything against us."

"Aren't we technically working for them?"

"*No.*" She raised her voice, as if the castle was intelligent and might be listening. "They're manipulating us and keeping us from going home."

As they passed the window, Frayvar looked grimly at the dead body on the forest floor.

Kaylina walked with determination toward the stairs while hoping her stubbornness wouldn't get them killed.

9

IN THE NORTH, SPRING SLOWLY UNFURLS ITS BUDS, MORE WARY OF FROST than floods.
~ *"A River Melts in Time" by the bard Velvenor*

Kaylina found a broom and some rags and spent the morning cleaning while Frayvar bought a newspaper and read up on current events in Port Jirador. He'd tried to go to the city library to get information on the castle, but it hadn't been open yet. Kaylina didn't know if she wanted more details on its past or not.

They'd survived the night huddled in a corner of the kitchen with the heavy frying pan and her sling and knife close at hand in case they were attacked. The enemies that had assailed them, however, hadn't been tangible. Every time they'd dozed off, and sometimes even when they hadn't, dreams—or maybe visions—had swept into their minds.

Kaylina had seen more deaths—more *murders*. Each time, they'd been committed by what should have been an inanimate object with no sign of a person controlling it in view. Twice more, she'd seen men die to the cobra-like vines. Once, a ceiling beam had fallen and crushed a woman. Another time, a branch had broken through a window and impaled someone in workman's clothes carrying two tankards down a hall.

Though they'd all been disturbing, that one had troubled her the most, because the man hadn't been a ranger, and there hadn't been any rangers in the vision to suggest an association with them. He'd looked like a customer at the old inn. Since Kaylina wanted to open a business in the castle, a customer-killing curse didn't bode well.

When dawn had come, its arrival announced violently by a chandelier crashing to the floor in the great hall, Frayvar's eyes had been as hollowed and haunted as hers. She hadn't needed to ask if he'd also experienced dreams—nightmares.

A yawn made Kaylina pause her cleaning, and she wiped her gritty eyes. A part of her wanted to curl up in a corner and do nothing—after all, they didn't yet know if Vlerion would be able to talk the owner into leasing the castle to them—but she had a vague notion that if this place *was* intelligent, it might appreciate being tidied up.

While she worked, she glanced out the windows often, waiting for Vlerion's return. Not because she missed him—hardly that—but because she wanted him to see that they'd stuck out the night. She might have bags under her eyes, dust in her hair, and cobwebs stuck to her clothes, but she hadn't left the premises.

Crunches came from the kitchen, Frayvar eating one of several apples he'd found while out. This far north, pickings were slim this time of year, only fruits that could store over the winter, but his munching noises implied he found them satisfactory. He'd brought her pastries and dried jerky, but he was, as always, unwilling to eat food that anyone else prepared. Unpeeled fruits and vegetables were okay, since nobody dusted them with nutmeg or other *toxic* spices, as he called them. There was a reason he was always gaunt.

As midday approached, one of Kaylina's glances out the window made her pause. Someone stood outside the wrought-iron gate, gazing at the front of the castle.

A woman? The person wore a fur-trimmed cloak with the hood up, so it was hard to be certain, but she was slender and not much taller than Kaylina. Snow wafted from the gray sky, so the outfit wasn't unusual, but the steady way the person gazed at the castle—and through the window—made Kaylina think she wasn't a casual passerby.

Kaylina put her back to the stone wall, wondering how long the woman had been peering in.

Frayvar walked out of the kitchen, waving the newspaper. "It's a good thing we didn't go with the people breaking out of jail, especially that one that was all beat up. It was Wedgewick, right?"

"The man who was being tortured? That's my guess."

"There's a reward for him and three other ringleaders of the rebellion. The *Virts.* I guess the newspapers call them that because they run around referring to themselves as the righteous and virtuous."

Kaylina nodded. She'd gotten the gist of the name.

"Those leaders are to be brought in dead or alive. If alive, they'll be hanged in a place called Mason Square." Frayvar skimmed the article as he spoke. "Anyone found associating with one of the ringleaders will either be jailed without chance of parole or, if they're found guilty of treasonous actions themselves, strung up with the others." Frayvar gave her a pointed look.

Since Kaylina had considered going with those people, she couldn't wave away the threat and say that such a fate never would have befallen them.

She looked out the window. Their watcher was gone. Good.

"We won't associate with anyone," she said.

"If we *were* going to associate, it would be safer to be on the side of the rangers."

"You just like Vlerion's taybarri."

"They're beautiful animals. And the ranger is..."

"Also beautiful?" Kaylina smirked.

He wasn't. Even *handsome* might be a stretch with that scar and severely short hair. Though he did have some kind of draw. Maybe it was his athleticism and fighting prowess. It was hard to put a finger on it, but she didn't think her wandering thoughts about sex during the questioning could be dismissed as entirely drug-induced.

"Uh, you'd have to be the judge of that. I..." Frayvar's gaze drifted toward the window.

Kaylina tensed. Had their watcher returned?

"Now, *she's* beautiful," he whispered, his jaw dropping as he gazed in appreciation.

A pale-skinned woman in a blue coat, matching dress, and fur-trimmed boots was stepping out of a carriage, her wavy blonde locks tumbling past her shoulders. Her green eyes sparkled as she considered the castle with a bemused expression on her elegant face.

The driver asked something, probably if she was sure she wanted to get out *here*. She nodded, gave him a coin, and removed a leather satchel before heading into the courtyard, stepping carefully. An inch of fresh snow made Kaylina realize she would have to add *shovel* to the long list of supplies and equipment they needed to open a restaurant. She didn't know how much money Frayvar had brought, but expenses would add up quickly.

Maybe they should have started with a vendor's cart and a tent instead of trying to lease a building. Especially a giant castle. But it was hard to cook out of a tent, and she needed space for the mead once she bottled it.

"She must be the Saybrook woman." Frayvar continued to gaze

at her.

"Pretty," Kaylina guessed, remembering Targon's descriptors.

"If there's a sister who's even prettier, I can't imagine it." Frayvar appeared ready to offer her his servitude, devotion, and complete control over his life.

"I don't think nobles date beneath them." Kaylina hoped her brother wouldn't have his feelings hurt. Even if they'd been societal equals, he wouldn't have had a chance with her.

"I'll offer to cook for her." Frayvar winked and ran to the doors, opening one wide with a smile. "My lady, come in to the Deep Sea Honeybee."

"We haven't decided on a name yet," Kaylina whispered.

"I like that one. You'll make mead, and I'll specialize in seafood dishes. It might be different fish up in these cold oceans, but I can adapt my recipes."

"Good morning. I'm Ghara Saybrook." She had a melodious voice, and Frayvar's eyes grew even more appreciative. "I brought a lease for you to look over and sign, if it's agreeable to you." She drew a few papers from her satchel. "You are the Korbians, correct?"

"Yes, I'm in charge." Kaylina tapped her chest, grimacing at a cobweb that draped one of the buttons of her blouse. She turned the tap into a brushing motion and noticed she'd buttoned the blouse lopsidedly in the dark that morning, leaving a gap of skin visible. Wonderful. "I'm Kaylina. That's my brother, Frayvar."

"I'm so pleased to meet you, ma'am. Lady. Uhm." Frayvar looked at Kaylina, as if she might be more versed in how to address the stuffy northern nobility, despite all the books he'd read.

Kaylina had a feeling most of Frayvar's knowledge had dumped out of his brain when Ghara walked in.

"The divine beauty that enraptures your soul?" Kaylina suggested.

Frayvar's cheeks flushed impressively red considering his dark skin.

Ghara blinked. "Lady Saybrook would be fine."

She peered around the vestibule and into the great hall, her gaze lingering on the broken chandelier on the floor. It was heavy, so Kaylina hadn't tried to move the frame yet. She had swept up the glass.

"Has the establishment given you any trouble? I understand from Vee that you spent the night here?" Her eyebrows climbed, as if she couldn't imagine it. She even shuddered.

"*Vee*?" Kaylina mouthed, though she knew who Ghara meant. Kaylina struggled to imagine Vlerion with a nickname, unless it was something like *Killer* or *The Beheader*. Not that those rolled off the tongue.

Ghara smiled and touched her chest. "Lord Vlerion."

"We spent the night here, yes. It was fine." Belatedly, Kaylina realized she shouldn't say that, lest Ghara think to increase the rent. "I mean, it wasn't *fine*. There's a creepy light in the tower, there were groans and other weird noises all night, we both had distressing nightmares, and someone was murdered out back yesterday." She hadn't checked to see if the body had been removed but assumed the rangers had handled it.

"That sounds about right. I'm impressed by your chutzpah." Ghara nodded, appearing sincere, and looked again at the chandelier. "Nothing hurt you?"

"No. Does that happen?"

"There are a lot of stories from the past, and, in my lifetime, a body was found. The cause of death was unknown. The curse is real."

"So we gathered." Had Kaylina been less fatigued, she might have reacted more strongly to it all. Or, if she'd been less determined to see her dream become a reality.

"I've never been in here before. My grandfather forbade it."

Ghara handed the lease to Kaylina, eyebrows raised, as if asking if she *truly* wanted it.

Kaylina took the papers without hesitation.

A cloaked figure much larger than the one who'd gazed through the window came in, not via the front door but from the kitchen.

Kaylina jumped and reached for her sling before the person pushed back his hood. Vlerion.

The quickest hint of amusement entered his eyes when their gazes met. Because she'd drawn the sling on him again? Or because—

His gaze shifted upward toward the top of her head.

"You have cobwebs in your hair," Frayvar whispered.

Scowling, Kaylina scraped them out.

"Vee," Ghara exclaimed with delight. "There you are."

She dropped her satchel, glided across the great hall while avoiding the chandelier, and approached him with the grace of a dancer. Without hesitation, she wrapped her arms around him, rose on tiptoes, and kissed him on the cheek, though something about the way she paused and checked his eyes said she wanted that kiss to go on his lips.

"Here I am," he agreed.

Frayvar's shoulders slumped.

"Maybe he *is* beautiful," he muttered.

"Handsome." Kaylina didn't know if they were a couple, but Ghara clearly adored Vlerion, so she patted her brother's shoulder.

"Really? Even with the—" Frayvar drew his fingers down the side of his face, mimicking Vlerion's scars.

"Yeah. And he's..." The memory of Vlerion's powerful arms around her, holding her against his hard chest—his entire hard *body*—jumped to mind. "Fit," she finished, though it was an understatement.

Ghara leaned into Vlerion and patted his chest without fear of rejection, then let her hand linger as she gazed at him. A twinge of envy plucked at Kaylina, but she scowled at herself and pushed it away. She didn't like Vlerion *or* want to pat his chest.

"Oh, right. The muscles." Frayvar gazed sadly at his own thin arm. "Women like those."

"Yup."

"I don't see why we couldn't have ridden together," Ghara told Vlerion. "Your company is much more compelling than that of my driver."

"I had Crenoch."

"You could have traveled the road beside us. I know he likes to run fast and flash, but you have before."

"Targon doesn't want rangers seen around here while these two are establishing their business." Vlerion waved to his cloak and hood, and Kaylina realized he wasn't wearing his black leathers.

"Are you going to tell me what that's all about? And why you wanted a special deal for..." Ghara didn't curl her lip in dismissal when she looked over at Kaylina and Frayvar, but Kaylina had little doubt she considered them riffraff.

"No."

"Mysterious as always." Ghara smiled up at him with the same longing in her eyes that Frayvar had possessed looking at her.

Other than to nod at Ghara, Vlerion didn't change his expression. His face remained as stoic and distant as when he looked at Kaylina. That surprised her. Since Ghara was a childhood friend —if not more—Kaylina would have expected her to warrant a warmer reaction.

His muted response didn't surprise Ghara. She only smiled sadly before patting Vlerion again and stepping back. "I gave them the lease to look over."

Vlerion looked toward the broken chandelier. "For five hundred a month?"

"Yes. I convinced Grandfather that it would be better to have someone using the place and looking after it than it standing vacant and attracting crime."

Vlerion grimaced—thinking of the dead lord? "Yes."

He moved away from Ghara and stood in front of Kaylina, glancing down at the lease, or maybe her crookedly buttoned blouse, for the hint of amusement returned to his eyes.

Scowling, she tucked the lease under her arm and unbuttoned the top of her blouse so she could fix it. If there were mirrors in the castle, they were upstairs in what she'd dubbed the haunted rooms.

His gaze caught on her fingers, or maybe the skin she briefly showed, before he looked into her eyes. "You spent the night here?"

Kaylina lifted her chin. "Yes, we did."

He looked at the chandelier again. "Huh."

The single syllable didn't convey admiration and respect, but at least she'd exceeded his expectations of her.

"I'll assume it wasn't that peaceful," he said.

"It was not. There are bones of dead people in some of the rooms."

"I'm not surprised."

She had been.

Vlerion smiled slightly at her. "Targon will be glad to know the newcomers he wants to use aren't easily scared."

"Yes, *Targon* is who I long to impress."

His smile widened, his face less restrained, and she decided he *was* handsome. Despite the scars.

"Vee." Ghara lifted a finger, beckoning. "A word?"

Vlerion nodded but bumped his knuckles against Kaylina's arm before walking away.

She didn't know how to interpret the gesture, but at least he'd acknowledged she wasn't *easily scared*. That was almost the same as calling her brave, wasn't it?

Ghara linked one of her arms with Vlerion's and guided him through the great hall and toward the dining hall. "Will you return to the mountains after this?"

"After Lord Darringtar's murderer is caught and the ring-leaders of the rebellion are dealt with."

Hanged, if the newspaper article was correct.

"So, you'll be in the city for a while? I could move a few things into my apartment here and visit with you when you're off duty. I miss having you close."

Kaylina didn't hear his response, but Ghara slipped her arm fully around him before they moved out of view.

Not my business, Kaylina told herself. Why her jaw clenched, she didn't know.

Frayvar joined her, sighing wistfully. "Is five hundred a month written on the lease? What's the length of our commitment? Will they do any repairs?"

Reminded of the paperwork, Kaylina held the lease out, but the rows and rows of tiny print blurred when she tried to read them. The night's fatigue was catching up with her.

"Check, will you?" She handed the pages to him.

Most people would find such a task onerous, but Frayvar pounced on the contract, taking the pages to the light of a window.

There was more to clean—*much* more—but Kaylina couldn't help but be curious what Ghara and Vlerion were talking about. If the topic was her apartment and how he was invited to visit any time... that wasn't anything Kaylina needed to know about. But if they spoke about what Captain Targon had planned for Kaylina's new meadery, wouldn't it be smart to gather whatever intelligence she could?

Yes, but if she sneaked closer to listen in, would Vlerion catch her? Probably. He had when she'd eavesdropped back at the jail.

Kaylina grabbed her broom and rags and headed through the library toward the kitchen. She paused inside the little well room to wet the rags. The water that came up from below was pure and delicious—she'd tasted some the night before and had been delighted. It would be wonderful for the mead.

She'd already swept and wiped the counters in the kitchen, so she pushed open a pantry door that creaked on its hinges and stepped inside. Light came through a narrow horizontal window near the ceiling, illuminating shelves that had mostly rotted away. They'd been made from a less resilient wood than the oak of the stairs and bookcases elsewhere in the keep, but once she repaired them, there would be room for dozens, if not hundreds, of bottles and all the spices her brother could ever need.

A few large glass jugs hunkered on the floor in the back, and Kaylina stepped fully inside, crouching to wipe them off. The door creaked, and she whirled, afraid of it locking, the way the front door had. But it didn't close fully, and she let out a relieved breath.

Wiping the jugs revealed that they could be used as carboys, and delight filled Kaylina for the first time since the rangers had shown up, interfering with her plans. She would need larger fermentation vessels eventually, but these would be perfect to get started. When she made specialty varieties of mead, she usually did small batches anyway.

She caressed the jugs with love. "Perfect."

Voices sounded in the kitchen. Vlerion and Ghara.

Kaylina froze. She'd thought they'd stopped in the dining hall for their private conversation.

"I can't believe you made those two sleep here," Ghara said. "They could have been killed. People have been, you know."

"Not for years," Vlerion said.

Kaylina stood, intending to step out and make her presence known, but the desire to hear what they would say stilled her feet.

"Only because people stopped spending time here."

Vlerion snorted. "Criminals spend time here regularly."

"In the catacombs, right? They don't enter the castle, do they?"

Vlerion hesitated. "I don't know. I'd assumed those two would be scared away and leave before anything happened to them."

Kaylina bit her lip, unable to make herself open the door wide and step out. Instead, she leaned closer to the crack, not wanting to miss anything.

"The girl has moxie."

"Yes." Vlerion sounded approving.

Because he liked that in a woman? Or because *Targon* would like it?

Kaylina bared her teeth at the thought.

"Why are you helping them if you want them to leave?" Ghara asked.

"It's Targon's plan. He'll do anything for the good of the kingdom."

"We want that in a ranger captain, don't we?"

"Yes, but his plans aren't always healthy for those who are swept into them."

"Do you care what happens to those two? If they might be useful to the kingdom..."

"They're just tourists." Vlerion stepped into view, leaning against a counter with the cabinet doors long since torn—or rotted—off.

Kaylina's heart pounded. Would he see her if he looked over? The pantry door wasn't open wide, but the window light might make her outline noticeable.

"They're barely even kingdom subjects," Vlerion added. "They don't have a clue what's going on up here."

"Is that why Targon thinks he can use them?"

"They have no affiliations, I gather."

"Will the rangers enjoy the offerings of this—what is it going to be? A winery, you said?—once it's open?"

"A meadery. The rangers won't have anything to do with it except to keep an eye on the customers."

"Ah, I thought you might want to keep an eye on *her*. She's comely under the dust and cobwebs."

"I'm not shopping for a lover," Vlerion said.

"Good." Ghara stepped into view, sashaying toward Vlerion. "I've missed you. You've been in the mountains so much these past years. You hardly come by anymore."

"I know." Vlerion didn't reach for her or beckon her closer, but that didn't mean he would stop Ghara if she pressed her body against his. She rested her hand against his chest and gazed up into his eyes. "I think often of the Solstice Moon Festival. For me, it was wonderful, but you... I always wished I could have made it better for you."

"It was fine." His words were clipped, like he didn't want to talk, but his gaze did dip toward her chest.

"Yes, that's the problem. You were so distant. I was thrashing like a maiden in an erotic poem, and you... I could only assume you weren't... that I wasn't..."

"Ghara," Vlerion said softly and took her hands.

Kaylina swallowed and looked away. She should have stepped out of the pantry as soon as they'd entered. Now, she might get stuck watching who knew what. *Relations.*

Being caught observing that would be far worse than being caught eavesdropping on a conversation. She glanced toward the window. There wasn't any glass in it, but with the shelves rotted or missing entirely, she doubted she could climb out without making noise. Was it even wide enough to crawl through?

"You were fine," Vlerion said. "*Good.*"

"I've gained some more experience since then," Ghara admitted. "If you'd like to try again."

"You've been taking lovers to learn better bedroom play?" He sounded amused.

"One has to learn somehow. So one can make sure her man enjoys his time as much as she enjoys hers."

"Your grandfather would be horrified to hear you speaking of pleasing a man."

"It's not proper to bring up elderly relatives during tender moments, Vee."

Kaylina crept closer to the back wall to consider the window more closely.

"This can't be a tender moment," Vlerion said. "It's safer if there's nothing between us."

"Safer?" Ghara laughed. "Are you afraid the curse of the castle will get worse if we're intimate in the kitchen?"

"No."

"From what I've heard, nights are worse, though I wouldn't want to be here alone during the day. Your tourists are either foolish or brave."

"Some of both, perhaps."

"Vee," Ghara groaned his name. As she slumped against him? "I've missed you. I *want* you."

They fell silent. Kaylina didn't return to the door to see if they were kissing. She didn't want to know.

Instead, she reached for the sturdiest of the rotten shelves. It was time to get out of there.

Before she could climb, the door creaked open.

She barely kept from blurting, "Shit." Instead of going up, she crouched, grabbing one of the carboys. With the heavy glass in her arms, she spun.

Vlerion stood in the open doorway, his face a mask. His cloak had been thrown back, and his shirt was untucked. Had Ghara been shoving her hands up there? Or going for his belt to show him what she'd *learned* from her other lovers?

Not Kaylina's business.

"Are you done out there? I didn't want to interrupt." Kaylina's words came out panicked, tripping over each other. She raised the carboy, half of it cleaned of dust. "Look what I found. I can use these for my first batch of mead. If you could refrain from having sex in the kitchen, that would be amazing. There's so much to do, and I need to focus on getting this room up to sanitary standards. I assume they do *have* sanitary standards up here in the north, right? This is the capital, after all, the heart of the kingdom. The epitome of civilization, one would assume."

Stop talking, the back of her brain ordered as Ghara peered around Vlerion to look into the pantry. Thankfully, nothing was untucked on her.

"I'll get out of your way." Giving up on the idea of the window —though it was tempting to flee that way and hide in the courtyard until they left—Kaylina stepped toward them.

If Vlerion didn't budge, there was no way she would get by him, but she kept walking, as if she fully expected him to. Would he move? Or grab her?

His eyebrow twitched ever so slightly, and he stepped aside. Ghara did too, though she was frowning deeply at this intrusion.

Still clutching the carboy, Kaylina hurried past them and fled the kitchen. She found her brother in the great hall, the lease in his hand.

Frayvar held it up. "We would only be committing to a year."

"That's not much."

"Not for a commercial endeavor, no." He sounded surprised. "Maybe she owes Lord Vlerion a favor."

Thinking of the conversation she'd overheard, Kaylina glanced back at the kitchen. "Yeah."

Vlerion wanted Kaylina and Frayvar to leave, or at least thought they would be better off if they did, but he had also done exactly what his captain asked. She would be wise to remember his loyalty was to his boss and his class, not a couple of *tourists*.

10

ALLIES AND ENEMIES TEMPT US BY DIFFERENT MEANS BUT TEMPT US ALL the same.

~ Kar'ruk High Commander O'tak

As noon approached, Kaylina tipped the pot toward the funnel, carefully pouring the must for her first batch of mead into one of the scrupulously cleaned carboys. Once finished, she stifled a yawn as she set the pot aside and grabbed the airlock, pausing to rub her gritty eyes.

She and Frayvar had spent two nights in the castle and hadn't been murdered yet, but they hadn't slept much either. Each evening, Kaylina dreaded twilight's approach and the return of nightmares, but she refused to leave. They *couldn't* leave.

In her mind, she'd proven her bravery—or foolishness—to Vlerion, and they didn't need to spend nights there because of him, but they'd sent five hundred liviti away with the signed lease, and they needed to buy so many things. They couldn't afford to spend money sleeping at another inn when they had dozens of rooms here.

She kept having to remind herself that goals worth having weren't easily achieved. They required sacrifice and work.

"So obnoxious."

Frayvar walked into the kitchen, yawning as much as she. "Have you noticed cloaked people coming to watch us through the windows?"

"Yes. Just one though." Kaylina looked at him to see if the numbers had increased. "How many are out there now?"

"One, but one's enough to be concerning, isn't it? Especially since she's hiding her face. It's not like we would know who she was if she showed it." He shrugged. "We don't know anyone."

"Yeah."

The words brought a pang of loneliness. It wasn't surprising that Kaylina would miss the rest of the family, and having more people around to talk with, but when she'd left, frustrated by being ordered around and unappreciated, she'd thought she would be happy once she had her freedom. Now... even though she was working toward her dream, she was more weary than happy.

"It's probably someone curious about us for staying in the cursed castle," she said.

"You think so?" The wariness in Frayvar's eyes meant he thought it was more than that.

"Who else would care about us?"

"The *rangers* do."

"Just the captain."

"Vlerion seems okay." Frayvar shrugged.

"But he doesn't *care*."

"Well, no, but it's concerning that the captain does."

"True."

Frayvar lowered his voice and glanced around, as if spies might be lurking behind a counter. "I'm glad they haven't been by for a few days. I don't think... What did you mean the other night when you said we can't leave? I don't want to, because I'm here to help you and see us be successful... but you said it like it wouldn't be an option."

"Apparently, Captain Targon ordered the shipmasters in the harbor not to give us passage if we try to book it."

"Oh."

"There's a highway along the coast," Kaylina said, "but I've heard it's rough because it goes over mountains that drop straight down to the water."

"Yes. There's a pass that way that will be blocked a while longer with snow. All freight comes in and out via the harbor. Can I send a letter? They're not monitoring our mail, are they?"

"I doubt it. Who would you send a letter to?"

"Grandpa and Grandma. We'll need more funds before long, and, if we're going to set up a serious meadery, we'll need a lot more honey. Each batch requires a substantial amount."

"I know, but unless I was going to bring a horse and wagon, I was limited by what I could fit in those trunks. Besides, I..." Kaylina shrugged away her hesitancy. Her brother already knew most of the details of her departure. "I didn't ask to take the honey I did bring. I wanted to be successful first, to prove I could do this, before asking for help." She'd also been afraid their grandparents would have said no. If her sister had wanted to do this, they would have supported her, but Silana was older. And perfect. Kaylina... was not.

"That's not logical. You didn't bring enough honey *or* money to do anything but start a hobby. If I hadn't come along with extra funds, you would already be scrubbing dishes in somebody's inn for paltry wages. You wouldn't be any happier doing that here than back home. Probably *less*."

"I don't need a lecture."

"You need something."

"Not from my seventeen-year-old brother." Kaylina scowled at him.

Frayvar frowned back in confusion. "From someone older? Silana?"

"*No.*" Especially not her.

A thud came from the courtyard out front. Though it was probably something dire and ominous, Kaylina leaped at the chance to end the conversation.

She grabbed her sling and knife. As she padded through the dining room and great hall, the thud sounded again. Something striking the door?

Afraid to open it, lest a horde of murderers be poised to kill, Kaylina went to the window and pushed open a shutter. Two loaded wagons waited in the street out front, tarps covering their goods. Thick black letters were visible on one: Saybrook Industries.

A girl about Frayvar's age held a rock in her hand, lifted to throw. She lowered it when she spotted Kaylina in the window and waved up to men in the drivers' seats.

Several other rocks lay on the ground in front of the door.

"Is there a problem?" Kaylina asked.

"The name's Milzy. I've got a delivery for this place." The girl tilted a thumb toward the closest wagon.

"We didn't order anything."

"It's from Lord Saybrook."

Kaylina was on the verge of saying it had to be a mistake—if anything, *Ghara* Saybrook would have been the one to have something delivered—but Milzy was already peeling back one of the tarps.

The fading light revealed piles of pots and pans—brand *new* pots and pans—as well as chairs, tables, and all manner of kitchen appurtenances.

Mesmerized, Kaylina stepped outside.

Had Vlerion arranged this delivery? Requesting another favor from Ghara? He didn't even want them to succeed.

The other wagon held a large crate that read *professional wine-making kit.* There probably wasn't a *mead-making kit* in the city, but the fermentation buckets, auto siphons, bottle brushes, and other tools were the same. This would be wonderful.

When she reached the wagon, Kaylina touched the crate with reverence.

"There's more stuff in the warehouse. And we're to grab two loads of firewood for you too." Milzy looked Kaylina over, as if silently asking who she was to be able to afford all this. "Once you unload the wagons, we'll get it, but me and the boys aren't going in that castle. No way."

Kaylina eyed the full wagons but could hardly object to unloading them. She whistled for Frayvar and wasn't surprised to find him peering out the window. He was far from being the *muscle* in the family, but together, they would be able to get the stuff inside. Eventually.

"Was this in the lease?" Kaylina whispered to Frayvar when he came out.

"No."

Despite Milzy promising that her team wouldn't help, the drivers climbed into the back of the first wagon and lowered tables and chairs down to the cobblestones.

"Are we going to get charged for it in the future?" Kaylina asked as she and Frayvar toted chairs through the gate. "What if the Saybrooks don't realize how little seed money we have?"

"I don't know. Maybe it's things they own already? The warehouse the girl mentioned could be theirs."

"I guess. After all, they have *apartments* in the city. You know, for when manor life on the estate gets too tedious."

"Given the favors they're doing for us, you probably shouldn't mock the nobles."

"Maybe not, but I'm afraid there's going to be a catch. A big catch."

Frayvar didn't disagree. The castle moaned loudly as they carried equipment inside.

"Shit," Milzy said, her gaze drawn to the tower window. With clouds darkening the sky, the red glow was visible. "You think people are going to come here for food and drink?"

"Sure," Kaylina said. "I've altered my vision a bit to add lots of tables and chairs in the courtyard. Maybe some warming tents so we can serve outdoors even in the winter. And for those who are brave, there's plenty of seating inside."

Still eyeing the glowing window, Milzy shook her head. When Kaylina returned for another load, the girl asked, "You get hired by the Saybrooks or what?"

"No, this is our own endeavor." Kaylina pointed to herself and her brother.

"You have the money for all this?"

"We're getting a good deal on account of the curse. And... our family back home has a successful eating house, so they're helping out." Sort of. If Frayvar sent that letter and convinced Grandma it wasn't a waste of money, they might. At the least, Kaylina thought Grandpa would send honey.

"Are you nobles?"

"Not even close. There's not much nobility in the Vamorka Islands. Our father was actually, uhm. He always told us he was a *buccaneer* and not a pirate." Maybe Kaylina shouldn't have admitted that, but Dad hadn't come around since she'd been a little kid. He was probably dead. "Either way, he was the opposite of noble."

"Oh, yeah? Good." Milzy nodded toward the closest driver, who gave a single nod back.

What was that about? Kaylina hoped these people didn't plan to swindle them, the way the supposed land agent had.

"We'll check you out when you open up," Milzy said as one of the now-empty wagons rolled away. In a softer voice, she asked, "Do you think you could get any intel on the Saybrooks?"

"Intel?" Kaylina asked.

"Like where their supervisors stay in the city, when the owners will visit their factories, and what the security is like on their warehouses. Anything that could be useful. We've learned a bit from doing this and a few other jobs for them, but we always need to know more. You know Old Geezer Saybrook orders his people worked until they're half-dead, right? Kids too. They don't get holidays off, and people get injured in his factories all the time, and nothing ever changes. The Saybrooks deserve for a couple of mishaps to happen. *All* the nobles do."

For a long moment, Kaylina could do nothing but watch her breaths fog the air. This sounded like the kind of information the rangers wanted, but she didn't want to be their spy. If she *had* to pick a side, she wouldn't pick theirs. With numbness, she realized the mead-making equipment was a bribe.

"What do you think?" Milzy prompted into the silence.

"I don't know any of that stuff yet, just—" Kaylina almost said that Ghara Saybrook would be staying in her apartment in town, but she caught herself as the voice in the back of her mind cried a warning. What would Vlerion do if cutthroats murdered his childhood friend? Someone who was *more* than a friend to him? If he found out Kaylina had been responsible...

"Yes?" Milzy asked.

"If I hear anything about our landlord's operations..." Even that sentence, Kaylina struggled to finish. If she heard things, what would she do? Report to this girl she'd just met? This girl who wanted for *mishaps* to happen? "Maybe I can share the details," Kaylina finished softly, sweat dampening her palms.

"Good. People like us gotta stick together." Milzy thumped her on the shoulder and hopped in the second empty wagon. It drove away after the first, horse hooves clattering on the cobblestones in the quiet night.

"Huh." Frayvar had come back out with a lantern. "Do you think Targon foresaw that?"

"I don't know."

Once the wagons rolled out of sight, Frayvar handed Kaylina a slip of paper and held the lantern up so she could read it.

I trust this will help get your meadery operational in a timely manner. ~T

"T?" Kaylina tried to remember if anyone had mentioned Lord Saybrook's first name. Would he have signed something so casually though? Something for them?

"I'm guessing Targon," Frayvar said.

"Oh." Kaylina lowered the paper, admitting that made sense, that the Saybrook Industry wagons were a front for the rangers. Or maybe Targon had enough sway that he'd made a deal with the senior Saybrook to have the equipment lent to them. Or *Vlerion* had. That seemed more likely. "This is getting complicated quickly."

"I noticed."

Snuffling noises at the side of the castle made them jump. In the shadows of the courtyard, a taybarri stood, snout in the air, nostrils twitching.

Alarm lurched through Kaylina. Was that Vlerion's mount? Crenoch? If the taybarri was here, Vlerion had to be nearby. What if he'd heard Milzy asking for *intel*?

Hand shaking, Kaylina rubbed her face. If she didn't step carefully, she could be caught in the middle of a budding war and killed. She didn't even want to be involved. All she wanted was to start a successful mead-making business.

After sniffing the air repeatedly, the taybarri turned and ambled toward the back of the castle.

"I think that's Crenoch," Frayvar whispered. "We might be in trouble."

"We haven't done anything wrong." Kaylina had *almost* blathered what might be considered intelligence, but she'd caught herself.

"That hasn't kept trouble from finding us so far."

11

WITH RESPECT AND FOOD, THE DEADLY BEAST IS WON.
  ~ Ranger Saruk

Instead of walking through the keep, Kaylina and Frayvar followed the taybarri through the courtyard and around the outside. Along the way, she expected to find Vlerion leaning against the wall with a stern expression on his face. But Crenoch ambled to the door between the kitchen and the well room, and there was no sign of his rider. The hinges on the rusty back gate stuck, so Kaylina wasn't surprised that it stood open and had allowed the taybarri to enter that way.

Their furred visitor butted the door with his nose, then looked expectantly at her.

"Are you *sure* that's Crenoch?" she murmured.

"No," Frayvar said.

The taybarri let out three whuffs like laughs, then butted the door with his snout again.

"But I think it is," Frayvar added.

The long-bodied furry creature was too tall and broad to enter the keep, but Kaylina risked stepping closer and gesturing that she would open the door. Crenoch wanted *something* inside. The rations they'd nibbled during the day? Frayvar's apples? That might be it.

The taybarri sniffed Kaylina when she got close, and she hoped he wasn't thinking of having *her* for dinner.

"I'm going to open the door for you." She pointed at it, but she also stood still to let Crenoch sniff her. His large nostrils created enough of a draft to stir her hair. "Are taybarri carnivorous?" she asked her brother.

"Omnivores, I think." He'd stopped by the gate. To watch for rangers? Or so he could flee easily if she angered the taybarri, and he shifted into battle mode?

"So fruits, vegetables, and humans are all in equal danger from those teeth?"

At the moment, Crenoch's fangs weren't visible, but she'd seen them and remembered their length and sharpness.

"I don't know enough about their eating habits to rank their favorite foods."

Crenoch finished sniffing her and butted the door again.

"Right." Kaylina pushed it open and stepped back.

The taybarri padded forward, sticking his long neck through, much as he had when they'd first met. It had been a window that time, and he'd been interested in her pack.

With a jolt, she realized it was on a counter near the door. There was honey in it, as well as a couple of her favorite books. The thought of the taybarri shredding the pages to satisfy his sweet tooth filled her with alarm.

She lifted a hand but hesitated to touch his furry shoulder without Vlerion along to make sure his mount behaved.

Crenoch withdrew his head, fangs now visible because they were clamped around her pack.

"That's mine, friend," Kaylina said.

The taybarri backed up, his broad tail stirring pebbles and bits of broken mortar on the ground. He dropped the pack but only so he could sniff it thoroughly. His broad tongue slid out between his fangs to prod it.

"Is there honey in there?" Frayvar asked.

"Yes. And books."

"I doubt he came for your romance novels."

"I wouldn't think an animal with fangs would want honey either. And they're romantic *adventures*, not romances. There's swashbuckling. And pirates."

"Yes, the literary value is immense."

Kaylina shot him the dirty look that comment deserved while the taybarri continued to prod, trying to figure out how to open the flap. "It's got to be the honey. You think he's like the bears that swim across the strait to raid Grandpa's beehives?"

"Probably. A *lot* of animals like honey, fangs or not. High-calorie foods are rare in nature, so they're a prize."

"Ranks higher than humans and vegetables, huh?" Kaylina risked creeping to the backpack, whispering that she would get some honey out for the taybarri. As if he understood, Crenoch stepped back and waited.

"You don't need me to tell you that," Frayvar said. "I've seen you feed your bok choy to the hounds while making lover eyes at Grandma's honey cakes."

"I *tried* to feed the bok choy to the hounds. They're not as keen on vegetables as you'd hope."

"Tell me about it. My attempts to get them to eat water spinach never went well."

Since they needed all the honey they had for their mead, Kaylina only withdrew a small piece of comb. She held it out to Crenoch, expecting him to sniff it, but he must have already determined he wanted it, because he didn't hesitate. Only when the big tongue came out—even larger than a horse's—with those teeth drawing near her hand did she realize she should have tossed it onto the ground at his feet.

Before she could pull back, the tongue swept across her palm, warm and moist and rough. It removed the honeycomb while leaving enough slobber to make her skin glisten.

She grimaced and wiped her palm while Crenoch smacked his blue lips and ran his tongue over his teeth, not wanting to miss an iota of the honey. He stepped closer and licked her hand again. His brown eyes considered her pack, and she had little doubt he could smell that there was more inside.

"I need the rest for my mead." Kaylina risked stepping forward and patting him on the neck. "You're a good taybarri and must want me to become a successful mead maker here in town, right? It's what your boss wants." Or what *his* boss wanted, anyway.

Crenoch's whuff sounded indifferent to his rider's wishes, but he didn't go for the pack again. Instead, he startled her by licking her on the cheek, leaving it as moist as her hand.

"Uhm, thank you."

His tail swished across the ground again.

"Grandma's honey-lavender lemon tarts are even better than her honey cakes." Frayvar didn't comment on the slobber—maybe he was too busy daydreaming about the food at the Spitting Gull to have noticed. "Is it too soon to feel homesick?"

"No." Kaylina was about to admit that she'd had such feelings —along with more doubts and regrets than she could name— when Frayvar jumped.

Vlerion strode through the gate in his ranger blacks, his hand wrapped around the hilt of his sword.

"There you are." Disapproval laced his stern voice.

Kaylina skittered back, dropping her hand, though she didn't know if the words were for her or the taybarri.

Crenoch swished his tail, looked over his shoulder at his rider, and lolled his tongue out. A laugh? Defiance? Whatever the gesture meant, it had to indicate a lack of concern.

Eyes narrow, Vlerion strode across the courtyard. He barely glanced at Frayvar, who scurried out of his way, before focusing on Crenoch. The taybarri licked his lips again.

Vlerion turned on Kaylina. "You fed him?"

"Not... exactly." She surreptitiously wiped her hand on her trousers again.

"What *exactly* did you do?"

Though she felt guilty, since she *had* given the taybarri the honey, Kaylina didn't appreciate his tone. She folded her arms over her chest. "Listen, pirate. He came here of his own accord and got my pack out of the kitchen. Also on his own."

Mostly on his own.

"Do not call me that." More irritation infused Vlerion's voice than he'd previously shown. The dangerous glint in his eyes that she'd caught a few times appeared.

Though it rankled, Kaylina attempted a conciliatory tone when she said, "It's a term of endearment in the south."

It was at least a *common* term there.

"It is not. You may call me Ranger Vlerion or Lord Vlerion."

"Oh, yeah, you'd like that, wouldn't you? Lord Superior and Special. Lording over all us peons." All right, she was *awful* at conciliatory.

"It is the appropriate way for a commoner to address an aristocrat. Especially after luring away his mount." Vlerion flicked an exasperated hand toward the taybarri, jaw clenching, and the dangerous glint in his eyes almost turned into more. She didn't know what exactly, but did his pupils dilate? Like a cat's? He took a breath, unclenched his jaw, and said, "We are attempting to keep people from noticing that there is an affiliation between the rangers and this project, and nothing is more *rangerish* than a taybarri."

Crenoch whuffed, then blew hot air across Vlerion's face. Sadly, his hair was too short to be messed up.

After giving the taybarri a sidelong you're-not-being-properly-respectful-either look, Vlerion dug something out of a pouch fastened to his belt. A flat oval that looked like compressed sawdust. He held it out.

Using his teeth instead of his tongue, Crenoch plucked it up and chewed it. He didn't lick his lips.

"What's that?" Kaylina asked.

"We call them protein pellets. They're desiccated elk and moose muscle meat mixed with liver and brain and held together with suet."

"Yum."

Vlerion's eyes closed to slits. "They're nutritious, don't spoil for a long time, and the taybarri like them."

"They like honey more."

Crenoch whuffed in agreement.

"*Honey* isn't nutritious." Since Vlerion glared at them equally, Kaylina didn't know if he was speaking to her or the taybarri. Probably both.

"It goes longer than suet without spoiling," she said. "It doesn't *ever* spoil. Maybe you should use it as the binder in your, ah, protein pellets."

Crenoch's second *whuff* sounded like a cheer.

Vlerion did not look amused.

Frayvar, maybe hoping to distract the ranger from his irritation, grabbed the pack. "I'll take this inside to protect the rest of the contents from uninvited marauders who were solely and completely responsible for acquiring their own honey."

Vlerion's lips twisted, as if he didn't believe that.

What, did he think Kaylina had spent the day wandering the streets of Port Jirador with honeycomb, looking for a taybarri to suborn?

Vlerion sighed and faced Crenoch, clasping him on either side of his broad snout so their eyes met. "Go back to the stables where the other taybarri are obediently staying without using their magic to pass through fences or unlock the gates. We don't want to endanger these people—" Without glancing at her, Vlerion pointed toward Kaylina, "—by letting others know they're associated with the rangers."

Remembering her promise to the castle that she *wasn't* associated with the rangers, Kaylina glanced toward the stone walls. Did the curse extend to the courtyard outside? Could the castle hear spoken words and understand them? She had no idea, but most of the murders it had shown her, all save the one in the forest, had taken place within its walls.

Crenoch let out a soft whuff that might have indicated an acknowledgment, then turned for the exit.

"And don't come back here," Vlerion added. "No matter how much honey she plies you with."

The taybarri's thick tail swung around, swatting Vlerion in the hip on the way out.

Kaylina wished it had been a swat on the ass, a thought that put a smile on her face. Vlerion turned in time to catch the expression.

She dropped the smile and asked, "You said he can understand us?" to distract him.

"They understand a lot. Crenoch will return to the stables."

"And not come back here to mooch more honey?"

"If he *does* come, you will give him nothing."

"Don't you think people would be more likely to comply with your dictums if you were nicer about them? Maybe throwing in a *please*?"

"It is for *your* sake that I make this *dictum*. As I pointed out, you may be in danger if people realize you're working, however loosely, with the rangers."

"I guess that's a *no*, huh?" Kaylina kept herself from pointing out that he was as obviously *rangerish* as his taybarri, and he remained in her courtyard. At least he wasn't fondling the hilt of his sword anymore. "Don't people already know that a lord owns this place? Won't they assume there's a link?"

"The aristocracy owns *most* of the buildings in town. Few will think anything of it, if they even know the Saybrook family claims the castle. It's been abandoned for many generations."

A woman following the river trail walked past the gate. Though she wasn't close—the pedestrians using the street and trail all made a wide berth of the cursed castle—and didn't glance in their direction, Vlerion put his hood up.

He extended a hand toward the kitchen door. "We'll go inside. You'll give me a report of the time you've spent here."

"Oh, goodie. Shall I call you *lord* after each sentence?"

His jaw tightened again. "At the end will do, when you respectfully express your gratitude that Captain Targon arranged equipment to facilitate this ruse."

"It's our dream, not a ruse."

"A dream you came ill-prepared to pursue in a land much harsher than your sun-soaked south."

Kaylina scowled, not wanting to admit that she *had* been naive and hadn't brought nearly enough money and supplies. If not for her brother, they wouldn't have been able to lease a chair, much less a building.

Vlerion's expression was irritatingly knowing, as if he could follow her every thought.

"We do appreciate the equipment," she made herself say. Grudgingly, she added, "my lord."

There wasn't any triumph in his eyes at the honorific. Maybe he simply thought it was his duty to educate her on how to act up here where nobles proliferated like fleas.

He extended his hand toward the doorway again.

"What do you want in my report?" Kaylina led him inside.

"Anything of note." Vlerion looked around, his brows rising in surprise at who knew what. That they'd cleaned up the place? Maybe he would tell Saybrook's granddaughter that they were good tenants.

"Such as that the castle moans all the time, weird noises come from under the floor, we see horrible visions, and the stairs leading to the red-light room are gone, and it's boarded up?"

"Anything of note that I'm not already aware of." His tone suggested he thought talking to her was a waste of time. His captain, she remembered, was the reason he was involved here.

"How am I supposed to know what you're *aware* of?" Kaylina turned, putting her back to a counter as she crossed her arms over her chest. "Have you spent the night here?"

"No. For me, that would be unwise."

"Because you're a ranger?"

Did he know about the visions of the murders? Or maybe he knew the history and that those murders had actually happened and were reported in books somewhere.

"Yes." Vlerion looked her up and down.

It wasn't a look of sexual perusal—it was more like he sought the answer to some question. Even so, for some reason, she remembered being in his arms in the jail cell, squirming and unable to escape after the ranger captain had drugged her.

"I'm surprised you've stayed this long," he added, his gaze settling on her face.

"Your expression is hard to read. I can't tell if you're implying that I'm courageous and admirable for sticking this out or an idiot."

"No?" A touch of amusement found his eyes. "Good."

"You're an ass."

"My lord," he corrected.

"You're an ass, *my lord*."

"If you're that mouthy to a less tolerant noble, you might end up back in jail."

"And flogged?"

"The law would allow it."

"It's a mystery as to why people are rebelling up here."

His eyes narrowed again, but he didn't object to the statement.

"As for things of note that you don't know, the girl who came with the furniture delivery wants me to give her intelligence on the Saybrooks if I learn anything."

Kaylina felt guilty about mentioning that—would Vlerion want her to describe Milzy so he could locate and arrest her?—but she also didn't want him to think that being here was a waste of his time. She had worth, damn it.

His eyes sharpened with interest. "Did you tell her anything?"

"No."

"Why not?"

"She hasn't won my loyalty with her wit and scintillating conversations the way you have."

He snorted. Well, at least he didn't accuse her of colluding with the enemy.

"What kind of noises did you hear from below?" Vlerion pointed at the kitchen floor and raised his brows.

"Clanks," Frayvar said from the dining room where he was scrubbing the flagstones, trying to remove what they were both pretending wasn't an old bloodstain. "And thumps."

"You've been down to the catacombs?" Vlerion asked.

"No." Kaylina had no idea *how* to go down to the catacombs. "There hasn't been anyone to give us a guided tour."

"That didn't keep you from trying to investigate the light."

"Do *you* know what makes it?"

Vlerion shook his head. "I only know it's been there as long as I can remember. Probably since the curse was placed two hundred years ago."

"What happened two hundred years ago?"

"Seven winters of famine." Vlerion walked toward the pantry and opened the door.

"Did that... answer my question?"

"I'll go down to see if the boarded-up tunnel leading this way has been un-boarded again."

"Okay." Kaylina hadn't moved and didn't intend to, despite now being curious if there was a catacombs entrance in the pantry.

Vlerion looked back and considered her thoughtfully. "Do you want to come along and learn what's down here?"

"I don't know. Are the catacombs included in the lease?"

"The root cellar would be." Vlerion waved toward the floor of the pantry. "The rest, likely not. The catacombs and sewers are owned by the king."

"What a thing to inherit along with the crown."

"If criminals are using this part of the catacombs as a thoroughfare again, and you've set up shop in the castle, you might be in danger from them."

"I'm in danger from a lot," Kaylina said.

"I've noticed. Perhaps your disrespectful tongue is the reason."

"I'm sure *your* tongue lands you in a lot of danger too."

"It is my uniform that does that." Vlerion gestured for her to join him.

Before, he'd asked if she wanted to come along, but something told her that she didn't have that much of a choice.

Kaylina caught Frayvar peering into the kitchen and said, "I'll be back soon. Will you finish arranging the tables and chairs?"

"Oh, sure. You know I love using my prodigious muscles to heft furniture." Frayvar curled his arm to flex his biceps.

"In exchange, I'll hold your groceries when you're ready to shop for provisions for your first meals, and I won't be snarky and roll my eyes at how long you take to decide between cumin and coriander."

"No eye rolling at all?"

"Nope."

"Will you sigh melodramatically?"

"You have to leave me something."

"All right, deal."

"If you're ready." Vlerion extended a hand toward the pantry floor.

"Yup, I can't wait. A trip into the catacombs with an uptight ranger sounds like a delightful adventure." Kaylina grabbed her lantern, her pack, and her sling and joined him in the pantry. "And not at all dangerous."

"Just watch your tongue." His look was grave, a warning in his blue eyes.

"With the criminals? Surely, I don't need to call *them* lords."

"No. But don't talk a lot."

A sarcastic response came to her lips, but the warning lingering in his eyes kept her from voicing it. A warning and... was that a hint of uncertainty? Like he thought taking her down there would be a bad idea?

Maybe she should stay behind. But she *would* like to know if danger could pop up from below, especially since she and her brother were sleeping on the floor in the kitchen scant feet from the pantry.

"No problem. I've got a romantic adventure novel in case I get bored without your melodious voice in my ear." Kaylina patted her pack. "It's good. Love, treachery, swashbuckling, and nobles who aren't full of themselves."

Vlerion used his sword to pry up a flagstone to reveal a ladder descending into darkness. "I doubt the catacombs will put you in the mood for romance."

She doubted it too.

12

PER THE ONE GOD'S INSTRUCTIONS, THE DEAD WILL BE GUARDED AS assiduously as the living.

~ Kar'ruk High Shaman Velkar

They didn't descend the wooden rungs into darkness as far as Kaylina expected. A scant six feet down, she landed on a flagstone floor similar to that on the main level of the castle. Vlerion had to stoop to keep from hitting his head on the ceiling.

Kaylina wrinkled her nose at the dust, the air damper and mustier down here than in the keep. Her brother would have been sneezing already.

Shifting her lantern around revealed a root cellar with wooden shelves lining one earthen wall and cask racks on the opposite. Surprisingly, they appeared to be in decent shape.

"That'll be handy when we increase our mead production and need more storage," she said.

Vlerion took a couple of steps, which opened up a view of a stone archway in the back wall and a skeleton on the floor in front of it. Rat droppings and gnawed pieces of clothing suggested whoever it was hadn't died as long ago as the people upstairs.

"That'll be less handy," Kaylina murmured.

Vlerion only grunted as he plucked a torch from an iron sconce mounted on the stone of the archway. When he lit it, the flickering mix of illumination and shadow emphasized the hard lines of his face. The flames reflected in his eyes, reminding her of the dangerous sparks she'd caught in them, and she wondered if she was crazy for coming down here alone with the man.

For a moment, he gazed at her, as if he could guess her thoughts. But if he did, he didn't comment on them, only turning toward the tunnel.

"Given the curse, people aren't inclined to enter to remove the bodies." Vlerion stopped in the next room and knelt to look at a scuff mark on the floor. Left recently by someone's boot?

Unlike with the dirt walls of the root cellar, time-worked stone lined the room and formed arches that supported the ceiling. More shelves and racks were inside, but they weren't part of the original construction. They might have been added later when someone had tried to expand the root cellar and had discovered the catacombs entrance.

"History tells us," Vlerion said, "that the druids who placed the curse didn't share a lot of details about how exactly their magic would plague the inn. Over the generations, people have come up with their own hypotheses and created rules that are supposed to help you avoid being affected. It's said that you might become cursed yourself if you handle the bones of those who die here."

"Oh." Kaylina didn't mention that she and Frayvar had moved the bones in the hearth. They hadn't wanted to burn them when they started a fire. It had seemed respectful of the dead. Hopefully, the cursed castle agreed. "You don't believe that?" she asked before remembering that he'd skirted the skeleton on the floor without touching it.

"I don't deny that it's a possibility, but I'm only aware of a couple of specifics about the curse, those that were recorded by the scribes of the time. Their writings are archived in the king's castle—and the family libraries of those people who were affected." His voice had turned grim at that last.

Vlerion continued toward another archway on the far side of the room that led into a wide tunnel. Kaylina paused to look at narrow chips in the stone support. It looked like someone had struck the archway with axes or swords, and she envisioned castle defenders fighting shoulder to shoulder to keep enemies at bay.

In the tunnel, towering stone statues depicted cruel-faced beings with horns that scowled down at them. The Kar'ruk.

She'd only seen a few of the warrior people and only at a distance. Sometimes, their ships sailed past the islands, or one would be spotted with a human pirate crew, but the Spitting Gull didn't serve their kind. The Kar'ruk had no respect for human laws or belongings—or lives—and they were rumored to kill and eat men when game was scarce.

"People were cursed?" Kaylina pulled her gaze from the unsettling statues. "Not only the castle?"

"King Balzarak and his descendants."

Kaylina remembered the name of the king as one of many in a list in chronological order that she'd been compelled to recite in school.

Vlerion crouched to touch the floor again. "People have been in here recently. When did you hear the clanks?"

"The first night and last night."

He eyed the walls, then walked to one that was empty save for the relief of a tree. He pushed on one of the branches, and a hidden door swung open with a grinding noise that made Kaylina jump.

Behind the wall lay a cubby with crates stacked inside, crates newer and less dusty than anything else around. There were also kegs that at first made her think of wine casks but, at a second glance, reminded her of the explosives the Virts had used on the jail walls.

Vlerion drew a dagger and used it to pry open a lid. "Powder and shot for muskets and blunderbusses."

There was also a crate of cannonballs, though not a cannon. Maybe they were what had made the clanks.

Vlerion tapped one of the kegs. "I'm tempted to use their own munitions to blow up the stash, but it might bring down the ceiling—and the castle and street above."

"Given the curse, I'm surprised someone hasn't *already* blown up the castle."

"In this part of the kingdom, we don't wantonly destroy historical structures."

"I was thinking more of controlled demolitions than wanton destruction. To get rid of a problem in the city. I'm glad they didn't, mind you," Kaylina hurried to add when Vlerion frowned back at her. "Where else would we have gotten such a deal on a lease?"

"Nowhere." Vlerion stepped back, leaving the door open. "I'll return with some men to commandeer this stash."

"What else are you expecting to find?" Kaylina asked as he continued down the arched tunnel.

He didn't answer.

She remembered she wasn't supposed to talk, but it was hard. She was curious to learn what she could about her new home—and the ancient passageways under it. Besides, the silence was unsettling, the stone statues disconcerting.

As they walked down the tunnel, the sound of trickling water grew audible. Kaylina thought of the river as well as the canals that sliced through the city.

Two more Kar'ruk statues loomed, built into the sides of the tunnel. These were even larger than the first pair with extra arms she was fairly certain the belligerent people didn't have.

When she and Vlerion walked between the statues, the eyes glowed red, and a hiss of vapor blew from the mouths.

Startled, Kaylina sprang closer to Vlerion and his sword. Her lantern bumped against him and tumbled from her fingers, hitting the floor with a clink. The flame went out.

The vapor expanded, clouding the air, and dimming Vlerion's torch—their only remaining light. Kaylina caught herself gripping his arm and shifting behind him. Her free hand strayed to her sling, but what would she do? Hurl a round at a stone statue?

"These figures represent Kar'ruk Defenders, powerful minions that serve their god." Vlerion showed no alarm, not even drawing his sword. He *did* arch his eyebrows at her grip, or maybe that she'd pressed close and half hidden behind him. His solid muscular form was reassuring, even if he was haughty and uptight.

"They serve their god by spitting steam into the air?" Admittedly, the glowing eyes concerned her more than the steam. She'd never seen such a thing. Until arriving at the cursed castle, her main experience with magic had been with edible altered plants that the bees foraged and that Grandma and Frayvar used in some of their recipes.

"They were built when the catacombs were and guard this entrance." Vlerion's torch hissed, the flame battling the mist in the air, bringing out the scent of the pitch mixture it burned. "They used to spit poison in the steam, a potent vapor that could kill humans as well as their own kind within a few minutes of exposure."

There *had* been a good reason to hide behind Vlerion.

"They... don't anymore?" Kaylina assumed he would have run if the steam was poisonous.

"Their reservoirs ran out long ago. There are other statues deeper in the catacombs that haven't been depleted. The traps are designed to protect the sarcophagi in the lower levels. Those passageways are rarely disturbed, even by the criminals who use the catacombs to avoid the law."

Kaylina made herself step back. "That's good information to know."

"Indeed." Was that amusement in his eyes?

Better than warnings and dangerous glints, but it made her bristle.

"I wasn't scared," she caught herself saying. "Just startled."

"Of course."

She scowled at him.

Vlerion lifted a hand and touched her arm. "Were you easily scared, you would not have spent the last few nights in the castle."

"That's right." Kaylina attempted to lower her hackles. Maybe she was being defensive without reason. She wasn't even sure why his opinion mattered, though the light touch on her arm was appealing, his skin warm through the fabric of her blouse. She caught herself tempted to step closer again.

"I apologize for snipping at you upstairs."

She was so surprised to hear the words—were aristocrats *allowed* to apologize to commoners?—that she didn't know what to say.

"I was worried when Crenoch went missing, then disgruntled that he'd disobeyed my command."

"You care about him."

"More than he cares about me." A rueful smile accompanied the words.

Kaylina didn't know what to make of it. Did humans typically bond more closely to their taybarri mounts than vice versa?

The cloud of steam dissipated, and Vlerion squeezed her arm lightly before lowering his hand. Only then did she realize she *had* stepped closer to him, inexplicably drawn by his gaze. By him.

Silly. A few moments ago, she'd been questioning her decision to come down here with him.

Shaking her head, Kaylina picked up her lantern. It had gone out, but Vlerion lowered his torch so she could use his flame to relight it.

"How come you know so much about this place?" she asked him.

"Port Jirador is my home. I've lived in the area my whole life, and my family knows its history well."

"I thought you spent as much time as you could in the mountains, away from pesky people who irritate you."

Vlerion gazed at her, and she thought he would state that *she* fell into that category. All he said was, "I know the mountains well too."

With her lantern relit, he headed off down the tunnel again.

"I've been sent down here to hunt criminals before," he added. "The graycoats—the Kingdom Guard—are always reluctant to come down here, but Captain Targon isn't one to let a bad element lurk below the city. Periodically, he sends rangers to clear out the catacombs. There are a lot of levels and warrens for people to hide in, so we don't always get them all. And the criminals make traps of their own. It's dangerous down here for all."

"Nice of you to think I'd like to see the place."

"You are a fan of adventure, are you not?" Vlerion looked back at her—or maybe at the pack with the novel she'd mentioned.

"When it happens to fictional heroines in books, it's wonderful. As I told you before, I'm just here to grow my family business and—" she almost added *prove myself*. But she didn't want to open up to him. He wasn't a confidant. "What's the deal with the rangers and the castle? All the nightmares I've had while sleeping in there have shown your people and—I think—allies of your people being horribly killed by vines and branches and nature. *Violent* nature."

"Yes, when the druids set the curse, they were particularly displeased with the rangers." Vlerion kept walking as he spoke, the sound of running water growing louder. "Generations ago, Stillguard River Inn was owned by a family who'd always supported the rangers. It was a place where they could drink and relax, almost an alternate headquarters. That is why it was targeted by the druids when they decided to punish humanity. The rangers were only obeying the king's orders, but the druids didn't care. They took their ire out on them and their favorite destination."

"What were the druids pissed about? And why didn't they go after the king instead of the rangers?"

"They punished the king as well. Trust me." Vlerion slanted her a long look laden with significance. "As to the crime, humans poached in the sacred forest preserve east of the city. A millennia ago, when the druids agreed to leave this land for our kind, part of the deal was that humans would never hunt there. But after seven years of famine, King Balzarak was in a difficult situation. His people were starving, and the preserve was the only place teeming with game. The druids hadn't been seen for centuries. He believed there might not be repercussions and was willing to accept the responsibility if there were. He sent the rangers to hunt, to find enough game to feed the people. Had he foreseen that the consequences would be widespread, that rangers would be killed even as he was cursed, Balzarak might not have made the decision. But he might have. As I said, there was little choice."

"Sounds like a rough time."

"The northlands can be brutal."

They passed between two more Kar'ruk statues. Again, they hissed steam and the eyes glowed.

Knowing their reservoirs were devoid of poison didn't keep Kaylina from jumping at the noise or flinching at the cloud of vapor that caressed her cheeks. If anything, it made the catacombs scarier. How many people had died coming this way *before* the reservoirs had run out?

"You visit Ghara in her apartment yet?" she asked, blurting the first thing that came to mind in an attempt to distract herself.

Judging from the cool look Vlerion angled back at her, it wasn't an appropriate thing to ask a lord. She didn't know why she'd thought about it.

"Is that the intelligence the Virt girl sought?" he asked.

"No, I'm making conversation."

"As I recall, Ghara and I did not include you in that discussion."

"No? That's weird. I remember it really well."

"Do your kin find you exasperating?"

"Is that your way of saying you do? My kin like challenging women who speak their minds." Well, that was an utter lie. Her tongue had gotten her in trouble plenty of times at home.

"Interesting."

"Yes, I am."

They rounded a bend, and light came from an opening ahead. Vlerion paused and fell silent.

It wasn't the creepy red glow of the statues' eyes but the warm yellow of torchlight. That wasn't that much more reassuring since it meant someone was down here. Even with a special pitch blend that burned a long time, thanks to altered cinderrock powder mixed in, torches rarely lasted on their own for more than a day.

Vlerion held a finger to his lips before continuing on.

"You're the one who was doing all the talking," Kaylina whispered.

He gave her another cool look over his shoulder. She nobly and respectfully resisted the urge to stick out her tongue at his back. Hopefully, his back appreciated that.

As he advanced, Vlerion drew his sword. Had he heard someone?

Kaylina pulled out her sling again. She couldn't attack a statue, but she would have no trouble pelting a thief or pirate.

Would she attack one of the Virts though? Someone from the working class fighting for better conditions in the factories? Even if their methods were illegal—and deadly—she had a hard time condemning them fully. She let herself fall a few steps behind Vlerion.

They passed a deep alcove with a Kar'ruk statue guarding a squat stone sarcophagus against the back wall. The eyes on the statue didn't light up, nor did it emit steam. Vlerion went by without commenting on what triggering its defenses might once have done.

He paused at the end of the tunnel, prodding broken boards lying on the ground. A wooden frame had been built against the stone wall, and more broken boards thrust out of it, nails bent or jutting out.

"Last week," Vlerion said softly, forgoing his no-speaking rule again, "this was barricaded."

"So whoever delivered those crates came through this way?" Kaylina hadn't seen any other exits along the way.

"They must have. They could intend to use the castle as a staging area for an attack." Vlerion leaned around the corner into the lit area.

His broad torso blocked Kaylina's view. She resisted the urge to crouch and peer under his armpit or jump to see over his shoulder, but her curiosity made restraint difficult.

Vlerion looked back at her. "You may return to your work. I did not want to endanger you, only for you to see what goes on down here so you would understand the threat—and perhaps drag heavy furniture onto the trapdoor in the pantry." He stepped aside to give her a view.

The tunnel opened into a natural grotto around a large pool with a placid river flowing away through a wide passageway on the far end. An ancient clay pipe jutting from under the mouth of a stone lion poured water in from the opposite end. A pathway carved in stone ran around the pool, passing a stubby wooden dock built near the river.

All around the grotto, torches burned in wall sconces, the flames reflecting yellowish-orange on the surface of the water. The dock held stacks of crates and kegs, as well as a sack slumped open to reveal thick books inside. How odd to find reading material among explosives.

"There's enough black powder there to destroy half the city," Vlerion said grimly.

"And instructions on how to use it?" Kaylina leaned past him, squinting in an attempt to read the titles on the book spines. Did one say *recipes*? Surely, a bunch of rebels weren't toting cookbooks along on their campaign of destruction.

Vlerion eyed her, and she reined in her curiosity and leaned back.

"The Virts know well how to employ their explosives." His tone was disdainful, but his eyebrows crimped as another expression entered his eyes. Pain? Loss? Regret? If his duty was to fight the Virts, he'd probably lost comrades to them.

"Then those must be romantic adventures to keep them entertained when their buddies can't muster scintillating conversation."

"That is doubtless what they are." Vlerion surveyed the river passageway, the stone walkway continuing past the pool and down it on one side.

Since it was less than a foot wide, it would be easy to fall in. The Virts probably carried their munitions up in boats.

"I must stay and deal with them. You will return to the castle." After a moment's hesitation, Vlerion bowed his head to her. "I should not have brought you down here. I didn't expect criminals to be in the middle of unloading cargo."

"It's fine," she said.

"They must also have broken through the barrier Targon's men placed between the end of that river and the harbor where it flows out underwater. There's supposed to be a ranger's apprentice keeping watch on that area. I hope he hasn't been killed."

"Are you sure you don't want me to stay and help?" Kaylina held up her sling. "Given how much cargo we've seen, there could be a lot of guys."

"I will be able to handle them sufficiently without the assistance of a neophyte rock thrower," Vlerion said dryly. And insultingly.

One minute he was decent... and then got haughty.

"They're lead balls." Wishing he would need her help and that she could save his ass, Kaylina bared her teeth at him the way the taybarri had. Except with more fierceness.

"Go back to safety," he ordered, undeterred by her teeth-baring. It had to be her lack of fangs.

"The safety of the cursed castle? That place is at least as creepy and dangerous as these catacombs. Poison-spitting statues notwithstanding."

Vlerion hesitated again. "Since you are not a ranger, and the curse hasn't bothered you yet, you may not be in danger there."

The curse hadn't *bothered* her? Kaylina balked at that notion but wondered if he meant it hadn't *killed* her.

"In the visions, we saw it murder people who weren't rangers. There was a girl serving a tankard of ale to one of your people, and *she* got killed. Horribly." Kaylina almost mentioned the gaunt man who'd been strangled in the forest—the preserve Vlerion had spoken of?—but realized that might have been a ranger who hadn't been in his armor.

"The curse has struck those who've worked for the rangers or proven themselves allies," he admitted.

"I thought so. And you keep showing up at the castle, so if it's smart, or if the *curse* is smart, it might decide we're on the same side."

"Are we?" His brows rose.

"Thanks to your boss making sure we can't go home, and bribing us with furniture and mead-making supplies, my brother and I don't have any choice but to be."

Not unless she ran away and joined the rebels. That didn't sound appealing though. Why couldn't these people have a nice negotiating session and make peace?

"Perhaps you should stay at the Headwaters Inn."

"Our money is for launching our business, not vacationing at competing inns. Perhaps *you* shouldn't come by to visit."

"I wouldn't have to come *visit* if you hadn't lured my mount to your door with your honey." Though Vlerion hadn't raised his voice, his body tensed, and irritation sparked in his eyes. Irritation and something more. That dangerous glint she'd caught a couple of times.

"I didn't *lure* him," Kaylina couldn't keep from saying, though her instincts warned her to shut up and let him have the last word. Somehow, she'd touched on a tender spot. Maybe someone *had* suborned his taybarri before. But she didn't want him to believe she'd tried to do that. Forcing calm onto her face and into her voice, she added, "He came of his own accord. Probably because he has good taste." Unwisely and impulsively, she added, "And your protein pellets look like pulverized dung."

His jaw tightened. Though he didn't move, he radiated coiled tension that made her wish she'd listened when he told her to leave. What was she arguing for? Beyond having some understandable curiosity about those books, she didn't *want* to stay in the catacombs.

Several long seconds passed with Vlerion as motionless as one of those statues, except that he was making a faint noise. Was that... humming? A tune?

She stared at him, but he'd closed his eyes. Finally, he stepped back and exhaled a long slow breath.

He opened his eyes and started to say something, but his head whipped around. He peered down the tunnel in the direction they'd come and raised his sword arm.

"What—" Kaylina started to whisper, but he stepped forward, wrapped an arm around her waist and hefted her from her feet.

She barely kept from gasping in surprise and only because she heard what he must have heard. Footsteps. Running footsteps heading their way.

13

Pressed against Vlerion's body, with her feet dangling in the air, Kaylina wanted to protest his manhandling, but the footsteps grew louder.

"Zerek?" the running man called.

Sword out, Vlerion had started to thrust Kaylina into the alcove with the statue, as though he would leave her and spring out to attack the man, but hearing the voice seemed to change his mind. With his arm wrapped around her waist, he stepped into the alcove with her. He paused only to lean out and toss his torch down the tunnel and into the pool. It hit the water and went out. He lowered Kaylina so he could snuff her lantern, then stepped as far back into the alcove as possible, pulling her with him.

She found herself in the dark, wedged between the horned Kar'ruk statue and Vlerion, with the sarcophagus close enough to use as an arm rest. What a cozy spot.

His body was almost as hard as the stone statue, and she would have shifted, trying to find a more comfortable position, but the footsteps were coming closer. The speaker slowed from a run. Had he sensed them?

Vlerion leaned his head close, his lips brushing Kaylina's ear. The intimate touch startled her, especially given their current situation. Her body responded in a most inappropriate way, with a tingle of warmth that shot to her core.

"I know the name he spoke," Vlerion breathed softly in her ear. Sharing information, not nuzzling her. He drew back once the words were out.

She didn't say anything back, not wanting to give away their hiding spot.

"Zerek?" came another call, closer this time. "Are you still in here?"

"Back here, Legdar," another man called from a distance. His voice came from the far end of the grotto or maybe the walkway along the river.

"I think those kids from the castle know about the catacombs," the first speaker—Legdar—said. A big man carrying an axe, he walked past the alcove without glancing in. "I heard the boy calling for his sister from the root cellar."

The realization that these people not only knew about Kaylina and her brother but had been watching them closely enough to know their relationship chilled her.

"Kids?" Zerek laughed shortly. "That sweet southern vixen is most assuredly a woman. I've been thinking of visiting her one night."

"Oh, yeah, she's a nice piece of ass. I'd take her against a tree in a heartbeat."

Horror and humiliation flushed Kaylina's cheeks as they spoke about her.

"It's her tits that make me hard, but I'd be a gentleman and offer her a bed."

A soft rumble came from Vlerion's chest. Or... was that a growl? His arm tightened around her. Protectively?

She looked up at him, a faint hint of light from the grotto letting her see that his face was toward the tunnel. The men had met near the entrance, and, unfortunately, Kaylina had no trouble hearing their words.

"Guess that's why you're the boss, Zerek. But I like the excitement of standing and taking 'em from behind."

That prompted them to share their preferences for positions and muse whether she was a screamer or not.

It was too dark to see Vlerion's expression, but he must have felt her gaze, for his head turned back toward her. He bent to whisper in her ear again. "This is not the conversation I hoped to overhear." His body was tense with that same irritation he'd radiated in the tunnel. This time, it wasn't directed at her, and she didn't fear it—or him. She was glad he was there and didn't even mind being jammed between him and the statue.

After hearing another comment about her tits, Vlerion shifted, raising his sword arm. To rush out and attack them?

"It's okay," Kaylina breathed, resting a hand on his chest.

It wasn't, but she realized he'd hoped to overhear useful information about the Virts and their plans. Assuming they could get over their obsession with her anatomy, they might yet share that. She leaned her face against Vlerion's shoulder, willing them to get on with it.

He shifted his arm from her waist up to gently cup the back of her head. To offer comfort? She hadn't expected solicitude from him, not for someone like her. For someone like Ghara, maybe.

Vlerion stroked the back of her head, and she melted against him. Damn, that felt good. She believed he meant to offer comfort, not turn her on, but his touch sent more tingles through her, and she almost forgot the conversation taking place twenty feet away.

"Milzy talked to them," Zerek said. "It sounds like they might be sympathetic to us. They were arrested by the rangers and only got out of jail because of the breakout for Wedgewick."

Vlerion's hand froze.

Kaylina's heart started galloping in her chest. Not because of humiliation this time but because she worried Vlerion would believe she'd been more interested in Milzy's entreaty than she had been. What if he thought Kaylina had agreed to spy for the Virts and planned to share everything she learned about the rangers?

"Good. They might have ties to the southern provinces. We could use some allies down there. You know Cougar's been trying to open up a supply line, get more food and munitions and men to help us. We outnumber the nobles a thousand to one. It shouldn't be this hard to recruit people to overthrow the king and elect one of our own to be in charge of the nation."

"People are afraid of the rangers. You know how savage and ruthless they are."

Maybe Vlerion forgot the insinuation that Kaylina had spoken with one of the Virt girls, or he simply found this turn of the conversation more agreeable, because he returned to stroking the back of her head. Was he still doing it to comfort her? The men were thankfully not talking about her now.

Maybe she should have pulled back, as much as she could in the cramped quarters, but her body wasn't interested in that. She slumped more fully against Vlerion and let him stroke her hair. After all she'd been through this week, she deserved a gentle touch.

Vlerion was probably thinking of Ghara, but that didn't matter. It wasn't as if anything would come of a few head touches. Even if Kaylina found them more exhilarating than she should have.

"That's the truth," one man said. "The rangers don't care that we're human beings and not those rabid mountain monsters."

Vlerion's hand lowered to rub Kaylina's neck. She barely refrained from letting out a groan of pleasure. Her muscles were knotted after nights of poor sleep on the castle floor, and when his fingers worked on the tight spots, she wanted to rub against him to demonstrate how amazing that felt. She didn't, but she *did* lift her hands to grip his shoulders, even daring to trace the hard muscles with her thumbs.

"They go into battle lust and lop heads off like you're nothing to them," one of the men continued. "Except for that Vlerion. He's a stone-cold killer. No lust there. He's like one of them Kar'ruk statues come to life."

"Wish we could talk him into joining our side. He's not as vocal about the superiority of the nobility as a lot of the rangers."

Sure, they talked about her anatomy and thrusting her against a tree, and they admired Vlerion and wanted to befriend him.

"He'd run you through as quick as he did Dededrak and Timmar."

"I know, but if we could turn him..."

Another faint growl rumbled from Vlerion's chest. Because they were talking about him betraying his people, Kaylina told herself, not because her shoulder rub excited him.

"Let's worry about our upcoming plans for now. One step at a time. We've got to get everything staged before Wedgewick is ready. You know he wants attacks and distractions from multiple fronts."

A distant call sounded. Someone else coming up the river?

Vlerion's hand on Kaylina's taut muscles stilled, and disappointment rushed into her. It wasn't as if she'd expected him to keep rubbing her neck while more enemies arrived, but she wished the rebels would go away and—

And what? She could get busy with a haughty ranger next to a tomb? Sure, that would happen.

The men spoke again, but they'd moved farther into the grotto. To join whoever was coming?

"Is Hazlin with you?" one called, the words clear.

The distant answer sounded like, "Next boat."

"Stay here," Vlerion whispered, his lips brushing Kaylina's ear again.

She was positive he didn't mean his whispers to be erotic, and he was brushing her ear because it was dark and he couldn't see where it was, but her body didn't know that.

"For your safety," he added. "From... everything."

From everything? What did that mean?

His lips grazed her cheek as he pulled back. An accident, she told herself, however appealing it had been.

When he stepped away, easing out of the alcove with his sword in hand, she grew starkly aware of the cool damp air and missed the warmth of his body.

Kaylina rubbed her face and told herself to concentrate on the situation. There were at least three enemies out there now, three enemies who considered rangers foes to be dealt with. Even if Vlerion had been dismissive of her offer of help, she *would* use her sling if she saw an opportunity to assist him.

Before, she'd been reluctant to raise a weapon against fellow commoners, but after listening to those two voice their crude desires for her, she would have no trouble cracking *them* in the heads with lead rounds.

But long moments passed without the sounds of a scuffle. Nor did the Virts say anything to indicate they knew Vlerion was about. They'd moved too far away for Kaylina to make out their words, but she heard their voices and a few bumps and thumps. It sounded like they were unloading more cargo.

Was Vlerion hiding somewhere and hoping to hear more

useful information? The torches were placed frequently enough in the grotto that there hadn't been deep shadows between them. She didn't remember seeing any other alcoves, but she hadn't gotten a thorough look around the pool.

Kaylina crept to the tunnel and risked peeking out. The thumps and voices continued, coming from the direction of the dock. If the men were all there, they wouldn't be able to see her leave and return to the castle. Which was what she ought to do, as Vlerion had originally suggested. Of course, his last order had been for her to stay in the alcove.

A distant scream chilled her blood.

A louder thump came from the dock, followed by curses.

"Was that Hazlin? Wrendon?" someone asked, his voice raised in alarm.

Kaylina had no trouble making out his words, but the response was muted.

"It *was* one of our men," the first speaker said, a hint of panic in his tone. "The other boat had more cargo and was lagging behind."

Maybe that was where Vlerion had gone. He'd recognized some of those names. He might have bypassed lesser men to go after one of the leaders.

Hoping her curiosity wouldn't get her killed, Kaylina crept toward the grotto instead of away. Another distant scream sounded.

"That's it." Another thump accompanied the man's words. "We've got to go check on them."

"You feeling that brave?"

"They're our allies. Besides, whatever's after them will come for us next."

Kaylina peered out of the tunnel toward the dock. A boat had indeed been rowed up to it, and more crates had joined the earlier stacks, though the two arguing men hadn't finished unloading. With screams sounding in the distance, she couldn't blame them.

"What do you mean *whatever*? It's got to be the rangers."

"Or one of those beasts."

Kaylina fingered her sling. These were the men who'd been musing about her anatomy, Legdar and Zerek. While they were looking toward the river, she was tempted to crack them in the skulls. Too bad her rounds were great for taking down pheasants and quail but only tended to bruise men—and piss them off.

"There are no *beasts* in the catacombs. Unless you count those ugly statues."

"It wasn't a sword that tore Penner's head off. Those were *claws*."

"Just grab what you can carry. I have an idea." Legdar picked up two kegs, tucking them under his arms, and turned toward Kaylina's tunnel.

She pulled back, hoping she'd avoided being spotted, and jogged back to the alcove.

"Your idea involves running from our friends who need help?" Zerek asked.

"Gonna make a big distraction. If there are rangers down here, they'll be compelled to leave our men alone and check on it." Their voices followed Kaylina. They had to be heading for the hidden cubby where the other munitions had been stashed. Or would they go all the way to the castle?

In the alcove, she squeezed between the statue and the sarcophagus, hoping the deep shadows would hide her if the men looked in.

"What *kind* of distraction?" Zerek asked.

"We'll blow some of the kegs and see if we can take down that castle."

Kaylina stared in horror at the tunnel as the men walked past, lugging kegs of black powder. They couldn't blow up the castle.

Even if she hadn't signed a lease and invested her dream in it, Frayvar was there, worrying because she'd been gone so long. She envisioned her brother being trapped in the kitchen or maybe the root cellar as an explosion boomed, making the ground shake and beams and rubble tumble down and kill him.

"Can you blow up a cursed castle?"

"We'll find out. Either way, it ought to bring the rangers running."

"What if the curse transfers to us?"

"Don't be a milksop."

The voices grew fainter as they walked farther up the tunnel.

Kaylina gripped her knees. What was she supposed to do? She couldn't let them set off explosives under the castle. But the sling and knife were the only weapons she had. She was a mead maker, not a fighter, damn it.

Shaking her head, she gripped the sling. She would have to use what she had.

She slipped into the shadows of the tunnel, stepping as quietly as she could. Since the men were lugging kegs, she soon caught up with them.

Sling loaded, she drew it back and took aim.

The tunnel wasn't wide enough for people to walk side by side, so they trod single file. Zerek, the man in back, was a larger target, so she waited until the head of Legdar was visible and fired at it first.

Before her round struck, she loaded a second. Legdar swore, dropped his kegs, and grabbed the back of his head.

"What are you doing?" Zerek demanded before thinking to look behind him.

He turned his head in time to take Kaylina's round between the eyes.

The blow was enough to knock Zerek back. He stumbled over the kegs his comrade had dropped.

Kaylina wavered between firing again and running. The first man she'd struck snarled and drew a sword. That made up her mind.

She spun and sprinted away, knowing she was no match for a swordsman. But if they chased her, it meant they wouldn't head toward the castle with those kegs. Frayvar would remain safe. She just had to make sure they didn't catch her so *she* remained safe.

As they abandoned their cargo and pounded after her with legs longer and faster than hers, she realized that might not be possible.

14

WHEN LUCK BLESSES YOU, DO NOT QUESTION IT.
  ~ Winter Moon Priest Dazibaru

Aware of the men gaining ground as she sprinted down the tunnel, Kaylina abandoned her idea of evading them by ducking into the alcove. They were too close behind. She would have to run past the pool, along the river, and hope to reach Vlerion before they caught her.

But as she exited the tunnel, rounding the corner too quickly, she slipped on damp rock and fell. Her hip struck the walkway, and she pitched into the water. The iciness of its cold embrace shocked her system.

"Got her!" one man cried from the tunnel.

With no time to climb out, Kaylina took a deep breath, ducked under the surface, and pushed off the lumpy rock side of the pool. Her clothing and shoes dragged at her, but she swam fast anyway, staying underwater as she put yards between her and the path.

A need for air would force her up by the time she reached the middle of the pool, but neither of those men had ranged weapons. If they wanted to get her, they would have to follow her in. She might not be a fighter, but she'd grown up around the water and played with and raced other children often. She wagered she could out-swim the northern men, and if she bought enough time, Vlerion might return.

Shouts came from behind her. The water garbled their words, but the men sounded pissed. Kaylina took more strokes, the chill of the water invigorating her.

Since the light from the torches didn't extend below the surface, she couldn't see a thing. As fast as she was going, she prayed to Anglari, the Sea Moon god, that she wouldn't smash into a rock.

With her lungs demanding air, Kaylina risked coming up and turned to face the tunnel. Zerek crouched there, glaring around the pool as he searched for her. Legdar had raced to the dock.

Though she wanted to suck in great gasps of air, she forced herself to breathe quietly. They hadn't figured out where she was yet. The light from the torches didn't stretch to the center of the pool. She treaded water silently.

"You see her?" Legdar grabbed something out of his boat. A blunderbuss.

Kaylina winced. She hadn't considered all the weapons they were stashing. Maybe she should have angled toward the dock and hidden under it. But they could have reached her more easily there.

"No, but she can't hold her breath forever."

"Why don't you swim out and get her?"

"Why don't *you*? I've got a concussion from that damn rock she hit me with."

"And be eaten by one of the fur sharks? That's worse than a crack in the head."

Kaylina wiped water out of her eyes and glanced around.

She'd never heard of a fur shark, but maybe she shouldn't have assumed the pool would be safe. The gods knew fresh-water lakes and swamps on the mainland back home were filled with alligators and turgoraks.

Near the pipe pouring water into the pool, the surface rippled, stirred by more than its flow. Was that a fin?

"There she is." Zerek pointed at her.

Keeping her head up, Kaylina treaded backward to put more distance between her and the men. The fin or whatever it was had disappeared. Maybe she'd imagined it.

On the dock, Legdar raised the blunderbuss.

Kaylina prepared to duck below the surface, but he called out instead of firing.

"Come on, girl. We don't need to be enemies. Come tell us what you know about the rangers, and we'll take you back to one of our headquarters. Our leaders might have a use for you."

Zerek looked toward the river. "You hear something?"

He jogged along the walkway toward the dock.

"No, I haven't heard anything since those screams." Legdar kept the blunderbuss pointed toward Kaylina as he responded.

"The other boat should have been here by now."

"Best assume it's not coming." Grim-faced, Legdar called into the water again. "Come tell us what you know about the rangers. How many are down here? Why are *you* down here? Answer a few questions, and we'll give you some coin or help you with your inn. We're not rich, but we've got connections. And we'll run the kingdom before long. It pays to pick the winning side."

Something brushed Kaylina's leg. Something large.

She kept from shrieking—barely—and swam several strokes to the side, making exaggerated kicks in case she needed to strike whatever that had been in the head.

A huge creature with oily black fur and a fanged maw broke the surface five feet away. She didn't know if it was the fur shark the men had spoken of, but that broad jaw and those long pointed teeth promised it could chomp her in half.

Giving up on treading water—and avoiding the men—Kaylina paddled as fast as she could toward the dock. The creature followed.

Something batted her foot. A fin? She kicked hard, splashing and praying to scare the creature away—also praying it wouldn't latch onto her leg.

Kaylina glanced toward the dock, hoping it was closer than she thought. Legdar aimed the blunderbuss, not at her but at the water behind her.

Knowing how inaccurate those weapons were, she ducked under the surface. That might have been a mistake because that was the creature's domain. She couldn't see anything in the dark water, but her instincts warned her of danger. She pulled her knife out, twisted, and slashed outward.

The blade connected, but it clinked off something hard. The thing's fangs?

The boom of the blunderbuss rang out, thunderous even with the water muffling sound.

Hoping it would scare the creature, Kaylina stuck her knife in her mouth to free up both arms and swam toward the dock. She looked up as she paddled and was in time to see someone in black spring upon Legdar. Vlerion.

His sword glinted yellow, reflecting the torchlight, as he swung it toward the man's neck. The blunderbuss and Legdar's head flew off the dock and hit the water.

Vlerion glanced at Kaylina, but Zerek was charging him with an axe, and he had to defend himself.

Water surged behind Kaylina. The creature hadn't given up. She was only fifteen or twenty yards from the dock and put her head down, stroking and kicking as hard as she could.

Jaws wrapped around her leg, halting her as pain erupted in

her shin and calf. She couldn't keep from screaming, water flowing into her mouth and half-choking her. Terrified, she grabbed her knife and twisted, stabbing wildly.

Between the frothing water and the poor lighting, she could barely see the creature, but she thrust around her leg, hoping to get lucky, hoping it wouldn't—

There. Her knife sank in deep, and the agonizing grip loosened.

A great roar came from the dock—what in all the altered orchards was that?—and the jaws released her completely.

Yanking her knife free, Kaylina swam away, praying she could reach land—and that the shark-thing couldn't walk.

A tremendous splash came from her side, creating waves as something plunged in. She glimpsed short, sleek auburn fur. *Another* creature?

With fear and pain making her frantic, she kept paddling, sprinting for what she hoped was safety. More splashes and another roar erupted from the water behind her. The two creatures were fighting. Whichever one was roaring sounded enraged.

Glancing back as she swam, trying to figure out what was going on, Kaylina almost crashed head-first into one of the dock pilings. With water surging all around her from the nearby battle, she had to grab it to keep from being batted around. She clung to it with both arms and looked for a way up, but the dock and the walkway were higher above than she'd realized.

A shriek of pain came from the fight. She had no idea which of the creatures had made it, but the splashes stopped, the water growing still.

Afraid the winner of the battle was swimming under the surface toward her, she stroked toward the boat. It rocked when she lunged up to grab the lip, but it was wide enough that it didn't tip. With all the strength she had remaining, she pulled herself out, flopping down in the bottom and crying out when her injured leg struck the side.

The wounds burned with agony, and she had no doubt as much blood as water was dripping off her. All she wanted was to curl on her side in the bottom of the boat and sob, but those creatures might be able to surge out of the water and pull her back in.

That thought sent energy into her limbs, enough for her to push up to her hands and knees. She gripped the edge of the dock and pulled herself out.

"Shit," she blurted in surprise when she bumped a person lying dead on the boards next to a crate and a pair of boots.

Legdar. She'd forgotten.

Trembling, Kaylina crawled off the dock and used the rock wall to pull herself to her feet. Her injured leg didn't want to take her weight, and she slumped against the wall for support as she surveyed her surroundings.

Zerek was also dead, floating in the pool near the edge, his axe on the walkway. She didn't see Vlerion. She also didn't see the auburn-furred creature that had engaged the fur shark. It, however, floated belly up not ten feet from the dock, one of its fins torn off and its head smashed in, as if a battering ram had struck it rather than claws. It was near enough to one of the torches that she could make out four parallel gashes in its flesh, the wounds deep enough that they'd half eviscerated it.

Remembering the enraged roars of the other creature, Kaylina rubbed her face with a shaky hand. Whatever it had been, it had saved her life, but that kind of fury and power was terrifying.

"Vlerion?" she called softly.

Were there more enemies about? Maybe he'd been forced to run into the tunnels to engage another group of Virts. But she didn't hear any sounds of fighting. She didn't hear anything except the trickle of water flowing into the pool.

Should she leave and limp back to the castle? Or wait for him?

"Vlerion, I'm craving your presence for more scintillating conversation."

Shadows near the river made her tense, lifting her knife.

Vlerion walked out of the tunnel. He was barefoot, and his clothes were torn, as if he'd battled one of the creatures himself, but his sword was sheathed and his face as calm and controlled as ever as he walked toward her.

"I'm here." He paused to put on the boots he'd left on the dock, then approached, looking toward her leg.

Her trousers were also torn, but she only glanced at the punctures, the throbbing telling her without an examination that they were deep. She would have to find a healer to clean them and sprinkle protective herbs over them to stave off infection. How was she supposed to open an award-winning meadery when she was hobbling around with a cane?

"You were injured." Vlerion shook his head as he stopped in front of her.

With little expression on his face or inflection in his voice, Kaylina couldn't tell if that head shake meant he regretted that he hadn't been able to help or thought she'd gotten what she deserved for not leaving when he'd ordered it.

That probably wasn't it—his eyes seemed more sympathetic than vindictive—but she couldn't help but defensively blurt, "They were planning to blow up the castle from below. To distract you from hurting their buddies. I couldn't let them do that. Frayvar is up there. And we have a lease." She winced at that stupid last sentence. As if *that* had been her primary motivation for going after the men. "I had to stop them," she finished.

"By leaping into the maw of a fur shark?" Vlerion knelt to examine her leg, thankfully not touching the throbbing bite wounds.

Kaylina didn't look forward to the healer cleaning them.

"I cracked them in the heads with my sling." Reluctantly, she added, "The maw-leaping came later. The men were chasing me, and..." Hating to admit that she'd slipped and fallen in the water, she finished with, "I didn't quite make it to their boat to escape."

"Ah." Vlerion touched the back of his own head. Maybe he still had a lump from where she'd struck him. "I'll take you to ranger headquarters. We have the best doctors. Our people are injured often in battle."

"That's not necessary. We have money. I can find—"

Vlerion startled her by lifting her into his arms. "You will not spend your coin on this. It is my fault that you were down here where you could be injured."

Kaylina gripped his shoulders. Though she was proud and wanted to tell him that she could walk, her leg burned like an inferno, and it was a relief not to have her weight on it. Let him carry her. As he'd admitted, he *was* the one who'd asked her to come down here.

Thankfully, he didn't point out that she needn't have left her hiding spot in the alcove. Maybe he understood her reason for doing it. After all, rangers looked out for their own, didn't they? The same way she had to look out for her little brother.

"Thank you," she made herself say as he carried her into the tunnel.

With her hands resting on his shoulders, the memory of caressing them in the alcove came to mind, but the rips in his clothing distracted her. Not only his tunic was torn but his trousers were too, and the straps of his leather torso armor had snapped so that it hung loosely. Yet he wasn't bleeding anywhere, not that she could see.

"What happened to your clothes?" And why had he taken his boots off?

Vlerion bent to grab her pack and lantern, managing to keep her in his arms as he did so. She tightened her grip on his shoulders to help him, and her cheek brushed his hair. Since it was so short, she hadn't noticed before that it was wet.

"Battle," he replied.

"You weren't wounded?"

"No."

"How did your hair get wet?"

"Splashes."

"Splashes?"

"Men fell in as they died," he said tersely, looking at her. Was that... a warning on his face?

As he continued up the tunnel, and they passed under the still-glowing eyes of the statues, their illumination shone on his hair, reminding her that it was reddish brown. Auburn. Like that of the second creature.

She opened her mouth, though she didn't know what query she wanted to voice.

"Ask me no more questions," Vlerion said softly.

Yeah, that was definitely a warning on his face.

She thought of the utterly destroyed fur shark, with its head smashed in and its guts dangling. "Okay."

15

THE OLDER ONE GETS, THE LESS ONE CARES ABOUT ENGAGING IN socially acceptable behavior.
~ Mendar the Crazy

A cold breeze swept off the snowy mountains and across the frosty cobblestones of the compound Vlerion entered, still carrying Kaylina. He'd done so the whole way, even climbing the ladder out of the root cellar while balancing her. In the castle, he'd stood patiently with her in his arms while she'd explained to Frayvar what had happened. Technically, she'd *downplayed* what had happened, not letting him get a good look at her leg and saying only that she'd hurt herself. Her brother had wanted to accompany them, but Vlerion had swept his hood over his head and reminded them that the fewer people who saw either of them with rangers, the better.

On the way to his headquarters, he'd avoided busy streets and had taken a roundabout route through alleys and sewer access tunnels. Only when they'd entered through the front gate of his walled compound had he pushed back his hood and walked openly through the courtyard.

A familiar ranger jogged up to Vlerion, falling in at his side. It was his handsome friend, Jankarr. He smiled at Kaylina, the gesture conveying reassurance and concern, before giving Vlerion a stern look.

"You went off to find trouble without me? And you got Targon's innkeeper wounded? I'm your riding partner. I'm supposed to be at your side when there's a fight." Jankarr noticed the rips in Vlerion's clothes, though Vlerion had pulled his cloak close, either because he was cold or to hide the damaged garments. Kaylina suspected the latter.

"I didn't intend to find trouble when I left. I went in search of my wayward mount." Vlerion looked toward a stable where numerous taybarri stood out front, noshing from buckets that were probably filled to the brim with protein pellets.

"That was three hours ago. *He's* been back for two." Jankarr thrust a finger toward the taybarri.

Until one swished his tail with a defiant cant while looking over at them, Kaylina couldn't tell one from another. But when the animal's brown eyes met hers, she knew that was Crenoch. He sashayed toward them while chewing his last bite.

"I decided to check the catacombs while I was at the castle. Go tell Targon I have an update on the Virts for him."

Jankarr opened his mouth, a protest on his lips, but Vlerion looked coolly at him.

Jankarr threw up his arms and trotted off.

Were they *partners*, as Jankarr had said, or was Vlerion his superior? Vlerion seemed the younger of the two, but Kaylina didn't know how quickly rangers could gain rank. Maybe it had more to do with deeds than years in service.

Vlerion veered toward a building with three herbs painted by the door, one of the kingdom's signs to indicate a doctor or herbalist, often someone who was both. Crenoch caught up with them before they reached it. He sniffed Kaylina's leg, fortunately from afar without bumping it, then looked at Vlerion.

"It's not my fault." Vlerion knocked on the door with the toe of his boot. "No, it *is* my fault."

Crenoch snorted, hot breath whispering across their faces.

"No, it's not," Kaylina said, bemused that the taybarri might understand, even though Vlerion had suggested the possibility. "He told me to hide, and I, instead, tried to brain people with my sling."

The door opened as she spoke, and a white-haired man with the scarred face and hands of a warrior raised his bushy eyebrows. "Sling's not a real powerful weapon for braining. Try a mace next time. Something with heft."

Kaylina thought of the heavy pots in the castle and wondered if the rangers had found whoever had killed that lord.

"Her rounds have decent heft," Vlerion muttered. "Need you to tend her, Doc."

"You and your posse?" The white eyebrows remained up as he looked past them.

Only then did Kaylina realize that not only had Crenoch followed them across the courtyard but three other taybarri had joined him. The large furred animals all gazed curiously at Kaylina. She didn't know whether to wish she'd brought honey with her or not. Vlerion hadn't approved of that, but she had a feeling Crenoch had conveyed to the rest of the herd that she was a honey dispensary.

"That's *her* posse. You know the taybarri don't flock to me." Only briefly did Vlerion's mouth flatten—was that bitterness?—before his usual mask returned.

"Well, you aren't the most charming, are you?" The doctor pointed a thumb toward several empty cots in the outer room.

"No." Vlerion carried Kaylina to the closest, laying her gently on it. When he stood, he didn't shake out his arms or give any indication that toting her around the city had been a strain. He pulled a stool over and sat on it.

That surprised her. Didn't he need to report to his captain?

"You've got wounds?" The doctor waved toward Vlerion's torn tunic as he collected towels, water, bandages, and a suture kit.

"No."

"No?"

"No."

"Your clothes wrestled with a windmill by themselves?"

"Something like that."

"You going to loiter around and watch?"

Vlerion opened his mouth to answer, but a thump against a window made him pause and look. Crenoch stood out there, his large nostrils steaming the glass.

"I guess we both are," Vlerion said.

"Nothing like an audience when you're mending wounds." The doctor opened a pouch and pulled out a pill made from something green, pulverized, and plastered together. Too large to swallow without chewing, it reminded Kaylina of the taybarri protein pellets. He offered it to her with relish, as if it were a delightful treat. "For the pain." Next, he pulled scissors out of a drawer in a table beside the cot. "I'll have to cut away your trouser leg."

"It was going to be hard to mend anyway," Kaylina murmured, settling her head on the thin pillow and looking at the beam-and-board ceiling.

She made herself chew the awful-tasting pill and swallow it while avoiding looking down. She would prefer not to watch the doctor suturing the bite wounds nor see how deep they were.

"The north is rough on clothing." The doctor glanced at Vlerion's rips but didn't comment further on windmills.

The door soon opened, with Captain Targon walking in, trailed by Jankarr.

"*Some* subordinates come to my office to report in when they arrive," Targon told Vlerion after glancing at Kaylina.

"They sound obsequious," Vlerion said.

"Proper and obedient, as rangers are supposed to be to their superiors."

Vlerion grunted.

As the doctor cut off Kaylina's trousers, leaving her bloody leg visible to all, Targon gave her—gave *it*—a longer look. Then he regarded Vlerion as if considering him and his seat beside her cot anew.

"How responsible are you for that?" he asked so quietly Kaylina almost didn't hear.

The doctor, now intent on washing the deep punctures, didn't glance at them.

"Responsible," Vlerion answered before looking at his captain and considering *him*.

Targon's expression had grown very serious, very grave.

"Not that kind of responsible," Vlerion said, as if that was clarification.

"Ah," Targon said.

Kaylina was missing something.

"She was in one of the pools in the catacombs," Vlerion said, "and a fur shark got her."

"How were you responsible for that?"

"She wouldn't have been down there if not for me."

"*You* were supposed to be on duty in the Warehouse District tonight," Targon said.

"But you wouldn't have learned about the new Virt movements if not for Vlerion going down there, right?" Jankarr, who'd stayed back and leaned near the door, raised his eyebrows. Before, he'd berated Vlerion for not taking him, but it seemed he would stand up for his partner to others.

Targon sighed, glanced at Kaylina, and walked to the far end of the room, gesturing for Vlerion to follow.

"Tell me," Targon said.

Vlerion delivered a report in a voice too low for Kaylina to hear. Too bad. She would have preferred to concentrate on their conversation—on *anything* to keep her mind off the doctor's probing, especially once he started suturing. Apparently, some of the punctures couldn't be stitched and would have to be cleaned and checked frequently for infection since they would take a long time to heal fully. The wider wounds did receive sutures, and Kaylina grimaced with each stab, fighting not to gasp or show weakness in front of the men. Even with the pill, the fiery pain hadn't dulled as much as she would have liked.

Jankarr came and sat on the stool Vlerion had vacated. He touched her shoulder. "Do you want a stick to bite on? Or something to squeeze? I'd offer Vlerion's balls, but he barely reacts when you hurt him, so it's not much fun."

"Are you supposed to hurt your partner?"

"Only in the sparring ring. And occasionally if he idiotically goes into trouble by himself." Though Jankarr hadn't raised his voice, maybe not wanting their captain to hear about that, Vlerion glanced over.

Kaylina almost pointed out that Vlerion *hadn't* been by himself, but it wasn't as if she'd been any help. If anything, she'd been an impediment. She might have stopped those two men from planting explosives, but it was possible Vlerion would have caught up with them on his own before they'd done anything anyway.

"You cracked some Virt heads with your sling?" Jankarr's eyes crinkled at the corners when he smiled, and he was even more handsome that way.

Kaylina caught herself smiling back, glad for the distraction from the doctor's ministrations. Even if she didn't appreciate that the rangers were all using her—at the least, *Targon* was, and the others were going along with it—it was nice of Jankarr to care enough to sit beside her.

"I worried they would hurt my brother," she said.

"You get them square on, the same way you cracked Vlerion?" His smile widened.

She could feel Vlerion's eyes upon them, even if he was reporting to his captain, so she downplayed that. "I usually hit what I aim at."

"Nice." Jankarr gave her an appreciative look. "That's not a typical skill up here. Where'd you learn? What prompted you to master it?"

Kaylina hardly considered herself a master of the sling, but it was nice to have someone give her a compliment. It had been so long. And her family so rarely thought she did anything right that her heart almost ached with appreciation. She caught herself blinking to keep moisture from forming in her eyes. How silly to react so.

"We serve a lot of poultry and fish at the Spitting Gull," Kaylina said. "All fresh. Grandpa's brother is the fisherman and runs the nets and boats, but Grandpa loves his hounds and hunting. I took to it too. Anything to get out of the never-ending chores of running an eating house. He taught me the sling when I was little, and we went out for all kinds of partridge, quail, and hoatzin on the marshy islands of our chain. I practiced a lot with my sling when I was, uhm, frustrated with things." How many hours had she spent, hiding out and targeting driftwood and buoys on the beach? An escape from older—and younger—siblings telling her what to do.

"You'd probably be good with a bow too. Once you've developed a marksman's aim, it translates to other weapons fairly well."

"I've never used one. I fired a crossbow at a pirate once."

"In the head?" The amusement returned to Jankarr's eyes.

"No. In the, uhm, lower area."

Grinning, Jankarr looked at Vlerion and Targon as they returned to the cot. "You'd better watch your head *and* your cock around her."

Heat flushed Kaylina's cheeks. This wasn't the distraction she'd wanted.

"Which head?" Targon smirked.

Vlerion sighed. "I should have taken her to one of the healers in town. She's heard enough male ribaldry for today."

When he met her eyes, Kaylina knew he was thinking of the comments they'd overheard from the alcove. It touched her that he'd been affronted on her behalf. Though it also chilled her that he'd killed the men. The memory of the head and the blunderbuss tumbling free of their owner flashed in her mind.

"Civilian healers aren't as practiced as I am," the doctor grumbled, "and my old lady smacks me if I get ribald around women."

"She smack you if you call her an old lady when she can hear it?" Jankarr asked.

"Mostly throws things at me."

"Your relationship is something to envy."

"Got forty years together this summer."

A thump at the door drew glances. Crenoch remained at the window, the panes so fogged Kaylina could barely make out his blue furry face. Targon went to the door and opened it, revealing another taybarri outside. Its eyes swung toward Kaylina.

"What is this about?" Targon looked to Vlerion.

"She gave Crenoch honey."

"And thus he's sworn his eternal devotion to her? And that of the herd?"

Warmth crept into Kaylina's cheeks again, though she refused to admit she'd done anything wrong. She didn't know why the animals were so interested in her.

"Apparently," Vlerion said.

"That can't be all that's going on," Targon said. "If honey was all it took to earn the loyalty of a taybarri, our enemies would have plied them with stolen beehives centuries ago and made off with the whole herd."

"Hukk gives his taybarri sugar cubes and apples and doesn't get such interest," Jankarr said.

"My family's honey is really good," Kaylina offered. "The bees forage on islands with a lot of altered wildflowers. It's why our mead is so good too. It'll be a number of days before some is ready to try, but you're welcome to come by for a tasting of the first batch."

"I'd love to." Jankarr smiled at her again.

Vlerion's eyes narrowed slightly. "The rangers are to avoid the castle so the Virts don't believe us associated with it."

"Which is naturally why you were there all evening," Jankarr said.

"I was in the catacombs, not the inn."

"Enough." Targon raised his hand, then gave Kaylina a long assessing look. It was reminiscent of the calculating look he'd had for her the night of the jailbreak, and it reminded her that he'd given orders forbidding ship captains from taking her and Frayvar onboard. "I'd like to see your sling work when your leg has healed enough for you to give us a demonstration."

"All right," Kaylina said, though she didn't want to perform for him. She was positive he was thinking of another way he could use her.

"You planning to recruit her, Captain?" Jankarr sounded like he approved of the idea. "It's been a while since we had any new female rangers."

Kaylina shook her head. The idea wouldn't have been appealing even if she hadn't had her own dream she was pursuing. Besides, the rangers didn't accept commoners, did they?

"We'll see." Targon waved at Vlerion. "Change clothes, take her back to her castle, and then I want you in the Warehouse District. I'll send men down to grab the munitions in the catacombs and do a thorough search. I'm glad you stumbled on that, even if you didn't have orders to check that area, but we have to assume there are more stashes around the city. They're getting ready for something big."

"They are," Vlerion said.

"We don't need any distractions." Targon waved at Kaylina, as if he hadn't *just* been plotting some way to use her, then at Vlerion's ripped clothes. What was that supposed to imply?

"She is not a distraction," Vlerion stated coolly.

Targon held his gaze for a long moment before saying, "She'd better not be," and walking out.

16

W E EASILY ACCEPT TRUTHS THAT MAKE SENSE, BUT THE UNIVERSE IS FULL of nonsensical realities.
~ Lord Professor Varhesson, Port Jirador University

It was late at night by the time Vlerion accompanied Kaylina back to the castle in a horse-drawn carriage, the painting on the side claiming it belonged to the Ice Creek Taxi Service rather than having anything to do with the rangers. She would have preferred to ride on Crenoch, especially since he and three other taybarri had followed her to the gate, as if they intended to go along. But Targon had commanded the animals to return to their stable, reminding them that the rangers—and their mounts—were not to visit Stillguard Castle.

Too bad. The carriage offered a bumpy ride that jostled Kaylina's bandaged leg as it rattled through the cobblestone streets.

Since Vlerion watched her from the bench seat opposite, she did her best to keep the pain off her face. He spoke little on the ride, and she resisted the temptation to ask him how the fur shark had died.

In her heart, she knew, but her mind had never heard of a man turning into a beast, and she struggled to believe that was possible. How could such a thing happen? It sounded like something out of a fairy tale. A very grim fairy tale.

"Am I in danger from your captain?" Kaylina asked instead, wondering if Vlerion would tell her.

His loyalty was to Targon—after all, Vlerion didn't even like her—but that first night, he'd admitted his captain had arranged things so she and Frayvar couldn't leave. Maybe it had been more a *warning* than an admission, so she wouldn't do something foolish, but Vlerion needn't have said anything.

"He is intensely loyal to the kingdom and its subjects. He'll do anything to protect them."

"Even if it means sacrificing an innocent person along the way?"

"If he deems it for the greater good, yes. He's made that choice many times." Vlerion touched his chest. To indicate himself? Or maybe the rangers? How many comrades had he seen fall over the years?

"If he remembers to call me back for a sling demonstration, should I deliberately miss the targets?"

"Would your pride allow that?"

"Maybe. To save my ass." Kaylina hesitated, not certain that was true. "To save my brother's ass, I definitely would."

"Targon doesn't have much interest in him."

"Lucky boy."

The horses pulling the carriage stopped, the driver keeping them across the street from the castle. The familiar red glow shone from the tower window.

Arriving didn't feel like coming home, but weariness and pain made her long for a horizontal position. Anywhere would do.

Kaylina grabbed the crutch the doctor had lent her. It was bigger and more unwieldy than the cane she'd imagined.

"I recommend doing your best to make him forget you," Vlerion said quietly as he opened the carriage door.

He hopped down and lifted his hands toward her. Though she hated needing help, the ache from her leg kept her from doing something dumb like swatting his arm away and jumping out. Instead, she didn't object when he gripped her waist and gently lifted her down.

As they stood close, his hands lingered, and the memory of slumping against him in the alcove came to mind. Of rubbing his shoulders and leaning into his chest, of him stroking her hair and kneading the taut muscles in her neck. Since he didn't release her and step back, she wondered if he might be thinking about that too.

"Wrap your honey so that it's difficult to smell, and keep it someplace safe," he said.

Kaylina blinked. "What?"

"So Crenoch and the other taybarri aren't drawn here."

That was what he was thinking about while tenderly holding her?

Exasperated, Kaylina stepped back, jamming the crutch down for support. "You tell me to avoid your captain's notice but also want to make sure whatever he's planning for me doesn't get messed up. Is that it?"

"The taybarri must be bonded to their riders and not have their attention—or loyalties—split between multiple people."

Craters of the moon, maybe Vlerion's words had nothing to do with his captain. Maybe he was irritated because his faithful mount wasn't as devoted to him as the men he worked with were. Too bad.

"If you want him bonded to you, maybe *you* should give him

honey from time to time. Do you want me to get you some of ours?"

"No." Vlerion stepped back. "It is not appropriate for a taybarri."

"You can't tell me they wouldn't suck down a beehive whole if they found one in nature."

"I am the one who must tend to his teeth if any need pulling."

"Oh gods. However would the valiant rangers ride into battle to slay their enemies if their taybarri had cavities?"

Vlerion took a breath. When he said, "You are an exasperating female," he sounded calm, not exasperated.

"And you're an ass."

"My lord," he said tightly.

"*Pirate.*" Kaylina would have stomped into the courtyard if she hadn't needed the crutch. She was the one exasperated as she struggled to make the dramatic exit her last word called for. Worse, she tripped as she crossed through the gatehouse, the uneven ground needing repairs. *Everything* about the damn place needed repairs. This entire adventure was exhausting, and if not for Vlerion watching, she would have cursed at the fates that had brought her to the doorstep of the castle.

But she clamped her jaw shut and made it awkwardly across the courtyard. Only when she reached the doors did she notice someone sitting against the wall under the overhang. She let out a startled squawk.

"What is it?" Vlerion drew his sword and stepped through the gatehouse.

"Just me." Frayvar threw his hands up.

"We're fine," Kaylina made herself say, though she was annoyed Frayvar had seen her arguing with Vlerion. Why was he loitering outside? "Go home, taxi service."

She doubted anyone was spying on them but, to please the

pompous Lord Vlerion, she wouldn't go out of her way to screw up the ranger captain's ruse.

"Very well." Vlerion sheathed his sword and climbed into the carriage.

Even though she'd spent far too much of the day with him, a pang of loneliness struck her at his departure. The castle felt safe when he was around. Everywhere did. She didn't understand it, but she knew he'd been the one to save her life in the catacombs.

"Nothing attacked you, did it?" she asked Frayvar.

"No, but the castle was being eerie, and that's harder to stomach when you're alone." He pointed at her crutch. "I didn't realize you'd been hurt that badly. Did something attack *you*? Or did you fall and break your leg?"

"I both fell *and* was attacked. No broken bones though. Hopefully, bites don't take long to heal." As appealing as having an excuse to curl up in bed with her books was, there was so much left to do before they could open their new establishment that she didn't like the idea of struggling to get around. It would be easy to feel sorry for herself and succumb to one of her *funks*, as Frayvar called them, but she couldn't. They didn't have a fallback plan. There was no one here to take care of them if they ran out of money and failed. And going home probably still wasn't an option.

"Attacked by what?"

"Have you heard of fur sharks?"

"Certainly. I've got books on marine life of the North Dakmoor Sea and the fresh waters of the kingdom and beyond. I did a report on furred water creatures in school."

"Of course you did. You probably wouldn't have been foolish enough to jump into an underground pool where such things live."

"No," he agreed. "Why did you?"

"I fell more than I jumped in. I was being chased by men who were going to..." Kaylina stopped, not wanting him to have reason to be even more concerned about the castle. "Well, they're rebels, and they're setting up for a plan that involves a lot of explosives. And I mean a *lot*."

"You didn't use your sling on one of them, did you?"

"On one? No."

"On two?" he asked.

"It's like you know me."

"We've been siblings my entire life."

"Huh."

"Keep in mind that we're not vigilantes or crime fighters," Frayvar said. "Leave that to the rangers. I put together a menu for our debut dinner and made a list of ingredients. Are you... still going to be able to carry my groceries?"

"Lopsidedly, probably, but yes. The ranger doctor gave me painkillers that taste like dehydrated horse droppings."

"If that's true, Grandpa's hounds would love them."

"Probably so." Though it was cold outside, the castle was rarely much warmer, and she noticed he had a blanket. She sank down beside him, sticking her leg straight out and leaning against the stone wall. "I'm feeling overwhelmed," she admitted.

In front of Vlerion and the other rangers, Kaylina had striven to appear strong, but she didn't feel as compelled to put up a facade for her brother.

"I've heard shark bites will leave one feeling daunted. And perforated." Frayvar shared half the blanket with her.

"I meant about our project here."

"I checked the mead earlier. It's doing fine. The first batch will be ready in time for me to make mead vinegar for my lamb recipe."

"The one with fennel and figs?"

"Yup."

"That sounds amazing." Kaylina's stomach rumbled. When was the last time she'd eaten? It had been a long day.

"Because it *is* amazing. Especially when I make it."

"Your self-confidence in your abilities is admirable."

"It's a hallmark of a good chef. When Silana made the recipe, I don't know *what* she did, but it was drier than a desert."

"Do you think we can pull this off, Fray?" Kaylina pulled her half of the blanket up to her chin while watching someone bundled on horseback clopping up the street. Despite everyone's aversion to the castle, it was in a busy part of the city. If they could lure people in—and keep them from being slain by a curse —it had potential to be a good spot for an eating house and meadery.

"Of course."

"Even though you're so afraid of our establishment that you were going to sleep outside in the middle of winter under the murder holes?" Kaylina looked up. "Or are those the... what'd you call them? Macho-things."

"Machicolations, yes. And I wasn't afraid. I was *wary*. Also, it's spring."

"Do the mounds of snow piled along the streets know that?"

"One of the locals said it can snow even in the summer here. But that bush over there is budding out. And we'll be successful. Don't worry. The curse will make people curious to come."

"The curse and the skeletons in the bedrooms."

"Well, we might want to remove those eventually."

Kaylina had been afraid to touch them. Nothing Vlerion had told her of the history of the place had changed that. If anything, she was *more* afraid to touch them now.

"Or people can sleep in the courtyard," Frayvar offered. "Ten liviti for a blanket in this prime location."

"Our customers will line up to take advantage of that deal."

He nudged her with an elbow. "The good food and our amazing mead will make them line up. They'll love it, and they'll put up with the quirks. Just like they do back home."

"The quirks back home are seagulls pooping on the railings and the tacky wind chimes made from seashells."

"Come on. We get *hurricanes*. Not to mention that pirates raid Vamorka at least quarterly. Remember when we fought them off with crossbows and blunderbusses while the mayor and his wife were dining?"

"That is true." Kaylina scratched her jaw. "Despite what these northerners and their beast-filled mountains—and catacombs— think, the south isn't all sunshine and sandy beaches. Coming to the Spitting Gull *can* be dangerous, and people brave it anyway for the very recipes we're going to make."

"Yes, they do."

"You've actually made me feel better, Fray."

"Are you sure it was me and not the nasty pills?"

"Pretty sure. I— Are you expecting someone?" The person Kaylina had noticed on horseback hadn't continued past like everyone else on the street.

The rider was a cloaked woman with a lean face and thick gray hair clasped on either side above her ears. She slid off her horse and walked through the gate with a lantern at her side.

"No," Frayvar said. "Other than the Saybrook wagon that came of its own accord, I haven't even been able to get supplies delivered. People don't want to come through the gate. The worker who brought silverware chucked the pieces at the doors like darts."

Though Kaylina's leg protested, she pushed herself to her feet and grabbed the unwieldy crutch she was already starting to loathe.

"Good evening," the woman said, lifting a hand. "You needn't get up on my account. I'm Jana Bloomlong. I've heard about what you're doing and wanted to introduce myself."

"What we're doing?" Kaylina tamped down panic that threatened to bubble up. Had this woman seen her with Vlerion and recognized him? Was she a spy for the Virts?

"Starting a meadery, right?" Jana hung the lantern on a broken post, part of a railing that needed to be repaired, and alternated gazing at Kaylina and Frayvar and up at the castle.

"Yes. I hadn't realized word was getting out." Kaylina looked at Frayvar, but he only shrugged.

"Someone moving into the old ranger inn is big news. You know it's cursed, right?" Jana's gaze shifted toward the tower, but the red glow wasn't visible from their position.

"We've heard that," Frayvar said dryly.

"Mead isn't as popular as ale in Port Jirador, but it does decently well, especially in the summer if you can serve it chilled."

"I can't imagine serving chilled drinks is hard here at any time of year." Kaylina already regretted that she'd left the blanket's warmth.

"Ice men come down from the mountains in the summer with wagons filled with blocks carved from the glaciers. You can have them deliver directly to your place for a fee, or there are ice houses in town where you can buy it by the pound. It *can* get warm here in the summer. Quite pleasant, really. You'll want to put in an outdoor dining area." Jana pursed her lips as she considered the castle and the courtyard. "You might want to have customers dine outdoors year around. With a few fire pits to warm the patios, people will do it. We don't mind bundling up to eat and drink around here."

"I'd had that thought," Kaylina said.

To keep inimical vines from strangling customers inside the castle.

"You're doing food too?" Jana asked.

"That's the plan," Kaylina said. "Are you in the business?"

"I'm your competition." Jana winked and offered a friendly smile, but a hint of calculation in her eyes reminded Kaylina of Captain Targon, and she had a feeling this wasn't a social visit. "My husband and I run Nakeron Inn about a mile that way." She

LINDSAY BUROKER

pointed south toward the Factory Quarter. "We get a lot of laborers on their way home from work. You might not think it from this run-down castle, but you're in a nice part of town. You're more likely to get merchants or maybe even aristocrats." Jana's eyebrows rose.

Wondering if that was the audience they *wanted* to serve? If Jana was friendly to workers, she probably stood on the side of the Virts and was inclined to dislike the nobles.

Kaylina thought of her dream to have the king and queen visit and enjoy her award-winning mead. "Well, we certainly won't try to entice rangers to visit. From what we've gathered about the curse, the castle doesn't like them much."

Jana snorted. "That castle doesn't like *anyone* much. My husband and I were debating if you're terribly brave for choosing it or young and naive."

It made Kaylina uneasy to think of others talking about them.

"The latter, I suspect?" She looked at her brother.

"Oh, absolutely," he agreed.

That earned another snort. "At least you're not in denial. I'll wish you luck, and maybe we'll stop by on your opening night." Jana grabbed her lantern. "Where did you say you source your honey from?"

Wariness stampeded into Kaylina. "We didn't say."

"No? I can give you the name of my supplier if you like. There aren't many meaderies in this part of the kingdom. We'll have to look out for each other." Jana smiled, but, again, Kaylina didn't think it was sincere.

"Of course," she said politely.

"Will you be using your grandmother's recipes?"

More than the icy air chilled Kaylina. "You know about our family?"

"Everyone in the industry has heard about, if not tasted, the award-winning meads from the Spitting Gull. It's hard to get them way up here, as I'm sure you know, so I look forward to trying them for myself."

"We'll be happy to share samples. Free of charge, of course."

"Wonderful. I'll bring by some of ours, and we can compare." Jana lifted a hand and headed for the gate.

"How many people have you told about Grandma and who we are?" Kaylina whispered to her brother.

"Not many," he whispered back.

"*Any?*"

"Not that I recall. It wouldn't have occurred to me that anyone here would have heard of the Gull or give us special treatment for our association with it, so I didn't think to share." Frayvar pointed at her. "You told the ranger captain everything when they drugged you."

"Yeah, but would he have gossiped our life stories around town? He wants to use us, right? We're his secret whatever."

"Maybe he thought we would be more likely to get visitors if people knew we'd be using Grandma's recipes. He wants us to succeed so customers will come hang out and blab for his spies, right?"

"I don't know exactly *what* he wants, but I—"

Squeaks came from one of the tower windows, and a pair of bats flew out.

Since Kaylina had seen them coming and going before, she hadn't thought much of their presence—it wasn't as if she could find stairs up into those towers to clean out the rooms they'd claimed—but seeing them depart after being close enough to listen to the conversation...

"You know those stories about herbalists and alchemists having animal familiars and using them to spy on people?" she asked.

"Those are just fairy tales. We've already discussed that magic doesn't work that way."

"Are you sure? We've got a curse in our castle and killer beasts in the catacombs. There may be more magic in the world than your books know about."

"My books know about a lot. I've read thousands of years of history."

"Well, *someone* is keeping an eye on us."

Frayvar shrugged. "There were other people in those jail cells, remember. Some of the Virts might have heard your responses during the questioning. You weren't being quiet."

"I suppose that's possible. We'll have to be extra careful though. A lot more people than I expected are interested in us, and we don't have any allies here."

"The rangers want us alive."

"For now. If they come to believe we're not on their side, that might change."

"I don't want to be on a side, Kay. I just want to make good food and not have to slink back home, feeling like a failure because we couldn't start a business. *Or* because you died."

"I don't want you to have to slink back home after my death either. Trust me."

17

THE PLEASURE FOUND IN ONE'S CUPS IS MORE A BOON FOR THE MIND
than the body.
   ~ Dainbridge III, the playwright

"This will be our outdoor dining area." The lack of a breeze almost
made the sun bathing Kaylina's face feel warm. *Almost.*

She and Frayvar sat at a table in the courtyard behind the
kitchen, with goblets holding samples from their first batches of
mead and bowls of an apple-cider beef stew he'd made. It was one
of the recipes he was trialing for their soft opening. He'd even
baked bread, and they'd gotten fresh butter from the market, so
Kaylina was chomping with pleasure, feeling optimistic for the
first time in days. She was deliberately not thinking about the
body that had been sprawled a few feet away the first time she'd
seen this place.

"Out back? By the kitchen?" Frayvar sipped the apple mead, a
classic cyser that complemented the stew. He'd always loved
recipes that incorporated fruit.

"It's protected from the prevailing wind, has a view of the river, and those trees will be pretty once they leaf out." Kaylina sipped the semi-sweet mead that was one of her favorites, pleased it tasted like Grandma's. She had assumed it would, since she'd followed the recipe precisely, but Grandma had never had to make mead in an environment like this. Who knew what weird flavors a curse could impart?

Earlier, Kaylina had been tempted to take a walk along the river, to see more of the town and mention their upcoming opening to anyone out, but her crutch still leaned nearby. She could move around without it, but the punctures ached if she used the leg too much. The morning before, the doctor had arrived in a taxi-service carriage, wearing clothing that didn't hint of a ranger affiliation. He'd checked on her wounds and given her a fresh bandage.

"I suppose," Frayvar said, "but if we put tables on the side near the street, passersby will see through the gate that we have customers, and they'll be enticed to stop in."

"They'll be able to see if we *don't* have customers too."

Frayvar frowned at her. "This morning, you promised you would be optimistic today."

"Sorry." Kaylina grimaced at the reminder that she'd struggled to get out of bed the last few mornings, with feelings of desolation, regret, and defeat weighing on her more heavily than the blankets. The past week's gray sky and another round of snow hadn't helped. This was the first day that had dawned clear and bright since they'd arrived in Port Jirador. "I will be. And I am. The sun feels good and is making me think my dream might be attainable. All morning, I've been envisioning our tables filled with people enjoying our food and mead. I also appreciate that no rangers, aside from their conscientious doctor, have come by to pester us since the night I was injured."

"Do you?" Frayvar arched his eyebrows. "You've mentioned Lord Vlerion a lot."

"Only to curse him for being pompous, I'm sure."

Had she brought him up often? She'd thought of him from time to time, but life was simpler when he wasn't around. When none of the rangers were. Left undisturbed, Kaylina and Frayvar had made progress cleaning, and a crew from Saybrook Industries had come to repair broken wood and missing stones, so their eating house could open soon. They'd agreed not to worry about the inn part for now, largely because of the curse and the skeleton-filled rooms upstairs. Someday, they would have to clean those out and figure out the glowing tower, but Kaylina first wanted to see if they could host an opening night without anyone being murdered by the castle.

"You've mentioned his muscles three times," Frayvar said.

"Are you keeping track?"

"I do like to collect and collate data."

"If I've brought up his muscles, it was only to say that it would have been useful to have someone strong to help us move furniture." Kaylina blushed as she remembered the alcove and being pressed against Vlerion for those long minutes while he stroked her hair. She didn't *like* him, so she didn't know why that memory kept popping up. It wasn't as if she wanted a relationship with a haughty ranger.

"Hm." Frayvar pushed a notepad toward her, columns of numbers taking up the top page. "I've put together our expenses for the last week, what a realistic budget would be, how much we need to gross to break even, and how many customers a day and the average ticket cost we'll need to see to achieve that."

"That's good." Kaylina sipped from her goblet while eyeing a spruce tree near the river. It wasn't one of the handful of evergreens that grew on the islands down south, but she'd once seen a recipe for a mead flavored with spruce tips and admitted curiosity.

When they had their flagship recipes perfected, she would experiment with some of the local ingredients.

Something moved behind the tree, startling her.

"We got our lease for less than I expected, not to mention all the free equipment and supplies, so we're under budget. I didn't anticipate that. Even so, my funds will only go so far. We need to start bringing in an income soon."

"Naturally." Kaylina leaned back so she could see... Was that blue fur?

"What do you think about printing up posters and distributing them in the markets? Maybe we can give away free samples on the first day."

"Good idea. We'll have to do some marketing in the beginning, until the magnificence of our food and word of mouth combine to make us a raving success."

A taybarri padded out from behind the tree and looked at her. Was that Crenoch?

"I take it back," Frayvar said. "You *are* in an optimistic mood today."

"You did request that."

"I guess so, but don't forget to be realistic. You've heard Grandma's stories about how it took five years for the eating house to turn a profit and *ten* before they started getting recognition and awards."

"It didn't help that pirates lit the Gull on fire twice during that time, and thieves robbed it every other winter."

Yes, that *was* Crenoch. He walked toward the open gate to the courtyard, his tail swishing and his nostrils twitching.

"Oh, we'll have our hardships too," Frayvar said. "I have no doubt."

Though Kaylina liked the taybarri, she set her goblet down and hurried to the gate, intending to close it. She would have loved to stroke that lush blue fur, but she didn't want the rangers irked with her. Nor did she want the castle to start thinking she was allied with them.

"Sorry, Crenoch." She gripped the rusty gate. "We can't serve furry people. Besides, I have a feeling someone is looking for you."

And that *someone* would be torqued with her if he found his mount in her courtyard again.

As Kaylina swung the gate shut, Crenoch sprang and *blurred*. That was the only word she had for it. He blurred and disappeared, appearing an instant later in the courtyard, right next to the goblet-laden table.

Frayvar cried out in surprise and fell off the bench.

For a moment, Kaylina could only grip the half-closed gate and stare. She had, of course, heard the stories of the taybarri's inherent power to do exactly what she'd witnessed—it was one of the reasons the rangers loved riding them into battle—but she'd never seen it before.

With Crenoch looming, Frayvar half-scrambled and half-rolled away, raising an arm defensively in case the taybarri attacked. But the only things Crenoch attacked were the goblets. And he did so far more gently than Kaylina would have expected. The tip of his large tongue dipped into them, and his tail swished happily across the pavers as he lapped up mead.

"Uhm." Kaylina hurried to help her brother up while debating if she had the power to stop the sampling. She had no idea how much Crenoch weighed, but taybarri were bigger—especially *longer*—than horses, and she had seen them carry up to four grown men. "I don't think animals are supposed to have alcohol, my friend."

She looked at her brother for confirmation.

"Are you asking me about taybarri dietary preferences?" Frayvar brushed dirt off his clothes.

"More about what might *kill* them. Like Grandpa's hounds can't have cacao. Is alcohol poisonous to taybarri?" Kaylina glanced through the gate, hoping to spot a ranger or someone else who could pull the big animal away.

"I don't know."

"None of the zillion books you've read covered that?"

"Sorry."

Crenoch hadn't finished the first goblet—his tongue was wide enough that he couldn't get it all the way in—but he moved on to another like a patron at a tasting. Contented noises that sounded like a mix between a cat purring and a chicken clucking came from deep in his throat.

Kaylina stepped forward and touched his neck. "That's probably enough, buddy. I don't know if that's good for you."

Crenoch paused long enough to wash her face with his tongue before returning it to the mead.

"I'm glad you like it though." She wiped the moisture away and plucked up the rest of the goblets.

"Maybe we can put that on the labels when we bottle some for selling," Frayvar said. "Approved by taybarri everywhere. People like taybarri, you know."

"Maybe so, but they don't want to eat what they eat." Kaylina hurried into the kitchen to put the goblets somewhere Crenoch couldn't reach. She well remembered that enough of his head and neck could fit through the doorway that he could grab things off the closest counters.

"Uhm, Kay?" A worried note filled Frayvar's voice.

Afraid irate rangers had come to pummel them for giving one of their mounts alcohol, Kaylina grabbed her sling and hurried back outside.

Crenoch had backed from the table, the remaining goblet tipped over with the mead spilled out. His great body swayed, his steps unsteady.

Kaylina swore, terror tightening her throat. Was he dying? Was the mead poison to him, as she'd feared?

She rushed forward, reaching toward the taybarri, but she had no idea what she could do. "Get some water, Fray."

The thundering of heavy paws on the ground came from the river path, and three more taybarri galloped into view.

"No, no," Kaylina called. "Don't come in."

Only after she spoke did she realize that these taybarri had riders, Vlerion behind Jankarr on one, and two rangers in black that she didn't recognize on the others.

"Rangers *come* where they wish," Vlerion said coolly, but he only looked at her for a second before the swaying Crenoch captured his attention.

His taybarri pitched onto his side, landing with a thud, his tail stretched out behind him.

"Crenoch!" Vlerion cried in alarm as he sprang from Jankarr's mount and ran into the courtyard. "What did you *do*?" he demanded, skewering Kaylina with an icy gaze as he dropped to his knees beside the taybarri.

Something surged in his eyes, that dangerous glint she'd seen before. No, it was *more* than a glint. She remembered the beast that had torn the fur shark to pieces and smashed in its head. A wildness in Vlerion's eyes promised that he could tear *her* to pieces.

Fear made Kaylina stumble back and raise her hands. "It was an accident. He showed up and drank the mead. I put the other goblets away and tried to stop him. I..."

She trailed off because Vlerion had closed his eyes and didn't seem to be listening to her. His face tilted toward Crenoch, and he was humming. It was soft, and she doubted the other rangers heard. They were slowly dismounting and walking in, their hands on their weapons. It was the same tune she'd heard Vlerion hum in the catacombs.

Since he wasn't listening to her, Kaylina addressed Jankarr. "I swear I didn't mean for him to get any of the mead. He showed up, and he even flashed through the gate. That's what it's called, right? Flashing? He's so big that I didn't know what to do, and I wasn't sure he would let me take the mead away. He has all those fangs." She could hear herself burbling, the panic in her voice. Not only did she fear what Vlerion might do to her, but she was horrified that she might, however inadvertently, be responsible for Crenoch's death.

"He okay, Vlerion?" Jankarr asked, only twitching his fingers toward Kaylina to acknowledge her words. "I can see him breathing."

"He still lives." Vlerion stopped humming and opened his eyes. His hand rested on Crenoch's side. "For now. I don't know if he is *okay*."

His tone was calmer than Kaylina had expected. Though he didn't look at her, he had found his equanimity.

"Bradnoray has given his taybarri ale before," one of the rangers volunteered. "It made him fall asleep."

"I shall hope the results of this... *mishap* are as benign." Finally, Vlerion looked at Kaylina again. The wild glint was gone, and his face was masked.

"I'm sorry," she said, "but I didn't invite him in. I—" One of the other taybarri padded between her and Vlerion and sniffed at the spilled mead.

"Get back, Zavron," Jankarr barked, lunging for the taybarri.

But the great tongue came out, and the creature didn't budge.

"Wipe that mess up!" one of the other rangers barked as his taybarri also trotted for the table.

"That's what they're doing," Frayvar muttered, but he ran inside for a towel.

Not wanting all the taybarri unconscious in her courtyard, Kaylina ran to the table and yanked out the hem of her shirt. She leaned in and attempted to wipe up the remaining spill without having her belly washed by a taybarri tongue, but the creatures had already slurped up the liquid, and she got only saliva and a splinter in her shirt.

The ranger who'd given the order lifted a hand as he glowered at Kaylina. Vlerion appeared at his side and caught his wrist as another of the taybarri stepped between her and the rangers.

"I wasn't going to hit her," the man muttered. "I was worried about Rugger."

A great moist snore came from Crenoch. Others followed, the taybarri's breathing deep and regular as he snoozed loudly.

"One wonders," Vlerion murmured, "if the Kar'ruk would have as much respect for us and our fearsome mounts if they saw scenes such as this."

The taybarri that had stepped protectively in front of Kaylina swished its tail and leaned on her. The creature was so heavy that she staggered back, her leg twinging as she put unexpected weight on it. She caught herself on the table. The unapologetic creature licked her, forcing her to again use her shirt to wipe up saliva, this time from her face.

"How long is yours going to sleep?" Jankarr glanced at Kaylina's bared midsection before looking at Vlerion. "The captain said to grab him and be back for weapons practice. That starts in ten minutes."

"You're welcome to carry Crenoch if you're concerned about punctuality," Vlerion said.

"*I'm* not Targon's favorite. I have to be."

"He likes you fine. You're a scrappy commoner who's overcome his modest upbringing to excel among the rangers and loyally serve the crown. He'd sleep with you if you had a bigger chest."

"Thanks for putting that terrifying imagery in my mind," Jankarr said.

Vlerion stepped around Kaylina's taybarri visitor as she was moving her foot to keep from being stepped on. He eyed her,

Crenoch, and her again, his expression dyspeptic. At least it wasn't scary, the way it had been before.

"They are drawn to you," Vlerion stated.

"They're drawn to my *honey*."

"They are also drawn to you. This is problematic." His lips flattened.

"I don't disagree." Kaylina moved her foot again. This taybarri hadn't gotten any mead, but it had also started purr-clucking. "But it's not like it's my fault."

Only when Vlerion's gaze shifted along her arm did she realized she'd started petting the creature. She yanked her hand back, but that wasn't her fault either. It was self-defense to keep from being knocked over. Had she been sitting, the huge taybarri would have been in her lap.

A moan came from the rooftop. There wasn't any wind.

Kaylina shifted, reminded that the castle didn't like rangers. And she had a courtyard full of them.

Vlerion opened his mouth, but a newcomer spoke from the gate.

"Would someone like to tell me how in all the altered orchards this is keeping the city from noticing a link between rangers and this new meadery?" That sounded like Captain Targon.

The rangers straightened to stand at attention as they faced their boss. Only Vlerion answered.

"The taybarri are drawn to Korbian."

"Tell me something that isn't blatantly obvious." Targon stepped up to Vlerion's side. "Is yours *asleep*?"

"Crenoch imbibed alcohol," Vlerion said.

Targon gave Kaylina an exasperated look, as if he knew without a doubt that *she* was to blame. Just because she'd poured the goblets and sat down outside with her brother to sample them and write descriptions for the tasting menu...

"We have to do something about her," Targon said.

A chill went down Kaylina's spine. What did *that* mean? That they would send her home? That they would *kill* her?

"What?" The wariness in Vlerion's tone suggested Kaylina had reason to be concerned about Targon's attention. *Had* the ranger captain made people who were no longer useful to him disappear before? How ruthless was he?

Targon eyed the taybarri shifting closer to Kaylina, wanting her to return to petting it. She kept her arms down. It moved its head to rest its broad jaw on her shoulder.

"You're not helping," she whispered.

It *whuffed* in her ear.

"I think she's an *anrokk*," Targon said.

A what?

"Likely," Vlerion said.

Kaylina looked for her brother, memorizer of encyclopedias, but he lingered in the doorway several yards away, a towel in his hand.

"As long as she's *here*—" Targon pointed at the ground, "—they're going to be drawn by whatever allure she's exuding."

"Just the allure of honey," Kaylina said.

"It's more than that." Vlerion looked at Targon. "Will you send them back south?"

"Oh no. *Anrokk* don't come along that often. Jastadar is the only one we have right now, and he'll retire soon, something that very few rangers get to do."

"Not many live long enough to," Vlerion said.

"Exactly. But if the entire taybarri herd is looking out for you in battle, your odds go up."

A couple of the rangers gave Kaylina dark looks that she couldn't interpret. Once they'd realized their taybarri were only at risk of naps and not death, they'd stopped glaring at her about *poisoning* them. So, what fresh irritation was gnawing at their insides now?

"Must be nice," Vlerion said softly. Wistfully.

Ah, was that it? They all wanted to be *anrokk*, whatever that was.

Targon snorted at Vlerion. "The herd would probably trample you if you fell."

"I'm aware," Vlerion said, that wistfulness lingering in his eyes as he looked from the snoring taybarri to Kaylina.

"Report to ranger headquarters at dawn, Korbian," Targon told her.

"Ah, why?"

His eyes narrowed. "Why, *my lord*. Do they not teach children in the southern province proper etiquette when addressing nobles?"

"At least she hasn't called you a pirate," Vlerion said.

That earned *him* an exasperated look from his captain. Good. Kaylina didn't know what was going on but didn't feel she should take the brunt of everyone's ire.

"Why, my lord—" Kaylina worked hard to keep her irreverence out of her tone, "—do you want me to come to your headquarters again? My injury is getting better—thanks for asking—but I don't think I'm ready to demonstrate my marksmanship abilities."

"My men will make sure you're ready for that and more. You're to train to become a ranger."

"*What?*" That wasn't what she'd come north for. They couldn't *conscript* her, could they? Women didn't even become rangers, did they? She hadn't seen any when she visited the headquarters. "You can't just— I have a dream. *This.*" She pointed to the castle and to the table where the mead had spilled. "You can't walk in and give me a new career."

A career where people didn't live to see retirement. She didn't know how to fight, and all rangers *did* was fight.

Vlerion didn't appear surprised by his captain's words.

"You're a kingdom subject, aren't you?" Targon asked.

"Yes, but—"

"Then you will do what your people need."

"The meadery—"

"Can be run by your brother. He's the brains, isn't he?" Targon pointed toward the notebook full of numbers still open at the end of the table, as if he was certain Frayvar had done that. Why did so many people know so much about them and their business?

"It's *my* dream." Kaylina crossed her arms over her chest.

"Now, you can have another dream."

"Captain," Vlerion said. "You can't force people to join the rangers."

"Watch me."

"If you want the meadery to be taybarri free, then move her and her projects into ranger headquarters. But there's no reason to—"

"There are *many* reasons to train and use an *anrokk*. Do not question me, Vlerion, or I'll flog you myself. No, I'll do one better than that." Targon looked at Kaylina, calculation entering his eyes, before pinning Vlerion with his stare. "*You'll* handle her training."

For a stunned moment, Vlerion didn't speak. When he did, it was only after he'd frowned over at Crenoch, who'd woken from his nap and lifted his head to gaze at Kaylina.

"I am not interested in that duty," Vlerion said stiffly.

"Too bad. While you're teaching her to fight, knock some respect into her. She won't make it long in the north if she can't learn to say *yes, my lord*." Targon waved at the taybarri and the rangers. "Everyone back to headquarters."

Targon stalked out, leading the way.

Vlerion, after helping Crenoch to rise, looked darkly over his shoulder at Kaylina as he walked out.

He might have tried to help her, but he did *not* want this duty.

"Do you know what *anrokk* means?" Kaylina asked after the rangers had cleared out and only she and Frayvar remained in the courtyard.

"It's an ancient Daygarii druid word. It's someone who has an affinity for animals. For their kind, it meant a magical link. Since humans aren't magical in any way that science has ever been able to prove, when we use the word to describe people, it means animals are drawn to them, usually for reasons known only to the animals."

"That's silly. The taybarri like honey and know we have it. That's it."

"None of them have licked *me*." Did he sound *envious*?

She would gladly give him this *affinity*. Then Frayvar could go train as a ranger. Except, he couldn't. With his frail frame, awkwardness, and wheeze that came on with exercise, he was a more unlikely warrior than she.

"I don't get it, Fray. I'm not an *anrokk*. I like animals, but it's not like they communicate with me or treat me differently than they do others."

"No? You've never noticed that *all* of Grandpa's hounds like to sleep in your bed?"

"I notice when there's no room in the bed for me."

"Even the bees like you. You've never been stung."

"That doesn't mean anything."

"Sure it does. I can't go near a hive without a smoker, whereas they let you amble up, stick your head in, and take out whatever honey you want."

"I use a smoker. You're being silly."

"Because Grandpa insists, but do you really think you need to?"

Kaylina wanted to continue to protest, but his words and frank expression made her pause. She *did* always get along with animals, unless one counted the fur shark that had tried to eat her. But it had been shot at. That might have made it inordinately cranky. It would have made *her* cranky.

"What am I going to do?" Groaning, she bent over and gripped her knees. "I came to make mead, not war. Do you think I can... not show up?"

"If you don't, one of them will be here five minutes after dawn to haul you off. They *know* where we live."

The blackness of despair crept into Kaylina. Since they'd arrived, nothing had gone right, but she'd still had a shot at her dream. Now... now...

She rubbed her face. She didn't know.

"If I were you, I would feign ineptitude," Frayvar said. "When Targon asks to see your sling capabilities, hurl every round over the wall."

"I hit Vlerion on the head with a shot the day we met. He *knows* my aim is good."

"Well, maybe you'll be lousy with swords. You've never picked one up before, right? You could cut off your own toe with your first swing."

"Thanks so much."

"You could *pretend* to be lousy, even if you're not."

Kaylina slumped down on the bench at the table.

"Or we could stow away on a ship and go home," Frayvar added softly.

"After we've done so much? We're almost ready to open."

"I know. I miss everyone back home, but after all this, I'd like to see it through."

"*You* still can." Kaylina couldn't keep the bitterness out of her voice.

The clip-clop of horse hooves on the river trail made Kaylina lift a wary head. Jana, their competition, rode slowly past, smiling and lifting a hand, as if she was out for a ride and had happened to come this way.

"You can, and you have to," Kaylina caught herself saying as the woman continued down the trail. "I don't want her feeling smug, like we left because we couldn't handle some competition. I don't want her *winning.*"

"I didn't know you were entering a contest."

"Looks like we both are."

18

YOU CAN'T STRIKE AT ANOTHER WITHOUT MAKING YOURSELF VULNERABLE.
  ~ Ranger Lord Vlerion of Havartaft

Kaylina arrived at ranger headquarters precisely at dawn and set her crutch against the courtyard wall inside the gate. Maybe it was foolish, and she should have pretended more feebleness than she felt, but her pride wouldn't let her hobble around in front of Vlerion and Targon.

To her surprise, the doctor was the first to greet her.

"Heard you're getting trained today," he said.

"Yes. Unless you want to examine my leg and declare me too injured to learn sword fighting or whatever happens on Day One."

"I examined it the other day. It's coming along fine. But Day One, as you call it, tends to be challenging. A lot of the early months are designed to improve your strength, endurance, and balance, so you'll be ready for long days of riding taybarri, surviving in the mountains, and going into battles when they come."

Kaylina shook her head, though the idea of riding her own taybarri was appealing. Other than a brief jaunt through town on Crenoch, she hadn't done more than pet them. Or be licked by them. What would it be like to ride on their backs as they loped across the miles and flashed to discombobulate enemies in battle?

"You'll want this. And I can also offer this." The doctor dropped two of his compressed-horse-dung pills into her palm, one the familiar green and the other orange. He also handed her a pouch that probably held more of them. "Take them twice a day. That one, you know well, and it's to help with the pain. That one isn't something I'd usually prescribe, but it lifts the mood a bit, helps everything seem less onerous. Might even make you laugh while you're doing push-ups with your trainer hollering in your ear."

Kaylina frowned at the orange pill and thought of her mother's reliance on tarmav weed to get out of bed in the mornings. She didn't want to be like that. "I don't want my mood altered."

Frayvar would have laughed at her words and probably told her to chomp down the orange pills like bacon-wrapped dates. No, that wasn't fair. Mom's reliance on the weed concerned him too.

"Are you sure? I haven't seen you without a glower."

"You haven't seen me at my best." Kaylina pointed to her leg.

"Suppose that's fair. You don't have to take it, but keep the pouch in case you change your mind. I understand you didn't volunteer for this." His tone was sympathetic.

She decided she liked him. A lot more than the other rangers. *Especially* more than his captain.

"I didn't," she said.

"If you're an *anrokk*, I understand why Targon chose you, but..." The doctor spread his hand. "It's not an easy life."

She eyed his scars. If even the healers got beat up here, she had no doubt of his statement.

"Do a lot of the rangers take the mood pills?" she asked.

"Some. Mostly it helps out the new recruits. The early months of training are hard."

"Does Vlerion take anything?" Kaylina thought of those dangerous glints that came to his eyes and what might happen if he lost his temper.

"Not that I'm aware of. Not even pain medication when he's injured. He says he doesn't want anything altering his mental state." The doctor shrugged. "You can ask him more about it yourself." He pointed across the courtyard, past the taybarri stable to where Vlerion stood alone, his arms folded over his chest.

That dyspeptic expression was back on his face as he watched them. Had he been there all along?

Kaylina chewed down the dreadful pain medicine, then eyed the other. "Would the orange pill make it easier for me to bow and say *yes, my lord*?"

The doctor snorted. "Probably."

Thinking again of her mother, she didn't take it. Jaw set, she strode toward Vlerion.

Before she reached him, Captain Targon stepped out of the shadows, startling her.

"Good morning, my lord." Kaylina made herself smile, but she doubted it reached her eyes.

Targon nodded at her. "Thank you for coming."

"I assumed I didn't have a choice."

"Vlerion and I had a bet about that. I thought you'd run."

Frayvar's words echoed in her mind: *We could stow away on a ship and go home.*

"He didn't?" Kaylina didn't confess that she'd been tempted.

"Nope." Targon held up a finger to Vlerion, who hadn't moved but continued to watch them.

Targon turned his back toward Vlerion, as if he didn't want his subordinate to hear his next words. Kaylina tensed.

"I'm not going to change my mind about having him train you, because he's one of our best, and I think Crenoch is going to *insist* on you being his rider one day, but..." Targon eyed her. "I advise you to be respectful, mindful, and obedient to him."

"I do love being obedient to men."

His eyes closed to slits, and he gripped her arm tightly. It wasn't quite painful, but it made her clench her jaw and want to jerk away.

"I suggest that, for your own safety, you *are* obedient to that man. However much it may cost your pride, do *not* argue with him or try to make him lose his temper."

The various long looks that Targon and Vlerion had shared the night of her questioning came to mind. That awareness that they shared some secret. About that beast in the catacombs, she wagered.

"He's actually much better at keeping his temper than most men, but you've a knack for irritating him." The twist to Targon's lips as he stared into her eyes made her believe he thought she irritated most people.

Kaylina resisted the urge to stick her tongue out at him. Funny how many rangers made her want to do that. "It's my southern charm."

"He says you call him a pirate."

"Charmingly."

"I'll bet."

"Do women actually pass the tests to become a ranger? I haven't seen any here." Kaylina waved around the compound.

"There are a few. The tests rely as much on agility, endurance, marksmanship, and riding ability as raw strength. They're passable by those who train hard and have some gods-given aptitude." Targon glanced at the sling on her belt. "I believe the need to sleep on the ground in mountains filled with man-eating beasts and man-slaying Kar'ruk are a deterrent to many of the fairer sex. At least among the aristocracy, from which the rangers have traditionally drawn, there are few women who've been eager to sign up."

Kaylina had thought *all* of the rangers were nobles, but hadn't Vlerion said Jankarr had a common heritage?

Targon looked past her shoulder toward the stable.

No fewer than five taybarri were gazing at them. Or... at her?

She rubbed her face, not wanting that many witnesses to whatever this training involved.

"You'll be paid," Targon said.

"Huh?"

"The stipend during training is small, but if you pass the tests to become a ranger, the pay is commensurate with the duties and dangers of the job." He nodded to her, as if he were doing her a favor.

She wanted to earn her *stipend* from mead sales, but she made herself say, "Okay," and add, "my lord," when his eyebrows twitched.

After that, she hurried toward Vlerion before anyone else could waylay her.

"My taybarri has a hangover this morning," he stated, his expression sour.

She'd been on the verge of offering him a polite, *Good morning, my lord,* but his words got her hackles up.

"Your *taybarri* shouldn't have imbibed so much mead."

In truth, Kaylina was surprised that the small amount had affected such a large beast. Had Crenoch gotten into a keg of alcohol, he might truly have been poisoned.

"He's young and doesn't know what's good for him yet." Vlerion leveled a flat glare not at her but toward the stable.

Crenoch—she was fairly certain that was he—swished his tail and turned his back.

"Do I get to ride him today?" That sounded like a far more appealing perk than Targon's stipend.

"No."

"Tomorrow?"

"No."

"Ever?"

Vlerion looked like he badly wanted to say *no* again, but he sighed. "He'll probably insist."

Something to look forward to then.

"Normally, we would start off with strength and endurance training, but Doc Penderbrock said to give your leg more time to recover."

"I like him."

"We all do."

"Because he gives out good drugs?"

"Among other reasons." Vlerion looked down. "How *is* your leg?"

"If I say it aches horribly and green pus is constantly oozing from it, will you let me go back to the castle to start a new batch of mead?"

"You're going to be a difficult student, aren't you?"

"Yeah, but you're going to be a loathsome teacher, so it'll work out."

"Or we'll kill each other." He smiled.

She didn't. She had no doubt he could kill her but highly doubted the reverse would be true.

"Come." Vlerion led her toward the far side of the courtyard where men grappled with each other in a sandy pit. "We'll work on balance, and I'll educate you on the various threats you'll face as a ranger. Ten years ago, most of them came from our borders. These days, as you saw in the catacombs, we must also be prepared to respond to threats within our cities. Our forces are spread thin."

"Is that why commoners, including snarky women from the far southern end of the kingdom, are being recruited?"

"*You* are a special case, but it is why commoners who've proven themselves loyal and exceptional have been allowed in, yes. It's an opportunity for them too. If Jankarr, for example, survives his full twenty-five years and retires with honor, he'll receive a parcel of land and a title."

"The king is okay with turning commoners into nobles?"

"The program was his idea, back when he was a little more..." Vlerion waved his hand vaguely toward the sky.

"Little more what?" Kaylina hadn't heard from the newspapers or gossip in the Spitting Gull that there was anything wrong with King Gavatorin, but the islands were far removed from the capital, and a lot of people didn't care much about the king or the kingdom as a whole. The fierce patriotism present in the north wasn't found as frequently in those parts of the nation more recently annexed or conquered.

"He's getting older," Vlerion said, then added in a quieter tone, "and less sharp."

"That happens to people."

Not her grandparents though. Thankfully, they were still in full command of their faculties. Mother, on the other hand... Well, the tarmav weed was her problem.

"Yes."

Vlerion led her through a wide open-sky corridor toward another large courtyard. Barracks, an armory, and an eating hall surrounded it, all with windows looking out on arenas, a track, and stations filled with training equipment. A few men were using the various apparatuses.

Vlerion led Kaylina to an aboveground pool with a long log mounted on a spindle above it, the bark peeled away. "Remove your boots and whatever else you like."

Whatever else she liked? In front of witnesses?

He tugged off his own boots, removed his socks, then pulled his black tunic over his head, tossing it onto a rack.

Kaylina stared at his lean ropy muscles, each one fully delineated, the dusting of red-brown hair on his chest doing nothing to soften his body. He looked a lot different from Domas—from *most* of the men back home that she'd seen shirtless. Of course she'd expected Vlerion to be fit, but even before he grabbed a staff and swung it in a few warm-up exercises, she was mesmerized. Scar tissue rose in several places, wounds that, like the ones on his head, had come from claws or fangs rather than blades. How many great beasts had he battled in his life? He wasn't that much older than she.

"You'll get wet," Vlerion told her, catching her looking.

"What?" she blurted, jerking her gaze away.

"From the pool."

"Oh."

She shook her head. The last thing she needed was for him to believe she was into him.

Fortunately, he didn't comment on her gawking.

"We usually remove all our clothing as practice for enduring the cold," Vlerion said, "but I'm told it's not polite to walk naked among women."

Kaylina refrained from replying that she wouldn't mind and would be curious to see the rest of him—comments like that couldn't *possibly* be considered respectful to lords.

"That's right," was what she said and took off her sling and knife before removing her boots.

Staff in hand, Vlerion hopped onto a stump acting as a stair step and padded barefoot onto the log. It wobbled, turning left and right on the spindle, but only a little. His steps barely stirred it.

Why did Kaylina have a feeling it would rotate violently and pitch *her* into the water?

"Do I get a staff for balance?" She eyed the rack of them.

"They're not for balance. They're for striking your opponent.

It's a contest to improve your balance and teach you how to keep your composure when you're in a battle."

"If we're going to battle each other, I absolutely need a staff."

Vlerion smiled slightly and held his staff out horizontally. In offering?

Glad there weren't many witnesses around, Kaylina climbed onto the stump and then more carefully the log. With its bark peeled, the wood had little texture and nothing to grip with her toes.

The log wobbled, affecting Vlerion as well as Kaylina, but he adjusted easily to the motion. *She* flailed, causing it to spin in earnest. His expression never changed as his feet shifted, and he took small steps to stay on top as it rotated. His upper body barely moved. She ended up sideways, flailing harder and feeling like a spectacle.

Vlerion sank low, shifting his weight downward, and the log slowed to a stop. At least she hadn't fallen in. He could as easily have made it spin faster, she realized. Or used his weight to send it rotating in the opposite direction. Maybe he would once they started their "battle."

She crept carefully toward him and accepted the staff. "I get to try to hit you?"

"If you can."

"It doesn't seem right to attack an unarmed man."

"I am not without my means."

Yeah, with those muscles, he could heft her over his head and throw her into the water—or over the courtyard wall.

"What do I get if I knock you into the pool?" Kaylina decided that swinging the staff like a club would cause her to lose her balance. Instead, she gripped it in both hands, holding it close to her body and pointing one end toward him. Thrusting would be less likely to upset her balance.

"If you remain on the log for five minutes, I will tell ten influential citizens about your meadery and suggest they might enjoy the fare."

Great, he knew how to manipulate her. Not that she was a hard person to read. During that drugged interrogation, she'd spewed everything not only about her dreams but her need to prove herself to her family.

"Ten influential citizens and the king," Kaylina countered, testing how fast and hard she could thrust without making the log rotate.

"The queen is the connoisseur of fine food," he said.

Ah, that was right. Kaylina had read the culture column the queen wrote for the largest kingdom newspaper. It was one of the reasons she'd chosen Port Jirador for her new business.

"Okay, tell *her* about my meadery. And that our beverages are fit for royalty."

"I already know they are."

"Oh?" She inched closer to him with the staff. "You didn't get a chance to try any, did you?"

"Crenoch did."

"And his taste is impeccable?" The image of Crenoch's huge tongue dipping into a goblet came to mind. Hopefully, Vlerion wouldn't tell the queen that taybarri lips had been all over the drinkware at the castle.

"His taste is highly questionable, but he is what humans would call a prince. His sire and dam are leaders among the taybarri."

"Well, there you go. You can honestly say that royalty *loves* my mead."

"Yes. Should you last five minutes."

"We're already down to three, aren't we? Maybe four since I got up here."

"The timer begins when you attack."

"Damn, I thought I just had to keep you chatting." Kaylina didn't see a *timer* at all.

"No." Vlerion flicked his fingers in invitation.

She eased closer, then thrust the staff toward his groin. Maybe not a fair target, but it would be harder for him to dodge his midsection out of the way than his head or torso. He also might want to protect that area assiduously. Most men did.

He didn't dodge, merely sweeping his hand in to catch the staff and keep it from connecting. He tugged on it, almost pulling her off balance.

Though tempted to let go of it, she didn't. She did wobble and had to take several fast sideways steps as the log shifted. Vlerion matched the movements, staying on without trouble. He could have ripped the staff out of her hands, but he let her regain her balance and back up.

The next time, she thrust faster, first feinting for his head before committing to another groin attack. He must have been able to tell the feint wasn't a threat, because he didn't lift a hand to block it, simply grabbing the thrust toward his midsection again.

"I'm fortunate your sling didn't target my balls," Vlerion said.

"Your back was to me when I fired."

"If I'd been turned toward you?"

"Any target is fair game when someone is after my brother."

"I see."

Kaylina set up again, feinting twice this time, then lunging for his abdomen. He shifted to the side, using his open palm to block and deflect the staff, then wrapping his grip around it. He yanked the staff—and her—toward him, and she stumbled into him. She might as well have rammed against a stone pillar. He didn't move, and she bounced back, losing her balance and tilting toward the water. She tried to grab him and take him in with her, but he glided back out of reach.

With a great splash, cold water enveloped her as she landed butt-first. At least there weren't any sharks in the pool.

"Whether you're attacking or defending, keep your knees bent and the core of your weight low." Vlerion touched his abdomen and demonstrated by crouching. "It'll be easier to keep your balance that way. When you're on a taybarri, you can only move your top half, but you'll find that you can still sink yourself low if someone is swinging at you with an axe. Since the taybarri won't abide stirrups, saddles, and bits, you can't rise up and move about as much as you can on a horse."

Kaylina wiped water out of her eyes and waded toward the side. "They sound uppity."

"What else would you expect from royalty?"

"They're not *all* from that same sire and dam, are they?"

"No, but they all think highly of themselves."

Kaylina pulled herself out, water sloughing from her soaked clothes, and padded back onto the log. She wanted another crack at Vlerion. Too bad her five minutes had probably started over.

Once more, he held the staff out horizontally for her. Her splash had gotten him wet. As she eased across the log, she decided one wasn't supposed to admire the damp, gleaming muscles of one's opponent.

This time, she used her weight to shift the log before attacking. She had to think of ways to distract him if she wanted to catch him off balance.

Vlerion moved his feet without glancing down, stopping her spin and rotating it in the other direction. Since he weighed more, he could take control of the log anytime. Watching her, he rotated it faster.

She crouched lower, moving with the spin and balancing effectively for a time, but as soon as she attacked again, he caught the staff and pulled her. She let go of it, hoping she wouldn't go in again, but he shifted the weapon in his grip and thrust it at *her*.

She bent her top half, trying to dodge, but the tip clipped her. This time, she landed on her butt on the log before bouncing into the water. That one hurt more than her pride.

"Never relinquish your weapon," Vlerion said when she came up, pushing hair out of her face. "And be mindful that committing to an attack always has the consequence of opening your defenses. You can't strike at another without making yourself vulnerable."

Kaylina should have offered an obedient, *yes, my lord,* as she waded to the side again, but what came out was, "I don't want to *strike* at anyone. I'm a crafter, not a fighter. I *read* about adventures; I don't go on them."

"Aren't you on an adventure now?"

"To *craft*. Fine alcoholic beverages. Also to hold my brother's groceries at the market. He's not a fighter either. It's not fair to—" As she heaved herself out of the water, she glimpsed several young men in ranger blacks watching from a dozen yards away, and she clamped her mouth shut.

They smiled as she climbed onto the log again. At first, Kaylina thought they might be sympathetic smiles, since they must have undergone the same training, and maybe a couple of them were, but one man eyed her chest and elbowed his comrade.

"Nice to have some female rangers-in-training again."

"Because the view is better?"

"Oh yeah."

Kaylina might not have taken off her shirt, but when she glanced down, she realized having her wet clothes plastered to her body didn't leave a lot to the imagination. Cheeks hot, she crept toward Vlerion again.

He waited in the same pose with the staff out in offering, but his head had turned toward their observers. No, *her* observers. She might enjoy looking at Vlerion shirtless, but the male rangers were more interested in ogling her. Now that one had drawn the attention of the others, they were *all* checking her out.

"You will return to your duties," Vlerion told them coolly.

"Yes, my lord," they said as one and trotted off, though not without a couple of backward glances.

The one who'd spoken first licked his lips and winked at Kaylina, as if to promise he would meet her alone later.

"I prefer the attention of the taybarri," she muttered to herself, giving the ranger a rude gesture to help him along his way.

Vlerion returned his gaze to her—to her *face*—and nodded for her to take the staff. Even though he irked her, she wouldn't have minded as much if *he'd* eyed her chest. But he didn't even want to be there training her.

Kaylina accepted the staff and backed up to reconsider her strategy. If she swung for his legs, he might have a harder time grabbing it out of midair.

"Targon wants you moved into the barracks here," Vlerion said.

An alarm bell clanged in her mind.

"I can't abandon my brother," she blurted.

"I told him it would be unwise." Vlerion glanced in the direction the men had gone. "For numerous reasons."

Even though she knew he was more concerned about her being pestered for sex if she slept here, she knew how to handle unwanted advances from men. The thought of Frayvar having to deal with the cursed castle alone was what made her shake her head.

"My brother would sleep in the courtyard and freeze if I wasn't there. He's scared of that place." Kaylina was too, but the castle hadn't killed them yet, and the nightmares had grown less frequent, so she'd grown less uneasy about being there. She did, however, worry that the curse's decision to leave them alone might change if rangers kept coming by. "Besides, it's my fault he's here. I can't let anything happen to him."

Vlerion's expression never changed. She might as well have been complaining to a stone wall.

Frustrated, even though it sounded like Vlerion might have

talked his boss out of forcing her to stay here, Kaylina lunged in, thrusting at his front leg.

He lifted it, balancing on his back leg, and kicked her staff aside. Though her arms were knocked out wide with it, she held onto it and kept her balance. She thrust again, feinting and swinging, trying anything she could think of to catch Vlerion by surprise.

The log spun under her, but she managed to stay upright as she attacked. Unfortunately, she *didn't* manage to connect.

Her last thrust was high enough that Vlerion could grip the staff, and he did so at the same time as he shifted his weight, setting the log to spinning. Fast.

Cursing, she struggled to keep up, moving her feet rapidly to stay vertical, but he shifted his weight again, altering the spin so abruptly that she couldn't adjust in time. Once more, she pitched into the water. Her leg caught the log as she fell, and agony lanced up from her wounds. She barely kept from screaming.

"In battle, it is natural for instincts to take over, for rational thought to be elusive. We will train you such that many defenses and attacks become automatic, but it is also important that you keep your temper, that you don't allow frustration or anger to make your self-control evaporate."

"Screw you, asshole," Kaylina snarled, wincing as she waded for the edge again.

With her back to him, she sensed rather than saw Vlerion moving. He trotted off the log and sprang to the ground to land near her.

She tensed, expecting retribution for her disrespect, for not making it, *Screw you, my lord.*

But he didn't look mad or even annoyed. He reached for a towel on the rack and handed it to her. "We will move on to another exercise."

"Good," she said, though she didn't know if it was. With the sun barely up, there had to be countless more training torture sessions in store for her.

As she wiped her face with the towel, she glimpsed someone in the passageway again, a man like the others, peeking out from around the corner.

Vlerion stepped closer to her and glared at the young ranger. He jerked back out of sight.

At least while Kaylina was training with him, she shouldn't have to worry about the untoward advances she'd been thinking of.

He rested a hand on her shoulder. "Family is important. I understand. We all do."

The gentleness of his touch and his soft tone sanded her irritation down, and she caught herself leaning toward him.

He froze, so maybe that wasn't the right move. When she glanced up, he was looking toward her chest. Between the cold water and the chilly air, her nipples were popping through the wet shirt. No wonder she had gawkers.

She didn't want the attention of the others, and she shouldn't have wanted Vlerion's attention, but a weird flush went through her, and she was tempted to turn toward him so he could see... whatever he wished.

Vlerion shifted his gaze away as he took the towel from her to drape it around her shoulders and cover her chest. Well, wasn't that noble?

She told herself not to be disappointed. What did she think would happen between them, anyway?

"I lost my brother when I was younger," Vlerion said quietly, and she forgot thoughts of wet shirts and being ogled. "It's good that you want to look out for yours. I wasn't there for mine when he passed, and I wish I could have been. That I could have stopped it."

"I'm sorry." Kaylina didn't know why he was opening up to her, but it warmed her that he felt he could, and she regretted cursing him. "Was he younger?"

"Older. Before I had the notion, he defied our parents' wishes and became a ranger."

"That's how he was killed? In the line of duty?"

"It was an accident, but it wouldn't have happened if he hadn't been here." His vague wave could have indicated the ranger head-quarters or the city as a whole. His face grew closed, and she had a feeling he wouldn't go into more details if she pressed.

"I'm sorry," she said again and rested her hand on his bare chest. "It must have been hard for you to lose him."

"Yes." Vlerion looked down at her hand but didn't remove it or suggest she should. His gaze shifted to her face, his eyes heated.

The temptation to let her fingers trace the hard lines of his pectorals swept over her. Would he let her? Did he want her to?

Movement in the passageway pulled their gazes from each other. It wasn't the horny young men this time but a woman of about thirty walking beside Captain Targon.

Vlerion stepped away from Kaylina, and her hand dropped. Targon smirked as he eyed Kaylina, and she pulled the towel tighter around herself.

The woman had lush brown hair, voluptuous lips, and wore a silk dress and golden necklace under a fur-lined jacket. A noble? Surely not a ranger.

The pair walked toward them, and Kaylina, dripping water onto the pavers, felt scruffy with her hair plastered to her neck. The woman looked at Vlerion and ignored Kaylina except to give her a once over and purse disapproving lips.

"I need to speak with you, Vlerion." She didn't comment on Kaylina or her damp attire.

"I assumed," he said. "Trouble at home?"

"Most of the family's troubles are centered around you."

"That sounds like a *no*. I'll stand relieved."

"It's nothing too worrisome, but we need to talk." The woman gave Kaylina another look of disapproval before scrutinizing Vlerion.

His face was masked, and if he gave anything away, Kaylina couldn't tell.

Vlerion nodded at Targon, then walked off with the woman without explaining who she was. Another noble who'd built forts with Vlerion in their youth and now thought he was a sexy hunk?

"If my instructor is busy, I can go home," Kaylina told Targon.

He snorted. "Have no fear. We've many capable rangers who can take over for the morning."

"Lucky me."

With her leg throbbing, Kaylina followed the captain off to whatever torture and humiliation was next on the list. She couldn't help but look back toward where Vlerion and the woman had stopped, their heads bowed in conversation. She touched his arm and pointed at Kaylina.

They were talking about her? Kaylina clenched her jaw.

Neither looked in her direction. Vlerion shook his head at whatever the woman said. She frowned at him. He shook his head again.

"This way, recruit." Targon gripped Kaylina's arm to get her moving again, determined to lead her away.

"Lucky me," she repeated softly.

19

May the gods favor the innocent fallen on the battlefield, as the monarchs choosing their fate did not.
    ~ Moon Priest Denugla, Prayers for the Dying

After dusk, an unmarked carriage took Kaylina back to the castle. Her entire body ached, her leg throbbed, and weariness weighed down her limbs.

She hadn't seen Vlerion since the morning, but numerous other rangers had given her private or group instruction, during which she'd discovered that quite a few other recruits were in training. Most had been male but there had been another woman, a tough-as-nails type with short hair and as many muscles as the men. Kaylina had spoken to her, thinking they might have a connection, but the woman worshipped the rangers and was voluntarily devoting her life to becoming one. Whether she was a commoner or noble, Kaylina hadn't learned, but *she* had no trouble with the "my lords."

When the driver stopped in front of the castle, its telltale red glow seeping from the tower window, it took a gargantuan effort for Kaylina to peel herself off the bench and climb out of the carriage. Once it took off, with no witnesses about to judge her for weakness, she leaned heavily on the crutch and walked slowly to the front door, pausing only to regard two signs that had been put out by the gate.

Menu:

Fennel and fig rack of lamb served with Warrior Red Currant Mead

Apple cider beef stew served with Full Moon Cyser

Honey garlic salmon served with Trappers Dry Mead

Tasting flights available

Kaylina smiled, touched that her brother had made progress, but she felt guilty that she hadn't been there to help that day. And wouldn't for many days to come. Not forever; she refused to believe that. Once Targon realized what a lousy ranger she would make, he would boot her out. Surely, it didn't matter how much the taybarri liked a person if they couldn't stand on a log without falling in a pool.

Frayvar wasn't leaning against the wall in the courtyard. Kaylina didn't know if that was a good sign or not.

"You alive, Fray?" she called as she entered the keep, not wanting to startle him.

The cavernous front rooms were dark, and she headed to the kitchen, expecting to find him there. She wouldn't mind tasting some of those recipes if he had anything on the stove, but she didn't smell any of the scintillating dishes. That was surprising.

When she pushed open the door to the kitchen, it was dark inside, the fire in the hearth down to embers. Several seconds passed before her eyes could pierce the shadows to spot someone lying still on the floor.

"Fray!" Kaylina sprang to his side and knelt to touch his chest. Images of finding a dagger thrust into his heart filled her imagination.

She didn't bump into a blade or anything else, but he didn't stir as she patted him. Nor when she shook him.

"Fray?"

Swallowing, she laid her hand on his chest to make sure he was breathing. Thank Luvana, the Luck Goddess, he was. When Kaylina checked his pulse, his heart beat calmly under her fingers. But what had *happened*? She shook him again, as if he were asleep and could be woken.

But it was nothing so benign. His eyes wouldn't open.

A sick feeling hollowed out her gut, the certainty that the curse had done something to her brother. Had a wind blown him against one of the travertine counters so that he hit his head?

"I am so tired of this place," Kaylina snarled, lunging to her feet.

She grabbed the fireplace poker, longing for an enemy to present itself. But the castle wasn't moaning, and no visions intruded upon her mind.

She stomped up the stairs with the poker, as well as her sling and knife, the glowing tower her destination. There *had* to be answers in there. Maybe whatever was making that glow controlled the whole castle and implemented the curse.

On the way, she thrust open doors, looking for a ladder or anything she could stand on to break the boards. A sturdy wooden chair in a nearby room was the best she could find. Not certain it would give her enough height, she dragged it scraping and thumping down the narrow hallway.

Maybe she should have spent that time finding a doctor for Frayvar, but her gut told her his ailment wouldn't be solved with smelling salts or a potion.

"This won't take long," she promised, shoving the chair under the boarded-up ceiling in the tower.

Enough of the iron brackets that had once supported the stairs remained to provide handholds. If she could make a hole, she thought she could climb up.

With one foot on the cushion and one on the chair back, Kaylina jammed upward with the iron poker. The nailing of the boards had been clumsily done, and she didn't think it would take much to bring them down. Even so, her first few angry thumps didn't dislodge anything. Wishing she had a crowbar instead of the poker, she focused on the nails and gaps wider than the others.

Red light seeped through one of those gaps. A warning? She hardly cared. She wasn't going to let the castle kill her brother.

Fueled by her rage and fear for him, she rammed again and again. Sweat broke out on her forehead, despite the persistent chill of the place.

One of the castle's eerie moans wafted down from above. Probably another warning.

"Too bad." With a final great thrust, Kaylina knocked one of the boards free.

It flew upward and clattered out of sight. Dust wafted down along with the musty scent of... dried vegetable matter? She wrinkled her nose.

The hole wasn't large enough to climb through, so she attacked the board next to it. With the first gone, the others were easier to dislodge, and she'd soon knocked away two more.

One fell, almost hitting her as it clunked off the arm of the chair. Dried leaves fluttered down with the dust. She sneezed, her balance faltering before she jumped down.

From the floor, she eyed the hole, trying to see into the tower. The source of the glow continued to be a mystery, but a branch hung in the air, the ominous red illumination painting it from behind. Some long-forgotten plant that had died, she assumed, its skeletal remains undisturbed for decades, if not centuries. Normally, time would have disintegrated it, but if it had been an altered plant, the magic embedded in its husk might have kept it from falling apart completely.

After pushing the chair out of the way, Kaylina leaned the poker against the wall and used the remains of the staircase to climb. She had to stretch to grip the edge of the hole, and the board creaked when she shifted weight to it. Would it hold her up?

"It's not that far of a fall," she told herself, thinking of Frayvar.

He needed her to figure this out.

With an awkward lunge, she pushed away from the wall and gripped the edge of the board with both hands. Her muscles weren't strong enough to pull up her full bodyweight, and she had to swing from side to side, hoping to create enough momentum to throw a leg up. The boards creaked riotously.

For some reason, Vlerion's lesson on the log came to mind. Probably because she anticipated falling. Hitting the floorboards below would hurt more than water.

But with one great heave, she managed to hook her leg over the edge. A leaf fluttered down, landing on her nose. She clawed and strained to pull herself up, her muscles quivering before she made it.

Targon was an idiot if he thought *she* could become a ranger. One of his trained fighters would have leaped up and landed in a crouch with a sword out. She flopped down like a dead fish, rolling onto her back, cobwebs begriming her face, and hit her shoulder against something.

A ceramic pot large enough that it could have contained a symba tree rested in the tower opposite the arrow-slit window. The red glow came from it—no from what was *in* it.

Kaylina patted for her knife and pushed herself to her knees, dried leaves crinkling underneath her. The plant she'd assumed was dead was alive, the growth rising from the soil in the pot greenish, though it emitted the red glow.

She stared in disbelief. The strange illumination that had

been, according to what she'd heard, seeping from the tower window since the curse was placed centuries ago came from... a plant?

An admittedly huge and evil-looking plant composed of both thorny branches and vines, the latter snaking over the edge of the pot and to the walls of the room. A few even trailed *up* the walls, as if they were trellised. Somehow, they adhered to the stone. Large star-shaped leaves grew from the branches. The vines were bare aside from suckers on the very tips.

Kaylina shifted on her knees, reminded of her visions, the visions in which rangers and their allies had been strangled.

"How can a plant have been alive for all this time? Even an altered plant?" She picked up one of the dead leaves. It was as star-shaped as the ones still attached to the branches. It was as if the plant had lived all this time, shedding leaves each autumn, and continuing to grow new ones in the spring. "How could you have gotten water?"

The eaves of the tower hung out over the arrow-slit window. Only a great storm with wind driving rain sideways might have brought water in. But how often could that happen? The boards were dry under the dead leaves.

Kaylina knew there were hundreds of species of altered plants in the world and that they all had unique properties, but she'd never heard of one that could grow without water. How much sunlight breached the tower? And where did the plant get nutrients? Whatever had been in the soil of the pot had to have long ago been used up.

"Probably no point in looking for logic when the plant is *glowing*," Kaylina muttered, rising to her feet.

Under the red illumination, the leaves and branches *did* look dry, as if the plant could use a good watering. The vines remained supple, but maybe it prioritized sending moisture to them.

"The better to kill intruders with..."

Knife in one hand, Kaylina risked creeping closer to the pot. It was as high as her thighs and much wider than she. The central stem of the plant could have been considered a trunk. It would take a saw, not a knife, to cut through it. Assuming some magic hadn't hardened it to withstand even steel. She had a feeling people had tried before to kill the plant.

Wanting to check for moisture, she touched her fingertips to the soil.

An electric shock coursed up her arm and through her body. Her heart fluttered in her chest, and she staggered back, dropping the knife.

Her knees hit the floor, and she pitched forward, barely managing to get her hands down and keep from striking her head. Red light flashed, and a vision filled her mind.

For the first time, she was featured in it. She saw herself and Vlerion standing by the carriage out front, the perspective from above. No, from the *tower*. The plant had been watching them.

An angry red glow outlined Vlerion. Was that the plant's way of saying it had seen him as a threat? Or it had identified him as a ranger?

In the vision, as Kaylina walked away from Vlerion and toward the front door where Frayvar had been, a vine extended out the window and down to the courtyard.

Had that happened? And none of them had seen it? The vine wasn't glowing, and in the dark, who would notice it?

It crept slowly toward the gate—toward where Vlerion had remained. Kaylina couldn't affect the version of herself in the vision, couldn't order herself to warn him.

But Vlerion, after she'd told him that Frayvar was fine and he could go, had left, walking to the carriage. When he'd departed, the vine had only been a few feet from his ankle. He'd never seen it, never sensed it.

The vision version of Kaylina sat down with Frayvar to share his blanket, exactly what had happened. The tip of the vine lifted, wavering in the air like the snake she'd likened it to, considering its target. The plant could have killed them both that night, but maybe it had decided they weren't allies of the rangers? Or didn't *know* if they were? The vine had withdrawn, disappearing back into the tower.

The vision released Kaylina, and the glowing room came back into focus. A few of the leaves had rotated toward her. *Watching* her?

"Not at all creepy," she whispered, then raised her voice. "Look, we're not friends of the rangers, okay? We're working-class people who run eating houses and make mead. We're not even from here. My ancestors never did anything to pester druids."

She didn't know that for a fact, but the druids hadn't left a lot of statues and ruins in the southern end of the kingdom to suggest they'd lived in the area. It was plausible that her ancestors had never encountered them.

A tip of a vine flicked, and another vision gripped her. This one was brief, a younger version of herself out hunting quail and pheasants with Grandpa, the hounds constantly running back to her for pets and to show her whatever they'd found, everything from prey they'd captured to delightful sticks for chewing. Their tails wagged happily as they bounded around her.

The vision faded, but not before she got a sense of mocking in it. It was something that had happened, and it disturbed her that the plant could see into her memories, but it must have shared that instance for a reason. Why?

"I don't understand."

The plant showed her the hounds bounding around her again.

Dear moon gods, was she having a conversation with the plant? Not only was it alive when it shouldn't have been, but it had a brain or at least some way of being intelligent, of watching over the castle and all who entered it. And of scraping through people's memories.

Kaylina shuddered at the omniscience, but if she could communicate with the plant, she might be able to convince it to release her brother.

Again, it showed her a hunt, a different day, with clouds in the sky, but with the hounds frolicking alongside her, largely indifferent to her grandpa walking nearby.

"Is this about me maybe being an *anrokk*?"

Wait, Frayvar had said the word came from the druid language, that their version of the *anrokks* had possessed magic. Did the plant think *she* had magic? Did it need something magical done to it?

"Help my brother, and I'll help you," she told the plant, though she had no idea what it needed.

Was it her imagination that the red glow brightened with skepticism?

"We're not your enemies. We're innocent visitors here, doing what we have to do to make it in this strange land. You can understand, can't you?"

The plant didn't react. No further visions came from it.

Kaylina groped for a better argument to sway it, but a distant call came from below.

"Kaylina? Are you here?"

"Frayvar!"

She snatched up her knife and rushed to the hole but paused before jumping down. She didn't know if the plant had released him from its hold, or he'd woken up naturally, but she blurted, "Thank you."

The red glow pulsed once.

Kaylina jumped down, afraid she'd promised a favor she couldn't deliver.

20

THE GREATEST FREEDOM, AND ONE ELUSIVE TO MANY, IS THE ABILITY TO say no.

~ Abayar, Founder Sandsteader Press

Outside, rain pounded down from low dark clouds, making it hard to tell when night gave way to day. Kaylina didn't care. Other than checking to make sure her brother wasn't seized by unconsciousness again, she didn't intend to do anything. She wasn't getting ready for the opening of the meadery—how could she invite people to visit this vile castle?—and she had no intention of showing up at ranger headquarters for training. She planned to remain wrapped in blankets, dozing and lamenting her foolish decision to leave home.

During the night, more nightmares had plagued her, all featuring that plant, and clanking had come from the catacombs. She'd barely slept. Her brother would tell her she was in a funk, but, in this case, it *had* to be understandable.

Frayvar sat up and stoked the fire in the hearth.

"I need to start prepping. I wish I had an assistant chef." He looked toward Kaylina, as if he might press her into the duty, but must have remembered she was supposed to be elsewhere. "You weren't ordered to report for training at dawn?"

"Screw the training."

"They know where to find you if they want you."

"Let them come. If they care. Vlerion is probably still busy with that woman. After she showed up yesterday, he blew off my training." The hurt in her tone surprised her. She hadn't truly cared about that, had she?

Once she'd had to train with others, she'd realized that Vlerion was a decent instructor. He'd been patient and hadn't laughed at her ineptitude or leered at her chest. It turned out that was rare among the rangers. They *did* need more women working with them, but only so they would smack the men and indoctrinate better behavior in them.

Other than the occasional lawless pirate, someone who pestered *everyone*, men hadn't bothered Kaylina that often back home. They'd known her family would protect her. Her grandparents weren't physically intimidating, but everyone on the islands knew who they were and respected them, and her brother-in-law and male cousins snapped at anyone who was rude to their female relatives. Maybe Kaylina had taken them all for granted.

What had she told Frayvar the day they arrived? *It's hard to get people to take you seriously when there's nobody behind you.*

"Is he a good trainer?" Frayvar asked.

"Vlerion? Yeah, I guess he is."

"I thought he might be hard on you. Because you hit him on the head and called him an ass and a pirate."

"He wasn't exactly un-hard, but he was... decent."

And he'd been sympathetic about her wanting to protect her brother. She wished she'd asked him more about *his* brother. She'd hardly asked him anything about himself. Maybe it wasn't any of her business, but her mother had often told her to stop living in her own head and show interest in others. That had been before the tarmav weed, when she'd cared about her children growing up to be good people.

"Well, if you're not going to train, you can help me peel vegetables."

"I will. I—"

A chime sounded, startling Kaylina into rolling away from the blankets to grab her sling. Thus far, none of the noises in this place had led to anything good.

"Is that... the door chime?" Frayvar asked.

"I don't know. Nobody has ever rung the chime when I've been here." She hadn't known there *was* a chime. "Or knocked. Unless you count the girl who pelted the door with silverware."

"People aren't eager to come up to the keep." Frayvar pushed himself to his feet, but he waved for her to go first to check on it.

After his night, Kaylina couldn't blame him. She straightened her rumpled sleep clothes, combed her fingers through her hair, and then did the same for Frayvar, who hadn't seen a barber since long before they'd left home and looked scruffy.

"Ew, touching." He tried to pull away from her.

"I'm not *hugging* you. Don't be so melodramatic."

"It's wonderful that you understand me and are considerate of my preferences."

"Oh, shush." She punched him in the shoulder before hurrying for the front door, though she didn't know if she cared about missing a caller. It might be that Jana, coming again to smile and wish them luck while spying on them.

When Kaylina opened the door, a tidy gray-haired man holding an umbrella and wearing a chauffeur's uniform stood halfway back to the gate, poised to flee the rest of the way. A silver-trimmed black carriage with four magnificent horses harnessed to it waited in the street. An emblem that was somewhat familiar—

had she seen it before in a history book?—marked the side with a sword crossed over an ancient war horn.

Since the chauffeur's gaze was toward the tower window, he didn't notice Kaylina. Thanks to the darkness of the day, the red glow was evident.

"If you're here for a meal or mead tasting, they won't start until..." Until when? If she or Frayvar had an inkling of sanity, they would call everything off until they could figure out how to remove the curse from the castle. Or at least ensure it wouldn't result in guests being stricken unconscious. Or worse. "Later," she finished.

The chauffeur looked at her, his mouth opening slightly—in surprise?—when he took in her rumpled sleep clothes. What had he expected? A perfectly made-up woman in an impeccable dress?

"Are you... Kaylina Korbian?"

"Yup."

"The woman who began ranger training yesterday with Lord Vlerion?"

"Yup." Kaylina tensed, realizing the man might have been sent to drag her to ranger headquarters. But this looked like a nobleman's carriage, not one of the city taxis.

The chauffeur looked her up and down again, as if he couldn't believe he had the right person. Kaylina was tempted to shut the door but noticed a second man waiting by the carriage. Muscular, scarred, and armed, he wore the same uniform but looked like someone sent along to deal with disrespectful commoners.

"Very well. I've been sent by Lady Isla of Havartaft to retrieve you for a meeting at her estate."

"Uh. Who is that, and where is her estate?"

The chauffeur blinked slowly a few times. "You don't know where Havartaft Estate is?"

"I'm not from around here."

After another moment of consideration, during which he

possibly noticed her darker skin, he said, "I see. The estate is approximately one hour's ride to the north in a rich agricultural valley that extends from the Strait of Torn Towers to the west and the foothills of the Evardor Mountains to the east."

That was more detail than Kaylina had expected. She didn't know if the chauffeur was precise by nature or wanted her to have an idea of how much land the Havartafts owned and be impressed. With the mountains looming close to the water in places, she wasn't sure it was as vast as it sounded.

"You may wish to change into more... respectable attire for the meeting," he suggested.

It wasn't enough to say *my lord*—or *lady*? Her *clothes* had to be respectful too?

"You don't think Lady What's-it would like my floral-pattern pajamas? These are Vamorkan trumpet flowers." Kaylina touched her hem. "Bees love them."

His lips pressed together. As a chauffeur, he probably wasn't nobility himself, but maybe he felt so deeply loyal to the Havartafts that he believed his life would end if he delivered an inappropriately dressed visitor to the estate. Or maybe they flogged servants who didn't perform adequately.

"Look, I don't know anything about a meeting, and I've got a lot to do today. I appreciate you coming all the way down to get me —" that was a lie, "—but I need to help my brother peel vegetables. We're opening our eating house tonight." Maybe. The courtyard part. "Oh, how about you tell Lady Havartaft about our mead? Do you want me to give you samples to take home? Maybe she won't be irked with you for not collecting me if you show up with a goodie bag." Kaylina remembered that Targon hoped her new meadery would attract commoners with ties to the Virts, not aristocrats, but she didn't care. *She* wanted all people to enjoy her mead.

"Ms. Korbian. You *will* come to this meeting. It is of grave importance."

"I don't know who Lady Havartaft is. How important can our meeting be?"

"She is Lord Vlerion's mother, and this is about your safety as well as his."

"Oh," was all Kaylina could mouth for a long minute. That changed things.

She turned to find Frayvar listening to everything from behind her.

"I can handle the vegetable peeling," he said. "Just... please promise to be back before serving time. I don't want to be knocked unconscious again. Besides, who other than you can tell people about tasting notes?"

"You know as much as I do about the mead. You know as much as I do about *everything*."

"Not about how to stay upright in our own castle."

She grimaced. "I'll be back as soon as I can." She eyed the horses as she lifted a finger toward the chauffeur. "Give me a moment to change."

"Yes," he said with relief.

He might be disappointed when he saw how modest even her good clothing was, but Kaylina jogged to the kitchen to brush her teeth and hair, change clothes, and grab a bag of honey drops that she'd made for treats. She'd intended to give them to the taybarri when Vlerion wasn't looking, but she might need to bribe one of the horses out front to help her escape later. Since she'd offered, she also grabbed two bottles of mead.

"My clothes might not impress any nobles, but *this* will."

The chauffeur raised his eyebrows when she came out with the bottles in her arms, but he didn't tell her to leave them, nor did he comment on the sling or knife at her waist. The muscled man opened the carriage door for her, revealing an empty interior. Blue velvet cushions offered comfort and immediately brought thoughts of naps to mind, especially if Kaylina would be riding alone. She would rather have asked the men questions. Primarily, why did Vlerion's *mom* want to see her? But once the carriage started up, with wheels and hooves clattering on the cobblestones, there wasn't any opportunity for chitchat with the men riding outside on the driver's bench.

Kaylina watched the castle as the carriage rolled away, the window glowing as ominously as ever. She vowed to return well before nightfall to do what she could to help and protect her brother.

21

MOTHERS KNOW BEST.

~ *Queen Henova*

Weary after so many nights of interrupted sleep, Kaylina dozed during the ride out of the city and into the countryside. The rain turned to snow and hail, leaving a dusting of white on the vineyards and orchards along the highway. She imagined the buds shivering as they struggled to find the energy to turn into leaves.

A few manors and castles were visible in the distance, none near the highway. They perched on hills overlooking it and their lands, with long winding drives leading up to their gates. As the carriage turned off the highway, Kaylina spotted a stone sign: Havartaft Estate.

Vast fields stretched to either side of the wide drive, some with hardy cold-weather crops already poking green shoots up through the snow. Orchards and rows of bramble bushes—raspberries and blackberries—remained dormant, the branches and vines skeletal. She noticed beehives between the fields, their designs different from the south, and eyed them curiously, wondering if Lady Havartaft would give her a tour.

She snorted to herself. The lords and ladies of the estate didn't likely go out to the farm. They would have servants for that. Indeed, she glimpsed long rectangular bunkhouses and little clusters of warehouses and stables, mini towns used by those who worked the fields.

The carriage entered a circular drive at the front of a stone manor much larger than the cursed castle. It was immaculate, no chips in the facade or missing mortar, no peeling paint on the perky blue shutters or trim. A matching stable to one side held healthy-looking horses, some of whom were out in pastures pawing for grass under the snow.

Another uniformed man stood waiting for Kaylina, an emblem on his chest showing the same sword-and-horn as on the carriage. Was he a butler? She only knew about such positions from books she had read.

After Kaylina stepped out, the chauffeurs remained with the carriage and drove it over to the stable.

The butler said, "Good morning, Ms. Korbian," and considered her bottles and weapons. He pointed at the alcohol. "If you've brought offerings, I can put them in the kitchen for the staff to taste and prepare for your meeting with Lady Havartaft."

"Uh, sure." Kaylina decided not to be offended by the implication that the servants had to *taste* her drinks to make sure they weren't poisoned. Or maybe only to ensure they didn't offer anything disgusting to their boss.

Let them taste the mead. It was fabulous, and the more people who knew about it, the better. Hopefully, the Havartafts paid their workers enough that they could afford to visit eating houses in town from time to time.

"Excellent."

The butler rang a bell sitting on a table inside the door, then took the bottles. No more than three seconds passed before a woman in a black-and-silver dress hurried out to collect them.

"This way, Ms. Korbian," the butler said.

"Any chance you can give me a clue as to what this meeting is about?" Kaylina followed him down a wide marble hall lined with paintings. Some featured snowy mountains or vast forests filled with game while others depicted ancient battles between men and Kar'ruk along rivers or in ships at sea.

"I am not privy to such information, Ms. Korbian."

"You can call me Kaylina."

"That would not be appropriate."

"Are you sure? I'm not noble. You may have noticed."

"You are a guest of the family."

Kaylina paused at a painting in a more modern style than the others with bright colors that hadn't faded with time. A lake with mountains in the background showed battles taking place on opposing banks. On one side, men with swords and bows battled beasts and Kar'ruk. On the other side, men in ranger blacks fought other men and used firearms and cannons as well as blades.

"That is a recent addition," a woman said from a nearby doorway. "We had it done to honor my son."

She was pale, a somber black dress making the lightness of her skin more pronounced, with her face lean and plain. Gray mingled with the auburn in her hair, the locks swept back to the nape of her neck in a ponytail. She didn't wear any jewelry, and the simple clothing didn't bespeak riches or pretension.

A couple of old scars—claw marks?—traced the side of her neck, one disappearing below the collar of her dress. Had the estate been attacked by the fearsome predators that came down out of the mountains?

"Vlerion?" Kaylina asked before remembering the lost brother he'd spoken of.

"Vlarek." She—Lady Isla of Havartaft, presumably—studied

Kaylina with the same curiosity that Kaylina studied her. "You are not what I expected."

"Yeah, I got that from the chauffeur who implied you'd be deathly offended if I showed up in pajamas."

Isla smiled faintly, no lipstick or other makeup brightening her face. "I am not easily offended. *My* mother attends many social functions and cares about such things, but after all I've endured, I am unconcerned by propriety."

Yes, if she'd lost a son, what would lesser things matter? And those scars... Maybe the estate was attacked *regularly.* The rangers had to protect the lands of the nobles, as well as patrolling the borders, but Vlerion had suggested there weren't enough men these days to handle all that their duties required.

"I'm sorry you lost your son," Kaylina said. "How long ago did it happen?"

"Oh, some years back now. Almost a decade. It's hard to believe it's been that long. Someone once told me that wounds heal with time, but I've found that scars never go away, and they often ache in the deep of the night. We lost Avaron in the same year. After his son's passing, he struggled to control his emotions, and... that is often the end for those cursed."

"I... don't understand," Kaylina said, though if Isla had lost her husband too, no wonder she was grim.

"I wondered if he'd said anything to you."

"Vlerion." This time, Kaylina felt certain of her guess. "I don't know him that well."

"No? Beatrada thought you might have become close." Isla considered her again. "I'm a little surprised, as he's usually wise enough to avoid female entanglements, and you don't seem... Well, no, you're beautiful, certainly, and there's an exoticness about you."

"Er." The assessment made Kaylina blush with embarrassment —and discomfort. "I think—who did you say?—gave you the wrong idea. Vlerion doesn't like me. When we first met, he *arrested* me and my brother." She didn't mention hitting him on the head with a sling round. A mother might not approve of that. "Then his taybarri kept coming to visit me, and that irks him. Now, I'm supposed to be training as a ranger, and he's supposed to be my teacher, and he doesn't want to do it. Really, I don't think he likes me at all. By the way, if you can do anything about it, I don't *want* to be a ranger. I'm a mead maker. I brought some if you want to try it."

"Certainly. We make mead here with the honey."

Kaylina kept herself from suggesting hers would be better since that would be arrogant. And who knew? Maybe there was a master mead maker among the staff or family. "I noticed the hives."

Isla's gaze shifted down the hallway as the woman who'd taken the bottles walked toward them with a tray holding four glasses, two filled with the lighter-hued dry mead and two with the darker sweet. There were also three small silver plates containing cookies and pastries.

"Mead that the lady brought, my lady." The woman ducked her head as she formally held out the tray. Her eyes twinkled, and she winked at Kaylina as she added, "It's very good!"

Apparently, she was the taster.

"Raldo agrees," the woman added. "And Trager."

"Trager the stallion?" Isla raised her eyebrows.

"He came to the kitchen door with his nostrils twitching."

"And here I thought only the taybarri had noses for mead," Kaylina murmured.

"Interesting." Isla took a glass of the dry, waving for Kaylina to have some, and sipped, then nodded. "Thank you for the gift."

"Our meadery and eating house opens tonight if you or anyone you know wants to come by." Kaylina probably shouldn't be marketing when she didn't yet know if the castle would allow guests, but... she couldn't seem to stop mentioning it. It was her dream, damn it. She had to figure out a way to make it work.

"Hm," was all Isla said in response to that. "Take the tray upstairs, Helda. I'm going to show our guest a few portraits and have a chat with her."

"Yes, my lady."

Weren't they *already* having a chat? What else was there to discuss?

Feeling the need for fortification, Kaylina took a long swallow of the mead.

"Come." Isla cradled her glass without taking another sip. Maybe she wouldn't be as easily won over as the horse and the maid. At least she hadn't curled her lip and returned it to the tray. "I will show you a few things while we discuss the matter further."

The matter. That she thought Vlerion was into Kaylina? Kaylina didn't want to discuss that further. She'd hoped she had straightened Isla out on the subject.

"Is your estate attacked often out here?" Kaylina asked as she followed Isla through a couple of seating areas to the back of the manor where private wooden stairs led to an upper level.

"It has been attacked by Kar'ruk and packs of northern wolves and yekizar numerous times over the centuries," Isla replied without looking back. "It's only been the animals since I married Avaron and moved here. The Kar'ruk rarely send raiding parties these days. Pirates and bandits occasionally try to sneak in from the sea, thinking the Torn Towers mean the coast is defenseless. I know the king would like to rebuild them, but such projects are more expensive in these times when men must be paid."

"As opposed to when the nobles had slaves?"

"Serfs."

Kaylina wasn't the history enthusiast that her brother was, but she suspected there wasn't much of a difference between those two terms.

"As with most of the coastal north of the kingdom," Isla continued, "this area was once inhabited by the druids. Thanks to the magic they left in the land, our harvests are still prodigious, with our farms and orchards very healthy and not prone to disease and pests. They also left a few traps to thwart intruders. Perhaps I should say to thwart anyone who was not of their kind, but those who grew up here know to avoid those places. Would-be thieves from far away do not. The manor hounds sometimes find bodies along the cliffs overlooking the Strait."

"Our hounds are more into pheasants and squirrels."

"Ours are fond of those as well." After leading Kaylina through another sitting room, Isla extended a hand toward an open doorway.

A large four-poster bed occupied the center, and bookcases lined one wall with plush reading chairs next to it. Dark blue wallpaper sprinkled with the family crest in silver made the room dim, but maybe it suited Isla. Even without her dark dress, she would have carried the air of a woman in mourning, a woman whose wounds refused to heal.

An orange tabby cat lounging against the pillows sat up and looked at them.

"Vlerion can appreciate art and craftsmanship in many areas." Isla waved to a glass cabinet with musical instruments from around the kingdom, and was that a Kar'ruk bone flute? "Have you heard him play?"

"No, he oddly didn't break out a violin while he was arresting me."

Isla tilted her head. "Ms. Korbian, are you being snarky with me?"

"No. I was told that isn't allowed between commoners and nobles."

"It is most certainly frowned upon."

"There won't be flogging, will there?"

"Since you brought a gift, I'll refrain from springing upon you with a whip."

"I appreciate that."

The cat hopped off the bed and padded toward them. Kaylina couldn't imagine that it would smell the mead and be interested— cats were almost entirely carnivorous, weren't they?—but maybe it had been lonely and wanted attention.

"I suppose, since I brought you here to impart upon you the need to avoid my son, I shouldn't encourage you to get him to play for you."

Avoid Vlerion? How was Kaylina supposed to do that when his captain wanted Vlerion to train her?

"He is quite talented though," Isla continued. "His father and I thought... We didn't expect either of the boys to buck tradition and join the rangers. To involve themselves in battles and combat of any kind. We forbade it, of course, but once Vlarek was sixteen, he joined. And after he fell... Vlerion followed in his footsteps, thinking he could accomplish what his brother hadn't. Hubris. Both of them were full of it. All the males descended from King Balzarak have been farmers, and occasionally poets and artists as well. They've been talented in that area. And it is... what is safest for their kind."

King Balzarak? Vlerion had spoken about him, the man who'd ruled when the druids had cursed the castle, but he hadn't said Balzarak had been his ancestor. At the time of her questioning, Kaylina hadn't thought much of Targon's comment about Vlerion's ancestors giving up the throne, but the pieces clicked into place now. Maybe it had been the druids' curse that had prompted the family to step away from rule of the kingdom.

Isla gazed bleakly at a portrait on the wall, a middle-aged man with the same broad jaw and blue eyes as Vlerion. His father? Though the man's hair was longer, and his face wasn't as lean and scarred as that of his son, he had a fierce visage. There was a hint of something that could turn savage in those eyes. The same as Vlerion.

The cat brushed Kaylina's trousers, then wove between her legs.

"When I lose Vlerion," Isla said softly, "I will have lost everything. The gods did not bless me with any daughters, any who might have avoided the curse."

"Why do you say *when*? I've seen Vlerion fight. He's very talented at *that*. And when I say talented, I mean kind of amazing."

Isla turned her gaze on Kaylina. She'd been about to crouch to pet the cat, who clearly wanted attention, but Isla startled her by saying, "You are attracted to him."

"What? No."

Kaylina remembered the way her body had heated every time Vlerion had touched her, and the way she'd struggled to look away from him shirtless. Heat flushed her cheeks. She shouldn't lie to his mother, but it wasn't as if Kaylina would act upon any instinctual attraction she might feel. She didn't *want* to be attracted to someone who insisted on being called *lord* and got huffy because his taybarri liked her.

"If you've heard the term *animal magnetism,* it applies perfectly to the men of Havartaft Estate. I understand it well." Isla's voice dropped to a whisper, and she touched one of the scars on the side of her neck. "You're drawn to them, even if you shouldn't be. It is not your fault. Many women are affected that way, attracted to the danger they instinctually sense in the Havartaft men."

"I'm not attracted to Vlerion," Kaylina tried to assure Isla, though her face remained warm. She caught herself watching Isla's fingers and examining those scars anew. Those *claw* marks. She remembered the utterly destroyed fur shark floating in the water, its head smashed in by raw power. Raw power and *claws*.

"Then you will find it an easy matter to avoid him."

"Captain Targon is making him train me."

"Targon should know better than that. Vlerion may excel at training men, but you are not a man."

"I've noticed."

"And you do not desire to be a ranger? I do not know what Targon is thinking, but I will speak with him. He can find another to train you or release you from the duty altogether. Why has he recruited you?"

"Because the taybarri like me."

Her eyebrows rose. Maybe that wasn't the *usual* reason one became a ranger.

"He thinks I'm an *anrokk*. I don't know if you know what that is. I'd never heard of it, and I really doubt I am one anyway. I just have honey, and everyone—and every *animal*—likes honey." Kaylina dug in her pocket for the honey drops. "I didn't intend to give any to the taybarri. I wasn't *trying* to suborn them, despite what Targon said. They showed up and helped themselves. Especially Crenoch."

"Hm."

Since Isla had only taken a few sips of the mead and didn't seem that interested in it, Kaylina didn't expect her to reach for the honey drops. But Isla plucked one out and slid it into her mouth before Kaylina could say she'd made the treats for the taybarri. Oh, well. It wasn't as if it was a recipe for animal treats. Grandma served the honey drops with tea and mead for afternoon snacks at the Gull.

Isla's expression didn't change much as the sweet melted in her mouth, but she did eventually nod. "You have a gift for working with honey." She nodded toward the glass of mead as well. "Quite a gift."

"They're my grandma's recipes. She's the gifted one in the family. And the bees forage on flowers from altered plants that grow wild on our islands. That's our real secret."

"You may sell yourself short. I believe, if you can avoid falling to the curse of that castle, you could succeed with your business endeavor."

"Thank you."

"Targon is foolish." Isla took another honey drop, even smiling slightly as she popped it into her mouth. "That is where you should focus your efforts."

"I agree wholeheartedly."

"There is no need for you to interact with my son at all."

Kaylina hesitated. It was... a true statement, but why did the thought of not seeing Vlerion again feel like a punch to the gut? They didn't like each other. Not having to interact again should be a relief.

Isla's eyes closed to slits as she regarded her.

"I agree," Kaylina hurried to say. It would be logical to avoid Vlerion, to avoid all the rangers and concentrate on her dream. Her destiny. And this woman might turn out to be an ally, someone who could tell Targon off.

"If you *are* an *anrokk*, that might explain what Beatrada witnessed."

"Who?"

"My niece. She went to ranger headquarters yesterday and saw you and Vlerion standing together. Closely."

"Oh, that was his *cousin*?" Relief swept through Kaylina before she could remind herself that she wasn't interested in Vlerion and might not see him again if his mother had anything to do with it.

"Yes. She brought him news of another lord who was killed, a tax collector who was visiting the Nockberry Estate." Isla waved, perhaps to indicate that was somewhere close.

"With a blunt object?"

"I'm not certain of the details. If you are an *anrokk*..." Isla repeated, then trailed off.

"I don't think I'm anything special."

Isla looked pointedly down at the cat weaving between Kaylina's legs and purring. When Kaylina looked down, it put its front paws on her thigh and gazed up at her.

"I..." Kaylina lowered her arms, not sure if she should pick it up when Isla was reading who knew what into the attention.

The cat startled her by springing into her arms, trusting she would catch it.

"They are almost entirely men when they are in their born forms," Isla murmured, watching as Kaylina had little choice but to hold and pet the insistent cat. "But there's a hint of the beast. It's always there. Powerful. Dangerous. Just under the surface."

Kaylina swallowed. She'd sensed exactly that numerous times when she'd been near Vlerion. "Especially when they get irked?"

"Yes. That is the nature of the curse. It is when their emotions are roused that the beast comes out. Strong emotions are what bestir it. Hate. Anger. Passion. Fear." Her voice grew soft again. "Lust."

"When you say bestir, do you mean..." Again, Kaylina thought of the catacombs, of the creature she'd seen.

"They turn from men into beasts."

Isla took a lantern burning low near the bed and pushed on a bookcase, revealing a secret door, a windowless office behind it. Maps of the kingdom and enemy territories were mounted on the walls, but she went straight to a desk, a sketchbook open on the surface. She held up the lantern, gesturing Kaylina over.

Kaylina stared at a black-and-white illustration of the beast she'd glimpsed in the catacombs. Whoever the artist had been wasn't as practiced as the people who'd done the paintings downstairs, but he or she had captured the predatory power and savagery of the beast. Sleek fur short enough that one could see every muscle underneath the pelt. Claws. Fangs. Genitalia close enough to human to be startling. But the eyes were wild. Crazy, one might even say. There was no hint of sanity in them. Of control.

"That's Vlerion?" Kaylina whispered. "What he becomes?"

"This was my husband. I haven't seen Vlerion when he's turned, and I don't want to since people inevitably die when it happens. Men, *good* men, lose themselves when they become the beast. They're like rabid animals, savage instincts driving their actions. Only when they've sated their great surges of emotion do they change back into men. It can be minutes later. It can be hours later. The magic that the curse brings is unpredictable."

Even though a part of Kaylina had grasped this in the catacombs, it was still shocking to hear the details.

"When they're beasts, they kill indiscriminately. They sometimes know friend from foe but sometimes do not. And *all* men target them. Understandably, I suppose, but—" Isla's voice cracked, and she took a slow breath before continuing. "That is how I lost Vlarek. His own comrades didn't know about the curse, and when he turned and attacked people, they thought he was a monster down from the mountains. It took a great many trained rangers, but they slew him. Only when he died and turned back into a man, his body stark naked under the moonlight, did they learn the truth.

"That is why Captain Targon knows of the family curse. A few other rangers were there and also know. Before that, hardly anyone did. The descendants of King Balzarak Havartaft have kept it secret for generations, most of the men in the family seeking quiet lives, so as not to have the beast roused, so as not to kill, to murder. When it happens, sometimes they remember what they did. Sometimes not. From what my husband said, changing was like a dream—or a nightmare. Afterward, he was never certain what happened and what didn't.

"As you might imagine, I was horrified to learn all this, only *after* my parents had promised me to Avaron. Our families were old friends, and my grandmother knew of the curse. Apparently, she promised me to Avaron because I was a bit on the dowdy side, someone she thought wouldn't stir much lust but who could provide children." Her lips pressed together. "You can imagine what an honor that was when I learned of it."

Kaylina couldn't help but stare as the story unfolded, absently petting the cat in her arms. If this was a huge family secret, why was Isla telling her? What if Isla planned to have her killed after revealing everything? Thus far, she'd seemed like she might help Kaylina, but who knew what was in the noblewoman's mind? It wasn't as if she had any reason to feel anything for Kaylina. Her *cat* might like her, but...

"You're wondering why I'm telling you this," Isla said, watching her.

Kaylina couldn't imagine what expression was on her face.

"Yes," she whispered.

Isla smiled thinly. "*You* seem like someone who would stir a man's lust. If not his ire. Or both at once."

What was Kaylina supposed to say to that? She couldn't speak to Vlerion's *lust*, but she'd irked him more than once. More than once a *day*.

"Even I did," Isla admitted quietly. "Not at first, not when I lay there and let him..." She waved. "I was inexperienced. A virgin when we wed. But I was enamored with Avaron and wanted him to enjoy being with me. I feared if he didn't, he would seek mistresses, so I... educated myself on pleasuring a man."

Never would Kaylina have expected to discuss such things with a noblewoman, especially one she'd known less than an hour, but she couldn't keep from asking, "Did he... change?"

Once again, the scars on Isla's neck drew her gaze. A shiver of dread—of certainty—went through her.

"Yes." Isla followed her gaze and traced the scars. "There are others." She gestured toward her breasts and lower.

"Because he was mad or..."

"Aroused." Isla flipped through the drawing pad, showing

other pictures of the beast, and some of the man as well. "He knew when he was in that state that I was his mate—his *female* that he'd claimed—and, believe it or not, he was gentle, at least compared to when he attacked enemies. *I* lived, after all. And I... stayed. I loved him. And I bore his sons, which I don't regret, but, eventually, he grew distant and slept in his own bed. I don't think he went to others. I think he chose celibacy to ensure nothing would happen to the mother of his sons." Isla stopped on an illustration of the father holding a baby and standing next to a boy of seven or eight. Vlerion and Vlarek. "Some of the men in the family have done that, choosing celibacy and refusing to take wives, not wanting to pass along the curse, but the beast has thoughts of its own when it comes to that. It seems to be embedded in them that the family line must be continued. The *curse* must be continued. Usually, at least one son carries on the seed, taking a wife and bearing children." Isla turned back to Kaylina and held her gaze, her eyes intense. "Not all of those wives have survived. Sometimes, the beasts aren't gentle, or there are accidents. They're so powerful, so deadly..."

Mouth dry, Kaylina set the cat on the bed for an excuse to step away from Isla's unwavering stare.

"Listen, I appreciate the warning." Though Kaylina might have preferred *fewer* details. She also felt like an intruder now, knowing this much about the family history. "But it wasn't necessary. I—"

"For Vlerion, there have been a few dalliances with women—it is hard to convince a young man that he should be celibate—and I don't *think* any have ended... disastrously. But I doubt he would have told me if they had. His brother was his confidant. Since Vlarek passed, Vlerion keeps everything to himself. It was on a hunch that I had you brought here, and now that I've seen you might be an *anrokk*—" Isla glanced at the cat, still purring as it flopped down on the bed, "—I'm glad I followed my instincts and gave you this warning. For your own health and his, stay away from him. Please. Do not flirt with him. Do not even see him. If he turns, it's dangerous not only for you but for him. As I told you, his brother fell to his comrades. His friends. I don't want that to happen again."

Kaylina licked her lips, not knowing what to say. "Isn't there anything that can be done?"

"He does his best. When he feels his emotions rising, he sings or hums to himself, favorite old songs that calm him."

Yes, she'd heard that. Now it made sense.

But what she'd meant was... "Isn't there anything that can be done to end the curse?"

Isla shook her head. "For generations, King Balzarak's descendants have tried. Some became scholars and dedicated their lives to nothing but researching the past, trying to find a way to appease the druids, but those who left the curse are, as far as anyone has been able to determine, gone again from this world. Perhaps forever. Most of the descendants eventually accepted that they were dangerous and they needed to lead quiet lives of farming or scholarship or the like."

"Is the curse why King Balzarak abdicated the throne?"

"Yes. And it is why none of his male descendants attempted to reclaim it, even when they wished it, when they longed for the family to return to power. Neither my husband nor his sons would have turned on King Gavatorin, even if he's not the man his father was, and his son is... a dubious choice for a future monarch. That family has known about and kept the Havartaft secret since the beginning, so we owe him."

Kaylina hadn't meant to suggest a rebellion or that Vlerion try to take the throne—the city had enough strife as it was. She'd only been curious. She couldn't believe there wasn't a way to end the curse. Why would the druids have condemned the offspring of those so far removed from the people who'd committed the original transgression?

Isla rested a hand on Kaylina's arm. "Stay away from Vlerion. I can't risk losing another son. You don't know what it's like... to outlive your babies." She swallowed, her eyes moist. "I'll speak to Targon."

A horse whinnied outside. While Kaylina groped for what else to say, she drifted to the window, wondering if the carriage was ready to take her back.

But when she looked out toward the stable, she saw what had interested the horses. A taybarri had arrived. Crenoch. And Vlerion sat astride him. As if he felt her gaze, he looked up to the bedroom window, and their eyes locked.

An anxious flutter took Kaylina's stomach. His face was unreadable, but her instincts told her he wasn't pleased to see her here. To have his *mother* sharing his secrets with a woman he barely knew. With anyone.

22

A GOOD FRIEND WILL RISK HIS LIFE TO DEFEND YOU IN BATTLE; A GREAT friend will hold your secrets even when drunk.
   ~ Dainbridge III, the playwright

Vlerion's face was still masked when Kaylina walked outside, his mother coming right behind her. Protectively, Kaylina thought. Did she need protection from Vlerion? Maybe if he thought she'd come up here of her own accord, though Kaylina couldn't imagine why he would believe she would. Or could. She hadn't even known his surname.

"Mother." He'd dismounted and stepped forward to kiss her cheek. "Are you meddling?"

"Certainly. It's my duty to watch over you."

"You are not a god."

"Nor would I wish to be one, unless I could rouse them to return from the moon and walk among us again. We could use their guidance in these trying times." Isla gazed sadly at her son, probably thinking about the curse rather than the strife in town.

"Indeed." Vlerion looked between his mother and Kaylina and back, as if he wanted to ask what they'd been talking about. But maybe he already knew? Without questioning his mother, he faced Kaylina. "You did not report to ranger headquarters this morning."

Kaylina snapped her fingers. "I knew I forgot something."

His eyelids drooped in disapproval at her sarcasm.

"Try this, Vlerion." Isla offered him the glass of mead she'd been nursing.

He accepted it without taking his gaze from Kaylina and lifted it to his mouth but frowned down at it before touching it to his lips. "This is alcohol."

"Mead, yes," Isla said.

"You know I don't drink alcohol." The look he gave her as he handed the glass back said they both knew why.

Now, Kaylina had no trouble guessing the reason either. Alcohol's effects would make it harder for him to maintain his equanimity.

"A sip won't get you drunk. Just taste it. Ms. Korbian brought it."

Vlerion opened his mouth, presumably to refuse, but Crenoch ambled over, his large nostrils twitching.

"My mother was not talking to *you*," Vlerion told him. "Don't you remember passing out the *last* time you had her mead?"

Crenoch swished his tail and showed his teeth. Or maybe his *tongue*. He batted it against his upper teeth several times.

"Is that... a threat?" Kaylina couldn't tell.

"He's letting me know he doesn't care about the consequences and wants to imbibe like a lush selling her body for booze in a back-alley tavern." Vlerion moved the glass away when the taybarri tongue drifted toward it.

"Here." Kaylina intercepted his mount and dipped her hand into her pocket, withdrawing the bag of honey drops.

Crenoch's twitching nostrils turned in her direction. Isla watched but didn't say anything as Kaylina doled out the same sweets she'd shared with her for the taybarri. Crenoch whuffed, clucked, and licked as he slurped them out of Kaylina's hand. As he savored the treats, he leaned affectionately against her with his great body and almost knocked her over.

Vlerion stepped forward to steady her. "He's a beast."

The memories of the conversation with Isla flooded her mind, and Kaylina didn't come up with a response. Maybe that roused his suspicions because he frowned at both of them.

"Yeah, but he's nice," Kaylina said to distract Vlerion.

She patted Crenoch's neck, which resulted in more agreeable whuffs.

"Exactly what rangers want. *Nice* mounts to ride into battle against enemies."

Crenoch bared his fangs at Vlerion and whuffed again.

"If you're ready to go," Vlerion told Kaylina, "I'll give you a ride back to headquarters."

"I need to help my brother. It's opening night."

"Targon wants—"

"Tames will return Ms. Korbian in the carriage to her establishment to prepare her mead," Isla interrupted her son.

"Mother. The captain—"

"I will speak with him on Ms. Korbian's behalf."

"You just *met* her. Why are you involved in this, Mother?"

"Taste the mead." Her tone made it an order, a sterner no-nonsense order than Kaylina had heard Targon give to Vlerion. Than she'd heard *anyone* give him.

He stared mulishly at her for a moment and finally sipped the mead.

"It's good." He shrugged.

"It is like the ambrosia the gods enjoy after their great battles over the territories of the moon," Isla said.

Kaylina blinked at the accolade. She hadn't thought Isla liked it much.

Vlerion took another sip, letting it linger on his tongue as he considered it further.

"It is her calling," Isla added. "She has no desire to become a ranger."

"I'm aware."

"I will speak with Targon myself," Isla said. "Do not concern yourself further with Ms. Korbian. Tames will return her to the castle."

"I can take her." Vlerion waved to Crenoch. "I need to return to the city, and she's been eager to ride a taybarri again. There's no point in two of us making the trip."

Crenoch whuffed and stepped closer—Kaylina almost lost her foot that time—so she could rub higher on his neck, right under his floppy ear.

"Riding bareback on a taybarri with nothing but you to grab onto isn't appropriate for a young woman," Isla said.

Abruptly, Kaylina realized why Isla wanted her to ride back in the carriage. Alone. Isla believed Kaylina wouldn't be able to resist her attraction to Vlerion. If they were on a shared mount, with her arms wrapped around him, Kaylina might... what? Be so overcome by his masculinity—no, Isla had called it *animal magnetism*—that she would start rubbing herself all over him until he grew lustful?

Kaylina folded her arms over her chest. That would *not* happen. She was tempted to assert as much but didn't want to state aloud what Isla was insinuating but not saying to her son. Besides, if Isla could get Targon off her back, Kaylina didn't want to risk irritating her.

"She's not a noblewoman, Mother," Vlerion said. "I *know* she doesn't care about what is considered appropriate."

"You know less than you think," Isla said softly, a hint of some past pain creeping into her eyes.

"Isn't there a rule against mothers insulting their sons in front of women?"

"Absolutely no rule anywhere, no." Isla waved to someone in the stable.

"Mother." Vlerion gently but firmly clasped Isla's arm and pushed it down. "This is silly. She will ride back on Crenoch."

"Will you walk?"

"What? Four grown men may ride on a taybarri."

"Were she a *man*, I would have no concerns."

Vlerion squinted at her. Catching on?

"Walk with me, Mother," he said coolly, lifting a hand in a silent command for Kaylina to stay where she was.

As if she planned to rush after them to eavesdrop on their conversation? She wouldn't do such a thing. Probably.

As Vlerion and Isla walked off together, Kaylina admitted to intense curiosity. Knowing she was the subject of the conversation made it hard to ignore.

Two horses arrived. Had they been let out of their stable? Or had they escaped? Their noses butted Kaylina as they sniffed the dwindling sweets in her bag. She withdrew a few more honey drops. Crenoch's big tongue came in, ensuring he also got more.

By the time Vlerion returned, another two horses had shown up for the sweets, and it was only between their legs that she saw his boots approaching.

"Sorry, my lord," a young man called, running to gather the horses.

Only with reluctance and backward glances at her empty bag did they allow themselves to be led away. Crenoch held his head up and swished his tail. Nobody would lead *him* away.

"My mother may not have as much success talking Targon out of his plan for you as she thinks," Vlerion said. "The animals *are* drawn to you. I'm convinced he's right that you are an *anrokk*."

"I'm not. It's the honey." Kaylina waved the empty bag.

"Was my mother's cat also a fan of your honey?"

"I don't think cats eat honey."

"So, no."

"No."

Vlerion gripped Crenoch's fur and swung himself onto the taybarri's back. "I will take you to the castle to assist your brother with the opening of the eating house tonight, but, unless Targon tells me differently, I will expect you at dawn tomorrow for training." He lowered his hand, offering her assistance.

Kaylina was tempted to refuse, saying she could pull herself up, but nobody had given her a lesson on mounting a taybarri yet —what if there was only a certain spot or certain way they allowed their fur to be grabbed as an aid for rising? She clasped his hand.

She expected him to pull her up behind him, but he lifted her with ease and settled her in front of him, wrapping an arm around her waist. What, did he think she might leap off on the way back and try to escape?

Maybe his grip should have felt like a prison, but her entire body flushed with the awareness of him behind her. This was a more intimate position than she'd imagined.

She looked around for Isla and found her standing in the doorway, watching with a deep frown, as if she was positive nothing good would come of them riding together. But Vlerion had apparently reached the age at which he would no longer obey his mother unconditionally.

Isla tilted her head back and swallowed the rest of the mead. Something told Kaylina she might get drunk today, a way to keep from thinking about losing another son.

But she wouldn't. At least not because of anything Kaylina did. She hadn't intended to fling herself at Vlerion, even before his mother had told her everything, and she wouldn't now. She would be a fool—if not suicidal—to ignore Isla's warning.

But when Crenoch started walking, and then loping with the ease of a wolf that could cover dozens of miles in a day, the jostling shifted her back until Vlerion's inner thighs rested against her outer thighs, the heat of his body intense even through his clothing. The muscular arm around her waist kept her in place. Maybe she should have requested the carriage ride.

But Vlerion had to know what he was doing. He hadn't succumbed to lust when Ghara Saybrook had propositioned him, nor had he let himself gaze salaciously at Kaylina during their training. If he was interested in her at all, which Kaylina wasn't convinced of, he could control himself.

As Crenoch galloped down the road, his powerful legs carrying them far faster than the carriage would have, Kaylina allowed herself to relax. Vlerion had said he would return her to the castle, and this would get her back sooner. It *was* logical. There was nothing to worry about.

"My mother thinks I'm drawn to you because you're an *anrokk*," Vlerion stated with disdain. "Like the horses and taybarri and her sloth of a cat."

"I... She mentioned having concerns like that, but you're not, right? You haven't— I mean, you don't even like me, right?"

"You are exasperating and irreverent."

"Yup, that's what I thought."

"But I *am* attracted to you."

Her heart skipped a few beats at the startling admission. What was she supposed to say to that? To *do*?

He shifted slightly behind her, and she could feel the evidence of his attraction through his trousers.

"*Not* because I'm a mindless animal drawn by some ancient magic in your blood," he added.

"I didn't say that," Kaylina whispered, the irritation in his tone making her uneasy.

What if it ended up being his *mother's* words that made him angry, that roused the beast?

"You don't even like my mead," Kaylina added, striving for a lighter tone, but it was hard to think about more than the arm wrapped around her—trapping her—and his hard body behind hers.

"I didn't *dis*like it."

"Such praise. Can I put that on the menu under the tasting notes? Rambunctious Red. Not disliked by rangers."

"I'll allow that."

"Magnanimous."

"Yes."

Crenoch crested a hill, and the city came into view. Kaylina breathed a slow breath of relief. The ride wouldn't take much longer.

"You needn't be concerned around me," Vlerion said. "I do not act on the animalistic urges of my body."

"Meaning you're not going to make a pass at me?"

"Correct."

"Good. I'm relieved."

He snorted softly. "*You* probably are."

Something about the way he said that told her that such wasn't his experience with most women. Kaylina remembered the way Ghara had expressed her longing to be with him again.

Vlerion might not be as handsome as his riding partner, Jankarr, and his scarred face might not bestir a sketcher's muse, but women were drawn to him. To the beast, as Isla had suggested, sensing it lurking even if they didn't know of its existence. As Kaylina had been drawn. And... as she still was?

She didn't want to admit it, but if Vlerion rode off into a forest, pressed her up against a tree, and kissed her, she might not stop him. She *should* after what Isla had said, but strange urges kept sweeping through her. Animalistic urges, as he'd said. Unwise urges.

They were descending down a long slope toward the city, not more than ten minutes from the outskirts, when Vlerion's chest pressed against her back, and he whispered in her ear. "What did my mother tell you?"

It was more fear than arousal that shot through her, though there was some of both. Isla hadn't admitted the topic of their conversation to him? She'd told him to mind his own business? Or did he know but he wanted confirmation? It was a secret—his mother had said as much—and he couldn't be pleased that someone like Kaylina now knew about it.

"Tell me." It was an order, not a request.

"Only what I already suspected. After the catacombs."

"I see."

Vlerion nudged Crenoch with his knee, and the taybarri veered off into a copse, the trees interspersed with ancient vine-draped statues. They overlooked the city from the top of a cliff, a drop-off of at least twenty yards scant feet from the path.

Kaylina's fear intensified. What if Vlerion decided that getting rid of her would be an easy way to keep his secret safe?

After he slid off, gazing up at her with a grim expression, she wondered if she could try a knee nudge of her own and convince Crenoch to leave him and take her to the city. Probably not. She was out of honey drops, and the taybarri was busy sniffing a bush.

"Speak with me for a moment." Vlerion lifted a hand, offering her help down.

Kaylina slid off on her own, but her leg throbbed when she landed on hard rock, and she wobbled. He steadied her.

"About honey?" she asked, nervous. "Or mead? What would you like to know? Mead is believed to be the first alcoholic beverage that humans intentionally fermented. People have long valued honey for medicinal purposes as well as eating it for enjoyment. We've even used it to fertilize plants." An idea struck her as that bit of trivia came out, but she was trying to divert Vlerion from his dark thoughts, so she filed it away to consider more thoroughly later. "Early humans may have learned the craft of mead making from the druids, back before the druids decided people were the bane of their existence and a plague on the land. Over the centuries, all manner of variations have been made. There's metheglin—spiced mead—and my brother's favorite, melomel—mead with fruit mixed in—although if you're talking apples, you call that cyser. Oh, and my absolute favorite is acerglyn, which uses maple syrup. That's harder to come by on our islands, so we have to trade for it, and acerglyn is something my grandma only made once in a while. I'm planning to do a batch soon. I've seen maple trees right in the city."

Vlerion tilted his head as he regarded her. At least he didn't look like he was contemplating her swift death. No, he was probably contemplating how exasperating she was.

"I'll send some to your mother," Kaylina added. "She's an unexpected fan."

Bringing up Isla was a mistake. His faint exasperation switched to jaw-clenching hardness.

"She should not have called you to the manor. And Beatrada should not have said... whatever she said. She must have misinterpreted us standing together. I don't know why. It is not as if we were *doing* anything." There was that exasperation again. "Even if we had been, it's none of her business. I can manage my... *issue* without my mother interfering."

"I didn't get much of a choice." Kaylina didn't want to pit Vlerion against his mother, but she wanted him to know she hadn't tried to wheedle that information out of her. "Her chauffeur and strongman showed up at the castle and insisted I come."

"Beatrada may have learned of Targon's belief that you are an *anrokk* and thought I would be affected more strongly by you than by normal women."

Kaylina shook her head, both at the term that now plagued her and the fact that yet another man didn't consider her *normal*. Domas's condemning words rang in her head again.

"But I am not an *animal*." Indignation flared in Vlerion's eyes— and that glint of savagery that she'd picked up on from the beginning, that promised he was... not normal either. *Dangerous.*

She tried to step back, but Crenoch was behind her, so she bumped against him. Finished sniffing, the taybarri regarded Vlerion. With wariness?

Vlerion caught the look and took a deep breath. For a moment, he closed his eyes and hummed so softly that Kaylina barely heard it. Now that she knew his reasons for doing that, it was far from reassuring since it meant he was on edge. How *much* emotion did he have to feel before the curse prompted him to change?

"I request that you tell no one of my... condition," he said when he opened his eyes.

The glint was gone. He'd regained control.

"I wasn't planning to. Who would believe me?"

"You will not speak of it to your brother?" His eyebrows rose.

"I..." Would she? Frayvar was her only ally here, the only person she could rely on. She didn't want to keep secrets from him, but this shouldn't affect him in any way. Unless Vlerion lost it in the middle of their kitchen and endangered Frayvar, she couldn't think of a reason he needed to know. "I won't."

His eyelids drooped halfway. "And the Virt girl who wants you to deliver information on the nobility to her?"

"I wouldn't tell her." That Kaylina could say without hesitation.

Judging by the way Vlerion continued to gaze at her, her lack of hesitation didn't matter. He worried it was a possibility. Because they were both working class and would be drawn to band together against the nobles? Against someone like him?

Kaylina spread her arms, not sure how to explain that she barely knew the girl and didn't feel any loyalty to her. So far, the rangers and commoners had annoyed her equally.

"It is the kind of information the Virts want and that they could use against me and my family. Maybe the entire aristocracy." Vlerion looked over the cliff toward the city. "Over the generations that my family has been cursed... the beasts have killed many. That is because you have no control over its cruel and savage instincts when you change, not out of any malice or evilness in you as a person. My brother risked his life fighting as a ranger. He never would have taken the lives of others who were no threat to him or the kingdom. Not intentionally. And it is the same for me."

"I believe you."

They stood close to the edge of the cliff, and she again hoped he wasn't contemplating that it would be safest for him to get rid of her. Easing to the side a few steps, Kaylina picked out the river in the distance and followed it to the castle, imagining she could see the red glow of the tower from there, though it faced the wrong direction to be visible.

"They would come for me en masse if they knew what I was," Vlerion continued, not commenting on her steps away from him. "They might come for my family and our lands too. Do everything in their power to end the curse—to end the Havartaft line forever." His voice grew so soft she barely heard him add, "I can't even say that it would be a bad idea, but I would have to defend myself and especially my family."

"I understand that." They'd discussed how much family meant to them.

His gaze returned to her. "Perhaps you do."

"Hopefully, you won't be offended if I don't swear my obedience and loyalty to you, but I didn't want to know that secret to start with, and I'll keep it for you, okay?" Kaylina willed him to believe that. "That beast, uhm... *you* saved my life in the catacombs. I owe you."

"As we've discussed, you were only down there because I took you."

"You don't think I could have been curious and gone down and gotten in trouble all on my own? You don't know me very well. Just last night, I broke into the tower and threatened a sentient plant."

"Oh?"

"Frayvar was in danger, and I thought the answer to how to pull him out of it might be up there."

"Was it?"

"Not really. He came around on his own. But there's a big gnarly plant in a pot up there, kept alive by who knows what. I sure haven't been watering it. It's the source of the red glow."

"You should leave it alone. There's a reason someone removed those stairs and boarded it up. It probably tried to kill them."

Remembering the flexing vines, Kaylina deemed that likely. "There's got to be a way to remove the curse though. And *your* curse. They're tied together, right?"

"Many in my family have researched our curse."

Yes, his mother had said that, but... "Have they researched Stillguard Castle?"

"I'm not aware. Perhaps not since it doesn't belong to our family."

"Well, *I'll* research it. I'll get my brother on it too. He *loves* books. Not good rousing romantic adventures but nonfiction." She wrinkled her nose. "He's weird."

"You'll involve your brother whom you're not going to share my secret with?" His eyebrows went up again.

"Yeah. He doesn't need to know about that part of the curse to do research. He'll do research because he thinks it's fun. Like I said, *weird.*" She tried a smile for him.

Vlerion only gazed back with somber eyes.

"I mean it." She made herself meet that gaze. "I owe you. You can trust me with your secret."

"I have no choice but to do so." He didn't sound pleased about that.

It stung a little that he didn't trust her, but they didn't know each other well, and she called him *pirate*. Why *would* he trust her?

"I thought you might have brought me over here to push me off the cliff." Maybe she shouldn't have said that and put the idea in his mind.

"No." Vlerion smiled faintly. "Crenoch wouldn't have allowed that."

Hearing his name, the taybarri whuffed and swished his tail.

"He likes you more than me," Vlerion added.

"Because you're haughty, uptight, and don't give him sweets?"

"Because..." Vlerion turned his palm toward the sky. "He senses what I am—what I can *become*. They all do. To the taybarri, I am a dangerous predator, not a simple rider."

Crenoch nuzzled the side of Kaylina's head.

"I understand, but it still..." Vlerion closed his open hand into a fist and lowered it to his side. "It is petty of me to be annoyed by that, but I always admired them. As a boy, I had a stuffed taybarri toy that I took everywhere. I wanted to be a ranger, partially to follow in my brother's footsteps, but partially so I could ride the taybarri."

"They are impressive animals." Kaylina stepped away from Crenoch, not wanting to give Vlerion another reason to be annoyed with her.

Crenoch washed her ear with his tongue.

"Though somewhat exasperating." She leaned away and wiped her ear.

"Indeed."

Her movement brought the city back into her view, and she

picked out black smoke that hadn't been there before. It was coming from...

"The castle," she blurted, pointing. Fear surged through her veins, not fear for herself this time but for her brother. "It's on fire."

23

THE PAIN OF A LOVED ONE AFFECTS US MORE GREATLY THAN OUR OWN.
  ~ Dionadra, Essays on the Motivations of Men

Kaylina rode behind Vlerion as Crenoch carried them at top speed down the slope toward Port Jirador. Arms wrapped tightly around him, she pressed her cheek to his back and willed Frayvar to be okay. Every time she left, something happened to him. Why was the world targeting him instead of her? This was her big dream, not his.

"There's too much smoke for it to be something burning in the hearth," Vlerion said as they rode through the city gates, cresting a hill that gave them another view of the castle.

"My brother never burns anything. He tends everything he cooks assiduously."

"The curse may add an ingredient not compensated for in his recipes."

If that ugly plant was responsible for lighting the castle on fire,

Kaylina would run up there with a sword and lop off every one of its branches and vines.

The air buzzed, and a sharp tingle ran through Kaylina as the world blurred. At first, she had no idea what was happening, but they went from running down a street to landing atop a bridge over the river. Crenoch had flashed.

The ringing of a gong sounded several blocks over.

"That's the fire wagon," Vlerion said. "I don't know if they'll be willing to step onto the premises though."

"*I'll* step on them. Just get me there."

He did. A few seconds later, they reached the back of the castle, and Crenoch surged through the open gate into the courtyard.

Black smoke billowed out the kitchen windows and choked the air, stinging Kaylina's eyes. She could feel the heat too, a sharp contrast to the cool air.

Flames licked at the edge of the high pantry window, and Kaylina wondered if someone had come up from the catacombs to start the fire. But why? The Virts couldn't blame her or Frayvar for the men and munitions they'd lost down there, could they? As far as she knew, none of the men she'd seen—and who'd seen her—had survived to talk about it.

Vlerion sprang off before Kaylina could dismount and landed with his sword in his hand. Maybe he also believed someone other than the curse had been responsible for the fire.

He reached the doorway before her, calling, "I'll look for your brother," over his shoulder. "Stay outside."

She ran to the well house and drew up a bucket of water but feared it would do little against a fire that had already grown large.

"Help!" came a pained cry from inside. Frayvar.

Kaylina almost dropped the bucket but kept it as she charged through the kitchen doorway, water sloshing over the edges. The smoke made it hard to see inside, and she almost tripped over pots and pans on the floor.

Heat roiled off flames burning tapestries, curtains, and the wooden cabinets. They also licked at the ceiling boards. She hadn't realized there was so much flammable material in the stone castle.

A cry of pain came from the floor between the island and the pantry. *That* was why pans littered the floor. The huge wrought-iron pot rack had fallen, and Frayvar was pinned under it, a broken piece of the travertine countertop on top of it, adding to its weight. The rack was too heavy for him to move. It would be too heavy for *Kaylina* to move, too.

Vlerion shoved aside a cast-iron pot to crouch beside the rack. He touched the metal, jerked his hand back at the heat, then removed his shirt. He wrapped the material around the edge of the rack and, with a great flexing of his shoulders, heaved it upward.

Kaylina rushed forward, afraid Frayvar had broken bones and wouldn't be able to move.

"I told you to stay outside," Vlerion said, his voice raspy from the smoke, his back and arm muscles bulging as he held up the heavy rack with both hands.

"I told *you* I wouldn't obey you." Barely glancing at him, Kaylina grabbed her brother and pulled him out from under the rack.

"Exasperating."

"As we've established!"

Frayvar groaned in pain, and Kaylina worried she was hurting him further, but she had to get him out of there and kept pulling. As gangly as he was, he was still tall and weighed a lot to her. Coughing from the smoke invading her throat, she struggled to drag him toward the door.

As soon as her brother had cleared the rack, Vlerion let it fall. He leaped toward them and lifted Frayvar in his arms.

"Out," he ordered Kaylina.

With tears streaking down her eyes, and smoke curling up her nostrils, she had no reason to disobey this time. As she ran out after Vlerion and Frayvar, she glanced at the pantry, lamenting that her mead might be destroyed. The charred door stood open, several shelves burning. The mead was down in the root cellar, but the heat might ruin it. The fire might even have started down there.

She shook her head, gasping in fresh air as she ran into the courtyard. Frayvar was alive. That was all that mattered for now.

The fire wagon had arrived—sort of. The horses pulling it had stopped forty yards up the trail along the river. They and the men looked at the castle with concerned eyes, the horses because of the fire, the men because of the curse.

"Come closer," Vlerion ordered as he lay Frayvar on the ground outside the stone wall of the courtyard. It provided protection from the fire and heat. "Get the hose out."

"Let the cursed castle burn!" someone watching from across the river called.

But the firefighters either recognized Vlerion or were trained to obey orders, because they brought the wagon closer, then leaped down. Two men pulled the hose toward the courtyard, and another set up a pump to draw water from the river. Vlerion joined them, pointing out the well as another water source.

Kaylina wanted to help, but she had to make sure Frayvar was all right. His skin was red and warm, his eyes glazed, and soot darkened his sweaty hair.

"Are you okay?" She knelt beside him and pushed his shaggy bangs out of his eyes. "I'm so sorry things keep happening to you every time I leave. I'm going to *kill* that plant."

Frayvar dragged a sooty sleeve across his watering eyes. "I don't think it was the curse." His voice was even raspier than Vlerion's had been. "I heard something below. Not *way* below, like the clinks from the catacombs, but it came from the root cellar." He coughed several times and wiped his eyes again before he could continue. "I grabbed the fireplace poker, opened the trapdoor, and went down. There wasn't anyone there, but some of your mead was missing, and someone had left a lantern. The arsonists had to have come in from below."

"Why would the Virts burn the castle? And steal my mead?"

Maybe they'd wanted their staging area back. And to drive out the pesky witnesses working in the castle.

"You didn't see anyone?" she added.

"No, but I didn't go exploring. My stew was on the fire." Frayvar grimaced. "All my meals will be ruined. The opening tonight..."

"I know. It's horrible."

"There were people out front looking at the menu this morning. I took mead samples out, and *more* people came. Some said they'd be back as long as they could eat outside. I showed them all the tables in the courtyard and said that wasn't a problem. They really liked the mead. It was all going to work. And now—" Another round of coughs took Frayvar.

"Relax." Kaylina patted him down, trying to figure out if he had broken bones. That he was talking was a good sign, but she wanted to take him to see a healer.

His face contorted when she touched what had to be a tender area. Broken ribs?

Kaylina drew back. Better to let a healer do the exam.

"I like your ranger more now," Frayvar admitted, closing his eyes. "He doesn't seem as stuffy and aloof when he's saving your life."

"Odd."

"Yeah. Though his face was the same, even when he was

heaving the rack off me." He opened his eyes. "Real steady and calm. You have no idea what he's thinking."

"He had to be thinking that someone was an idiot for crafting such an obnoxiously heavy pot rack."

Crenoch walked over and stood beside them, his tail brushing the pebbles of the trail as he looked up and down the river. Why did Kaylina believe he'd decided he needed to guard them?

"Probably," Frayvar said. "It *was* heavy. I've been told I'm not real expressive. Maybe Vlerion is like me. And grandma too. She laughs and jokes sometimes, but she's usually got a blank face when you're talking to her. I guess I do too."

"We're not the most normal family. Except for Silana, maybe."

"Yeah. She takes after Dad. What I remember of him."

"She's not a deadbeat who abandoned his family because he couldn't handle doing mundane chores and having Grandma tell him what to do." For the first time, Kaylina realized that *she* had left the family too, drawn by something intangible. Needing to prove herself, yes, but maybe also feeling it would be easier without so many eyes upon her, without her loved ones worrying about and judging her. The realization that she might have some of their father in her was disturbing.

"I don't remember much about him," Frayvar said. "He played wooden snakes and rabbits with me."

"He hugged you too. You hated that. You always tried to squirm away."

"I prefer games to hugging."

"You prefer everything to hugging. You're never going to get a girlfriend."

"I guess I should stop dreaming about Lady Saybrook then."

"I think so."

Vlerion stepped out of the courtyard, soot streaking his bare chest, his damp trousers clinging to him. He looked heroic. And hot.

Kaylina swallowed and pulled her gaze from his chest, glad that fires didn't rouse the beast. Most battles didn't either. She wondered what had happened in the catacombs, why he'd lost his equanimity down there.

"How is he?" Vlerion pointed to Frayvar.

"Broken. Would your doctor be willing to treat a young chef?" Maybe she should have asked about another healer, one not associated with the rangers, but their doctor was experienced, and she wanted the best for her brother.

"I'll ensure he is," Vlerion said. "Crenoch can carry the three of us."

The thought of returning to the taybarri's back with Vlerion's arm wrapped around her again had some appeal, but...

Kaylina bit her lip and peered through the gate. She should go with her brother, but she wanted to figure out what had happened here. And, if it was possible, she wanted to salvage her mead. *Especially* if someone lurking below had stolen some. What if they came back for the rest?

"The fire is out?" Kaylina didn't see any more flames, only sooty stone and water dripping from the eaves and streaking the walls. The heat had dissipated.

"It is."

"Thank you for your help." Though it was difficult, she made herself add, "My lord."

His eyebrow twitched, and she knew it had sounded like a cat had dragged that honorific out of her throat with its hind claws.

"Frayvar likes you now," she added. Maybe that would mollify Vlerion.

"Only Frayvar?"

While she groped for a witty response, a firefighter walked out.

"Flames are all out, my lord. We found this in the pantry." The man lifted the remains of a broken bottle. "It smells of kerosene. Looks like someone started this intentionally."

Vlerion took the bottle, sniffed the interior, and nodded. "The Virts have been down in the catacombs, making trouble lately. I'll send men to do another flush."

The firefighter's sooty face blanched, making Kaylina wonder if he was associated with the group. All he said was, "Yes, my lord. If there's nothing else?"

"No. It's Sergeant Tannerhook, right?"

The man blinked. "Yes, my lord. I didn't realize..."

"I'll tell your superior that you did good work today."

"Thank you." The firefighter bowed before rounding up his men and equipment.

"There was an explosion too," Frayvar said. "That's how it started and when the rack fell."

"The Virts are good at explosions." Vlerion gathered Frayvar in his arms again and hoisted him to Crenoch's back. "Can you roll over and hang on?"

Frayvar hissed in pain at the jostling to his ribs but nodded. "Yes, my lord."

His *my lord* was a lot more sincere than Kaylina's. Maybe if Vlerion had pulled her out of danger, she would have an easier time with the words. Or... maybe not. For some reason, his insistence that she use them rankled. She *did* appreciate that he'd saved her life in the catacombs, and she would keep his secret for him.

"Do you need a hand up?" Vlerion turned toward Kaylina after he'd settled Frayvar astride.

"I'll stay here. Someone should let the people who show up for dinner know there's been a slight delay with our opening."

"You don't think the charred wood, sooty walls, and smoke hanging in the air will tell them that?"

"I prefer the personal touch."

"She wants to check on her books, my lord," Frayvar said.

"That's not it." But his words sent a surge of alarm through

Kaylina. "Why, what happened to my books? They're upstairs, not in the kitchen. The fire didn't go up there, did it?"

"I don't think so."

"Good. It's the *mead* I was planning to check on."

Vlerion pressed his lips together. "The arsonist may still be around. You shouldn't stay here alone."

He lifted a hand, as if he would grab her and hoist her up behind her brother, whether she wanted it or not.

Kaylina skittered back, and Crenoch stepped between them before Vlerion could decide if he seriously wanted to go after her. The furry blue snout turned left and right as Crenoch considered them both. His eyes seemed to say, *Be good.*

Vlerion speared his mount with a dark glare. At least he didn't give Kaylina an irritated one. His admission that it bothered him that the taybarri was more into her than him floated through her mind, and sympathy welled up in her. He hadn't asked for that curse. With that beast always lurking within, threatening to come out, he was forced to be a different man than he should have been, all because of a choice a long-dead ancestor had made.

Kaylina stepped around Crenoch and clasped Vlerion's hands. "I want to look around. I'll be okay. I'll crack any arsonists I see in the head with a lead round. And," she added, thinking it might please him, "I'll come for training in the morning." On impulse, she rose on her tiptoes and kissed him on the cheek.

As she drew back, his mother's words came to mind: *Do not flirt with him.*

But a kiss on the cheek wasn't flirting. It was showing gratitude. And Vlerion's visage softened.

"I'll send someone to help you look," he said, swinging up behind Frayvar.

"A ranger?" Kaylina gazed toward the opposite side of the river. The man who'd shouted to let the castle burn down was gone, but other onlookers remained, drawn by the action.

Vlerion followed her gaze. "Someone who won't attract notice. Jankarr, if he's around. Wait until he arrives to go inside." His tone made it clear that it was an order, but the squint that accompanied it suggested he wasn't positive she would obey it.

"Of course." She smiled.

His squint deepened, but Frayvar groaned and gripped his ribs. Vlerion nudged Crenoch into motion.

Only as they rode away did Kaylina realize she recognized one of the onlookers. The woman's hood was up, but it didn't quite cover her face. Jana.

24

ENEMIES AND ALLIES TEST US IN DIFFERENT WAYS, BUT THEY TEST US ALL the same.
~ Lord General Menok

Water dripped onto Kaylina's head as she looked through the wreckage in the kitchen. None of the food would be salvageable, unfortunately, and she frowned at the thought of having to buy all Frayvar's ingredients to start again. She hadn't asked him how much money he had left, but she'd recently caught him looking into his ledger and scowling at the numbers.

Surprisingly, the fire in the hearth was still burning, happily gnawing at logs with red embers. A layer of soot floated in the pot of apple-cider stew that still hung above the flames. She put on mitts and removed it. Like everything else, it would have to be thrown out. Frustrating, but, if the firefighter was right, she couldn't blame the curse.

Reminded of her earlier musings about the plant, Kaylina filled another pot with water and hung it lower over the flames so it would boil. Despite the fire that had burned in the pantry, the jars of honey hadn't broken, and most were still sealed. She took one and grabbed a spoon, intending to make the fertilizer she'd been thinking of earlier. As far as she recalled, Grandpa had mixed a few tablespoons of honey in a gallon of water. She didn't think there were any other ingredients.

While waiting for the pot to boil, she peered into the root cellar. Tiny shards of glass lay on the stone floor below. From the broken bottle of kerosene the fire sergeant had found?

She crouched by the ladder and debated whether to investigate further but decided to be wise—*not*, she told herself, obedient—and wait for whoever Vlerion sent to help her. She didn't need to run into vengeful arsonists lurking in the catacombs.

After stirring her honey into the heated water, she grabbed a rag and debated how to clean up the kitchen. Everything was sooty, and the thought of tackling the chore was daunting. That niggling feeling that they should give up and go home returned. This was turning into so much more than she'd planned for.

Some instinct told her to check the window, to see if Jana had disappeared or was still watching. Yes, the older woman remained across the river, now standing in the shadows of a tree, twilight creeping over the city and helping to hide her. If Kaylina hadn't spotted her earlier, she would have missed her.

Deciding to be cheeky, Kaylina lifted a hand and gave a hearty wave.

Jana didn't react.

"Doesn't that woman have her own inn to keep her busy?" Kaylina hadn't verified Jana's story by going to see if the establishment she'd mentioned existed. She made a mental note to do so.

"Hello?" came a young woman's voice from the vestibule.

"We're closed due to fire." Kaylina assumed it was someone who'd planned to enjoy dinner here, but hadn't Frayvar said that none of those people had been willing to come inside?

She abandoned the rag to check on the visitor and found the girl from the delivery wagon in the great hall. Milzy.

Vlerion's concern about what Kaylina might tell Milzy filled her mind, and her first urge was to shoo the girl out. What if the ranger, or whoever Vlerion sent, showed up and found them chatting together? Milzy might be a known Virt spy.

"I heard about that," she said. "I came to see if you're okay. Is your brother..." Milzy looked around.

"Gone to see a doctor. Broken ribs. A heavy iron pot rack fell on him."

"Oh, that's awful." Milzy lifted a hand to her mouth and appeared genuinely distressed.

"He would agree. It'll be all right though. We'll get the place cleaned up and do our opening another night." Kaylina smiled and waved Milzy toward the front door, hoping she would take the hint and leave.

But Milzy looked around, from floor to ceiling, and didn't notice the gesture. "I heard there was a ranger here. Lord Vlerion. He's a scary bastard. Killed a lot of the righteous and virtuous." Milzy touched her chest. "They say he doesn't blink when he drives his sword through people. A real stone-cold killer."

"He is... effective."

"What was he doing? Is he gone?" Milzy lowered her voice to a whisper. "Is it safe?"

"As safe as it always was." Kaylina glanced in the direction of the glowing tower. "I'm surprised you came in."

"I wasn't going to, but two other rangers on taybarri were riding down the street out front. I didn't want them to think I was lurking or loitering. Whatever they call it. I've been arrested before, even though I wasn't doing anything."

"They like to throw people in jail."

Milzy looked at her. "That's right. You were there that night.

When the ranger captain and Lord Vlerion were killing our people outside."

Our people. Kaylina had already known Milzy was allied with the Virts, but the words voiced out loud where anyone could hear them made her nervous. She glanced toward the kitchen, half expecting to spot Jankarr in the shadows listening.

"I've heard they're interested in this place. And you."

Milzy's expression was curious rather than accusing, but it also made Kaylina nervous. She didn't want to be known as being aligned with the rangers and not only because it might ruin Targon's plans. For whatever reason, she and Frayvar—especially poor Frayvar—were already targets.

"Not so much interested in as mistrustful of," Kaylina said. "Their taybarri have come here of their own accord for my honey and mead."

Milzy blinked. "What?"

"Apparently, they like sweets, and the rangers only give them protein pellets."

"Huh. That's interesting. I wonder if you could intentionally lure their taybarri out of the stables with such things."

Kaylina didn't point out that Vlerion had brought up that very notion. He'd seemed certain that honey alone wouldn't draw them.

"The rangers are dangerous all on their own, but they wouldn't be quite as effective without their fearsome mounts. And they wouldn't be able to get across the city so quickly." Milzy's eyes had grown speculative.

Kaylina wondered if Milzy was older than she'd originally believed. And higher up in the Virt organization than one would think?

"I don't know." Kaylina glanced toward the kitchen again. She didn't see anyone but had the feeling of being watched.

"Would you be willing to try it? Luring the taybarri out of the city? On a particular night when it might be useful to those who want to change things and make it better for people like you and me?" Milzy pointed to Kaylina and herself.

"Look, I'm sympathetic, but I can't get involved. My brother and I just suffered a financial blow, not to mention the blow to his ribs, and we need to focus on making the meadery work before we run out of money. We don't have a backup plan."

"You're sure? If things changed and Port Jirador was less oppressive, and factory owners had to pay more, there'd be a lot more people who could afford to eat fancy food and mead."

"Our food won't be that expensive."

"The menu looked fancy."

Did that mean Milzy had been by earlier? How many people were keeping an eye on the castle?

"That's only because Frayvar can't write anything down without using big words." Kaylina gently took the girl's arm and walked her toward the exit. "I need to clean. Thanks for checking in. Come on by for the opening. I'll give you a free cup of mead."

If her mead was still palatable. She needed to check it more thoroughly.

At first, Milzy let herself be led, but a few steps from the door, she rooted her feet to the floor. "Are you sure you can't help us? There's going to be a night soon when we'll really need some distractions. Having all the taybarri escape would help."

Kaylina started to shake her head, but if she could get the date the Virts were planning something and give it to Vlerion, he might trust her more. Maybe she shouldn't *want* his trust, especially since Milzy was right, and, logically, Kaylina should be on the side of the underdog workers.

But Vlerion deserved to have something go his way. Her desire to make that happen had nothing to do with his class. Just with him.

"What night do you need the distraction?" Kaylina asked

quietly, hoping she'd been mistaken about someone watching her. Even though she planned to give the information to Vlerion, if she were heard asking, it might sound condemning.

The girl smiled. "I *knew* you were with us."

"I'm not. I just... want to help."

Help Vlerion, she added silently, but Kaylina wished she *could* somehow help the girl and the workers in general. Couldn't both sides come together and negotiate for improvements without warring with each other? Without blowing things up and killing people?

"Tomorrow night," Milzy said.

"That soon?"

Milzy nodded. "It's long past time for a regime change. If you're thrown in jail, we can get you out."

"Thanks," Kaylina murmured and opened the door, the fresh air that wafted in making her realize how smoky and stuffy it was inside. How would they ever get this place fit to serve people?

Milzy, in a far brighter mood, skipped as she left the property.

Kaylina closed the door and rested her forehead on it. *Regime change.* Maybe she should have tried to get more details, but that might have been suspicious. Less than an hour after an arson, Kaylina wasn't inclined to raise anyone's suspicions and inadvertently turn herself into an enemy. A target.

"You know they're planning to assassinate the king, don't you?" a male voice spoke from behind her.

Heart leaping into their throat, Kaylina whirled. It wasn't Jankarr but Captain Targon.

His face was hard, his eyes icy, and she knew he'd heard everything.

25

AN IDEA MAY SPARK A MOVEMENT.
  ~ *Lord Professor Varhesson, Port Jirador University*

"I didn't know that, no." Kaylina willed calm into her voice as she answered Captain Targon. The ranger wore a cloak, but his black leather armor was beneath it, a sword hanging from his belt. After seeing the veteran fight, she knew he was almost as dangerous as Vlerion. "You're not Jankarr."

An obvious statement, but she was nervous.

"You think he would have minded less that you were talking to a Virt spy?"

"I think he would have come out, flirted with her, and helped me learn more information."

"The flirting part might be right." Targon walked slowly toward Kaylina, considering her.

"I only asked because I thought Vlerion would want to know what night they're planning things."

"And you've sworn your loyalty to him now?"

"Well, he saved my brother's life." Kaylina pointed toward the kitchen. "And his mom likes my mead."

Targon stopped, his eyebrows drifting up. Maybe there hadn't been time for Vlerion to give him a lowdown of the day.

"You spoke with Lady Isla? At Havartaft Estate?"

"Yes. She sent a carriage for me."

"Why?"

Kaylina opened her mouth but paused. Isla had said Targon knew Vlerion's secret, hadn't she? And Kaylina had caught the two men exchanging long significant looks she believed had been related to it. Even so, she worried she'd misremembered something, so she hesitated to speak it aloud, lest she betray Vlerion.

"Lady Isla is a mead enthusiast," Kaylina said.

"Not that I've heard."

"Maybe she doesn't confide her drink preferences to you."

Targon walked closer. "In the jail, under the influence of the kafdari root, I believed you were a foolish tourist, as Vlerion said, and nothing more. But now I wonder... I've recently grown aware of Virt factions forming to the south, in cities far removed from the capital. You did nothing but babble about your family when we questioned you."

Kaylina winced, well remembering how she'd revealed far more about her fears and dreams and regrets than she ever would have wished to tell a stranger. She didn't tell her closest family members that much about her thoughts.

"That's because that's all I know about. Honest."

"Honey alone wouldn't lure away the taybarri. They're not dumb animals, and they're not trapped in our stables. They could *escape* any time they wanted." Targon had heard every word of that conversation, hadn't he? "But as an *anrokk*, you might be able to do what that girl was asking. The Virts have their own spies. A lot of them. I wonder if they've figured out what you are."

"I'm not anything. I swear."

"By now, even you can't believe that."

Kaylina spread her arms helplessly. What did he want from her?

"What were you trying to learn from Lady Isla?" Targon asked.

"Nothing. She invited *me* up to her estate."

He stopped in front of her. Close enough to grab her. Kaylina was tempted to reach for her sling, but he had that deadly blade and might decide her usefulness had ended.

"Is that so? How did she hear about your mead? You haven't opened yet, and she lives an hour to the north."

"Vlerion must have told her." Kaylina shrugged and groped for a way to end the conversation or divert his attention. She hadn't meant to, but she'd started lying, and Targon was the type who might sense that and get her tangled up in her mistruths. "Look, I was being sarcastic. It wasn't about mead. She warned me to not flirt with Vlerion."

"Oh?" Targon had lifted a hand, as if he were on the verge of grabbing her, but he lowered it. "Did she? Maybe Beatrada said something."

"Yes. His cousin, right? I guess she saw us together in the arena and thought there was something there that wasn't and told Vlerion's mom." Kaylina shrugged. "I get that I'm a commoner, and I'm not *appropriate* for her son, but I had no idea the mothers of nobles were so nosy."

"Hm." Targon regarded her thoughtfully.

Trying to discern if she was telling the truth?

"You can question me with that drug one more time, if you want," she found herself saying, though the thought made her cringe. What would she babble this time?

"Perhaps we will. For now, I came to check on the catacombs and find out why people want to burn down this castle. And what else they want." Targon backed away from her.

Kaylina was careful to make her sigh of relief soft so he

wouldn't notice it. "Good. Thank you. We'd appreciate it if no more arsonists crawled up out of the catacombs."

"We *sealed* those damn passageways." Targon shook his head and headed for the kitchen.

Kaylina trailed him at a distance and only because she wanted to see if the pot of water had cooled enough to use. When she stepped into the kitchen, Targon was in the pantry doorway, but he'd paused to look back at her.

"Vlerion said I shouldn't leave you here alone."

"I'm not going back down there." She pointed at the trapdoor and then at her calf. "It didn't go well for me last time. Besides, I have a plant to fertilize." Kaylina mixed the contents of the pot again.

He eyed the jar on the counter. "With honey?"

"My grandpa used to do it. It worked well in the garden. Honey has lots of nutrients in it. And it's not like that plant can get any crankier." She pointed through the ceiling toward the tower.

"There's a plant up there?"

Something flickered in the shadows along a wall, making Kaylina jump. But when she looked in that direction, she didn't see anything. Targon looked too but soon turned back to her. He must not have seen anything either.

"A plant?" he prompted.

"Yeah. I went up there last night." Kaylina described what she'd seen, the angry writhing vines.

"And you're going to fertilize it? To make it grow bigger?"

"To make it *happier*." All right, that sounded dumb. "To give it some nutrients," she corrected. "Like I said, honey is rich in them, and I thought... Well, it couldn't make things worse."

"I wouldn't count on that." Targon stepped away from the pantry and pointed at the staircase. "I'll go with you."

"Uhm."

"Vlerion wouldn't be happy with me if a plant strangled you

while I was supposed to be keeping an eye on you. He'll be on his way back soon. We'll check the catacombs then."

"Suit yourself." Kaylina didn't want the captain's company, but maybe it wasn't a bad idea to have someone nearby if her experiment went awry. She didn't *think* things could get worse, but that was a big assumption to make about this place.

After mixing the honey water again, she grabbed a ladle and a lantern, and headed for the stairs. They creaked as Targon came up behind her.

As if to verify her doubts, another flicker along a shadowy wall drew her eye as she climbed.

She paused. "Did you see that?"

"All I can see is your ass."

That made her walk faster, to remove her rear anatomy from his line of sight.

"A gentleman wouldn't look at that," she muttered.

Targon scoffed. "That's not true—he might not *tell* you he was looking—but I'm hardly a gentleman."

"Aren't you a noble?"

"The bastard son of King Gavatorin's now-dead younger brother, which makes me... not much of anything. I was lucky to get invited into the rangers. Twenty-five years ago, when I joined, even a lot of full-blooded nobles weren't accepted in."

"How did you end up in charge?" After they reached the landing, Kaylina led the way down the hall and turned toward the tower.

"By being stronger and more ruthless and useful than my contemporaries. Most rangers strive to be honorable and noble of heart as well as blood, but my predecessor knew the troubled times we were entering. He knew it would take someone who wasn't afraid to do dirty work."

The boards that Kaylina had pried free remained on the floor where she'd left them, and red light seeped down through the hole. Most of the plant wasn't visible from below, but two vines dangled through the opening. She hadn't left them that way and eyed them, waiting to see if they twitched or whipped about. They hung limp.

As she looked up, she realized it would be hard to replicate her climbing feat while holding the pot. "Will you hand this up to me?"

"Not only haven't you called me *my lord* once since I arrived, but you want me to be your lackey."

Kaylina thought about asking if bastards were considered aristocrats, but he probably merited the title for being in charge of the rangers if not fully for his lineage.

Despite his sarcasm, Targon held his hands out for the pot. "Vlerion hasn't trained much respect into you yet."

"We didn't get to work together for more than an hour."

"Had you been at headquarters today instead of chatting with his mother, he might have had time to whip some discipline and respect into you."

"What a shame I missed that." Feeling self-conscious with Targon watching, Kaylina picked a careful way up the stone wall, thinking that she should have found a rope to make her second ascent easier. Of course, she hadn't originally planned to return, not until she'd had this silly idea.

Maybe she could have climbed one of the dangling vines, but touching any part of that plant did not seem wise. Watering it might be foolish. It might not have been watered in two centuries, and it was doing fine.

After she swung her leg up and pulled herself through, Targon probably watching her ass again, Kaylina knelt beside the hole. The red glow was bright enough that she didn't need her lantern. The large pot remained in the same place, but the gnarled branches and vines had rearranged themselves, not only the two that had lowered through the hole. One was poised in the air, like a whip about to crack.

"You're an interesting plant," she murmured. "What species were you before you were altered, I wonder?"

Chilly air whispered in through the window, and a leaf rotated toward her on its stem.

Creepy.

Kaylina dropped to her belly on what she hoped was sound wood—the original flooring, not to mention the staircase, had been torn away. Someone must have been trying to remove the plant. Had its pot remained, floating even after its support was gone?

Careful not to brush the vines, she said, "I'm ready for the pot."

Grumbling, Targon came closer. He also eyed those vines. Since entering the castle, had he been gifted any of the visions about rangers being killed?

He lifted the pot overhead, and she stretched down, flexing her core for support as she gripped it. A leaf twitched on one of the vines, and she almost dropped the honey water on Targon's head. A few drops sloshed out of the pot. He cursed and stepped back, but he was looking at the vine, not her.

"Is that plant *alive*? Or what?" He dropped a hand to his sword.

As Kaylina hefted the pot onto the boards next to her, she thought about saying all plants were alive, but she knew that wasn't what he meant. "I think it's in the *or what* category."

Targon grunted and took another step back.

"You might want to go," Kaylina said. "Based on the visions I've had while sleeping—and not sleeping—the castle doesn't like rangers."

"So the stories say." Targon glanced toward the exit but, hand on his sword hilt, remained where he was. "Do what you need to do. I said I'd keep an eye on you."

Something brushed Kaylina's back, and she rolled away, barely refraining from screaming. One of the branches had shifted toward her, leaves flexing. She scurried toward the wall, though she was tempted to dive through the hole and get out of there.

But the branch didn't reach farther for her. It hovered over the pot, one of the leaves dipping in, reminding her of Crenoch's tongue.

"You all right up there?" Targon asked.

She'd kept from screaming but wasn't surprised he'd heard her rapid roll. "So far. It just… moves."

"I noticed. I'm debating cutting off those dangling vines, but I've seen enough in my life to know that curses and magic are real. We probably shouldn't have let you set up here."

"*Probably*," Kaylina mouthed and rolled her eyes.

From below, he wouldn't be able to see her disrespect.

"But Vlerion doesn't think the *curse* started that fire."

"No, someone is after us. Or wants us out of here, more likely."

"You have any suspects?"

Two more leaves dipped into the pot.

Kaylina rose to her feet and grabbed the ladle. "The Virts, I'd guess. People who want to use the pantry as an entrance and exit to the catacombs without witnesses around. I suppose Jana might be involved."

"Who?"

"She's an older lady who introduced herself as one of the proprietors of the Nakeron Inn. I guess they make and sell mead, so she's our competition." Kaylina avoided the branch and ladled her honey concoction onto the soil of the plant. The liquid disappeared immediately, as if she were pouring water into a parched desert. She spread it all around. "She's come by a couple of times that we know about, and I've gotten the vibe that she's spying on us. She was watching the fire from across the river."

"Hm."

Kaylina stepped back, wondering if she should leave the pot

up there. A few more branches had draped over it, and a vine had slithered across the floorboards and over the lip.

Nothing more substantial happened, not that she could see. The glow didn't change, and she couldn't tell if the plant's magic altered. One of the familiar eerie moans wafted from the rooftop, so probably not.

"What kind of magic have you seen? In your twenty-five years with the rangers?" Kaylina wondered if Targon had seen Vlerion change. Or maybe he'd been one of the men responsible for killing Vlerion's brother when he'd been in beast form. If so, could Vlerion have forgiven him?

"More than can be explained by books," was all Targon said.

Kaylina looked out the window, not surprised to spot snowflakes falling from the dark sky. Spring was slow coming here. Maybe those frigid mountains always kept their frosty grip on the land.

A startled gasp came from below.

"Targon?" Kaylina looked at the vines dangling through the hole, but they hadn't moved.

A choking sound followed the gasp, then a growl and a thump. Finally, the faint rasp of a sword being drawn.

Kaylina dropped to her hands and knees by the hole.

Just like in her visions, a thick vine had snaked out of a stone wall to grab Targon around the neck from behind. Like a viper.

Sword in hand, he hacked at it, but the sharp blade barely nicked the rubbery green vine.

Kaylina drew her knife and was about to jump down but, on a whim, she grabbed the ladle, spooned up the honey mixture, and flung it at the vine.

"Suck that down, plant," she growled and swung down, landing in a crouch.

Targon had twisted about so he could swing more effectively at the vine, but it still had him by the neck. Kaylina rounded him so she wouldn't be in the way of his sword arm and lunged in with her knife. She stabbed the vine near the wall, thinking it might be weaker there. But the blade didn't cut in. In addition to being tough and rubbery, the vine was slick from her water.

"So much for that idea," she said.

Rustling came from above—the vines that hung through the hole stirring. Would they jump into the fray? Grab her as well?

Kaylina stabbed again, afraid Vlerion would blame her if Targon died at her feet. He might think she'd colluded with the curse—or the Virts somehow—and that she'd wanted this.

Stabbing harder, she nicked the vine, but it didn't let go. Targon, his face turning red, had more luck. His slashes weren't wild and frantic but precise as he methodically struck it up and down, seeking a weak spot.

Unfortunately, the vine didn't seem to have weaknesses. It had grown straight out of the stone. How could that be?

Footsteps pounded on the staircase, and Kaylina whirled, afraid of who—or what—might show up next.

Vlerion ran into view, cursing when he saw his captain in trouble. For a second, that savage glint entered his eyes, and Kaylina worried the beast would erupt. If it did, going by what his mother had said, it might not only destroy the vine but kill Targon *and* her.

Vlerion started humming as he ran. By the time he reached his captain, sword swinging toward the vine like an executioner's axe, his calm mask had taken over his face.

Kaylina backed away so the men would have room to wield their blades. Since he wasn't constrained by a vine around his neck, Vlerion's movements were freer and more effective. Or maybe he was simply stronger. His sword cut deeper into the vine, and, on the third stroke, he cleaved it in half.

Targon dropped his blade and grabbed at the end wrapped around his neck. As if that part of the vine was alive independent of the rest, it continued to squeeze. Targon's face turned redder and redder. His earlier methodology abandoned, he clawed at it, desperate to pull it off as his end neared.

Vlerion raised his sword, slashing again. Though careful not to cut Targon, he came alarmingly close. The blade sliced deeply into the vine, less than an inch from his captain's neck.

It weakened, giving slightly as Targon continued to pull. Vlerion dropped his sword and grabbed the vine with his bare hands. He ripped it away from Targon's neck.

The captain collapsed to his knees, wheezing as he gasped for air. Vlerion rested a hand on his back and looked at Kaylina.

"Are you all right?" he asked.

"Yes. It didn't attack me."

"Because *she's* not a ranger," Targon rasped.

Vlerion opened his mouth, a *yet* forming, but he glanced at the walls and didn't voice it.

Yes, Kaylina would prefer the curse not know she was training for that...

"If any other man had been swinging that close to my throat with a sword," Targon said, knuckles pressed into the floor for support, "I would have wet myself."

"I'm surprised you didn't do that when the vine first wrapped around your neck." Vlerion looked around. "It *is* damp here."

"That's the girl's honey water."

"If you say so."

They shared grim laughs and thumped each other's fists.

"I left your brother in Doc Penderbrock's infirmary," Vlerion told Kaylina. "His ribs have been wrapped, and he's received painkillers. I thought about bringing him back to the castle but figured he might rest easier elsewhere."

"If I'd known free lodgings were involved, I would have gone with you." Kaylina closed her mouth. She shouldn't complain or even joke about the castle. It hadn't tried to kill *her*.

"Offer the girl a bed, Vlerion," Targon said. "She helped me. She might have stood back and cheered that thing on."

Kaylina grimaced. She hadn't cheered, but she hadn't been effective. If Vlerion hadn't shown up, she would have been forced to watch Targon die, exactly as the rangers in her visions had.

Vlerion smiled, meeting Kaylina's eyes. "She's a better person than that."

She didn't know what she'd done to deserve the look, but it warmed her.

"You think so?" Targon didn't sound as appreciative. "She's incapable of saying *my lord* without being sarcastic. I insist you instruct her on proper respect."

"There's not a lot she says without sarcasm."

"That's a *fault*, not something to admire."

"Sorry, Captain." Vlerion's smile shifted to a smirk.

"Let's check the catacombs." Targon used the wall for support as he grabbed his sword and pushed himself to his feet. "Never thought I'd say they sound cozy and appealing after being in here, but I'll joyously leap into them tonight."

"Yes." Letting Targon lead, Vlerion reached for Kaylina before following. "What do you want to do? Not go back down there, I suspect."

"No, but if you find out who started the fire, I'd like to know." She stepped closer, and he rested a hand on her shoulder. She had to resist the urge to lean against him.

"Of course." He squeezed her shoulder. "The barracks are an option if you want to sleep elsewhere."

"Let me think about it."

Kaylina looked at the hole above, but the plant continued to glow red. Nothing had changed.

26

As surely as drink, fatigue brings honesty and a lowering of defenses.

   ~ Spymaster Yeroknor the Senior

Kaylina sat on the ground with her back to the courtyard wall, the castle dark and quiet behind it, the river rippling softly as water flowed past in front of her. Snow dusted her shoulders, and cold seeped into her from the ground and the wall, but she felt numb to it. Maybe it was fatigue, but she felt numb to everything.

The carboys and bottles of mead she'd salvaged from the root cellar lined the wall beside her. The fire hadn't damaged them, but someone had indeed stolen several bottles. Another bottle had been cracked and was leaking, so she'd grabbed a mug and was drinking the mead. More than she should, most likely, as she'd given herself a buzz, but the thought of letting her grandpa's prize honey go to waste disturbed her almost as much as everything else going on around her.

The part of her mind that nagged her to be a normal, functioning human being kept telling her to put the mead away and go check on her brother. But such weariness cloaked her that even getting up felt like an impossible task. Besides, Targon and Vlerion hadn't returned from the catacombs.

But would they? They might not return through her root cellar, instead coming up in another part of the city, off to handle whatever new mess they'd unearthed down there. Maybe they would forget about her. She didn't know why they wouldn't. What was she to them?

She took a long drink from her mug, the sweet mead chilled by the same air that seeped into her bones.

"There you are." Vlerion stepped through the gate, his cloak and hood hiding his features as he looked down at her.

"I've heroically salvaged the mead." Kaylina raised her mug.

"A noble deed, I'm certain."

"Yup." She drank again, welcoming the fuzzy numbness creeping into her mind.

"We didn't encounter anyone in the catacombs, but the barricade was broken again. We'll have to bring masons down to build a more substantial barrier. We should have done that to begin with, but we've been inconsistent about defending the castle access point. Some felt it was better to know where the criminals were coming and going rather than forcing them to use another exit we didn't know about. Catacombs access points are all over the city. A nursery on Fountain and Second has one in the basement."

"Any evidence that the arsonists came in from the catacombs?" Kaylina suspected so, but the broken kerosene bottle in the pantry didn't prove it.

"We did find a half-empty bottle of kerosene and some matches at the dock. Also another crate of munitions. Targon used the supplies to burn down the dock, though that will only inconvenience the Virts slightly. He took off to gather some men to flush the cata-combs completely. Or as completely as one can. Between all the levels down there, there are probably more miles of tunnels than there are roads in the city." Vlerion cocked his head. "You told Targon the Virts are planning to assassinate the king tomorrow night?"

"The girl—Milzy—told me something big is going to happen then—a *regime change*. I think your captain already knew they were planning an assassination. Milzy wanted me to use my vast powers of befriending animals with honey to let all the taybarri out of the stable and distract you rangers."

"So Targon said." Vlerion's tone was neutral, and he gazed down at her. "Did you know he was listening in on the conversation? Did *she*?"

"I had a hunch, a feeling that someone was watching me. I don't know if Milzy did or not. I'm not sure why she would have expected the ranger captain to be skulking in my kitchen."

"It depends on how much the Virts know about our relationship with you and the castle. We haven't done a good job of staying away, and you told Targon some other woman has been spying on you?"

"Jana. A mead maker. My competition."

"I know who she is. She's not known to have a connection to the Virts, but it may only be that we haven't discovered it yet. If the information this Milzy told you *is* accurate and the Virts *don't* know you've been working with us... it's invaluable. We've known they're preparing for an attack, and that they want to overthrow the existing regime, but we haven't been able to find out when they're going to strike. Tomorrow night, we can have men watching the harbor and lying in wait in the royal castle."

Kaylina raised the mug again in a salute. "Then I'll hope it's accurate information and you're able to save the king."

"Yes, though they must plan to do more than assassinate him.

Otherwise, Prince Enrikon will take over, and that might be even worse for what they want."

"Maybe they're going after both."

"That's possible, but there are dozens of people with blood ties to the crown who would be available to step up. The Virts want a whole new system of government. Though I suppose they could have ties to some of the potential heirs. Maybe they've got someone in mind who will agree to make changes if they're put in power. I don't know. I'm away on the border a lot and am not as in the loop on government matters as I should be."

The discussion was giving Kaylina a headache. In all her years, she'd never had to pay attention to the monarchy or care who was in charge. Keeping the Spitting Gull in the black and fending off pirates were her family's primary concerns.

"The Virts must be the ones who stole my mead. Bastards." She took another sip. The back of her mind spoke up again, suggesting she shouldn't let herself get drunk around Vlerion. She might do something foolish.

"Naturally. Planning assassinations and insurrections is thirsty work."

"Try some?" She held the mug up toward him.

"No. Do you wish to visit your brother and spend the night in the barracks? I don't want to leave you here alone."

"What about my friends?" Kaylina patted the nearest carboy.

"I can get a wagon so you can bring them. Or did you mean to imply the alcohol would keep you safe if you stay here tonight?"

"It's not *that* wondrous." She closed her eyes and leaned her head against the wall. "Sorry. Am I being exasperating?"

She didn't know why she asked. If the answer was *yes*, she would feel stung. After the day's events, her emotions floated near the surface, raw and abraded.

"No. You're exhausted." Vlerion spotted someone in a uniform crossing the bridge a block away, held a finger up to Kaylina, and trotted off to talk to the man.

She couldn't hear what he said, but he soon returned and settled next to her on the ground, his back to the wall, his shoulder brushing hers. That was nice. Too bad he didn't want to join her in a drink.

"A wagon will come soon," he said.

"Thanks. You're right. I am tired." She let herself lean against his shoulder.

At first, he stiffened, and she thought he would shift away. But he looked at her and must have reconsidered. He draped an arm around her shoulders.

Oh, that was *more* than nice. She slumped more fully against him.

"Everything is screwed up," Kaylina whispered. "If I'd known we were coming north into the middle of a rebellion... Oh, I don't know. I might still have left. I lost my temper with my family and stuck my foot in my mouth, said some things I regret—*you've* seen that I'm good at that. I think I fled because I was too proud to stay after my defiant blathering. It wasn't that premeditated. If Frayvar hadn't come along and brought some funds, I would have starved by now. In my dreams, I always have these grand ideas, but in reality, I'm..." She swallowed, aware that the drink was making her overshare, much as she had under the influence of that drug. But it was hard to stop speaking. She needed to confess to someone, and Vlerion was here. "I'm a screwup who can't get her act together."

"You have the potential to be many things." Vlerion pushed back his hood to reveal his short hair and face. "A mead maker, certainly, but during the brief time we spent together training, I saw your athleticism. You were also smart enough to realize you couldn't take a huge swing at me with the staff without upending yourself and falling in the water. You'd be surprised how many recruits don't have the foresight to understand that before they try. Then there's your marksmanship ability. And your knack with the animals... It may not matter what my mother says, however influential she is, to Targon. He wants you in the rangers. He sees your potential too."

"Potential isn't the problem, though I appreciate you thinking I've got some. It's keeping from sabotaging myself. I don't know why that's so hard."

"I know all about self-sabotage," he said dryly.

Puzzled, Kaylina looked at him. It took her a long moment to realize he had to be talking about the curse, about how he sometimes failed to maintain his equanimity and keep the beast from taking over. That hardly seemed like a fault though, since it was something he couldn't fully control. He was human, and humans weren't perfect. She understood that and could forgive others their flaws more than she could herself.

"You almost lost it in the castle, didn't you?" Kaylina whispered, studying his face though his mask was in place again. At first, she'd found it infuriating. Now she understood why he so carefully kept it up.

"Yes. And if I had, I might have killed you and Targon as well as shredding that plant."

The blunt words were chilling, even though that was exactly what she'd worried about. But she didn't want him to think she'd been concerned at the time—or was uncomfortable being beside him now—so she strove for a light tone when she said, "Who would have guessed that a wayward plant could infuriate you more than a horde of men trying to kill you?"

His response was serious. "People, animals, or *plants* trying to kill me—that last being admittedly rare—don't typically present a problem. I have a lot of practice keeping my calm in battle. And I can deal with the irritations of human beings in general." An eyebrow twitch was his only indication that he referred to some of their conversations. "I've had practice at that too. But no amount of practice prepares you for the overwhelming emotions that arise when someone you care about is in danger."

"Ah. I didn't realize you felt that strongly about Captain Targon. He's... kind of a dick."

Vlerion snorted. "I've known him a long time."

"You're not that old are you?" She'd thought they were similar in age, that he might have two or three years on her but not much more. "How long have you been a ranger?"

"Six years, but my brother was one before me, and I knew Targon before he became captain. They were friends, and he's especially watched out for me since my brother... passed."

Was killed, her mind corrected. "Did Targon have anything to do with that?"

His mother had said rangers had taken his brother down.

"Not directly, but he felt responsible. Once he was made captain, Vlarek told him our family secret. Vlarek felt the captain of the rangers needed to know."

"I guess that makes sense. How many people know?" Kaylina wondered how rare of company she now kept.

"The king and some of his aides and confidants. Probably the prince, though I'm not certain. We haven't spent much time together, but it's a matter of kingdom security since, when we change..." Vlerion spread his palm.

People died. Right.

"Among the rangers, not many," he continued. "Among the aristocracy, even fewer. Among the proletariat, I hope none, but, as I told you, I worry about the Virts discovering the secret and using it against my family. Maybe even to rally their own people. Generations of Havartafts have killed innocents when the beast has taken over, *murdered* them essentially." He winced. "It's unacceptable. We should have been put to death long ago. All of us. The curse could be ended by destroying every male Havartaft."

Kaylina shook her head, horrified by the idea that Vlerion might be killed because of something he had no power to stop, something he was only affected by because a distant ancestor had wanted to feed his people during a famine.

"It's not your fault." She caught herself lifting a hand to touch his jaw before remembering his mother's words, that she could be a danger to him as surely as an attack in battle. "And it's not fair."

"A gripe I've often made," he said. "Especially after I lost my brother. I struggled to control my emotions then and spent a lot of time as the beast. The memories of what I do in that state are always vague and blurry, but I don't forget completely. It's hard to forget when you wake in your human form the next day with someone's blood dried on your bare chest. The horrors of what I did are what forced me to get myself together, to lock away my feelings about my brother's end. I cried at the funeral pyre but not after that, though my mother railed at me for being distant. Even though she understood, she struggled to accept it. Then, at least. Now she knows and does her best to protect me."

Kaylina almost drew her hand back, but she didn't want him to feel it was a rejection, that she blamed him for the curse.

"It's not your fault," she murmured again. "It's not self-sabotage."

She brushed her fingers along his jaw, feeling the late-day beard stubble, and longed to let her hand drift higher. To stroke his face, to push her fingers through his short hair, to rub his warm scalp...

Vlerion closed his eyes and lowered his head toward her, as if *offering* it for a rub. She ran her fingers over his scarred scalp, wanting to soothe him, to promise she wouldn't judge him. Maybe she should have, if innocent people had died to his deadly claws, but she couldn't find it within herself to do so. He'd *saved* her with those claws.

He exhaled slowly, as if relaxing under her ministrations, but there was a hint of a rumble to his breath, almost a growl. She flashed back to his neck rub in the catacombs and of sitting in front of him on the taybarri with his hard body behind hers. Heat crept into her. *Desire.*

By all the moon gods, she wanted to scoot closer and kiss him. To have him touch her. But they couldn't risk doing anything. He probably didn't even have feelings for her.

Or did he?

Kaylina knew that she irritated and exasperated him, but he was sitting here with her now, far closer than he needed to be while they waited for the wagon. That was evidence of caring, wasn't it?

"You changed in the catacombs." She spoke the words as a realization. "I'd assumed because fighting those men made you lose control, but you've since said..." She raised her eyebrows.

Vlerion lifted his eyes to meet hers, his gaze steamy through his lashes, steamy and intense.

A longing to kiss him rose up from her core, spreading heat throughout her body, but that glint had entered Vlerion's eyes, the one she now recognized as danger. Maybe she had all along.

Her hand stilled, her entire body freezing. His mother's warning rang in her mind. She was playing with fire.

Stupidly, that knowledge didn't steal her desire to kiss him. His lips, slightly parted, drew her. She longed to crawl into his lap and—

Vlerion closed his eyes. He didn't hum this time, but she sensed him withdrawing, gathering his calm, reaffixing the mask.

"Are you asking if I feel as strongly about you as I do Targon?" He sounded dry, even amused, as if she'd asked a silly thing.

"Well, I'd hope they would be a different *kind* of feelings." Kaylina struggled not to be stung by the implied dismissal.

Vlerion leaned back, removing his arm from her shoulders. The distance made her hand drop from his head.

"My mother raised me to be disturbed by seeing women in danger, to want to protect them." He shrugged.

"Ah." That was noble, she supposed, but such disappointment swelled in her that it surprised her. She hadn't consciously realized she wanted him to say he cared, but she must have. Why, she didn't know. She hadn't known him that long, and they were different. Too different. "So any girl being chomped on by a furry shark would have made you turn?"

"Likely so."

A clattering of wheels on cobblestones alerted them to a wagon approaching, and Vlerion rose, lifting a hand to the driver.

Kaylina blew out a long breath. She was slower to rise, and when she did, she needed the wall for support. The mead had made her unwise, and she was glad she hadn't succeeded in doing... whatever the libidinous part of her brain thought it wanted.

"Maybe I'll stay here," she said.

"Your brother needs you."

"I thought he was safe?" She searched Vlerion's eyes.

"He's been tended, but he's bereft without your companionship."

"I'm positive he didn't say that."

"I could tell."

Kaylina did feel obligated to check on Frayvar. "All right."

"I've observed something about you." Vlerion picked up her bottles of mead to load carefully into the wagon.

"I'm not sure whether to ask what or hope you won't tell me." She didn't want to be analyzed.

"You'll move the world to help those you care about. You have a hard time moving even your own body to help yourself."

"That's not true," she said more out of reflex than because he was wrong. When he looked frankly at her, she amended her statement. "That's not *always* true. Sometimes, I'm full of energy, and I have these great dreams and visions of a future I can make. Then I can move myself. But other times, I'm too tired, and everything is much harder. You can't blame me for being tired after this day." She flung a hand toward the castle, then immediately felt guilty. *He* was the one who'd risked his life to heave that rack off Frayvar. And *he* was the one who spent every day concentrating on staying calm in a world full of angst, lest he turn into a beast. "I'm sorry. I shouldn't complain. A normal person wouldn't complain about little things."

"It's all right."

"Domas always told me I'm not normal."

No, he'd asked *why* she couldn't be normal.

"Who is that?"

"Someone I had a relationship with. It's over."

"Ah." As they finished loading the mead, Vlerion said, "For what it's worth, I've observed that *normal* people complain a lot."

"I suppose."

"I'll come for you at dawn for training." Vlerion helped her into the wagon, then stepped back. Maybe he needed to return to the catacombs. "The king has a speech at noon, after which the Spring Salutation Holiday starts, and the rangers will need to position themselves in case there *is* an attack tomorrow night. We'll work out early. As we discussed, you have potential we must unlock."

"Won't that be fun?" she murmured.

Unfortunately, she knew it wasn't her mead-making ability that the rangers wanted.

27

After checking on her brother and collapsing into a barracks bed a ranger had guided her to, Kaylina slept straight through the night. Unfortunately, thanks to her overindulgence in mead, she woke with a headache and wasn't refreshed at all when Vlerion knocked and called for her through the door.

The sky was *barely* getting light, and two inches of snow smothered the courtyard outside the window. She didn't want to train. Further, she worried that Vlerion would say something about her head rubbing the night before, about how it had been foolish and he shouldn't have let her touch him. Sure, he had put an arm around her shoulders, but it had been an act of sympathy, nothing else. Apparently, he didn't even feel as much for her as he did for Targon.

"Like you should expect that," she muttered, rolling out of bed. "They've known each other for years."

Kaylina was nothing more than a random woman who'd stirred his emotions because she'd been in danger.

Since she hadn't thought to grab her pack or her pajamas—only the mead, the priority, of course—she'd slept naked, letting her smoky clothes air out. Had she been in the warm climate of her homeland, she would have washed them, trusting they would dry by morning, but her experience with wet clothes here was that nothing dried quickly.

When another demanding knock followed the first, she wrapped the blanket around herself and shuffled over to answer it. "I'm coming, I'm coming."

Vlerion stood in the hall, his mouth open to call again, but his lips froze as he considered her.

She hadn't thought she had anything hanging out or drooping, but the tops of her breasts were showing. Grumbling, she pulled the blanket higher, though that made it gap open at her hip. Damn it.

Vlerion recovered, lifting his gaze to avoid seeing anything below her neck. "Dress. The queen wants to see you."

"Uh?"

"The correct response is *yes, my lord, right away.*" He was in a snit this morning, wasn't he?

"Okay." Kaylina was about to point out that the only clothes she had were the rumpled smoky ones she'd worn yesterday, but he thrust a folded garment at her. Was that a *dress*? And slippers? Maybe her regular trousers and shoes, even if they'd been clean, wouldn't have been deemed appropriate to wear in a queen's presence. "Thanks."

When she reached for them, the blanket drooped again. Maybe she should have hunted for a clothespin...

He glanced down at her bared skin but only for an instant before pulling his gaze to her eyes. "I suggest you rein in your snark and add *Your Majesty* to the end of most of your sentences. The queen is no one to be trifled with."

Concern darkened his eyes for a moment, and that made her uneasy.

"Is she... a threat? She likes food and drink and music, doesn't she? She writes that culture column for the newspaper. I think I told you I'm hoping she might come to my meadery one day."

"She does like those things, fine dining and the symphony and plays, but she has also made women disappear."

"Disappear?" For some reason, Kaylina thought of the plant in the castle, vines snaking out to wrap around the necks of rangers.

"She's the queen, so nobody has ever made a formal accusation against her, but she's rumored to have knowledge of poisons and be vengeful when her husband's eyes wander."

"How much *wandering* can the king's eyes do? Isn't he in his eighties?"

"His late seventies."

"*Such* a difference."

"He had many mistresses when he was younger, before and after he took her as his second wife. That has never sat well with her. Be respectful, and keep the buttons on that dress fastened to the collar."

Trepidation crept into Kaylina. Why wasn't the north anything like how the newspapers portrayed it? She'd heard nothing about the bad traits of the king and queen, nor had she known anything about the rebellion brewing.

"The newspapers are *not* accurate," she protested before realizing Vlerion might not follow her train of thought.

But he nodded, as if he understood perfectly. "The crown controls the press. The journalists aren't foolish enough to irk the king or queen with anything they publish. Dress." He pointed at the clothes.

"I will, but why does she want to see *me*? How does she know about me? And, uh, are you going to stand there and watch?"

"Only if you continue to ask me questions." Vlerion gripped the edge of the door, prepared to depart, but he answered her other queries first. "Targon likely reported your existence to the king when the queen was nearby. It's still required that the ranger captain gets permission to allow a commoner to train. He would have mentioned your *anrokk* trait as a justification."

"And the queen would care about that? Why?"

"I don't know, but it's the only thing I can imagine catching her interest. I doubt my mother told her about your mead."

"You don't think that's a possibility?"

"They're not friends. It's through my father's side of the family that the curse exists and that my family has ties to the crown."

Kaylina nodded. She'd assumed that.

She shook out the dress to look at it. The pale-blue fabric with white trim and lace around the collar reminded her of something she'd worn to Gods Day when she'd been a girl. The hem of the dress would go past her calves, if not trip her as she walked.

"I don't think the king's going to ogle me," she said.

"Then I chose correctly. Don't arrive in the blanket, or there *will* be trouble." Vlerion stepped back to close the door but not before glancing toward her chest, where the blanket had sagged again. A brief hungry look gleamed in his eyes before he disappeared.

The threat of the beast might have been there as well, but all Kaylina could focus on was that he, whether he *cared* for her or not, wanted her. She tried to tell herself that wasn't a good thing, that it would lead to trouble, but she couldn't help but feel titillated that the stiff and aloof Lord Vlerion might have woken up thinking about her, a lowly commoner from a remote part of the kingdom.

"Focus," she told herself, shaking out the dress again.

If the queen was dangerous, Kaylina would have to be careful this morning. She couldn't imagine why such an important woman would want to see her when her husband might be attacked by assassins that very night. The queen might be a target too. Shouldn't concern about that be consuming her thoughts?

Unless the rangers hadn't told her about the possibility of an assassination? Because they didn't want her to worry?

Well, if they hadn't, Kaylina would. The woman had a right to know she might soon be in danger.

28

'WARE THE WRATH OF THE INSECURE.
~ *"Foundations III" Scribe Menalow*

When Vlerion returned to escort the now-dressed Kaylina to a carriage waiting in the main courtyard of ranger headquarters, two taybarri bounded out of the stable and into their path. Crenoch and a slightly smaller creature that Kaylina had seen before but didn't know the name of. A female?

"She's getting a ride in the gilded carriage that was sent for her," Vlerion told the taybarri, guessing their intention before Kaylina did.

Crenoch swished his thick tail across the snowy cobblestones and whuffed. The other taybarri ambled up to Kaylina, resting a broad jaw on her shoulder.

"Sorry," she said, giving her a pat, "but I didn't bring any honey drops."

The tail and ears drooped in disappointment.

"I'll make some more as soon as people stop lighting our kitchen on fire," she caught herself promising.

Both taybarri looked pointedly toward a building she hadn't been in before.

"Our mess hall and kitchen," Vlerion said dryly.

"Is it available for guests to cook in?"

"Rarely. Maybe the captain will make an exception." Vlerion looked at the taybarri. "*After* her meeting with the queen and after we thwart the Virts' plot."

Crenoch opened his jaws and flicked his tongue against his teeth. The other taybarri did something similar.

"Do they not know the rules about respecting nobility?" Kaylina asked.

"They don't feel human rules apply to their species. Sadly, there's nothing in the treaty between our people and their elders about respect." Vlerion lifted a hand to make a shooing motion and pointed past them to the carriage, but he paused and considered the taybarri thoughtfully. "Actually, it might not be a bad idea for you to show up at the royal castle riding one of them. I assume that's what they're offering."

Crenoch sniffed Kaylina's pockets, but the borrowed dress had never carried a honey drop. "I wouldn't assume that."

Vlerion snorted. "They'll do whatever you wish."

"Are any people besides rangers allowed to ride taybarri?" Kaylina patted the female wistfully.

She would *love* to ride a taybarri by herself, without hanging on to Vlerion. But was this the time? She wanted her mead to stand out and earn the attention of royalty. Not herself.

"Anyone the taybarri allow on their back can ride one," Vlerion said as if he were stating the obvious.

Kaylina rolled her eyes. "Well, yes, I'd assume so, but don't they usually let only rangers ride them?"

"Rangers and *anrokk*." Without asking her *or* the taybarri, Vlerion boosted her onto the female's back.

The dress made it awkward, and she ended up with it hiked to her thighs. Kaylina gripped the blue fur and watched the female, worried they'd misread the offer and that the taybarri would buck her off. But the female held her head high, swished her tail, and made a *phhhtphhht* noise with her tongue against her teeth as she looked at Crenoch.

Crenoch whuffed. In indignation?

"At least let Kaylina finish her training before you abandon me for her," Vlerion told him. "Of course, you may have to tail wrestle with some of your buddies to figure out who gets to carry the honey lady into battle."

The female swished her tail again.

"What's her name?" Kaylina patted the strong, stout neck while Vlerion mounted Crenoch, then let her fingers twine into the thick luxurious fur as the taybarri started moving.

"Levitke."

Their taybarri strode for the gate, walking side by side.

Kaylina's only experiences riding them were on Crenoch with Vlerion, and she'd been distracted, at least the last time, by his body pressed against hers. Even so, she was fairly certain the male taybarri hadn't had a sway to his gait. She looked back to find Levitke's tail swishing back and forth. It had the effect of her hips swaying as she walked.

"Do all the female taybarri... sashay?" Kaylina asked.

Vlerion looked over at them. "I believe she's proud to carry you."

His gaze shifted to Kaylina's bared legs and snagged. "The carriage might have been more practical in a dress."

"I did not insist on this."

He cleared his throat and looked forward.

Kaylina smiled, liking that he found her attractive, but her lips turned down when she remembered what his mother said, that the beast within him might be drawn to her because she was an *anrokk*. The thought saddened her, even if it made sense.

Ranger headquarters wasn't far from the royal castle, and it was visible on its clifftop perch as soon as they exited the compound. Kaylina forced her mind to more practical matters. Like how she was going to keep her speech contrite and proper and stay out of trouble.

Why did the queen want to see her anyway? Since nothing had gone her way lately, Kaylina couldn't imagine that good luck was about to befall her. Even if she'd been someone prone to optimism, Vlerion's grimness when he'd come for her would have squelched it. He believed she was in danger. She made a note to shove her dress down as soon as she arrived in the castle, lest the queen think she was female competition who needed to be poisoned.

As they traveled along the road that switchbacked up the steep ascent to the royal castle, they had a view of the entire harbor, the city sprawling to the south, and the snowy mountains to the east. Unlike farther north, the towers and walls overlooking the harbor were in good condition and manned. She glimpsed blue-furred taybarri as well as men watching ships coming and going. From those walls, they could see ten miles or more up and down the strait.

"Targon stationed a lot of rangers with the Guard." Vlerion was also looking at the towers. "I assume he's not taking what the girl said as a certainty. It's possible the Virts plan to attack during the speech. A lot of people will be in the area, listening to the king and preparing for holiday celebrations. Explosives could do a lot of damage—they could *kill* many. Indiscriminately." His gaze shifted to the city, especially squares and streets with views of the cliff and the castle.

Since Kaylina had never heard the king speak, she didn't know where he stood to address his people, but on a still day, his words might carry from one of the balconies down to the bottom of the cliff. Especially if he used something to amplify his voice.

Blue-furred taybarri padded through the city streets as well, the rangers keeping an eye on everything.

"There wouldn't be any of them left in the stable for me to let out, even if I were so inclined," Kaylina said.

"By tonight, there might be. Usually, there are only a dozen of us on duty then, though Targon will keep more out and ready in case that intelligence *was* accurate."

"Do the catacombs run under the royal castle?"

"No. They end down there." Vlerion pointed toward buildings a couple of blocks from the base of the cliff. "I doubt the king who chose the location for his domicile would have wanted it perched above ancient Kar'ruk sarcophagi."

"I'm not that delighted that my new meadery is above them, but if the skeletons inside don't bother me, I won't bother them."

"I wish the Virts had the same philosophy."

Kaylina shivered at the idea of being caught in what might turn into a city-wide battle. She was glad her brother was in the infirmary in the ranger headquarters, but what if the compound was a target? The Virts might want the king dead, but the rangers were his loyal and deadly troops, a threat they could also want to deal with.

Vlerion and Kaylina rode onto the plateau outside the castle, the view even more spectacular from there. Two guards at a closed portcullis in a gatehouse watched them approach.

One man eyed Kaylina's legs. On the ride up, she'd smoothed the dress over them the best she could, but the salty sea breeze had ruffled it upward again.

Vlerion scowled at the overly observant guard, then nudged Crenoch closer to Levitke. The two taybarri stopped as Vlerion brushed the hem of the dress downward, his touch sending a zing of pleasure up Kaylina's leg. She had to resist the urge to shift it closer to him so he would have fuller access. The guards were watching.

"I should have insisted on the carriage," Vlerion muttered.

Kaylina told herself not to be turned on as he attempted to defy the wind to arrange the dress to cover her legs. He might have been more effective if he weren't simultaneously glaring at the guard. The man looked away under his withering stare.

Kaylina rested her palm on Vlerion's hand to stop his fussing. She knew he didn't mean it to be arousing, but her body came alive at his touch, and this wasn't the place for that.

"Thank you for trying to protect me," she said so he wouldn't feel disgruntled that she'd stopped him. She had the greater dangers in mind, not the guard checking her out, and hoped he understood.

With his hand resting on her leg, its heat noticeable through the fabric of the dress, Vlerion met her eyes. "I wasn't honest with you last night."

"Oh?" Nervous anticipation filled her, and she caught herself leaning closer, longing for him to admit... Oh, she didn't know. That he cared? That he felt something more than an attraction? That he didn't find her irritating and exasperating?

"Not any woman in danger would have made me turn," Vlerion said softly, the words for her alone. "You've... interested me since you were brave enough to stay the first night in the cursed castle. More than I should have allowed."

"I've... liked your interest. More than I should have allowed."

"I know."

She snorted. "You're arrogant and pompous."

"You don't mind." Smiling slightly, Vlerion looked at her hand holding his to her leg.

Kaylina should have pushed him away, but she didn't. If they'd been alone, she would have been tempted to guide his hand higher.

"Nothing can happen between us. It's too dangerous." His eyes grew intense as they captured hers. "But I will protect you."

A shiver went through her, and she shook her head, about to tell him not to do anything that would get him in trouble, especially here, in the royal castle, but he released her leg with a final brush of her dress and rode resolutely toward the guards.

Kaylina nudged Levitke to follow him and hoped nothing would happen inside to cause him to *need* to protect her.

When they reached the gatehouse, one guard bowed politely to Vlerion and looked curiously at Kaylina. "What is your business, Lord Vlerion?"

"The queen has requested to see the mead maker Kaylina Korbian."

"And this is she?"

"Yes."

"She's young."

"There's not an age requirement for getting into mead making," Kaylina said.

"And forward," the guard added.

"The lips of commoners are loose in the south," Vlerion said.

"I suppose one can't expect much from wilders annexed in recent centuries."

Wilders? Kaylina had never heard the term and scowled. Did northerners think her people lived in caves and gnawed raw meat while grooming each other with fish-bone combs salvaged off the beach?

"One cannot," Vlerion agreed mildly.

Kaylina shot him a dirty look.

The silent guard stepped into the gatehouse and withdrew a clipboard. "She is listed here. An appointment with the queen." He looked at Kaylina. "Interesting."

"I've found her to be so," Vlerion said in the same mild tone.

Yes, he'd just admitted that, and she treasured her new knowledge of his feelings.

"There is no mention of you having an appointment today, Lord Vlerion," the guard said.

"I'm accompanying her."

"A mead maker rates a ranger companion? On a day when... We've been told enemies might strike tonight."

"She does." Vlerion's tone was firm now, and he regarded the men through slitted eyes. "I trust the meeting won't take long," he added. "I'll have plenty of time for my other duties."

The guards exchanged looks.

"The queen would have added *and ranger companion* if she wanted to see both of them," one murmured.

"Are you going to say no to him?" the other whispered back.

"The rangers are loyal to the king. He wouldn't attack us. Whereas Sergeant Madrik might flog us for letting someone in without an appointment. Especially now when there are spies about."

"Lord Vlerion isn't a *spy*."

"Are there no rangers on the grounds currently?" Vlerion asked, as if he hadn't heard the rest of the conversation.

"No, my lord. As far as we've seen, they're all patrolling the harbor and the city for threats."

"*Some* should be within the royal castle. The king is a target."

The guards straightened, their chins rising.

"The royal guard has extra men on the grounds today and is capable of handling riffraff trying to storm the castle."

"Nonetheless..." Vlerion looked around again, including at the towers along the castle wall. "I'll talk to Captain Targon after the meeting. Open the gate."

His voice was firm, and the guard who'd objected that he wasn't on the schedule was the first to move to obey. He gestured to whomever inside controlled the portcullis. Only after it started to rise did he look at his comrade with uncertainty.

"It's fine," the other guard said. "I'd rather have Lord Vlerion inside if something happens than not."

Nothing about their demeanor or the looks they shared made Kaylina think they knew Vlerion's secret. They were probably aware only of his fighting ability and based their comments on that.

"We're capable of handling insurrectionists. It's not like hordes of Kar'ruk are on the horizon." Despite the words, the guard stepped back and waved for them to enter.

"You don't need to stay with me," Kaylina quietly told Vlerion as they rode through a courtyard twenty times the size of the one at Stillguard Inn. "Especially if you think something is afoot and need to talk to Targon."

"It can wait."

"Are you sure? I don't want to be the reason..." She flexed her hand in the air, not sure how to finish the sentence. "I don't want to cause trouble. Or delay you if there's trouble."

Vlerion regarded her as the taybarri padded across the courtyard toward a stable where horses were kept. "As I said, I will protect you."

"All right." Kaylina didn't truly want him to leave her alone here.

"Besides, you don't know where her quarters are."

"Is there no directory? Primitive. So strange that the guard called *me* a wilder."

"You'd prefer a sign in the courtyard pointing enemies toward key locations in the castle?"

"It could be removed during invasions." Kaylina swung down from Levitke's back and patted her. "Thank you for the ride. If I'm offered any sweets today, I'll pilfer some for you."

The taybarri swished her tail and blew hot breath over Kaylina's face.

Kaylina pushed down the hem of her borrowed dress and smoothed the fabric. Maybe the steamy breath would help iron out the wrinkles from the ride.

They left their mounts near a hitching post, though the taybarri didn't have reins and there wouldn't have been a way to tie them even if Vlerion had been so inclined.

Kaylina followed him toward one of several open doors in the courtyard, some leading to gardens or stairs up to the walkways and others into the interior of the castle. They'd only taken a few steps before a woman in a gold-trimmed green dress appeared. Her eyes widened when she spotted Vlerion walking with Kaylina. Her mouth opened and closed a couple of times.

"I'm getting the feeling nobody expected you to come," Kaylina murmured.

"I'm getting the feeling it wasn't *desirable* that I come," he murmured back as he looked alertly around the grounds and up to the towers, barely acknowledging the woman.

"Lord Vlerion," she said, ineffectively hiding her dismay. "It's always a pleasure to receive you in the castle. Are you here to see the king? I hadn't heard that he had any appointments this morning. He's receiving his fortifications and rehearsing his speech."

Fortifications? What did that mean?

"Medicine," Vlerion murmured for Kaylina's ear only. To the woman, he said, "I'm accompanying the mead maker. The rangers have an interest in her."

"I—" The woman gave Kaylina a bewildered once over. "Why?"

"She has a way with the taybarri."

"I... hadn't heard that."

"What *have* you heard?" Kaylina asked, still wondering why she'd been summoned.

"That you make mead. Come this way. I'll take you to the queen." The woman lifted a hand toward Vlerion, as if she wanted to ask him to wait with the horses and taybarri, but she lowered it and headed into the castle.

He looked pensively at the woman's back as they followed her through halls with great arched ceilings and past open doorways to vast rooms, most painted with murals and trimmed by intricate moldings or friezes. Huge chandeliers dangled from gilded chains, and Kaylina's feet were tempted to stray when she spotted a library with more books than she'd ever seen in one place.

Maybe she *did* veer in that direction, because Vlerion touched the small of her back to keep her following the woman.

"You could be wrong," Kaylina whispered to him, "and your mother *did* share my mead with the queen, and now she wants to order some directly from me. And write about its wonders in her column for the Kingdom Crier. The Queen's Corner."

"The citizens in the south haven't heard about the revolution brewing, but the Queen's Corner makes it to your islands?" Vlerion asked.

"Yeah."

"I suppose I shouldn't be surprised. As I said, the crown controls which newspapers are distributed kingdom wide and what's in them."

"It's important that we know which eating houses and play-houses the queen finds acceptable this season." Kaylina said the words with a modicum of sarcasm, but she *did* enjoy reading that column, especially when it covered food and drink.

They ascended stairs wider than most rooms to a landing full of furnishings that appeared more decorative than functional. A hall led them to an office, guards stationed to either side of the open door. Within lay numerous desks, bookcases, and several sofas and divans arranged around two fireplaces.

A handsome black-haired woman of fifty-ish sat at one desk,

her back to a ceiling-high window with a view of the harbor. Head down, she gripped a quill and wrote without looking up.

Was this the queen? Penning her next column?

Someone else sat in a nearby chair that was turned to look out the window. Only the top of his or her gray-haired head was visible, but the age of the first woman was in line with what Kaylina had heard about the queen. The king's first wife had passed without providing an heir, and he'd married Petalira afterward, a woman thirty years his junior.

The guards trailed Kaylina and Vlerion in, though they watched him warily and gave him a wide berth.

"Kaylina Korbian, the mead maker, is here, Your Majesty," their female guide reported with a curtsey. "And, ah, Lord Vlerion."

Petalira looked up and smiled at him. "Ah, Lord Vlerion. I've no need of a report from the rangers, as I've been apprised of recent developments already this morning. Perhaps you could wait outside." She looked at but did *not* smile at Kaylina.

Right away, Kaylina knew her dream was not to be. This woman was not a mead fan who wanted to put in a special order. For some reason, Kaylina was in trouble. Again.

"I will wait here, Your Majesty," Vlerion said.

Petalira's brows rose. It had been a suggestion, not an order, but, without a doubt, people rarely failed to heed the suggestions of royalty.

Kaylina shifted her weight, torn between wanting Vlerion to stay and not wanting to get him in trouble.

"It's okay," she whispered, waving for the door. If something *did* happen to her, he would be close.

He didn't move.

"This is a private matter." Petalira put down the quill and stood. "Between women." She glanced at the person in the chair, then gazed at Kaylina.

"I will wait here," Vlerion repeated, flicking a hand toward the sofas. To suggest they could speak privately over there while he stood by the door?

The room was large enough for that...

Petalira frowned at him and looked at the sword at his hip before turning the frown on the woman who'd guided them in. "Why is he armed?"

The woman blanched. "He's a ranger."

"So naturally it's acceptable for him to come to my office bearing blades."

"No, Your Majesty." The woman curtsied deeply while keeping her head bowed.

Kaylina's sling and knife were in the dress pockets too. Should there have been a search before they were allowed in?

"Perhaps he is an ally of hers in this matter," the woman in the chair spoke, "and should be considered with suspicion."

Kaylina gaped. She recognized that voice.

Jana rose from the chair and faced them while taking a step closer to the queen's desk. When Kaylina met her eyes, Jana smiled in triumph, as if the victory she'd sought all along was finally hers.

29

THOSE YOU'VE NEVER WRONGED MAY YET SEEK YOUR DOWNFALL.
  ~ *"Sorrows of Men," by the bard Nogorathi*

"The rangers are above suspicion, ma'am," the female guide whispered, though she kept her head down.

"A spy may come from any quarter," Queen Petalira said.

"In this case," Jana said, "a *poisoner* may come from any quarter."

Uh, poisoner? Kaylina didn't know what to say.

"Of what do we stand accused?" Vlerion didn't sound shocked or outraged. No, he was calm, that mask he'd practiced donning so often securely in place.

Good. The last thing Kaylina wanted was for him to lose his calm in here. By all the gods, if he turned into the beast and killed the queen... There would be no saving him after that.

"Poisoning the mead that was delivered as, according to the message accompanying it, a gift for the queen," Jana said.

Even though Kaylina had figured out right away that Jana was up to something—and probably behind this—she couldn't keep from blurting, "Delivered? What gift? I didn't send any mead." She looked at Vlerion, more worried that *he* would believe the lie than that the queen would. "When would I have had time to *do* that? I don't know anything about poisoning."

Vlerion's face remained masked, and he kept his gaze on the women and the guards instead of Kaylina. He hadn't moved his hand to the hilt of his sword yet, but it was open beside it.

Jana lifted something that had been hidden by the chair. One of Kaylina's bottles of mead. One of the *missing* bottles.

"I thought the catacomb bandits took that." Kaylina stepped toward Jana, anger driving away wisdom—and her self-preservation instinct. "Did *you* start the fire in the castle? My brother almost died in that."

She crouched, fantasizing about springing over the chair to throttle Jana. But two more guards surged out of a side room, stepping between Kaylina and the queen and Jana. They drew their swords and faced Kaylina grimly.

Vlerion stepped between her and them. He didn't draw his own sword, but his hand did rest on the hilt.

Kaylina swore to herself. She had to keep her cool lest she endanger him—in more ways than one. Besides, this was idiotic. She hadn't done anything wrong. She had to be rational and defend herself logically. As Frayvar would be the first to advise.

"I know nothing about the origins of that fire," Jana stated calmly. Almost *smugly.* As if she knew she'd already won.

Gritting her teeth, Kaylina eased out from behind Vlerion so she could see the two women. Petalira observed her through slitted eyes.

"Are you sure?" Kaylina asked. "Because I saw you there, watching from across the river."

"You are mistaken. I was at work creating mead that *isn't* poisoned."

"Mine isn't poisoned either."

"How did you acquire that bottle?" Vlerion asked.

"*I* acquired it," the queen answered. "As I said, it arrived via a messenger with a note suggesting the king and I would enjoy sipping it during the holiday celebration."

"Was it a Virt messenger smelling of the catacombs?" Kaylina suspected Jana had paid someone to steal it, rather than wandering through the dark and monster-filled passageways herself, but she had to be responsible.

"It was a known messenger working for a reputable service," Petalira said.

"I didn't send it, Your Majesty. Someone's trying to frame me." Kaylina looked at Jana.

"Why would a proprietor who's lived in Port Jirador her entire life and been supplying mead to the castle kitchen, among other reputable establishments, for decades seek to incriminate you?" Petalira asked. "A newcomer working out of a cursed building that nobody with common sense would ever visit."

Unfortunately, that was a good question. Kaylina had no idea why Jana had ever been concerned about her.

"Because I make wonderful mead using my grandmother's famous and award-winning recipes," Kaylina said, though she struggled herself to believe that was the reason. "She's threatened by me."

Jana looked at the queen sidelong. Watching for her reaction? To see if she believed that?

Could Kaylina have stumbled upon the truth? Maybe Jana had, from the beginning, given Kaylina more credit than anyone else had and thought she did have what it took to be legitimate competition. Maybe she thought Grandma and the family were backing Kaylina and would send their support to make sure the meadery was a success.

"That's laughable," Petalira said. "Besides, Jana has nothing to prove to me. *She* did not send me poisoned mead."

"Neither did I. And it's not poisoned." Kaylina couldn't keep the exasperation out of her voice.

Irritation flickered in the queen's eyes, but all she said was, "If you are certain of that, then you won't hesitate to enjoy a few swallows."

She pushed the bottle toward the edge of the desk and beckoned Kaylina in invitation.

"Of course not." Kaylina stepped forward.

Vlerion held out a hand to stop her. "The bottle has been out of your possession for many hours."

Yes, *and* the cork had been removed.

Kaylina froze, noting how Jana's eyes sharpened. Did she *want* Kaylina to drink it and collapse on the rug? What had Kaylina done to her to make the woman want her dead?

"If you will not sample from your own bottle," Petalira said, "I must assume that you know it's poisoned and sent it as part of the Virt plot to assassinate my husband and me. I understand witnesses have also seen you speaking with a young woman who works for one of the freight transportation companies and is a known Virt operative."

Witnesses? How many people had been spying on the castle? Targon knew about Milzy, but he wouldn't have helped frame Kaylina. He wanted to use her.

"The punishment for attempting to poison royalty," Petalira continued, "is death for you and exile for your entire family."

Kaylina shook her head. How had this gone so wrong so quickly?

"What is the name of the messenger service that brought the bottle to the royal castle?" Vlerion asked. "The rangers will visit them, find out who delivered the mead, and question the person to learn who dropped it off and paid the fee. *I* will visit them."

"Why are you involved in this, Lord Vlerion?" Petalira asked. "The rangers aren't known for defending commoners."

"The rangers defend the innocent, no matter what class they're in. Also, my taybarri likes her."

Jana grunted. "More likely, *he* likes her. He is ruled by his penis, as all young men are."

For the first time, Vlerion's back stiffened, and his jaw tightened.

The guards remained between Vlerion and Kaylina and the two women, their swords out. They noticed Vlerion's reaction and lifted those blades, though they also glanced at each other, not looking like they wanted to fight him.

"You will not harm Korbian," Vlerion stated. "The messenger will be found and questioned."

"With a ranger hand wrapped around his throat?" Jana asked. "If you're looming over him, he'll say whatever you want him to say."

"He will be questioned under the influence of kafdari root to ensure he speaks the truth."

Kaylina leaned forward with hope. Yes, that could work. If the messenger was found and could point to Jana or, more likely, someone she'd hired, it might save Kaylina. Maybe the underling could even be traced to Jana.

"Seek him out if you wish." Jana waved her hand airily, not looking concerned by the idea.

That was unsettling. Had she already anticipated someone would want to question the messenger and arranged for the man to leave the city? Or... He wasn't floating dead in a canal, was he?

"You could, however, simply drink the mead if you wish to prove your innocence." Jana turned to the queen. "That is the most logical course, is it not?"

"Not if *you've* poisoned it," Kaylina said.

"Do not compound your foolishness," Petalira told her, "by accusing an upright kingdom subject of plotting murder."

Kaylina clenched her jaw.

"Lord Vlerion," Petalira said. "If you wish, go out and seek the messenger. I am familiar with kafdari root. Your people may question him under its influence. I will refrain from passing a death sentence on this girl until you've concluded your investigation."

Kaylina blew out a slow breath. That was something.

Vlerion looked at her, his face still grim. Did he not see this as a victory? Or did he also suspect the messenger had disappeared?

He glanced toward the window overlooking the harbor, and Kaylina remembered that he wanted to speak to Targon about positioning more rangers in the royal castle. Being forced to spend time here with her was keeping him from a far more important duty. She grimaced with guilt.

"I will find him and bring him for questioning in front of whatever witnesses you choose, Your Majesty," Vlerion told the queen. "It may take some time to ferret him out, especially on a holiday. Until her innocence can be proven, Ms. Korbian may be held in one of the cells in ranger headquarters. You can trust it as secure as any other cell in the city, including the castle dungeon."

Kaylina almost groaned at the revelation that the castle had a dungeon, but she couldn't be surprised. Even before the queen spoke, her gut told her she would end up held there.

"Your offer is magnanimous," Petalira said dryly, "but she will stay here under the supervision of guards who are not motivated by..." She glanced at Jana.

"Their penises," Jana offered.

"Indeed."

"That is *not* what motivates my actions," Vlerion said coolly.

"What other explanation could there be?" Petalira asked. "This newcomer from a land scarcely within our borders has only recently arrived and isn't properly respectful."

Damn it, Kaylina had said all the *Your Majesties*. How hadn't she been respectful?

"There is no reason a noble and a ranger would defend her so assiduously," Petalira added.

"I told you the reason, Your Majesty," Vlerion said.

"Your mount likes her?"

"*All* of the taybarri like her. Targon believes she's an *anrokk* and wants to train her to serve as a ranger."

Jana didn't hide her scoff.

"I am merely obeying his orders when it comes to her," Vlerion said.

Petalira considered Kaylina a little more thoughtfully, but she didn't look like she would relent about anything. "If she is loyal and wasn't the one to send the mead, then Captain Targon may keep her and train her."

Jana's eyes closed to slits, but she didn't object.

"Find the messenger, Lord Vlerion," Petalira said. "Ideally, before nightfall. I understand the city may be in for some excitement, during which all the rangers could be pressed into service."

"I am aware." Vlerion held the queen's gaze, and Kaylina thought he might ask for her word that no accidents would befall Kaylina on the way to the dungeon, but maybe one wasn't supposed to extract promises from royalty. "I will do as you say." His bow was stiff, but he removed his hand from the hilt of his sword and nodded to the guards. "I will leave as soon as I see her safely escorted to a cell."

"That's not necessary, my lord," one of the guards said—he hadn't sheathed his sword yet. "There aren't any vats of molten lava or pits of spikes along the way that she might fall into."

"I understand those were removed from the castle centuries ago," Petalira murmured.

"Nonetheless, I will accompany her," Vlerion said.

"It's your time."

The guards shrugged and led the way out. Six more armed men stood in the hallway outside. Had they been called up in case Vlerion started something?

Kaylina didn't feel reassured about her situation, but she was glad he hadn't been forced to choose between defending her and attacking his own people.

Jana wore a dour expression as Kaylina and Vlerion walked away surrounded by guards. A dour look but not a worried or defeated one.

Something told Kaylina that Vlerion wouldn't find that messenger. What would happen to her then?

30

JUST AS NOT ALL TRIUMPHS ARE EARNED, NOT ALL DEFEATS ARE deserved. In the face of either, we must endure.
    ~ Ranger Sergeant Myorkdar the Grim

The guards led Kaylina and Vlerion down numerous levels of wide stairs and ramps that wound deep into the cliff under the castle to a cave that appeared half natural and half hollowed out by tools. The guards walked about, lighting lanterns dangling from rusty hooks embedded in the stone walls. Along one side of the cave, stalagmites rose around a pool with stalactites hanging above it.

Kaylina thought of the fur shark. No rivers flowed into or out of this pool, so she hoped that meant nothing lived in the dark waters.

Alcoves had been carved into the cave wall opposite the pool. Cells. Iron bars with gates secured the fronts.

At the beginning of the row of cells rested a desk and chair in front of a nook filled with tools. Or were those torture implements? Kaylina didn't peer too closely into that nook, instead noticing a small bookcase that held a number of tomes. Reading material for the guards who were stuck on the subterranean duty? Or maybe prisoners were allowed a way to pass the time.

The lead guard grabbed keys from the desk drawer and unlocked a cell. None of the others were occupied.

"At least I get a private room." Kaylina tried to smile for Vlerion, who hadn't stopped looking concerned.

"Search her before putting her in." One of the guards pointed to a bulge in Kaylina's dress pocket—her sling.

"I'll search her," one man volunteered, leering at her chest.

"*I* will search her," Vlerion said. It was almost a growl.

"My lord," the lead guard said. "We have to—"

"I will search her," Vlerion repeated, his voice quiet and dangerous as he held the guard's gaze. "You may watch, though I assure you that rangers are capable of this task."

The guard sighed. "Yes, my lord."

Vlerion also sighed as he faced Kaylina, putting his back to the guards so they could have a semblance of a private moment.

"My instincts told me something like this might happen," he said softly as he withdrew her weapons from her pockets. "I apologize for bringing you here. It crossed my mind to help you and your brother to the harbor and onto a ship."

"I can't leave," she said, though the words sounded asinine as they came out. Her *life* was in the balance. If she had an opportunity to escape, she would be a fool not to take it.

But she would rather clear her name and stay. To go home would be to admit defeat. Besides, that wasn't even an option now, not if the queen believed Kaylina had tried to poison her. A warrant would be put out for her arrest, and she would be hunted if she stayed in the kingdom. Further, her family might be exiled. That would be even worse than Kaylina's death, at least in her eyes. If she had come here to prove herself only to destroy the livelihoods of every person related to her...

The thought brought tears to her eyes. Not wanting Vlerion to worry, she blinked them away.

But he was standing close enough to see everything, even in the dim lantern light. After setting her knife, sling, and pouch of lead rounds on the desk, he lifted a hand to her cheek and brushed away a single tear that had slipped from her eye.

"I'll find the messenger," Vlerion said. "If I can't, I'll drug and question every server and dish boy at that woman's inn. Someone helped her with this. I'll find out the truth and clear your name."

"Thank you," Kaylina whispered, closing her eyes and leaning into his touch. "I don't know why you're going out of your way to help me, but I... thank you." It occurred to her that if she died, he wouldn't have to worry about a commoner knowing his secret, a commoner who, as far as he and the rangers knew, might be tempted to join forces with the Virts.

She didn't think he believed she would do that, but... he could make sure. Instead, he was helping her.

The guard cleared his throat. "Proper search procedure checks more than *pockets*, my lord. And I don't believe the books mention cheeks."

"Criminals sometimes stash items under their tongues to assist in thwarting locks," Vlerion said.

"Then you can stick your hand in her mouth to check."

"That's not what he wants to stick in her mouth," the guard who'd leered—he was *still* leering—said.

"Be professional, Toks," the leader said. "Or I won't stop him if he clobbers you."

"Would you stop a ranger anyway?" one of the others asked.

"From clobbering Toks? No."

Vlerion might have ended the search with Kaylina's pockets if not for the guards watching, but he probably didn't want to do anything—or *fail* to do anything—that would prompt them to do a second search after he left. He knelt, squeezed her slippers to look for who knew what lumps might be hidden in them, then brushed his hands up her legs as he checked the inside of the dress for secret pockets. He'd given it to her, so he had to know there weren't any, but the guards didn't.

Kaylina closed her eyes, trying to ignore them watching, and trying *not* to be turned on by Vlerion's touch. He kept the search professional, his hands never straying beyond what the duty required, but every bump and brush ignited fire in her nerves.

This was Vlerion, not some guard she'd never met, and she'd found his touch arousing from the beginning. Whether she'd admitted it or not, she'd longed to have his hands run over her body, whispering over her bare skin, stroking her hip, trailing along her side, touching... whatever he wished. Never had such simple brushes raised gooseflesh while stoking heat that made her body tighten with painful longing.

If he died—or she was killed—she would be disappointed that they hadn't ever kissed.

"She has no weapons or anything that would be useful in breaking out," Vlerion declared.

"Put her in then."

On impulse, Kaylina wrapped her arms around Vlerion and hugged him. He returned the embrace without hesitation, pulling her close, molding her against his body. Only then did she realize he'd also been aroused by his professional pat-down.

That urge to kiss him returned, especially if it might be the only chance they got, but she sublimated it and rose on her tiptoes so she could bury her face in the side of his neck. Her lips brushed his warm skin, and she breathed in his masculine scent.

"I keep meaning to drive you off, for your own safety," Vlerion murmured, his lips brushing the top of her ear, making pleasure streak through her. "I keep failing."

Kaylina hugged him tighter, kissing his neck and wanting...
what they couldn't have.

"I'm not great at self-preservation," she admitted, half-forgetting that the guards were there watching. She wanted to show
Vlerion that she appreciated him, that it meant a lot to her to have
him stand up for her. To want to protect her.

He exhaled slowly, almost a growl, and it reminded her of the
danger. Of the beast.

His hand slid down her back, pressing her tight against him.
Would his desire make him forget the threat of what he could
become?

If she roused the beast, he might kill all the guards, but that
wouldn't be a victory. For punishment, he would be killed himself,
just as his brother had been. And once he changed, he might not
recognize her as a friend. He might kill her too.

Maybe that crossed his mind, because he unhooked her arms
and stepped back.

"The cell," he said, a rasp to his voice.

That glint of savagery she'd seen before in his eyes was there,
more than a glint, and she realized how close he'd come to being
overtaken by his emotions. A trickle of fear joined her other anxieties, and she nodded and hurried into the cell.

He shut the gate firmly. To protect her from the guards? Or
from himself?

Before letting go of the bars, Vlerion closed his eyes, took a
deep breath, and hummed a stanza of his song.

"What is that noise?" one of the guards whispered.

When Vlerion opened his eyes and stepped back, he'd reaffixed his mask. He nodded at Kaylina, as if to say he was under
control.

"I'll be back for you," he said quietly.

"I know." She might not know why he cared, other than his
admission that he'd liked her bravery, but she trusted that he did.

"Any chance I can have a book and a lantern? Assuming you don't think I can use the pages as instruments to effect my escape."

Vlerion walked toward the case, plucking a lantern from one of the wall hooks on the way.

"She doesn't need a book," the lead guard said with exasperation.

Vlerion looked coolly at him, and the man lifted his hands.

Surprisingly, Vlerion considered the titles on the spines instead of grabbing one at random. He withdrew a thick tome and gave it and the lantern to Kaylina.

"*The Ranger's Guide to Honor, Duty, and Tenets?*" she read off the spine. "Seriously?"

"You might as well educate yourself while you wait."

"I was hoping for a romantic adventure."

"Dungeon reading material is limited."

"No kidding."

After giving her a nod—and a glance at her lips that promised he would rather leave her with a kiss—Vlerion walked away with the impatient guards.

Fortunately, they all departed. As unpleasant as her new circumstances were, they could get worse if the leering guard was left with her. She doubted the queen had cared enough to stipulate that her new prisoner not be harassed. *Jana*, Kaylina was certain, hoped she never walked out of the dungeon.

She rested her forehead against the cool bars, trying to figure out how she could avoid that fate.

31

FORTUNE FAVORS THOSE WHO PREPARE THEMSELVES TO RECEIVE IT.
  ~ Summer Moon Priestess Tya

Kaylina had only been alone in the dungeon cave for ten or fifteen minutes when a soft scraping came from the far side. She lowered her lantern—and the *extremely* dry reading Vlerion had given her —and peered into the gloom beyond the pool. Or had that come from *in* the pool?

Thoughts of deadly water animals returned.

But it sounded like it came from behind the pool. Maybe on the cave wall? Or *in* it?

If Vlerion hadn't said the catacombs didn't run anywhere near the royal castle, Kaylina would have guessed Virts were back there, planting explosives, as they'd planned to do under her meadery.

Maybe those sounds came from someone tunneling in from another cave to rescue her. She snorted. Right. Besides Vlerion and her brother, Kaylina couldn't imagine anyone bothering. Vlerion was searching for the messenger, and Frayvar didn't know she was in trouble. She didn't know whether to be relieved or glad she hadn't gone to visit him before leaving to see the queen. He had a noble enough heart that he *would* try to rescue her from trouble, but he wasn't strong enough to implement a plan that didn't involve numbers and ledgers.

The scrapes stopped, then started up again, then stopped permanently. An hour or more passed without a sound, and Kaylina's hopes that someone would break her out died. It might have been an animal moving in the little forest of stalagmites. Though if she was the *anrokk* that people believed, an animal ought to come over, say hello, demand pets, and filch the cell key for her.

The soft clanks of armor sounded on the stone steps leading to the dungeon. Kaylina closed the book she hadn't made much progress in and braced herself for her next trial.

A guard walked into view, the one who'd been leering at her.

Kaylina gripped the book, the closest thing to a weapon she had, and vowed to club him if he entered her cell.

Someone walked into view behind him. Jana. Her hood was up, but Kaylina knew her cloak and furtive walk right away.

"If you've come to let me out to pee, I appreciate it," Kaylina said out of a notion that she shouldn't show fear, shouldn't give away that her belly fluttered with nerves. "The guards didn't make a latrine stop on the way down, and there isn't so much as a bowl in my cell."

"If you hadn't been busy rubbing up against the ranger, you could have asked to go," the guard said.

Jana grunted. "I knew they were sleeping together."

If only...

"It was the only explanation for how she got a ranger wrapped around her finger so quickly." Jana pressed a gold coin into the guard's hand and pointed at the stairs. "Stand over there. Let me know if anyone is coming."

"For the mead maven? Anything." He winked and gave *her* a leer.

"I'm married and old enough to be your mother, you oaf," she said but sounded as if she liked the attention.

Kaylina curled her lip in disgust at the thought of liking *anything* from that man.

"I'd enjoy you," the guard said. "I'm still hard from watching them hump."

"Disgusting. Over there." Jana pointed at the steps again.

After giving her another leer, as if any of her anatomy were visible under that cloak, the man obeyed, walking far enough up the steps to be out of sight.

Jana stopped in front of Kaylina's cell. "The problem with the ones who are amenable to bribes is they're not exactly the best of the best."

"Why are you doing this? I never did anything to you." Kaylina looked toward the far side of the cave, but it had been a while since she'd heard any scrapes. Maybe they'd been her imagination.

"I told you we were competitors. Competitions can be ruthless up here."

"I hadn't yet made my first batch of mead when you said that. You couldn't possibly be worried about me."

"I've been to the Spitting Gull." Before, Jana had said she hadn't. "I don't know where your grandmother gets her honey or the secrets of her recipes, but her mead is the most exquisite I've ever tasted, and I've tasted a lot. You will *not* open a meadery here. I've worked my whole life to establish my business, win supply contracts with the royal family and other monied nobles, and make enough to buy land for my family, to ensure my children and their children won't grow up in poverty, like I did. Do you have any idea how hard it is to have a successful business and buy land as a commoner?"

"I've got some inklings." Kaylina knew how hard it had been for her grandparents. "Are you seriously trying to get me killed because some competition might cause you to earn a little less?"

"To lose all my contracts would be more than *earning a little less.*"

"But I haven't even—"

Jana's voice rose as she snarled, "I *tasted* your mead."

"The mead you had someone steal from our root cellar?"

"I tasted it," Jana repeated softly without admitting to the rest. "It's the same as I had down south. It might even be better."

This was not the time to feel pride, but Kaylina filed that comment away to enjoy later... if she survived until later.

"Your ranger won't find the delivery boy." Jana slid a hand under her cloak.

"Did you kill him after he did your awful work?"

"Of course not. I am, as the queen said, an upright kingdom subject. I'm not a murderer."

"But you would have no trouble killing me."

"You're a girl venturing into a world you're ill-prepared for. If your grandmother wanted to extend her empire, she should have sent someone with more experience, someone with more than a child's toy for a weapon." Jana glanced at the sling on the desk.

Likely so, but Grandma hadn't sent Kaylina. She didn't point that out to Jana.

"The dose in the mead wouldn't have killed you. Just confirmed your guilt while giving you crippling abdominal pain and explosive diarrhea. At the queen's feet."

"I'm extremely disappointed I didn't try it."

Death might have been more merciful.

"*She* might have killed you afterward. Likely would have. She has a history of getting rid of people."

"So I've heard."

"The funny thing about those who use poison to solve their problems is that they're quick to believe others will do the same."

"Did you start the fire in the castle when you were stealing my mead?"

"I did not. I believe that was a test." Jana withdrew her hand, a small vial of a purple liquid inside. "The Virts wondered if they could trust you or if you were feeding information to the rangers that people kept noticing at your side."

Yes, they hadn't done a good job of feigning there was no link between Kaylina and the rangers. Kaylina and *Vlerion*.

"Had the castle burned without intervention, they would have believed you were an entrepreneur working on your own. After all, not even the fire brigade would go near that cursed place." Jana squinted. "Not unless they were *ordered* to. Not only did the fire brigade assist in putting out the flames, but Lord Vlerion himself did."

"If the Virts had burned the castle to the ground, even if I weren't working with the rangers, I wouldn't have been eager to jump in bed with the arsonists who targeted me."

"A risk I believe they were willing to take. You'd have to speak with their leaders for the details. I suspect they mostly wanted the catacombs and that exit into the city to remain unwatched." Jana set the vial on the crossbar next to the gate.

"Is that the same poison that you sabotaged my mead with?" Kaylina glanced toward the stairs, wondering if the guard was listening, or cared if he was. Probably not. He'd been paid.

"In this small concentrated dose, it would be fatal," Jana said. "I'll leave it there in case you want to end things instead of getting your ranger killed."

Kaylina looked sharply at her. Did Jana know about Vlerion's secret?

"I saw the way he looked at you. When he doesn't find the messenger, he'll be driven to do something foolish. Ask yourself if you want him to give up his career and probably his life for you." Jana raised her eyebrows frankly. "If he attacks and kills guards to break you out... even if he only defies the queen's wishes... it'll be the end for him. Even nobles aren't above the law."

"I'm innocent. Breaking me out wouldn't be a crime."

"Except that I've ensured that it would be." Jana smiled, bowed, and backed away.

"Because you're too much of a coward to compete fairly with me for customers?"

"I haven't gotten this far in life by being *fair*." Jana pointed at the vial. "I suggest you make your decision quickly. That guard has some notions about what he'd like to do with you. Acts that might also drive the ranger to rage-fueled slaying if he returns at an untimely moment. Love prompts young men to make poor decisions."

"He doesn't love me."

Kaylina had little doubt about that, but if Vlerion was drawn to her because she was an *anrokk*... might that not be as powerful as love?

"We'll see." Jana turned toward the stairs. "Unless you make the selfless choice and end your life before he can lose everything."

After planting her vile seed, Jana walked away without looking back.

Alone again, Kaylina stared at the vial. A tremble went through her. She wouldn't consider the horrible woman's offering, but... Could she live with herself if she did get Vlerion killed?

"Gods," she whispered.

A clank from the stairwell made her realize she wasn't alone. The guard hadn't left.

Kaylina plucked up the vial and slid it into her pocket.

Gripping the book in both hands, she stepped back until the cold chiseled stone wall pressed into her shoulder blades. The guard sauntered into view, his expression smug, that of a man who had dastardly plans in mind and knew he wouldn't get caught.

Kaylina didn't know whether to wish Vlerion were there to protect her or not. Seeing the guard approaching her might cause him to turn. The man might deserve an end at the claws of the beast, but... the queen wouldn't see it that way. The law wouldn't see it that way. And then there was the possibility that the beast would kill her after killing the guard.

"The king is giving his speech," the man said. "Hearing him stumble through his rehearsed words isn't that scintillating, but people are supposed to listen. I doubt anyone will come down here for the next hour or so."

"Maybe you should go up and listen too. Prove yourself a good guard deserving of a pay raise."

"I've already been paid more today than I make in a month." He showed the gold coin, bit into it to dent the metal, and slipped it into a pocket. "And if I'm reading the moon craters right, the only one who cares what happens to you is that ranger, and he's not here." The guard opened the desk drawer and pulled out the keyring.

Nerves dampened Kaylina's palms as she gripped the book. If he opened the gate because he wanted to rape her, and she could avoid that fate, she could get out. Escaping from the rest of the castle wouldn't be easy, but if most people were watching that speech, maybe she had a shot. She would have a much better chance of clearing her name from outside the dungeon than in it.

But the guard stood between her and escape.

He stepped close to the gate, slipping the key into the lock. He was tall, muscular, and broad-shouldered, with a flanged mace at his hip and chain mail protecting his torso. And she... she had a book.

Nonetheless, she lowered into a crouch, Vlerion's lesson on balance coming to mind. She might not be able to beat the guy, but she had to try.

"You going to club me with that?" Amusement gleamed in his dark eyes.

The lock clinked.

"As many times as I can."

"Exciting." He gave her a long look from head to toe, his gaze lingering in select spots.

Fury flowed into Kaylina's limbs, making her believe that maybe she *could* get the best of the guard.

He opened the gate and strode toward her.

Instead of taking a swing, she threw the book at him, hoping to startle him.

He raised an arm, deflecting the heavy object. She rushed in, trying to take him off guard, and turned and dropped her shoulder, aiming an elbow to his groin.

But he was fast and shifted his body. Her elbow struck his hip, jarring her and not hurting him. He grabbed her and spun her, thrusting her against the bars and pressing his body against hers from behind.

"*Very* exciting." He laughed and bit her ear.

Pain sent another blast of fury into her. She screamed, more rage than a cry for help, and stomped down, catching his instep. But she wore only slippers, and his boots protected him.

She grabbed the bars, trying to push and twist away, but he used his greater weight to keep her pinned. One hand snaked down, jerking her dress up.

Kaylina whipped her head back and caught him in the nose so

hard that cartilage crunched. His grip loosened. For a second time, she threw her head back, clipping him again.

He cursed and let go, tears springing to his eyes.

She whirled and reached for the vial in her pocket, but unless she could force it down his throat, what good would it do? Instead, she lunged for the mace at his hip.

The guard recovered enough to stop her, grabbing her wrist. She kicked him in the shin and jerked her arm away.

Doubting she could win a fight, she spun toward the open gate, intending to run instead.

But a tremendous boom came from the far side of the cave, from where the scraping had been.

The ground quaked, and the cell gates rattled as rubble flew. It splashed into the water and clunked to the ground. Smoke blew over the pool, filling the air, and men's voices sounded as the noise of the explosion dwindled.

The guard swore and thrust Kaylina aside as he lunged for the gate. She had her second chance to grab the mace and snatched it from his hip. This time, she was successful.

With the weapon in her hand, she backed away.

"Damn it." The guard spun toward her, reaching for it as he glanced at the smoke, the shapes of men visible streaming into the cave.

Kaylina swung the mace at his head.

If he hadn't been distracted, she wouldn't have gotten the best of him, but she cracked him square above the ear. He pitched to the ground.

Armed men ran around the pool and toward the stairs. Virts? Here to assassinate the king? There were dozens of them, and they carried swords, axes, maces, and crossbows. She was positive they hadn't come to hear their monarch speak.

Kaylina crept to the open gate, hoping that the smoke would

keep them from noticing her. Then she could escape and... and what? She didn't know. Find Vlerion.

But two men in the lead paused to look at her.

"Didn't we rescue you once before?" one asked with a laugh. His face was vaguely familiar. He must have been at that first jailbreak.

"I rescued myself, thank you." Kaylina admitted their explosion had helped with that, but she raised the mace, hoping she looked capable—and that they didn't have any notions of capturing her.

He laughed again. "Yeah, you did."

"Shit," someone closer to the stairs barked, pointing in that direction. "Ranger!"

Vlerion.

At first, Kaylina's heart soared. But he was alone, and there were at least forty men, with more rushing into the cave. Even he couldn't win against such odds.

A snarl from behind startled Kaylina. The guard.

He sprang on her, smashing her against the bars again and grabbing her wrist. She tightened her grip, refusing to let go of the mace, and cursing herself for forgetting about him. She'd *thought* she had knocked him out, damn it.

Her dress ripped as he pawed at her with one hand and twisted her wrist with the other. The tear of fabric was audible in the suddenly silent cave, and Kaylina looked toward the stairwell, afraid Vlerion would shift.

Utter rage filled his eyes. Kaylina clubbed the guard with the mace, knocking him to the ground again. It didn't calm Vlerion. He transformed right before her eyes.

His clothing ripped, his skin sprouted short auburn fur, and he grew even more muscular and powerful, the laces of his leather armor snapping under his bulging torso. Claws thrust from hands that had turned paw-like. When he threw his head back to howl, his jaw broadened and his teeth elongated into fangs.

By all the altered plants in the world, that change had to hurt.

Between the shadows and smoke, a lot of the invaders might have missed Vlerion's shift, but every head turned at the roar. When the beast charged into the cave, half the men yelled and scattered. But half the men raised their weapons, aiming to kill him.

32

FEAR FOR THOSE WE CARE ABOUT STEALS OUR WISDOM.
  ~ Dionadra, Essays on the Motivations of Men

"No!" Kaylina shouted and hammered the mace against the metal bars.

She didn't expect the men to listen, not when the beast was springing into their midst, claws slashing and jaws snapping. But she hoped to distract them, to keep the ones with crossbows from firing. Nobody had muskets or blunderbusses, but those quarrels could drive through an eye and pierce a man's brain. Pierce *Vlerion's* brain.

He didn't look at her as he tore into the men. Weapons slashed for his head and torso, but he moved so quickly that she couldn't follow his blurring claws. And the power he struck with... Men flew backward into each other and the cave walls. An arm torn free from its body thudded to the ground not five feet from her cell, blood spattering the bars and her dress.

Horrified—and *terrified*—Kaylina backed up. Since transforming, Vlerion hadn't looked at her and didn't seem aware of her at all. His eyes were the same blue as when he was a man, but there was no recognition in them, no indication of thinking at all. Only the killer instincts the curse had embedded in him.

The druids must have wanted this, Kaylina realized numbly as the beast beheaded a man before springing toward another. It was their revenge, that a human turn into an animal to slay his own kind, whether those people deserved death or not. The druids must have felt that *all* men were a blight on the world.

"What *is* that thing?" someone yelled.

"A gorilla?" another replied, aiming at Vlerion's head.

By accident or instinct, the beast sensed the threat and ducked. The quarrel skimmed through his fur without digging in.

"Not with those claws!"

A blade struck the beast, leaving a bloody gash in his shoulder, but he didn't slow. He slashed, enemies falling with each blow.

Crossbows fired. Most of the quarrels went wild, but Kaylina winced when one gouged deep into the beast's thigh. He roared but, again, didn't slow down.

The men who'd yelled and scattered when Vlerion transformed ran for the stairs.

"Run, you fools," one called back. "This isn't the battle we came for."

But the beast blocked others who tried to run. Another crossbow quarrel took him in the back of the shoulder. His armor, loose but still on, protected him from a third. His shredded clothes hung limply, no help at all. His boots were missing entirely.

The number of enemies had dwindled, but Kaylina worried the beast would be overcome. If one of those quarrels found a vital target...

She stepped toward the gate, tempted to help, even if she could only thump one or two crossbowmen in the backs of their heads to keep them from firing. But when the beast's gaze swung in her direction, it was devoid of humanity, and she knew without a doubt that he would kill her just as he was killing the men.

Swallowing, Kaylina backed up and closed the gate. If she could figure out a way to help from within the safety of the cell, she would, but going out there would be suicidal. That frustrated her enough that she also wanted to roar and howl.

The guard had left the key in the lock of the gate. She turned it and removed it, ensuring nobody could enter unless she let them in.

More intruders scurried up the stairs, abandoning their comrades. The beast was down to three enemies. So many men lay dead on the ground that Kaylina couldn't count them all. Twelve? Fifteen? More? Blood washed the stone floor like someone had hurled paint buckets about.

As the beast sprang onto another man, one who'd tried to escape but hadn't made it, Kaylina caught movement behind her. The guard was stirring again.

Though he lay on his belly, brow creased with pain, he looked at her with fury in his eyes. His focus was so pure that he didn't seem to see what was going on outside the cage. He drew a dagger from his belt and pushed himself to his elbows.

"Are you *still* going after me, you bastard?" Kaylina hefted the mace.

He pushed himself up, raising the dagger to throw. She sprang forward, fear more than bravery motivating her—she *couldn't* deal with a threat within as well as one without—and she kicked. Though he saw the attack coming and tried to pull his arm back, her fear made her fast, and she connected with his wrist.

The blade flew from his grip and clanged off one of the bars, the sound loud in a cave that had grown quiet. The guard looked at it and started to lunge after it. She swung the mace, striking him in the head again.

Once more, he pitched to the ground. After as many times as

he'd risen, she didn't know if she had finally knocked him unconscious.

Mace aloft, she watched him for movement.

The beast sprang from the shadows and landed halfway up the front of the cell, furred paws wrapping around the bars. Startled, Kaylina skittered away as he rattled them, powerful muscles rippling under that sleek fur, his form huge this close.

She trembled, almost dropping the mace, but she made herself tighten her grip, terrified she would have to defend herself against him.

Wild fury burned in his inhuman eyes. Though his enemies lay dead behind him, the beast wasn't done killing.

"It's me, Vlerion." Kaylina made herself meet his gaze, hoping to get through to him.

Snarling, he pulled at the bars. Metal groaned, and a bolt tore free, clinking on the ground. By the gods, he was strong. There was no way she could defend herself against him. She *had* to get through to him another way.

She tried to hum the tune she'd heard from him numerous times, but she didn't have any musical experience and hadn't paid that much attention to the melody. Could he even hear her over his attempts to break the bars?

She tried singing a nursery rhyme from her youth about fish and eels, but her voice cracked and quavered. Even when she wasn't afraid for her life, she didn't have a knack for song.

The beast shifted to the gate, trying to yank it open.

As Kaylina backed farther, her heel hit something on the ground. The book.

Without dropping the mace, she grabbed it and opened it.

"Proper behavior for young rangers," she read, hoping vainly that hearing the words—and the mention of rangers—would get through to Vlerion, would remind him that he was, at the heart, a brave and noble warrior with honor and ethics. He wasn't an animal.

With a great wrenching of metal, the beast tore the gate off the hinges. He flung it to the ground ten feet away and sprang into the cell.

Fumbling the book, Kaylina almost screamed. The guard lifted his head, eyes bleary with confusion. The beast sprang not for Kaylina but for him. With an enraged roar, he hefted the guard to his feet and used those preternaturally powerful muscles to rip the man's head off.

This time, Kaylina *did* scream as the head landed on the ground between her and the beast. She backed until she struck the cell wall and could go no farther, raising both book and mace though neither would defend her from his might.

The beast crouched, his chest heaving from the long battle, his eyes locking onto her. But he didn't spring. He stared intensely at her, fangs and claws dripping blood.

Though Kaylina had never been more afraid in her life, she lifted the book again. The tremor to her hands made it difficult to read but she did her best.

"Proper behavior for young rangers... is to be respectful toward fellow humans... whether noble or common." She licked her lips. Why was her mouth so dry? "And also to honor the ancient treaty with the taybarri."

The beast's eyes remained locked on her. He hadn't moved and did seem to be listening.

"Upon return from battle, tend your mount before feeding yourself. Wash, groom, and give it sustenance. This duty shows respect and strengthens your bond with the taybarri while also calming the mind of the ranger, so often agitated after battle. No kidding," she muttered, glancing into the eyes of the beast, hoping to find Vlerion in there somewhere.

"My," he rasped in an inhuman voice, the word barely understandable.

Kaylina stared. Somehow, she'd never imagined the beast would talk.

"What?" she whispered.

He reached toward her while looking her up and down, his gaze lingering on the tear in her dress. With a possessive glint in his eyes and his voice a snarl, he said, "*My* female."

"Uhm."

He glanced at the dead guard. "My female."

"That's right." Kaylina decided agreement was a good idea, but the thought that the beast might want to celebrate his triumph with sex made her tremble with fear. The memory of Isla's scars came to her. Scars her husband had left on her when he'd been the beast.

Kaylina jerked the book back up and continued reading, emphasizing the words *ranger* and *respect* and *honor* when she crossed them, hoping they would bring back his humanity. Hoping—

The beast growled and stepped toward her. It sounded more like a contented growl than a savage growl, but that didn't reassure her. She kept reading and wondered if she should try singing again.

He took another step. And another. He was close enough to touch her—to rip her head off or do whatever he wished to her. The book shook so much that she couldn't read the words any longer.

He reached out with a claw and traced her cheek, as he'd done with his finger earlier to brush a tear away.

"Vlerion," Kaylina said softly, again making herself meet his eyes.

For the first time, something was there, something human. Then he collapsed at her feet.

33

A SMALL WEAPON PRECISELY PLACED MAY DEFEAT MORE ENEMIES THAN A tool of great destruction.

~ Ranger Lord Vlerion of Havartaft

Kaylina stared down at the beast, the great furred body unmoving at her feet. Faint pops and groans sounded as he transformed back into Vlerion, the shredded remains of his clothes barely covering him. He didn't stir except for the faint expansion and contraction of his ribcage with breaths that had grown soft and even.

The crossbow quarrel that had struck him in the shoulder remained, embedded deep in his flesh. Kaylina put aside the book and mace and rested a hand on his back.

"Vlerion?"

He didn't move.

In the catacombs, the last time he'd changed into the beast, he'd disappeared after killing the fur shark, then soon returned as himself. If he'd fallen unconscious after that battle, it couldn't have been for long. But this battle had been more extended and, with so many foes, it might have taken more out of him. Maybe the powerful magic that infused the beast drew upon Vlerion's own stamina and constitution. Was it possible that if he had to fight long enough and hard enough, it would kill him?

"He's not dead," she told herself.

Kaylina eyed the quarrel and thought of the invaders that had made it up the stairs and had to be, even now, fighting the castle defenders and trying to reach the king. When he came to, Vlerion would want to help, but having a quarrel embedded in the shoulder muscle of his sword arm would impede him.

Though it might not be the most medically sound thing to do, she tore the remains of his shirt to create bandages and gripped the quarrel. Better to remove it while he was unconscious and couldn't feel it. His ranger doctor could fix the wound later.

She pulled out the quarrel, wincing as his muscle spasmed.

"Vlerion?"

Maybe that had woken him. But, no. His eyes didn't open.

She tied the strips of the shirt around the wound as a bandage.

Remembering the quarrel in his thigh, Kaylina summoned her strength to roll him over. He wasn't as big when he wasn't the beast, but he was still a tall and muscular man, and she grunted with the effort. When he flopped onto his back, she could see the quarrel through a great tear in his trousers. It had broken off, and she couldn't tell if it was near a vein. Reluctantly, she left it in.

A faint groan came from Vlerion.

"There you are," Kaylina whispered, shifting closer to his head and watching his eyes. "Time to wake up, Vlerion. Your people need you."

She needed him too. She touched his jaw.

"I would kiss you, to see if my lips have some magic to them, but your mouth was dripping blood a minute ago, and there are bodies everywhere. I'm not feeling moved to romantic overtures." Despite her attempt to keep her tone light and avoid looking at the carnage, her voice had an edge of hysteria to it. She needed to get out of the gory dungeon. Badly.

In case it would help, Kaylina kissed Vlerion on the blood-free forehead.

His eyelids fluttered. She trusted he'd been about to waken anyway and that her lips were not magical.

"I was hoping... you'd read to me more." Vlerion turned his head left and right, enough to glimpse some of the bodies, and he winced. From more than physical pain, she knew. "I was also hoping... you'd never see me... see this."

Kaylina had seen the beast in the catacombs already and almost said so, but this had been far worse. Far gorier.

"I didn't particularly want to." She helped him sit up. "A lot of the Virts ran up the stairs. Hopefully, the castle guard has already rounded them all up, but they might need your help."

Frowning, Vlerion looked around the cave until he saw the hole and rubble on the far side of the pond. "I briefly had time to wonder where they came from before..." He waved vaguely at himself, then stood, wincing again when he put weight on the leg that had been shot. His pain didn't keep him from looking her over. He lifted a hand toward the flap dangling from her torn dress, but didn't touch it. "Are you injured? Were you...?"

"Just a couple of bumps. But I need to get out of here." She also needed to clear her name, but if assassins were in the middle of trying to kill the royal family, this wouldn't be the time to plead her case again to the queen.

Vlerion eyed the front of the cell, the warped hinges all that remained of the gate. "Someone already opened the door."

"*Someone* has strength that makes the Kar'ruk seem puny."

"Yes," he murmured, looking at her again. "I'm glad I didn't hurt you."

"Me too. You'll have to teach me the lyrics to that song later so I can sing it to calm you if need be."

"It's called 'Lake of Triumph and Sorrow.'" Vlerion stepped over the body of the guard and limped out of the cell, finding his sword lying on the ground. He pointed toward the stairs. "My brother wrote it. He could play numerous instruments and had the soul of a poet. It still surprises me that he wasn't any better than me or our father at controlling the beast."

Kaylina returned the book to the desk and grabbed her knife, sling, and pouch of rounds. "It's hard to thwart a curse."

"It is indeed."

A distant boom reverberated through the cliff. It sounded like it had come from farther away than the castle, but it was hard to tell from deep underground.

"You're right." Vlerion picked up his pace, gritting his teeth against his leg wound to take the stone stairs three at a time. "They may still need help up there."

"I'm ready." Kaylina hurried after him. "But what should I do if we run into the queen?"

"She won't be out in the middle of a battle."

"Her guards might be."

Vlerion paused to look back at her. "Maybe you should stay down here. Or better yet, leave through that hole. It must connect to the catacombs. According to the maps we have of the city underground, there's almost a mile between the end of the tunnels and this cliff, but the Virts could have been excavating a new passageway for a long time. There are so many tunnels and hidden doors down there that the patrollers might not have noticed another one."

"I'd rather stay with you."

"To read to me if I go berserk again?"

"Well, I returned the book to the jail library. I'm not a thief. And that didn't work as well as one might have hoped." She raised her eyebrows. "Are you likely to, uhm, go berserk again?" Become the beast. "It seemed to take a lot out of you."

Vlerion straightened his spine and lifted his chin, as if to deny that he was anything but hale and full of vigor, but he did say, "Usually, at least a few hours have to pass before it can happen again. Sometimes, even days. I haven't attempted to test it fully, for reasons I trust you understand, but turning does bleed off the dangerous edge for a time, even if my emotions are roused again right after I change back into myself."

Another distant boom sounded, the stone walls vibrating with the explosion. Vlerion looked up and then back at Kaylina.

"I'm sticking with you," she said firmly. "Besides, there could be a second wave of invaders waiting in that tunnel, and I'd run right into them with only my sling and this little letter opener to protect me."

Not that she thought she would be in much danger if she did encounter the Virts. Their mission had little to do with her. She didn't want to think too much about how the beast had killed a bunch of men motivated by a desire for equality and better working conditions, not, as far as she knew, real malice or a craving for power and wealth. Still, someone on their side had burned her castle, so she wasn't inclined to feel immensely sorry for them. Assassinations also weren't an acceptable way to work toward one's goals.

"All right." Vlerion returned to taking the stairs three at a time.

Kaylina hurried to catch up.

When they pushed open the stone door into a hallway on the ground floor of the castle, it was empty, but shouts and clangs came from the direction of the courtyard.

An animal roared. Was that a taybarri? Maybe the rangers had gotten in and were battling the invaders. Maybe Vlerion and Kaylina wouldn't be needed.

The smaller booms of muskets rang out from the walls and the courtyard. Another greater boom sounded in the distance. From the harbor?

"They're attacking from multiple fronts." Sword in hand, Vlerion ran toward the courtyard. "Or there are ships in the harbor raising a distraction."

"I thought they were supposed to attack tonight." Kaylina raced after him, but she was ill-prepared for a battle against men with firearms.

"They may have been testing you by feeding you that information." He glanced back as he ran.

Yes, if the fire had been a test, the information could have been too. That made sense. Nobody trusted Kaylina. Except maybe Vlerion.

He paused in the doorway leading to the courtyard. Blue fur streaked past not five yards ahead of them.

"Crenoch!" Vlerion called softly, his voice almost drowned out by the boom of a cannon firing from the castle wall.

His mount spun and came back to the doorway. Kaylina peeked under Vlerion's arm and glimpsed a second taybarri across the courtyard, the great beast biting one of the invaders.

"Is that Levitke?" Kaylina didn't see any other taybarri or rangers, though numerous castle guards fought intruders both in the courtyard and on the castle wall.

"Yes." Vlerion swung up onto Crenoch's back and offered a hand to her.

But a roar came from the other taybarri. After biting and trampling the intruder into the stone pavers, Levitke charged across the courtyard toward Crenoch. No, she was coming toward *Kaylina*. Their eyes met, and Kaylina somehow grasped that the taybarri was glad to see her and expected Kaylina to ride her.

"I'll go on that one," she told Vlerion.

Vlerion didn't look like he wanted to let her get that far from him, but Levitke butted Crenoch out of the way to get close to the doorway and Kaylina.

"So I see," Vlerion said as she gripped the thick fur and pulled herself astride. "Be careful. Stay on the outskirts. This isn't your battle."

No sooner had the words come out than Levitke surged toward a knot of intruders fighting guards near the castle gate.

"Tell her that." Kaylina alternated gripping her mount and loading her sling while trying not to fall off. The meager weapon might not help much, but she didn't feel as useless with the great muscles and fangs of the taybarri under her.

Vlerion grunted and nudged Crenoch to ride at Levitke's side.

Kaylina used her sling to fire at one of the intruders, but she'd never before shot from horseback—and certainly not taybarri back. The round went wide.

"This is going to take a little getting used to," she muttered.

The world blurred, and Levitke flashed, magically disappearing, then reappearing twenty yards ahead, in the middle of the fighters.

Heart pounding, Kaylina found herself surrounded by swords and maces whipping through the air. A shield slammed into Levitke's side. She spun and bit it, then tore it from the invader's grip. It flew ten feet and clanged against a stone wall. Next, the taybarri lunged into *him*, jaws snapping for his throat.

Levitke's swift movements made it hard to stay on her back, much less contribute to the battle. Kaylina almost lost her sling as she was forced to grip fur with both hands.

"A *lot* of getting used to," she corrected.

Crenoch smashed into a pair of invaders that had been fighting as a team. He snapped for the throat of the one on the left as Vlerion, face set in his usual expressionless battle mask, slashed at the one on the right. The invader jerked a shield over his head to deflect the sword blow, but Vlerion shifted his grip and swept the blade in again, this time slipping under the man's defenses. It cut deep, and the invader pitched backward, losing his shield. Crenoch trampled him.

Levitke was relentless as well, biting and often lifting a front limb to claw at the invaders. Unlike normal animals, the intelligent taybarri knew exactly who the enemies were.

Feeling she should do something to help, Kaylina lifted her sling and sought a target she could hit even with her mount gyrating about. Vlerion's lessons on the importance of balance came to mind again. If only she'd had more than one day of training.

"Get the ranger," someone from the wall called. An invader. He'd downed one of the guards firing a cannon toward the harbor and looked to be sabotaging the weapon.

Another invader with a blunderbuss crouched beside him. He lifted his firearm toward Vlerion, who was still swinging his sword, trying to make his way to the gate.

Kaylina couldn't take the time to think or aim. She loosed a round at the man targeting Vlerion, doing her best to compensate for Levitke's movement. Fortunately, the invader had to wait to fire to make sure he didn't hit his allies, and he didn't notice her—or, if he did, didn't consider her a threat. Her round landed before he pulled the trigger.

Her aim was off, but it still struck him, hitting him in the chest instead of the forehead. The blow was enough to startle him, and he dropped his blunderbuss. It went off, scattering shot, before it bounced off the wall and into the courtyard.

"Thanks." Vlerion had seen the threat—and her hitting it.

Pleased, Kaylina nodded and looked for another target.

One man noticed she was armed and sprang for her, an axe raised. Levitke charged at him. He swung the weapon toward the taybarri's shoulder.

"No," Kaylina barked, aiming her sling at him.

But Levitke was so fast that she whipped her neck about to catch the swinging axe by the haft before it connected. When Kaylina's round hit the man in the forehead—it was much easier to target someone so close—his hands spasmed, and he released the weapon. Levitke hurled it across the courtyard.

"Someone get that portcullis open," came a yell from outside the castle walls. Was that Captain Targon?

Kaylina glimpsed more blue-furred taybarri charging up the ramp, a few bumping into armed men on the landing outside, trying to get in to help.

"It's stuck," a guard crouching near the gate, staying out of the battle, yelled back.

One of the invaders gave him a quick nod. Was that guard also being bribed? He looked like he was blocking access to the portcullis rather than trying to get it unstuck.

Frowning, Kaylina lifted her sling. Levitke raced in the opposite direction, toward double wooden doors across the courtyard that two intruders had entered, but Kaylina managed to twist and get a shot off. It struck the guard in the face as Targon appeared at the portcullis.

Kaylina winced. If she'd guessed wrong about that guard, the captain of the rangers had witnessed her shoot an ally.

"Open the gate," Targon barked.

One of the other guards, realizing Vlerion, Kaylina, and the taybarri had taken down all the invaders around him, ran to obey. He frowned at the man on the ground, who was gripping his forehead where the lead round had struck, and stepped over him to pull the lever. It wasn't stuck. The portcullis rose, and uniformed men and black-clad rangers on taybarri rushed inside.

"Take back the cannons!" Targon yelled. "And someone make sure the king and queen are defended."

Levitke ran through the open doors, her size making the wide hallway seem small. Kaylina caught herself ducking under the ceiling beams as the taybarri raced after the invaders that had run inside. She glanced back, having no idea where they were going, and was relieved to see Crenoch and Vlerion pounding after her.

Levitke turned into another hallway, this one equally wide, and, when they crossed an intersection, Kaylina recognized the area. They'd exited the dungeon near there.

The hallway opened into a great chamber with wide stairs at the end. The two intruders had reached the landing at the top.

A boom from somewhere nearby made a chandelier above their heads tremble and clink, but it was Levitke that drew the men's gazes and made them gawk.

Certain they were up to no good, Kaylina lifted her sling, but the intruders darted into a hallway behind the landing and out of view.

"The royal rooms are that way," Vlerion said as Crenoch caught up. "The king and queen."

Both taybarri sprang up the stairs but couldn't fit into the narrower hallway at the top. Kaylina slid off and let Vlerion take the lead. Without the fearsome Levitke, she was only a girl with a sling.

Outside, the booms dwindled, and Kaylina trusted Targon and the rest of the rangers were securing the defenses.

At the end of the hall, two castle guards lay dead before a splintered door that had been knocked partway off its hinges. Vlerion rushed into the spacious sitting room of an opulent suite with multiple fireplaces, but the rugs were askew and furniture knocked over. An older man with a confused and terrified expression crouched between two guards, who were fighting off the intruders, swords clanging against maces and shields.

Vlerion rushed into the fray, springing upon the invaders from behind. Kaylina lifted the sling in case they needed help.

Someone ran out of a bedroom with a woman slung over his shoulder. The queen. She wasn't moving and had to be unconscious. Hopefully not dead.

Kaylina fired at the kidnapper. With her feet on solid ground, her aim was impeccable, and the round took the man above the ear. He dropped the queen and whirled toward Kaylina as he grabbed the side of his head.

She readied another round, but the kidnapper had drawn a throwing knife, and he hurled it at her. She dropped flat to the floor to avoid it, but it grazed her shoulder, burning as it sliced through her dress and cut flesh.

He yanked out another knife. Kaylina rolled behind an upturned divan as someone leaped over it and her. Vlerion.

The intruder shifted his aim, hurling the knife at Vlerion. He whipped his sword up and deflected it with a clang. It struck the brick of a hearth across the room.

Vlerion reached the intruder, sword again ready to attack. The man must have realized he couldn't win against a ranger because he spun and tried to run. But he tripped over the unmoving queen. She groaned at the contact—at least she was alive—but didn't otherwise stir. Vlerion plunged his sword deep into the man's heart.

The suite fell silent, the intruders all downed. A guard gripping his side with blood streaming between his fingers staggered out of the queen's room. He started to nod at Vlerion but then spotted Kaylina. His eyes bulged.

"The queen's poisoner! Pargorak, get her." The guard ran to stand in front of the queen but pointed at one of the two guards protecting the king in the corner, their elderly monarch on the floor with his hands over his head.

"I came to help." Kaylina opened her hand and held up her sling.

The two guards rushed toward her.

"No," Vlerion barked and intercepted them. Even as he bowled them over, he waved for Kaylina to get out of the suite.

Though she wanted to defend herself, to say she'd helped Vlerion and therefore *had* to be innocent, the queen hadn't seen her fighting at his side. She wasn't even awake. And the king? He wasn't looking at anything but the floor. As far as the royals knew, nothing had changed since Kaylina had been thrown into the dungeon.

Swearing, she ran out into the hallway. She didn't know where to go but thought if she reached the taybarri, Levitke might help her escape.

She and Crenoch were still on the landing, but two other taybarri had arrived and brought more rangers. Kaylina almost crashed into Targon when he stepped in front of the hallway exit. She flailed to a stop, but he grabbed her arm.

Would he believe the queen's guards and take her personally back to the dungeon?

Vlerion caught up with Kaylina, looming at her shoulder and meeting Targon's gaze. "She's helping us."

"I saw." Targon released Kaylina.

"But a mead maker framed her, convinced the queen she's trying to poison her." Vlerion glanced back down the hallway. He might have delayed those guards, but he wouldn't have severely hurt someone on his side, and Kaylina wasn't surprised when one surged into the doorway. "She needs to get out of here," Vlerion added to the captain. "I'll explain later."

"I'll hold you to that."

"Get her, Captain Targon," the other guard yelled on his way out of the suite. "Don't let her go!"

Targon stepped aside so Kaylina could pass while the taybarri shifted to block the hallway, to buy time for her to escape.

She appreciated that, and that Vlerion ran at her side to make sure nobody impeded her, but as they sprinted back to the dungeon—and the escape tunnel the intruders had excavated—she feared she was about to be labeled a criminal and a fugitive.

"You're still alive," Vlerion said softly, as if he could guess her thoughts. "There's always hope. I'll make sure Targon knows the truth, and I'll do my best to explain it to the royals."

"Thank you."

Vlerion smiled and patted her shoulder as they descended into the dungeon. "After this, Targon would be a fool not to want to continue your ranger training."

"After I hit a couple of people in the heads with sling rounds?"

"After you managed to shoot a weapon without falling off your taybarri. That's an advanced skill." He winked. "You're a natural."

"I just want to make mead."

"You're destined for more."

EPILOGUE

DREAMS WON WITHOUT A FIGHT AREN'T WORTH HAVING.
   ~ Grandma Korbian

The long trip through the excavated tunnel the Virts had made, into the catacombs they connected to, and under the city to a squat stone access building beyond its walls took hours to traverse. Kaylina couldn't complain, not when the wounded Vlerion was trekking at her side. He'd even had her wait while he slipped out near ranger headquarters, detouring to collect Frayvar and gather some supplies for them. The fact that he'd needed to do that alone, that it wouldn't be safe for Kaylina to be seen even by the rangers, was depressing.

Night had fallen by the time they stepped out of the building on a hill overlooking the city. Snow drifted from the cloudy sky, dusting the earth and suggesting winter might never end, budding bushes nearby or not.

Shivering, Kaylina looked back across the city toward the royal castle. Frayvar had suggested they go to the harbor instead of in this direction, a direction that headed toward the druid preserve and the mountains beyond. After all, what did either of them know about surviving in the wilderness?

But Vlerion had promised that, thanks to the assassination attempt, every vessel attempting to leave the harbor would be searched. Across the miles, Kaylina could make out the lights of warships guarding the route out to sea. It might be weeks or even months before anyone could leave that way, and she doubted the passes were yet accessible for the land route.

"We should have come in the summer," she muttered. "Or not at all."

"At least we know people here think our mead is good," Frayvar offered.

During their long trek, Kaylina had told him most of what had happened with Jana and the queen. Vlerion had glanced at her a few times as she'd relayed the story, but even without his presence, she wouldn't have told Frayvar about the beast. She'd promised she would keep that secret, and she would.

What would the newspapers report about the day's events? Maybe nothing. Maybe they wouldn't print an iota about the insurrection, simply distributing the Queen's Corner and her latest recommendation for a play to see.

"The only one who's tried it is Jana, and she wants me dead." Kaylina bent and gripped her knees, struggling not to give in to the despair that wanted to consume her.

"And my mother." Vlerion had spoken little on their journey, leaving Kaylina and Frayvar to converse while he led the way. His expression had been grim, and it still was as he gazed toward the city instead of looking at her.

She wondered if he'd been disturbed by the carnage he'd wrought as the beast. Based on the man she'd come to know, she had to believe so. Even if those had been enemies that he would have fought as a ranger—and he *had* fought once they'd reached the courtyard—to tear their heads and limbs off... That was horrifying. She couldn't blame him for it, but she had to admit that it would be good to have a few days away from him, to ponder her feelings and the future. Whatever future she could have.

"I also sampled it and enjoyed it," Vlerion offered. "My mother is right. As is the dreadful woman who framed you. You have a gift." Now he faced her. "You have many gifts."

"Thank you." Kaylina still felt like a screwup, that all of this had been her fault.

"Do you have a plan yet?"

"A plan?" She looked blankly at him.

"I briefly saw Targon when I collected your brother, and he forbade me from disappearing into the wilderness with you, but you must clear your name so you can return to the castle and open your meadery." Vlerion held her gaze.

He *wanted* to disappear into the wilderness with her? Maybe that shouldn't surprise her. He'd been protecting her all along, even when he'd claimed she exasperated him.

"I..." Kaylina hadn't yet considered more than escaping with her life.

"I assume you aren't giving up." Vlerion set the pack of supplies he'd been carrying by her feet. "You'll fight and find a way to return triumphant."

Frayvar raised his eyebrows. Waiting to hear her response?

"Is that what a ranger would do?" Kaylina asked.

"Certainly. And I believe it is your fate."

"People like me don't have *fates*, Vlerion. I'm not a noble or a great warrior."

"No? You've already changed the city."

Kaylina thought he referred to the battle in the castle, but she'd done little to impact the outcome of that, unless seeing her in danger had been what caused Vlerion to turn into the beast and singlehandedly destroy half of the invasion force. But he pointed toward the city, his finger following the river toward a dark structure along it. Stillguard Castle.

She started to say that she hadn't done anything there—thanks to the fire, it was in worse shape than when they'd leased it—but she started when she noticed a certain tower window. Not a red glow but a *purple* glow emanated from it.

"What does that mean?" she wondered.

"That plant may have liked your honey a lot more than it liked Targon."

"My honey is much more appealing than Targon, but... that doesn't mean... I mean, is a purple glow better than a red one?"

It *was* less ominous. She would admit to that. But had anything about the curse changed? And would the new glow last for a long time? Or only until the honey water she'd given the plant dried up?

She itched to go check on the castle. But she couldn't return to the city. Not unless, like Vlerion had said, she could enact a plan to clear her name.

"I've never heard of the glow changing color. It's been red for as long as I can remember." Vlerion extended a hand in the direction of the castle. "It's almost an invitation, isn't it? For your heroic return."

"You think so?"

"I do." He clasped her hand, sending a warm tingle through her. *He* wanted her to return.

"It's easier to be heroic for others than yourself," she said, though some of her feeling of defeat was waning, replaced by growing resolution. Maybe she *could* deal with Jana and somehow make everything work out. Achieve her dream.

"I've found that to be true. If doing it for yourself isn't enough, do it for me." His eyelids drooped as he gazed at her.

Kaylina wished she knew if she had truly changed something about the curse, because if it was possible to alter the castle, might it also be possible to alter him? To lift *his* curse? So he could have the life he deserved and be the honorable ranger he wanted to be? That he *was* when the beast didn't take him.

"Okay," she found herself saying as she returned his gaze.

"Good. Even though you are a terribly exasperating woman, I would be distressed if I never saw you again."

"I'd kind of miss you too, even though you're a haughty aristocrat. I'd *especially* miss your taybarri."

"The entire stable would be bereft if your absence were forever."

"Ugh." Frayvar turned his head and walked behind the stone building.

"What?" Kaylina called after him.

"You're going to kiss, and I don't want to see it."

"We're not going to kiss. We can't..." Kaylina trailed off, wishing they *could*. But the last thing she wanted was to prompt Vlerion to turn into the beast again. She'd seen exactly how terrifying that was, how deadly.

"No," Vlerion agreed softly, but he took her hands and continued to gaze at her. "But I do wish you to have a reason to return."

Did that mean... he *would* kiss her? Hope and nerves teased her belly. She should step back so that he wasn't tempted, so there was no danger.

But her treacherous feet took her closer to him, and she tilted her head back to search his eyes, though his face was hard to read in the dim night. The snow on the ground was bright but not enough to illuminate his features.

"You don't think the mystery of the purple glow is enough to draw me back?" she murmured.

"It may be. I can tell you're intrigued." Vlerion lifted his hand to her face and threaded his fingers through her hair, brushing her scalp, his touch stirring pleasure in her entire body. "But you will also return for me."

It was a statement, a cocky and arrogant statement, but when he bent his lips to touch hers, she couldn't argue with it. His kiss was gentle—*careful*—and she knew he didn't want to rouse his lust —to risk rousing the beast. It was for her. He wanted her to enjoy it.

And she did. Her heart ached with how much it meant that he cared, especially since the last man who'd kissed her had wanted to know why she couldn't be normal. Vlerion would never ask that. Because *he* wasn't normal. He understood what it was to have a dark side. But his was too dark, something no man should ever have to endure.

As she sank into his embrace, returning his kiss and wrapping her arms around his shoulders, she wanted nothing more than to fix his life. For his happiness and so he wouldn't have to be the beast. And for this, so she could kiss him without worrying. So he could kiss her *and more.*

Heat spread through her body, images of what that *more* might entail creeping into her. The restraint faded from his kiss, and his hand drifted down her back, as it had in the dungeon, and he cupped her, pulling her into his hard body.

Desire flared within her, and she struggled to tamp it down, to keep their emotions in control. She'd never been so drawn to anyone in her life, never needed a man's touch so much.

She curled her fingers into his hair, not wanting to break the kiss, to break away from him. There was hardly anyone out here. Maybe it wouldn't be that bad if...

Vlerion broke the kiss with a growl that mingled frustration with desire.

"You are dangerous to me," he whispered, his voice hoarse. Instead of pulling back, he nuzzled her ear, his lips and beard stubble brushing her, sending such delicious sensations through her that she almost groaned.

His arms still held her close, and she had to fight her body's urges to keep from rocking into him, imagining him taking her to the snowy ground and making her cry out in exquisite pleasure.

"So dangerous," he added.

"Do you still want me to come back?"

"You *will* come back." He nipped her earlobe, sending a sharp stab of desire through her, before releasing her.

She gripped his shoulders, not wanting to let him go, not even able to object to the order. She *did* manage to infuse a hint of sarcasm in the, "Yes, my lord," that she gave him.

Vlerion snorted, catching it. "You will also return to my training so I can drill respect into you."

"I look forward to it."

He took her hand, brushing her knuckles with his lips, before stepping back out of reach. Even that slight contact made her close her eyes and long for more.

The snow crunched under his boots as he walked into the stone hut, then climbed down the rungs, leaving her.

But not forever. She would be back.

THE END